For my mum, whose dreams and imagination are the same as mine.

Man is least himself when he talks in his own person. Give him a mask, and he will tell you the truth.
Oscar Wilde.

Prologue

Some people think I'm strange. Strange because I see things other people don't. Things that shouldn't exist.

I remember it being a strangely hot summer's day. I was ten years old clutching my mother's hand whilst crossing the busy road. All day I had a headache that made me dizzy and disorientated. Everything seemed to be brighter more into focus compared to what my light blue eyes were used to. My mother a petite woman with a fiery temper that matched her hair marched me across the road with my older brother in tow. My brother was only two years older than me, but with his strong build and tall body you would have guessed him to be older. I was the middle child; my younger sister who was three at the time was most probably sat on my father's knee screaming for her lost care bear.

The hot summer air was stuffy, and was only making my headache worse, I was becoming irritable. We were on our way back from school when I first noticed it. Sliding my hand from my mother's grasp I stopped to look across the road. Oblivious to what I was seeing my mother stopped and tapped her foot impatiently waiting for me to join her again, my brother ran on ahead. My attention wasn't on my mother's scowl as it should have been but on the giant dog that stared back at me from across the road. He didn't look like a dog; he was large with a stormy grey coat flecked with mud and piercing blue eyes. He looked more like a wolf, but that was impossible. No wolves lived in our small village in the middle of nowhere. The dogs eyes bore into mine as they did I felt like energy had been drawn from me, I was suddenly very weak, my legs beginning to shake underneath the weight of my body. When I looked back the dog had disappeared.

Something changed in me that day, that's when I figured I was different. Because I saw things other people didn't. Things that shouldn't exist.

Part 1.

Six years later...

Lily

I stumbled through the trees as the darkness swallowed the night. I didn't know what I was doing out here but apparently my feet did. The woods were thick and smelled damp from a previous storm. There was no light around just darkness. I could hear twigs being snapped from behind me. I looked over my shoulder to find millions of eyes on me, I knew the wolves were here somewhere but I couldn't see them. A pale lady with a willowy figure stepped out of the darkness. Her white dress was patterned with gold gems that seemed to glow in the eerie night. Her eyes as clear as day settled onto mine 'Lily today is the day' she sang in her lovely soft voice.

I woke like I normally wake, eyes to the ceiling. The same picture that's been plastered up there since I was ten stared back at me. Since the first time my eyes caught sight of the wolf his image has haunted me. Countless times have I tried to draw him, but never quiet getting the right colouring of his fur, or the pure density of his eyes. The drawing of the wolf clung to the ceiling like the mud on his fur when I first saw him. His bared teeth gave of a malicious but goofy grin; despite myself I smiled back and willed myself out of bed.

I guess I didn't explain something, my gift, or what I call my sight of seeing things that should only exist in the fairy tales my father used to read to me before bed. In the whole world there are only two people who know about what I used to see on a regular basis. My brother Leo and my great grandmother Amelia. My brother because he's understanding and irritatingly protective of me, my grandmother Amelia because she sees things too. It gives me hope that I may not be crazy after all. When I was younger I would dream vivid dreams that felt like reality; the next day the characters from my dreams would star throughout my day. However, I had managed to shake the dreams, the characters. I hadn't had a dream like that since I was ten, and I was thankful. Those dreams were like torture through the night, my only release was waking, and even then I had to face the demons in my consciousness.

I managed to slowly pull myself into my dull green school uniform that should have been outlawed in the eighteen hundreds. My mind started to focus as the smell of caffeine wafted under my closed door, my dream clung to me as though it was afraid to let go. I clung to myself. I hadn't had a dream like that in six years, why were they now suddenly returning? I thought I had finally found my freedom. I descended the stairs.

Our red tiled kitchen was set alight as the morning light seeped through the open blinds. Mum was busy by the toaster with little Leah around her ankles. My younger sister was my mother's copy, pale complexion with rusty coloured curls. I sat down. My Dad sat across from me propped up with a couple of cushions to support his frail frame. He managed a small smile in my direction before closing his eyes, softly falling asleep. It's still hard to imagine him being healthy, how he used to be, before he was diagnosed with cancer. I watched his eyelids flutter while he slept, I tried to look past the visible effects of his disease. How his light brown hair used to be carelessly spiked, or how his smile could light up a whole room. My memories evaporated when Leo walked through the door, taking the seat next to me. He smiled at me as though he knew what I had been thinking.

The early morning light was bright when I walked out of the front door. Leo had already left five minutes earlier to walk to school with his friends that lived close by. I walked alone. Leo and I were close, no sibling conflict between us. I will miss him terribly when he leaves for university in a few months, I would never admit this to him but I am incredibly proud of him.

He deserves to go to a top university he worked so hard for it. All the times his friends got him into trouble, and was able to put that behind him, show the teachers he was perfectly capable of obtaining an A. Even though he desperately wants to go, I also know how much he wants to stay. How much he will miss our small three bedroom house where it always smelled of burnt toast, no matter how much Febreeze mum used. Or the small structure of a school we attended where he was popular and had a girlfriend.

The males in our family were well trained in locking their emotions away, however Leo seemed to lack the skill. He always held what he was feeling in his eyes making him incredibly easy to read. If you knew him well enough. You could see it that day when he read out his acceptance letter, the dazzle of happiness only dimming when he turned to our terminally ill father, another thing he will miss.

The sun's rays made the concrete path sparkle as I walked along. The cloudless sky was an amazing shade of blue, odd as it was the middle of September. The school came into sight, the grey stone in which the school had been built with did not sparkle in the light as the concrete did, instead it stood tall and dull, as though it too was dreading the day ahead.

Cole

I was bleeding. I tried to run but a wound in the leg made it drastically harder. Every step sent a hot searing pain through my left hind leg. Yet I still ran. I didn't have a choice, I was being pursued by a hunter. I was losing grasp of my wolf, I didn't have enough energy to stay animal, but if I shifted I surely would be dead. I yelped as loud as I could, my distress call to the pack. My body began to tremble as the pain increased. A brown wolf answered my call as she trotted to my side. Managing to put my head on her shoulder I collapsed to the ground my body beginning to shake. I couldn't hear anything or see anything, I felt totally blind. All I could feel was the damp earth brush against my fur, then, everything went black.

Lily

I didn't care for school; it didn't matter to me what grades I got at the end of this year. My aim was to be an athlete, a sprinter, not a doctor like my mother, or an engineer like my father had been. This is what I wanted, and nobody could stop me.

Practice with Mr Light was intense. Timed sprints numerous crunches and laps, every muscle in my body screamed at the end of it. I had one last timed sprint to do before I could go home, I needed to beat my best score of thirteen seconds. I got down into my starting position my carves screaming as I did. 'Just one more Lily then you can go home and relax' I told myself. I looked around the red track with its ivory painted lines, Mr Light stood at the end of the 100m straight with his stop watch in hand. His sun baked face looked strained as he attempted to set the timer back to zero. Even though I had done this race a million times the adrenalin never faltered, as it pulsed through my veins taking the aches away.

Mr Light raised his arm the orange shot gun in his shaking hand. I focused. Bang! I ran faster than I had ever run before the only thing I could feel was the slight breeze around me and the soft track against my feet. I stepped over the line. As I stopped I could feel the burn in my chest as I greedily gulped in oxygen. Adrenalin fading, the aches in my body returning. I looked over towards Mr Light, he stood looking at his stop watch like he had won the lottery.

'You're definitely going to championships' he said as he showed me my time. 00.12 I smiled smugly at my achievement. Nobody could stand in my way now.

Even after training mum refused to come and pick me up, therefore I had to walk. I walked slower than usual taking larger steps to undo the tightness of my muscles, I ached. It was getting dark when I made it home. The cloudless sky was now a collage of colour in the slow sunset. The bare branches glowed against the violet clouds; it was beautiful. Sunset was my favourite part of the day, halfway between a day ending and halfway between a day starting. It was also magical how the sun could paint the world in various shades of oranges and purples.

Our house wasn't much to look at from the outside. It was small redbrick, attached to others identical to it. Mum tried last summer to make it look nicer, she added window boxes and a lawn. For a while it worked, the roses she had planted bloomed into exquisite reds and whites, the lawn grew into a lush green. Then autumn came sweeping the colour away.

I didn't go in, instead I sat on the grey steps that led up to the scarlet shaded door. I didn't know how much longer I could stand living in that house. Pretending everything was alright. Pretending dad was getting better, pretending mum wasn't close to having a mental breakdown, pretending that Leo leaving wasn't having an effect on all of us. Somehow my little sister Leah was the only one who wasn't pretending, too young to understand the problems that surrounded her she was protected by the bubble that was childhood. There will eventually come a time when that bubble will burst exposing her to reality, and in the end she too will have to start pretending.

Inside the fire glowed and the log sizzled. The living room was small but cosy. The walls were beige wallpapered with photos, memories. Dad sat in the corner of the room in his favourite chocolate leather recliner. He was asleep. I watched his chest rise and fall, I gently moved the hair that was stuck to his forehead. Leo looked so much like him. I fetched Leah's baby pink crotched blanket and draped it over his thin body. I turned to leave when he spoke in a small voice. "How was training?" It was dad who supported me on my running, he was the one who always believed I was good enough. He was always there at my competitions, always the first one to congratulate me or console me if I hadn't placed. He was the one I was mainly for filling my dream for. "Great dad I beat my best score". He smiled as best as he could at me, his eyes began to close again without his consent. 'I always knew you could do it, my little sprinter' my eyes pricked with tears at the mention of my childhood nickname. Then sleep invaded him.

Cole

The last thing I remember was the sensation of falling. When I awoke I was sprawled across my bed, the sheets ruffled underneath me. My sight was slightly fuzzy and wouldn't focus, my leg seared with pain. What was going on? My room looked unfamiliar in the early evening glow. I guess it was because I wasn't used to being home at night. Night allied with sleep, and sleep was my enemy.

I'm a werewolf, bred to defend humanity and kill vampires, or anything else that breaches the security of humans. I was built to be strong, brave, invincible, but I was not. The pack were superior where as I was the inferior one. The only one who was afraid of who I was, of what we do.

The clouds rumbled across the twilight sky a storm brewing somewhere faraway. I tried to stand but my weight was too much for my leg to hold, I crumbled to the floor. 'What are you doing'? I looked up to my mother's confused expression. "What's it look like I'm doing? I'm hugging the floor!" I answered sarcastically. Her smile told me she was amused. Unfortunately I didn't look like my mother. She had striking emerald eyes whereas mine were a dull blue, her light brown hair was long and curled around her angelic heart shaped face, mine was jet black, short and spiky with annoying dishevelled curls. "Well can you stop hugging the floor and come downstairs, your father's waiting". My breath caught for half a moment before I replied. "Mum can you help me please, my leg…" before I had finished my sentence she had grabbed me up under my arms. She slung one arm around my back and pulled my arm around her shoulders. I kept my injured leg of the ground afraid to put weight onto it, it would've healed by now if the wound wasn't so deep. "Cole are you okay?" My mother's tone was laced with worry, it scared me a little bit. Being a werewolf I was used to having a minority of injuries, she never seemed fazed before, she would just shrug and say 'You'll heal'. Now she was worried, maybe because nobody had ever taken a shot at me and succeeded. If only she knew half of the things I've had to experience. I squeezed her hand to indicate I was fine as we made our way towards the stairs. "Cole" my father's voice cut through me like a knife, I began to tremble, knowing what comes next.

Lily

Nobody talked over dinner. Dad hardly ate any of his food so mum put him to bed. He was exhausted. That was the lie mum made up as she wheeled him out of the kitchen. It was more for Leah's benefit than mine and Leo's. Still nobody talked. The three of us sat in comfortable silence, each of us thinking the same thing. How to demolish what was on our plates without actually eating any of it? She had burnt the pasta again. We needed a dog, like the ones you see in films. A dog that would hide under the table and eat the kid's vegetables as they passed them under so they could have dessert. We needed one of those dogs, but with mum's unpredictable culinary skills the dog maybe at serious risk of food poisoning. Yet we still didn't talk.

Mum returned to do the dishes, I vacated to my room before I got roped into doing them a second night. It was Leah's turn. Therefore I had our shared bedroom to myself for a few precious moments. Our room to my utter dismay was bright pink with purple butterflies plastered onto the walls. Nowadays the butterflies looked as if they wanted to fly away; I didn't blame them, given the choice I too would choose to fly away. The rest of our room was pretty simple, two single beds lodged on to opposite sides of the room, two faded oak wardrobes, and a small TV on the back wall. What I liked most about the room was the double window that looked out towards the forest in the distance. It was an amazing view in the spring and summer, in autumn and winter there wasn't much to look at. Leah's toys were scattered about the room like the auburn leaves outside.

My eyelids suddenly felt heavy. I was physically drained from training earlier but sleep seemed far away. I then felt a sudden urge to do something, to go somewhere. Mum would probably kill me if I left the house now. However, she probably wouldn't even notice I was barely a blip on her radar these days. I grabbed my favourite long blue jacket that was thrown across my bed and unlocked the window. My old track trainers were by my wardrobe so I quickly pulled them on, my heart was racing. Was I actually going to do this, sneaking out of the house? I had never done anything like this before. Maybe this was my rebellious teenage stage mum was so worried about. Our window was just a few metres above our garage so I gently pulled the window closed and jumped down onto the garage roof which was situated round the back of the house. Slowly I crawled myself to the other end where the gate was, I clambered onto the gate and climbed down. Relief released her shaky hold on me as my feet hit the ground. The cold breeze began biting at my cheeks as Goosebumps traced my arms and shivers raced down my spine. I zipped up my jacket pulled up my hood and carefully jogged away from the house. Hopefully nobody would notice my absence.

The trees were like silent soldiers standing guard over me. Even in the slight breeze the naked branches didn't even twitch, they were eerily still. The street lights helped guide me through the darkening night, I had been walking for a while now, just letting my feet wander. Looking up I found myself at the edge of the wood that bordered our small community. In all the time I've lived here I've never dared to enter. It was dense and menacing. The way the trees seemed both protective and foreboding at the same time was petrifying, leaving me feeling intimidated. I took a step closer, then stopped when I got the undeniable sense that someone was behind me.

Cole

Somehow I had made it outside. Dragging my leg along behind me. I sat down on the deck laying my throbbing leg out straight in front of me. The chilly wind made my body shake with shivers, my eye stinging from dads punch. He was angry with me, and being shot obviously wasn't punishment enough for him. It was the first time mum had ever seen him lay a hand on me, she was still inside screaming at him, punching him too. Knowing this argument was far from over I stayed put. For a moment I thought when he did punch me that I saw a glint of guilt in his pale blue eyes, then I remembered dad never felt guilty, he never regretted anything he had ever done.

Mum didn't know that this wasn't the first time he had hit me, no she didn't know the regular abuse he had inflicted over the past six years of my life. He only ever hit me when I broke the law, or if he was in one of his moods. The first time he ever hit me was when I was ten; to young and naïve to think about the consequences of my actions. It happened completely by accident. We were out running when I lost the pack. All my survival training evaporated into the humid air. Suddenly I felt an urgent pull in my chest, compelled by its tug I followed it out of the woods, and the security of the trees. There I stood on the side of a road. Cars passed on by oblivious to my presence. It was then I remembered they were Mortalis (human). Humans couldn't see our world without having some sort of sixth sense I guess you could call it. There was a physical barrier between our worlds the only way for humans to pass through is if they believe, if you didn't believe in, let's call it magic, you can't see us. Young children who hadn't been influenced by adult's thoughts could see us, parents just thought their child had some imaginary friend whenever the child mentioned one of us, not bothered their child was friends with a dangerous mythical creature. I've always thought humans were stupid.

Back to my story, the human family that walked on by seemed utterly ordinary. There was a small woman with burnt coloured curls who pulled her two children across the road at rapid speed. The woman and the tall boy who I assumed was her son seemed un fazed by my presence like normal humans. However, the girl on the other hand intrigued me. The way she scanned everything around her, the way she watched everything was interesting. Then her light lupine gaze landed on me, the tug that had brought me here vanished. The girl stayed glued to the spot, the lady tapped her foot impatiently waiting for the girl to join her again. But the girl stayed still and returned my un wavering stare. She could see me, did she believe or was she something else? Alarm bells started ringing in my head, my pack wasn't allowed to be seen by humans, we weren't allowed to interact with them. This was the oldest law enforced by the very first alpha, and I just broke it. The current alphas son. My heart thumped loudly in my chest, I managed to step back into the undergrowth and disappear, never looking back. She didn't follow.

When dad had found out he was beyond furious, and when he struck me across the face I thought for a stupid split second he regretted it, that it was by accident. Then I saw the fire blazing in his eyes, I knew he meant it. After that day I promised myself I would try not to face my father's wrath again, to keep out of trouble. It hasn't worked so far.

Lily

A warm breath tickled the back of my neck. The world around me began to spin faster. My heart beat rapidly in my chest. I turned to face whatever was behind me. There was nobody there, the street was empty. All I could see was the intimidating night stretch out before me. Did I imagine the breath on my neck? No. I knew better to think it was just a figment of my imagination. No. something was out here sharing the night with me. Something not entirely human.

Cole

When the arguing had died down I slowly limped back into the warmth of the house. "Cole?" I turned to the sound of my name. Stood in the dim light from the window was my little sister. Her long curly ebony hair was messy from sleep; their shouts must have woken her. The moonlight from the window made her skin look pale and transparent, as though she was a ghost. Her bright blue eyes looked glassy and scared as she began to shake with silent tears. I opened my arms wide to her, she crashed herself against me. Her salty tears staining my faded black polo, yet she didn't make a sound. Like me she had learned to keep quiet, carefully locking emotions away, only then to be released when nobody was around to witness them.

Even with a weak leg that was healing remarkably slow I managed to lift up her small frame and carry her back to bed. Her bony arms were linked around my neck like a clasp, refusing to let go. "Cole can you stay in here tonight?" Her voice was small and shook with emotion. I nodded to her and went to collect a spare blanket and pillow from the dresser, to make my makeshift bed for the night.

I lay facing the ceiling. Like my own room, Skyla's walls were a plain cream colour, cracks cascaded down the walls into the floorboards like a water fall plunging into the pool below. We moved around a lot so we were used to having hardly anything, we were used to having a small box shaped room with only a window (if we were lucky). I remembered a time when we didn't have to move around, a time when we were a proper family and had a proper home.

My room had been green like the grass in summer, bright. My toys were constantly thrown across the floor mum always tripping over them as she came to wake me for school. It was a time when dad would push me on the swing set that stood on our large back garden. A time when he would come home and swing me around as he hugged me, a time when he loved me.

I looked up to my sister her eyes were closed, her breathing slow and even moving the flyaway hairs that hung round her face. Her tattered teddy buried into her neck. That's all she had, one teddy bear. She was five and that's all she had, no other toys to spend her days with. We didn't have friends, we didn't go to school. She was alone, I was too. I closed my eyes and let her slow breathing lull me into a hopefully dreamless sleep.

The forest that surrounded me was dense and menacing. The wind blew whispers through the violent sky. My bones began to ache as they changed into a different form. The forest called to me along with the dangerous night. I looked back at my house with wolf eyes, cracked walls that had been seriously weathered. I could see a shadow behind the dull curtains of the downstairs window. He was coming for me. I ran as fast as my fury legs could carry me. I had angered him badly this time, there was no way he was letting me get away. A shot rang out. He was hunting me, adrenalin pumped through my veins, but it wasn't enough. Pain blared through my hind leg rendering me helpless. I managed to drag my changing body into the shadows of the trees hiding from my hunter. I refused to be the prey!

The first time I changed into a wolf was when I was seven. I had always known I would eventually become a werewolf. It was a gift according to my grandfather, which was passed down through the family. It was then I learned that you could only be born a werewolf not bitten or turned. At the age of seven I was truly fascinated by the dynamics of the pack, how everything worked. I learned that our wolves were strongest after sun set and weaker when the sun rose. However, what got me most hooked was the pack itself not our wolf quirks, well there were plenty of those. But to be ruled by one Alpha was like bowing down to your king, you had to follow his every command, pledge your allegiance or face the consequences. The Alpha was our king which evidently made me their prince. I learned about Omegas and Betas of the pack. Omegas had extremely calm wolves, they never entered a fight unless they were putting a stop to it, they were all about peace and harmony. Even to be in the presence of an Omega you would be able to feel their calming effect wash over your wolf settling your animal instincts, well that's what I felt in the presence of our Omega Carmen. She was the only female in our pack so we knew she was special even before she came into her power. I always thought her name was ironic considering she was the calm wolf. Our Beta was one of the stupidest wolf's I've ever met, his name was Hector Moon. Beta's were supposed to be a buffer for the pack if they ever got angry they would take that anger out on the Beta instead off the others, however our Beta was there mostly for entertainment, taking our minds of our anger with laughter.

Strangely I wasn't the youngest in the pack, no there were two other boys one the same age, the other a year younger. They were like brothers to me, I hardly get to see them what with moving around all the time and not being able to go to school, to be normal. My father held my future in a glass bottle, one wrong move he would drop that bottle, my future and dreams would lay scattered among the glass shards, broken and gone forever.

Lily

I could feel the wet forest beneath me, the smell of damp leaves and dirt was potent in my nose. I was cold. Slowly opening my eyes I looked to the sky. Expecting to see a dark sheet of sapphire blue to be present up there, I was pleasantly surprised to find the light mirage of dawn. I didn't move. Not because I didn't want to, I just physically couldn't. My brain silently screaming at my body to move, but my body lay immobile. The hair on my arms began to stand on end and I knew I wasn't alone. I could only stare at the sky and watch the sun trace its path across it. I closed my eyes preying I would make it through alive, for my dad, I wanted my last thought to be of my dad. I opened up my eyes again to say my goodbye to the sun, but my eyes never locked onto the sun but onto a familiar pair of blue eyes...

I woke with a start. My heart beating hard against my chest. I hadn't realised I was screaming until I ran out of breath. Chest aching as I breathed in more air. Mum crashed into my room with a panic stricken face. Her expression softening as she caught sight of me. She padded to the side of my bed and planted herself on the edge, her feet not touching the floor. I crawled to her needing my mother's warmth and comfort after still feeling cold from my dream. She wrapped her arms around me pulling me closer, her perfume disintegrated the smell of the damp leaves that was trapped in my sinus. She stroked the top of my hair as she spoke "you haven't had a bad dream in nearly six years, are you okay? Do you want to talk about it?" She spoke so quickly her words tumbling out in a rush, she knew I wouldn't talk about the dream, I never did. "I'm okay mum, just a dream." She kissed the top of my head before letting me go, she stood running her fingers through her curls and rubbing her forehead like she did when something was bothering her. "Ok well if you're not feeling too good maybe take the day of, maybe Mr Light is training you to hard." She was babbling on, she never let me take the day off unless I was seriously sick as in on the verge of dying. She was right I hadn't had a dream like that since I was ten years old and it scared me, so it must have shaken her a little. I smiled a small smile at her and nodded my head indicating I agreed with what she was saying, I needed a day of.

I then realised she was still in her pyjamas. She was always impeccably dressed and up before all of us, I can't remember a time I've ever seen her not dressed in her normal attire even on Christmas morning. I looked at the battered clock on my chipped bedside table 5:30am so it was just a tiny bit early even for her. She began playing with her wedding band whilst she moved towards the door to leave. "I'm going to get ready and start some breakfast, call me if you need anything." She was gone before I could tell her it was just a bit early to be starting breakfast, Leah and Leo wouldn't be up till seven. Thinking about Leah I looked over to her thinking with my scream I should have at least woken her. She lay facing me in deep sleep earphones stuck in each ear.

While everyone got ready for school I was able to think. I couldn't grasp what was going on with mum, she never acted that way, even when I would dream when I was younger she would still send me to school. Maybe because it's been years since I had one of my dreams she might think they were coming back with vengeance. But why now were my dreams returning, the day I saw the wolf was the day they disappeared, like him? Something's changed.

Lily

I slipped in and out of consciousness throughout the day. Mum checked on me every hour even when I was asleep, she probably thought I wouldn't notice but I could feel her lingering stare as she closed the door behind her. I felt like a science experiment constantly under the looking glass. It was then my memory remembered that I had gone out last night, how did I get home? My memory came up blank as though someone had taken a chunk of it away from me. I now had three problems, one my dreams were back and I had no idea what that meant, two, I had lost a whole night from my memory with nobody to explain to me if it was just my imagination, and three no matter how much I didn't want to believe it but maybe just maybe I had finally gone crazy.

Cole

I ran alone. I had always liked to run on my own, I had time to think. Nowadays all I did was think. In all honesty I didn't have much to think about, but I liked the idea of being free with nothing else to worry me except my thoughts. I may not like being a wolf, or the job I have as a wolf, I do however like the freedom that comes with being a wolf. I like that I can change into a different form and escape into a world where my worries don't exist. Tonight I wasn't running for myself. My father had ordered me, yes ordered me! To go and collect a new member of our pack. He didn't express any details on this individual just that I was to go to a specific place in my wolf form, and they would be waiting. I didn't trust him, meaning I didn't trust whoever he had found. I knew mum didn't either, she hadn't said anything though but the purple bruise around her eye was a hint to her silence. She had looked at me with her imploring green eyes, begging me not to say anything, and for her sake I kept my fist down. It was one thing to hit me, it was a completely other to hit my mum. I hated him, yet I wanted to love him.

I stood in the clearing only slightly out of breath. The trees jostled in the slight breeze, the clear starry sky shone brilliantly on this cold autumn evening. I waited. I could detect the slight crunching of leaves as someone progressed towards me. I could hear their rapid heartbeat which pounded furiously in their chest. Looking towards the trees a small figure emerged from the shadows. A girl. Her scent was carried to me in the chilly wind, she smelled of cinnamon and blood... human blood. She was Mortalis?

The girl by now had made it out of the trees and stood shaking in the clearing before me. Her thin tanned arms wrapped tightly around her torso, blood seeping through her fingers, she was hurt that's how I smelled the blood. She didn't smell afraid, though she looked it. My father told me I was picking up a new pack member but this girl was human? The girl's dark maroon gaze fell onto me, I slowly began to approach her with caution. She tilted her head to me, a small shy smile creeping into her expression. The wind blew her hazel curls onto her face. Yet she didn't attempt to move them back into place, instead, she took a step closer to me.

Lily

I had never liked visiting my Great Grandma Amelia's house, but here I was anyway. The house she lived in was old and decrepit, with long vines of weeds scarring the faded bricks. Amelia was a kind and devious character, who always had an opinion on young adults these days. Her favourite topic was style of clothing "why do those young boys pull their under garments up like that, they're not called underwear for nothing?" Of course there would be a range of profanities launched into that sentence, it wouldn't be an Amelia quote without any. Cursing was sort of second nature to her, mannerisms were never her forte.

However she did have a very loving and sweet side to her too, you just had to offer her something that in her opinion was worth showing that other hidden side that she kept locked away. You never arrived at Amelia's house with nothing to offer if she saw you with nothing she wouldn't even let you step over the threshold, instead it would be a door slammed in your face. This is how I currently found myself at her small oak table in her tiny kitchenette slowly consuming the chocolate gift we had brought. "So Lily when do you start secondary school?" Unfortunately for Amelia she had a disease that affected her brain, especially her memories. "I've already started remember, I'm in my last year." I smiled back at her. She smiled back more brightly "of course dear, sorry." Although her smile was bright, I saw the dim darkness that lay behind the blue in her eyes, it wasn't really darkness. It was hurt. She hated herself whenever she forgot the simplest things such as my schooling.

Amelia was like me in a lot of ways, I even looked like her when she was younger. The same pale blonde hair and dubious blue eyes. She was the only family member that had any sort of resemblance to me, I was a complete opposite to my mother and father, and saw none of my features in my siblings or other grandparents. She also had dreams too, when I was younger she would share her dreams with me, hers were always imaginative and beautiful, whereas mine were dark and daunting. Since her memory started to fade she stopped sharing those dreams with me.

When it was time to go Amelia grabbed my wrist, her grip strong for an old lady. "Our dreams are changing Lily; we need to figure out why." She knew, hope flared inside of me, finally maybe I could get the answers I was looking for. "Come back in a week bring Leo too!" And with that she let go of my wrist and shut the door behind me.

Cole

The girl stretched her hand towards me; I bowed my head to her as she placed a cold palm against my skull. "My name is Rain, you are Cole right?" Her voice echoed through the night, her voice sweet and soft with a slight trace of an accent. I nodded against her hand, her smile was sad. "Take me home." My body twitched under her statement, home? She must have read the question in my eyes as I faced her. "Your home, where you just came from. That is my home now." Her face looked pained. I sucked in a breath and started to walk, cautiously she followed.

Lily

When I failed to have another dream episode that night mum evidently found I was well enough to go back to school. I was so tired that I barley registered I was in class, until the teacher called on me. Wait which class was I even in "Lily what's the answer?" The teacher stared at me with his grey eyes that were held captive by his wire framed glasses. I think his name is Mr Roberts. The fluorescent classroom light was reflecting on his shiny bald head, it was rather distracting. He asked me again "Lily what's the answer?" He started to tap his foot impatiently the percussion began to drill into the back of my head. I could feel my classmates stares bore into me as I stayed silent, I felt faint. Suddenly the classroom began to turn fuzzy a ringing sound shot through my ears. Then, I was sucked into the unknown, a dark abyss, the muffled voices of my classmates following me.

"Lily can you hear me? Lily wake up!" Leo's panicked voice seemed faraway, I tried to focus on it, his voice was the light that was going to pull me out of my temporary darkness. My eyes carefully peeled open to the dazing lights of the nurse's room. The smell of vomit enveloped my senses. Leo grabbed me by the arms pulling me into a crushing hug. He was squeezing so tight that I thought I might faint again from lack of oxygen. He finally let go. "Lily what happened are you okay?" His eyes were sad he looked like he could burst into tears at any moment. I pinched his arm like I used to when I was younger to indicate I was alright, "I think I'm just tired." I lied. Relief swept the sadness of his face as he smiled back at me. The nurse came to take my temperature "we've called your mum to come and pick you up" she whispered it as though she was telling us a secret.

When mum arrived ten minutes later Leo seemed to come to the conclusion that I was incapable of walking to the car unaided, therefore he carried me to the car (firemen style). Mum was silent on the way home, I could tell she was worried as she kept glancing at me from the corner of her eye, biting her lip. Something was seriously bothering her. "Just say whatever it is mum" I sighed. She hesitated before answering me. "I've booked you an appointment with a doctor, don't get mad let me finish!" She screeched as I was about to protest "you've not had a dream like the ones you've been having since you were ten, now fainting in class. I just want to help you Lily". Her voice broke on the last bit. I could tell now she was internally struggling with this, she wouldn't cry because she always had to be strong for us. I leaned across the console and squeezed her hand that was gripped tightly to the steering wheel. Even though I was the one who fainted I was the one to do all the comforting today, and even though she thought talking to a doctor would help, I had no intention of going.

At home I spent the rest of my day with dad watching daytime TV. He sat on the corner of the sofa with me next to him holding his calloused hand. "What you thinking about Lil?" His barely there voice asked. "That life could've been so much easier." He smiled. "If life was easy there would be no test, if there is no test where would you learn the lesson?" I looked at him, thin worn down yet he still held the same smile that he always had. How could he be so philosophical? "Don't you wish things were different?" He looked away from me his gaze now on the yellow leaves outside twirling in the twilight. "Yes there are things that I wish to be different, but in life you have to accept the things that you can't change that's just the way of life." He turned back to me looking me in the eye, ignoring the tears that were brimming. "I look back at my life and I have nothing to be ashamed of, nothing I wish I could do again. I have an amazing family, three beautiful children. Heaven has been gracious to me and now it's time to pay the price." I didn't believe in God, but I'm sure if there was he wouldn't have agreed with my father in that moment. He would have said something even more philosophical like, life doesn't have a price, life is just about living in the moment. However, I didn't believe in god, which meant as much as it broke my heart I knew my father was right, nothing in life is free.

Cole

Rain had been asleep for fourteen hours. How? I didn't know. All I knew was that she was asleep and had no intention of waking anytime soon. "She's dying you know." Mums voice seemed loud in this vacant living room. I didn't look up at mum when she spoke. Instead I kept my gaze carefully locked onto Rain, afraid that she might disappear. She looked more fragile in sleep, compared to how she looked when I first met her in the clearing. I had to admit she was pretty; her tanned skin looked pale under the dim chandelier light that dangled above us. Her dark hair curling from the heat of the blazing fire next to her. She had only been in the house ten minutes before sleep claimed her fatigued body. "Why is she here?" My voice quiet so I wouldn't wake her. "He thinks he can save her...by biting her." She came to stand by me, placing her warm hand on my shoulder. "And how's he going to do that? You cannot become a wolf by biting, unfortunately you're cursed to be this way when you're born!" She closed her eyes as if she was fighting tears that tried to break from her eyes. "It's not a curse Cole" she coughed as though it physically hurt her to say it. "And how would you know mum? You're not like me or him for that matter!" I stood quickly and walked out of the room. I let myself out of the house onto the deck that sat on our back garden, I let the refreshing air cleanse me of my anger.

Lowering myself down onto the deck I laid back, the cold wood hard on my spine, yet it wasn't entirely uncomfortable. The sky was a sheet of black highlighted by the stars, the moons face illuminated the night. "Cole." I looked up to see a familiar face. "Reeve long time no see." I stood to greet my fellow pack mate. Reeve was the same age as me, and we had a year on his cousin Jett. Reeve had light brown hair with matching brown eyes, Jett had similar features, his hair was the same light brown, however his eyes were an abnormal shade of green, like his mother's. "Yeah it's been too long, what have you been up to?" Reeve didn't know about my dad, none of the pack did. As our pack leader everyone looked up to him for guidance, he was a role model to the younger wolves like Jett and Carmen. He was like royalty to them, because of this I lied. "Oh you know helping dad about the house, were trying to make the house look a little less depressing." As anticipated Reeve laughed enjoying the simple talk between friends.

Even though Jett and Reeve were part of the pack they weren't like me. Their fathers wanted them to have a future, to go to school and get an education. Whereas mine was held captive in the hands of my father, who wanted me home, where he could still control me.
 "So... There's this girl I like... and I don't know how to tell her I like her, she doesn't seem the type that's interested in boys you know?" Reeve blurted out his problem as he took a seat next to me. "So are you saying she's into the opposite gender?" I laughed. His brown eyes looked at me amused but serious at the same time. "No! I mean she doesn't seem the type that likes to date. She's all about her running, I mean she's really good too got a chance at championships and everything, but..." he stopped.
"You wish she would just stop for a moment and notice you" I finished for him.
"Exactly."
"You do realise we sound like a bunch of girls right?" He laughed playfully shoving me with his shoulder. "Yeah I know, she fainted in class today and I had to carry her to the nurse's office. She was completely out of it."
"Well there you go, you can go ask her if she's okay now that's your conversation starter."
 "But what I else do I say?" He looked away from me into the wood.
"Are you afraid to talk to her, Reeve you're a werewolf, you shouldn't be afraid of anything especially a girl, a human girl." Saying this it dawned on me that even though I was a werewolf there was still things out there that frightened me too, does this make me a hypocrite?
"Yeah you're right, I am a werewolf I can talk to a girl. Thanks Cole you always did make things easier." He got up ready to leave already.
"You're welcome what are brothers for?"
 "Brothers" he mimicked as we fist bumped. I then watched him disappear into the mist that had by now surrounded the perimeter of the wood.

Lily

School wasn't exactly the most exciting thing in the world, especially if you really didn't care about the things you were learning in the first place. However, Fridays were the best. Only four periods of work, a free period, then escape. Well for the weekend. It was currently two o clock therefore it was free period. Study period. Unlike my fellow classmates I didn't use free period to study for my upcoming exams that could determine whether I would be a fully qualified doctor, or a wag. Instead I was on the schools worn athletic track, warming up. My two best friends Lexi and Sky were seated on the banking sharing bemused looks as they stared at a physics question. I knew it was physics because Lexi looked as though she was about to cry.

Lexi was extremely tall. Her legs were longer than my entire body. She had short brown choppy hair that only someone like her could pull of, complemented by big doleful eyes that were constantly hidden under dark shaded glasses. Where Lexi was tall Sky was her polar opposite. Small and dainty, with masses of long black hair that curled just short of her waist. Lexi was loud and confident, where sky was shy and quiet. I guess you could say I fit somewhere in between the both of them, fairly loud yet shy around new people. Sky I knew was only shy due to the constant snide remarks she has received over the years about her eyes, there was nothing wrong with having one blue eye and the other being brown. Even though there like my sisters, I would never tell them about my dreams. I don't think my heart could take it if they didn't believe me or worse wouldn't be my friend anymore because I was a freak.

I had known Sky the longest, we had been best friends since nursery, even our parents are good friends. Since then I had become fiercely protective of her. Lexi came later when we were around ten. She had just moved here from the city her parents wanting a simple quiet country life. Lexi had seen a boy about to put chewing gum in my hair when she tripped him over causing him to have a large cut along his face from falling, she had gotten a few detentions for that one but gained an ever grateful friend. She was protective over us both having no siblings of her own to look after she settled for us to be substitutes. Six years on she would probably do the same, tripping over anyone who dared do anything mean to us. It made me smile our own personal bodyguard.

Today the sun had been taken prisoner by the dark grey clouds. I quickly pulled my hair up in a bun so it wouldn't bug me whilst I ran, I started my laps around the track never realising I was being watched.

It was on my fourth lap when I noticed Lexi's attention had zeroed onto something, and it most definitely wasn't physics. Higher up the banking sat a boy, a very good looking boy. His light brown hair tousled in the wind, his dark chocolate gaze followed my progress around the track. Swinging my attention back to the track to stop myself gaping at the boy I hadn't realised my stupid shoelace had come undone. I soon found myself in a daze, my body on the floor. I never fell over! The bumpy turf on the track rubbed uncomfortably on my bare stomach. Embarrassment swept her claim over my cheeks. A warm hand held my elbow and slowly helped me to stand. The hand was definitely not Lexi's or Sky's, it was a boy's hand.

The boy kept hold of my elbow as though he was afraid if he let go I might fall on my face...again! I looked up and to my utter embarrassment I gasped. The hand belonged to the beautiful stranger that had been sitting on the banking. He smiled an award winning smile at me, my heart stuttered as it skipped a beat. "Are you okay?" He asked. I didn't trust myself by answering, knowing my voice would portray what I was feeling at this very second. What was I feeling? Deciding not to use my voice I smiled shyly and nodded my head. He smiled brightly back at me and released my elbow to take my hand instead, he then formally shook it as he introduced himself. "I'm Reeve." Still holding his hand I actually did gape at him. No way was this Reeve Skies standing in front of me and shaking my hand! He was in the same year as me, insanely popular, incredible at sport, and possibly one of the most talked about boys in the whole school. Add amazingly nice and gorgeous to that list too. I felt stupid for not recognizing him. Then again I don't think I had any classes with him. I suddenly realised I hadn't answered him, just stared at him like the goofy idiot that I am. I shook his hand with a smile "Lily."

"I know who you are, are you sure you're okay I can take you to the nurse's office if you like." He genuinely sounded concerned about me. Wait he knew who I was? I mentally kicked myself for being an idiot get a grip Lily!

"I'm fine but thank you." I smiled a tad brighter at him this time.

"For today…or yesterday?" He asked as he picked up his bag that had been carelessly flung to the ground.

"Yesterday?" I repeated.

He frowned before he answered "oh I thought maybe you might have remembered. You fainted in class; I was the one to carry you to the nurse's office, everyone was really worried." His brown eyes looked sad for a moment then he blinked it away.

"Well thank you for today and yesterday, but you're not even in my class why did you carry me?" I remembered fainting but I didn't remember being carried, yet I hadn't occurred to me how I got to the office still unconscious. Maybe I did know, no, I definitely would remember Mr tall and good looking carrying me.

"I was just passing by when Mr Roberts ran out of the classroom looking all panicked, nearly ran me over. When he saw me he pulled me into the classroom and told me to carry you. By then you were already unconscious." He looked me straight in the eye and I knew he wasn't lying.

"Well thank you, I guess I owe you one."

"What was wrong?" My heart began to beat fast I knew I had to lie.

"I…was just over tired…from training. Yeah too much training" so it wasn't completely a lie. He nodded at my explanation, something in his expression told me he didn't entirely believe me.

"Well no problem, you don't owe me anything. I don't mind saving someone as pretty as you." My heart stopped. I could feel the heat of a blush on my face. He smiled a dazzling smile at me before turning away towards the school building. He thinks I'm pretty? What was he drunk? I looked down at my clothes rolled up grey soft cottons with a mint green crop top. Let's face it I looked a mess, that was putting it mildly. I probably looked like I was on crack and hadn't had her daily fix yet!

Before my confused mind could come up with anymore insults towards my ratty appearance I was tackled to the floor by Lexi. "Wow Lily, I thought when you got a boyfriend he would be one of those guys that was slightly ugly, and you went out with them because you felt sorry for them. Never did I think you would pull the hottest guy Ever Green School has ever seen!" She screamed at me, I tried not to take offense to her words I knew she was joking.

"I didn't...I haven't...Lexi shut up!" Instead she giggled.

"What did he want?" Sky the grown up in the situation asked quietly.

"He wanted to check I was alright, because if you too hadn't noticed I fell straight on my face, which is not attractive what's so ever, and you two didn't come to my rescue!"

"I wanted to but Lexi held me back, she said Reeve was going to." Sky said as she looked down to the floor, ashamed she didn't help a friend in need. Standing up I put my arm around her shoulder to forgive her; she returned the gesture but put her arm around my waist as she couldn't reach my shoulder without it being uncomfortable. "Did you two know he carried me to the nurse's office?" The two nodded in unison.

"Why didn't you tell me?" My voice higher than I would've liked.

"We actually thought you knew. Anyways that's not the important thing right now, the fact that Reeve Skies likes you is!" Lexi squealed.

 "He doesn't like me like that."

"Then why did he ask me for your number?"

"Well... did you give it to him?" Apprehension tickled the pit of my stomach. Lexi began to smile a sly smile, a smile I had come very accustomed to by now. It was the smile she pulled when she had a plan, it was the smile that always got us into trouble. Sky even had a good mind to look a tiny bit worried.

"What do you think?"

Cole

Two things were waiting for me when I arrived home. A TV that dad has obtained from Hector Moon, the packs Beta. The other thing was Reeve. He sat waiting on the decking, his foot tapping out his anxiety that I could smell rolling of him. To see Reeve twice in a week was a true rarity. When he saw me progressing towards him he stood a smile sliding across his face. "I talked to her". I laughed at his goofy grin. "So her friend gave me her number...what do I put 'hey this is Reeve'?" Who did he think I was some kind of girl expert? Didn't he have any friends at school he could've asked? "Why are you asking me?" Reeve looked at me as he answered "because you're like my brother, you're supposed to be there when I need your help. Besides all my friends at school like her too so they wouldn't help." Who was this girl, who had caught Reeves attention when nobody else could? I had seen some of the girls Reeve went to school with when they walked past the wood towards their homes, they definitely weren't ugly. "Why are you so nervous? It's supposed to be easier to text someone, because you're not actually looking at them." He shook his head at me. "What if she doesn't want to talk to me?" I sighed frustrated, he was such a girl.

"If you don't, you will never know."

"Ok, any advice?" He pulled his mobile out of his back pocket looking at the screen as he answered a text. What was that like texting? Having no friends there was really no point in having a phone, so I had never text anyone before. "Don't be creepy."

"Don't be creepy" he repeated "got it" and just like that he was gone.

I shook my head, his troubles amusing me, I took a step onto the deck about to grab the door handle...when I heard a scream.

Lily

Deciding I didn't want to sit around all afternoon waiting for Reeve to contact me I decided a walk might clear my head. Maybe. Our small community was just that, small. The village was called EverGreen. We were in the middle of nowhere countryside. The nearest city was an hour away by car. The people who lived here either worked in the quaint shops on our small high street, or braved the city. Evergreen was stuck in the middle of a circle surrounded by the bordering forest, cutting us of from the rest of humanity.

The wood looked drastically different in the day compared to the night. It seemed friendlier, more inviting. Then again everything looked friendlier in the day. September had begun to paint the leaves, stripping away their vibrant greens, replacing them with golden browns. The sky was clear of clouds. Still, summer had long gone, substituting the chilly autumn nights in its place. Autumn however, was my favourite time of the year. Summer brought bright colours, winter vast empty spaces, spring the beginning of every life cycle. Autumn reminded me of myself, always turning away from the present and past, looking forward to the unknown of the future.

I was like a leaf shedding its colours, trading in my brightness, so I could seep into the vast unknown that the next season brings.

Walking I contemplated heading home. A scream pierced the silence that had surrounded me as I walked, not even thinking about the impending danger the scream had entitled, I ran towards it.

I stumbled through the wood like Bambi on ice, constantly tripping over my feet. "Come on Lily you're a runner for goodness sake!" I scolded myself. It had only just occurred to me that the person who screamed might be in some sort of danger. What was I going to do against an attacker? At the height of five foot one I was small. My only advantage was my legs, I had no upper body strength what so ever. If someone went to punch me, my only defence would be to duck and run. Hopefully my attacker would be fat, middle aged who happened to be a heavy smoker, only then would I stand a chance.

I crashed into a clearing. It was still and quiet. The grass was bronze and worn away. There was no flowers, no sign of life, just eerie stillness. My ears detected the slight cry of someone near. Peering further into the clearing my eyes sought out a figure laid upon the grass. Their body shook with tears. Slowly approaching the figure I came to realise that the person was a girl, also that she wasn't clothed. My mind hastily jumped to a million different scenarios of what may have happened to her. I carefully bent down to be at her level so I didn't look intimidating, reaching out I touched her arm. She flinched at my touch, her eyes shot open.

Familiarity shot through me like a lightning bolt. The girl wasn't much older than myself. She had big brown eyes that stared up at me with pure innocence. Her extremely long hair was spread around her, it was light brown with golden highlights. I shrugged of my jacket and placed it over her attempting to cover her shaking body. She looked from me to the jacket and back again. "Thank you." Her voice was weak and brittle as if she had been crying for a while.

"You're welcome, I'm Lily" she shook my out stretched hand eagerly. Her hand was cold.

"I'm Carmen."

"Pretty name" I smiled at her.

"My parents seemed to think so, Lilies are my favourite flowers." It should have been weird to be sat here talking to a complete stranger in the woods, a naked stranger. Yet, it wasn't. I was smothered with this utter calm sensation that I had never felt before.

"Carmen are you okay?"

"That's not the question you want to ask." She was right I wanted to know what she was doing out here stark naked and crying.

"What are you doing out here?" I asked softly. She sniffed back tears that brimmed her eyes.

"I got shot." My heart stuttered in my chest as panic began to settle in.

"You were shot!" I let worry lace my tone.

"Yes, didn't you hear me scream?" she moved her body to show me her leg. Blood and dirt smeared her bare skin, a gaping whole oozed crimson. I hated blood. Quickly I stood, beginning to pace, my face most probably going the sickly sheen of green. Carmen lay still, never once portraying she was in any sort of pain. It was like she was they eye of the storm, and I the thunderous tornado. "I need your help Lily, I need to get home...will you help me?" her familiar eyes pleaded with me. I nodded to her, of course I would help her. "Shouldn't we get you to hospital or something?" I said as I fumbled to get my phone out of my back pocket of my jeans. "No! No hospitals. Please Lily just help me get home, my father will know what to do." Nodding I sucked in a long breath to calm my nerves. Carmen carefully pulled her arms though my jacket, zipping it up. The jacket came just short of my knee on me; thankfully she was shorter than me and helped cover the majority of her body. I pulled her up and she leant against me, she felt like dead weight. She kept her injured leg levitated, pointing in the direction of her house with a shaky finger.

I took a while to get to Carmen's house, with our snail like pace. Carmen lived in the cluster of houses that stood in the middle of the wood. There was about four rundown homes here, all big and old fashioned. A man with grey streaked hair and a friendly face stepped out of one of the derelict houses. Again, like Carmen he struck me as familiar. "Carmen!" his voice alarmed. He ran towards us, Carmen reached past me to the man, tears trailing down her face. The man grabbed her before she fell enveloping her in a careful hug. "What happened?" he looked her dead in the eye and I could see he was scared for her. "I was shot" she whispered. He shook his head and I heard him mumble under his breath "she's the second to be shot this week." Carmen then looked over at me, as did the man. The man then straightened his shoulders, replacing his worried expression with a careful and polite smile. "Dad this is Lily, she 'helped me'." Carmen explained. The man then broke out into a glorious smile, he stepped towards me. Clasping his hand in mine he shook it "very nice to meet you Lily, my name is Dean, Dean Skies." Skies? No wonder they both looked familiar this must be Reeves family. God I hope he isn't home. Dean carried on ignoring my stunned expression. "How can I ever thank you for helping my daughter?" Recovering myself I replied. "You don't need to thank me Mr Skies, I just wanted to make sure Carmen would get home safely and that she would be okay."

"Well thank you anyways, would you like to come in?" I looked towards Carmen she smiled at me, gratitude shining in her teary eyes. "That's alright Mr Skies I better get home, it's getting late my parents will be worried, but thanks."

I waved at Carmen who beamed at me and waved eagerly back. "Well... don't be a stranger Lily, pop round anytime." I smiled at him and turned to leave.

"Lily?" Recognising the voice that had spoken I turned towards him. Just stepping out of the wood was Reeve looking rumpled and confused. Next to him stood another boy. His piercing blue eyes locked onto mine. His expression told me he recognised me, and I recognised him. However, the last time I saw him I was ten, and he was...a wolf?

Cole

Running into the wood I found Reeve. He stood still as a statue, listening. I strained my ears to hear more than just the forest. "It was my sister." Emotion was breaking down his voice. I didn't ask how he knew it was Carmen, just offered my suggestion. "Sounded like she was near the southern border, near the clearing, I'll help you look." We both looked to the sky; sunset was about an hour away, our wolves would be too weak to run until then. "We better stay human, our wolves won't be able to last long running" Reeve voiced what we both were thinking.

We sprinted through the forest. Side by side. Pushing ourselves faster. We would have probably been there already if we had four legs instead of two. When we finally reached the clearing it was empty, desolate. September had taken everything in her sudden arrival; all that was left was a puddle of blood. Fresh blood. Dread and a tinge of fear claimed me. "You don't think…?" Reeve cut in before I could voice my fear. "No, they promised to only hunt at night, when the sun goes down, when we can protect ourselves".
"But they could've lied."
"The Lamia know not to break their promise, they know what the consequence will be if they do." I knew he didn't truly believe what he was saying. We both knew the Lamia knew how to twist the rules. "Let's try back at yours she might have made it back to your dad." He nodded at me.

We heard voices as we approached Reeve's house. Two I knew, one I didn't. From our vantage point at the edge of the wood we could see Dean holding onto Carmen, talking to a girl who was just turning away. Reeve must have recognised the girl as he called out "Lily?" the girl quickly spun round to face us. She was pretty, with long blonde hair and big blue eyes. She smiled at Reeve then her lupine gaze settled onto mine, I was then suddenly sucked into the past.

The tug was urgent in my chest, as it pulled me out of the woods. The humidity clung to my fur. Daylight shone on the busy road. A Mortalis family walked on by, completely ordinary and in conspicuous. Comforted that the passer-by's couldn't see me I looked on. The girls azure eyes scanned the forest, then they found me. She stopped twirling, I stopped breathing, the tug in my chest dispersing. She saw me. Sinking back into the forest I ran.

Thrown back into the present, her eyes still locked onto mine. Six years later here I was, staring at the only human that had ever seen me. I blinked breaking the connection. Did she recognise me? "Hey Reeve...I was just leaving" her voice was as soft as honey.
"I was just going to text you actually" Reeve smiled. Wait, this was the girl Reeve kept talking about, who I helped him talk to. If I had known I don't think I would've helped him. Lily blushed. "Well you still can" she smiled a sweet smile towards him then turned on her heel and left. My gaze followed her progress through the wood. "That's the girl Cole! I guess she does want to talk to me after all." Reeve smiled broadly.
"I guess" my answer curt.
"She's pretty isn't she?" Reeve ignored my tone.
"Yeah, she's something else." He laughed and went to join his dad and sister. I needed to speak to her, I had lost her once when I had to leave, I wasn't about to make the same mistake.

Lily

I dreamed. Dreams more vivid and surreal than before, it was scaring me. Things were changing; I didn't know how to prevent what was coming. I didn't even know how I knew something was coming, all I knew was that it was bad, I could feel it in my bones.

A week had passed since I had found Carmen in the wood. All week I had hidden myself from Reeve, answered his texts as briefly as I could, I was too scared to talk to him. How could I talk to him when all I could think about was his friend? The boys eyes were ingrained in my memory, my brain had worked overtime for the past week trying to figure out the clues that had been left for me. It didn't matter what I came up with because it all came down to this, I was afraid. Afraid to accept the truth.

Currently I found myself standing next to Leo on Amelia's doorstep. A freshly baked Victoria sponge in my arms. My hearing could faintly detect the slight shuffle of her red velvet carpet slippers trying, in slow succession to get to the door. Most probably swearing in the process. She finally managed to pull open the door, her pale wrinkled face lighting up when she saw...what I was holding. Feeling the love here Amelia. Her eyes glazed over for a fraction, she then focused on me and Leo. "Leo, Lily come in, come in!"

Amelia busied herself by putting on the small plastic kettle, while doing this she had managed to snatch the cake from my hands, bread knife already at the ready. She obviously needed her sugar hit. "Did Nurse Sally say no sweets again?" Questioned Leo. The old lady didn't even bother to look up to answer, to fascinated by the sponge. "Yes she spouted some crap about our bodies being temples, and that we had to look after them. I almost believed her until I watched her get in the car and rip into a packet of bloody iced doughnuts!" Amelia's face had gone red with anger. "It was almost comical." I knew not to laugh, that would just fuel her anger. It was better to eat the cake rather than wear it. Leo let a smile slip from his lips, lucky for him her attention was still on the dessert.

"So you wanted me to come back, to talk." I prompted or else we could be here all day.
"Yes I did...well I wanted to discuss our dreams." Surprised she remembered I was too stunned to answer. She carried on. "Yes, well you know our dreams are changing correct." I nodded "well mine have changed, yours have only just returned right?" Confused I nodded. I didn't want to say anything just in case she lost her train of thought. "Mine vanished as well when I was younger, I never did understand why. I was thankful though, when they returned." She thought the dreams were a gift, I thought they were a curse. "Lily there's something you need to know, there's a reason why you dream about the world others can't see, because you're a part of that world Lily!" I felt my eye brow furrow I looked to Leo who wore a similar expression, except he looked slightly afraid. "What do you mean?"
"I mean you have magic, or whatever it is that makes us dream, we're one of them!"
"One of whom!"

"They call themselves as a whole Evers. They're people who have magic or they're not quiet human."

"I don't understand" she huffed in frustration at me.

"The things you dream about Lily, they're real! You and I dream about the world they belong to, you dream about Ever!"

"So you're telling me when I dream about wolves, vampires, witches you're telling me they're all real, and nobody else can see them?"

"Yes". Panic settled in now, all these things existed, and nobody could see them. The world had just become a much scarier place in the past two minutes. "So what does this make me?"

"They call people like Leo Mortalis, which means human, they call people like you and me Somnium Ruptors."

"What does that mean?"

"It means Dream Breaker." Astonishment tapped me on the shoulder.

"So what I destroy dreams now?" She closed her eyes squeezing her eyes shut, she was forgetting.

"Amelia?" I grabbed her hand. She shook her head clearing her thoughts. "Sorry dear, yes you destroy dreams but not in the sense you're thinking, you simply crack them open to discover the truth in them, but your ability can stretch further than that like..." Her bright irises clouded over, I knew now she had forgotten. I couldn't help but realise she was going to tell me something important. I simply looked at Leo who returned my look as though I was looking in a mirror. I came here looking for answers, only to leave with more questions. And with Leo's worried and slightly petrified look, I think it was time to stop telling him things.

Cole

A week, seven days, one hundred and sixty eight hours.

Obsession, I didn't fully understand the concept until I was undeniably under its power. For many years I had watched obsession become a person, such as my father and his craving for power, or my mother's compulsion with cleaning. Two obsessions, yet two completely different purposes. My obsession however wasn't like my parents; I wouldn't even say I was even obsessed merely intrigued. The girl, Lily was my obsession. She haunted my dreams awake and asleep. She stole my every thought; I couldn't accept it as an obsession, not really. Maybe it was and I was just kidding myself. A week, seven days, one hundred and sixty eight hours.

My footsteps were loud against the silence. It was daytime, a time where the living strived and hoped, but the world was filled with silence, it was almost deafening. She held my hand, if she let go, I would disappear.

I had only known Rain for a short period of time; therefore I couldn't judge her character properly without it being some form of prejudice. However, I had narrowed it down to two things; slightly insane, and stupid. After sleeping for nearly two days she woke in a mood I could only explain as chaotic. She ran about the house ignoring my mother's pleas to stop. I watched from the doorway as she trashed the living room, destroying all she could. My father stepped into the room his penetrating stare held her still, anger bubbled beneath his skin. I suddenly felt sorry for Rain. "Rain I command you to stop!" I watched my father's order ripple through her body, taking away her will. He was using his Alpha tone, the tone that forced you to obey. I didn't even know that his wolf power could work on a human. "What have you done to me?" She whimpered.

"I've accepted you into my family that's what I've done, your father came to me and asked me to help you. I agreed but if you carry on messing up my house, so help me Rain I will take you back, you know what happens then!"

"I...die" she whispered.

"Exactly you die. Now tidy up this mess!" He paused "Cole will help you" and with that he left the room in a thunderous stomp, mum trailing softly behind him.

Rain crouched down to begin picking up pieces of the glass from a vase. I bent next to her "stop you'll cut yourself, let me". Her maroon eyes looked up at me.

"Thank you." She smiled before getting up to put the cushions back on the sofa.

"No problem." I didn't take long to tidy the room as there wasn't much that had occupied it in the first place. After I went to sit outside on the deck, watching the day pass. Rain joined me. "Is your mum a wolf like you and your dad?" She had laid down next to me eyes to the sky. Pulling my knees up to my chest I answered. "No it's just me and dad."

"Do you wish she was a wolf?" Thinking about it sometimes I had wished she was a wolf, only then would she be strong enough to fight against dad, but then I thought that she probably wouldn't be the same as she is now if she was a wolf. Warm and approachable. "No she wouldn't be the way she is now if she was a wolf."

"Do you want to know why I'm here?" She had turned to look at my curious face, I nodded to her. "I'm dying, but you knew that already. Your dad thinks he can save me by turning me into a wolf, I knew you knew that already as well. What you don't know is that my Grandfather was a wolf, so your dad thinks a bite might work as I'm a descendant of a wolf." This intrigued me, there was only three wolf families left now, ours, the moons and skies. Which family did she belong to? Once upon a time there had been hundreds of us, back when the world was a lot simpler, but as our enemies grew, our numbers dwindled. It was just us now.

"What's your family name?" She looked away from me into the forest yearning clear on her face. She wanted what my father had told her to be true, that she didn't have to die. Even if it did mean living her life as a monster, under the control of an even bigger monster. "Ok don't laugh my parents were a bit eccentric, my family name is Cloud." She cringed away waiting for my impending laughter, but I didn't. The last time I had heard from a cloud was from the daughter of Jack Cloud which I'm guessing was Rains Grandfather. Alice had informed us that Jack had died therefore there was no other wolves from the Cloud line. After that my father knew that we and the other two families that made up our pack were the last wolf families. "Is your mum called Alice?" Rain stopped cringing and shuffled closer to me attention fully on me. "Yes but she left a few days after I was born, did you know her?" Her eyes imploring. "Yeah I only met her once. She came to tell my dad that your Grandfather had died." Recalling the image of Alice I remembered her to have a swelling round stomach. She had placed my hand on her stomach once, I remembered laughing as the baby kicked beneath my palm. "She was still pregnant with you." Rain smiled at me the first real smile I had seen from her since I collected her from the clearing. "She looked a lot like you, maybe a bit taller, she had a nice voice." Talking about her I remembered her more clearly, she had the same tanned skin and long dark hair, the only difference was that she had one blue eye and one brown eye. She had stayed with us for a few days, read me stories, told me what her home was like and how much she missed it, even though she had only been gone a few days. "She used to tell me stories of her home, her family, she even told me about you." Rain was practically beaming at me by now.

"What did she say about me?"

"She said she couldn't wait to tell you stories, she told me you were special." Rain turned away from me and stood up, I could hear the sadness in her voice. "She didn't tell me stories. I don't even know what she looks like. She left a few days after she gave birth to me. All that she left was a note to my father saying she was sorry and that she needed to leave. She left me this locket with the family crest on it, nothing else." I stood up to stand next to her she turned to me holding out her locket. It was a large faded golden oval with the words *Nos quoque nebulae* in scripted around a cloud. "We keep the clouds" she spoke then turned and walked back into the house. I didn't follow her, it seemed strange to me that Alice would just leave, leave her new born baby too. Something didn't add up, if Rain had to become a monster just to carry on living, the least I could do was find out the truth about her mother.

Lily

I found myself knocking on Reeves door early Saturday morning. After avoiding him for a week I felt as though I owed him an apology. As it was a Saturday it was unlikely he would answer the door, or be happy to see me for that matter. Knocking two consecutive knocks I stepped back, suddenly nervous. A lady answered the door. She looked a lot like Carmen only older, her features more fierce. I hazard a guess to say this was Reeves mother. Her dark eyes scanned me, her once frowning face turned into a glorious smile. "You must be Lily I'm Carmen's mother Delia!" Before I could answer she had me in a crushing hug. "I heard you saved my little girl I am ever so thankful!" I smiled a shaky smile towards her, the word 'ever' stuck out of that sentence more than it would have before, Amelia's words were on a continuous replay in my mind. *You dream about Ever.* Quickly taking hold of my hand she pulled me over the threshold.

The doorway led straight into the living room. Unlike my own living room it was large and spacious occupied by two ivory leather sofas accompanied by a huge plasma TV. The house screamed ultra-modern on the inside which completely contradicted its appearance on the outside. Dean Reeves father who I had met the week before sat comfortably in one of the sofas enjoying reading a paper. He looked up as I entered "Lily good to see you again." Reeves mother who insisted I call her Delia disappeared into the kitchen to start a round of drinks. This definitely wasn't what I was expecting. The stairs creaked as someone progressed down them, it was Carmen. When she saw me a loud scream shook the house as she tackled me into a hug "Lily you came back!" I laughed at her. The loud scream that Carmen had let out must have woken Reeve. He descended the stairs looking tired and rumpled. For a moment he just stared at me as though he couldn't quite believe what he was seeing. He soon consoled his features giving me a blank smile. I must have hurt him, way to go! "Lily what are you doing here?" He stepped of the stairs and waited at the front door, as though he was ready to bolt or drag me through it. "I needed to speak to you." I smiled shyly nodding my head towards the door, hoping he would take a hint. I wasn't about to talk to him about this in front of his family. He nodded his head to me opening the door, leaving it hanging open; I guess that was my cue to follow. I smiled back at Carmen who looked back at me confused and sad that I was leaving, but she did let me go despite her face telling me she didn't want to.

Outside he sat on the porch waiting patiently for me to join him, closing the door behind me I sat down. The sky was a cloudy grey, the wind kept my jacket wrapped firmly around me. "I wanted to apologise face to face, I never meant to hurt you in anyway and if I have I'm truly sorry." I let my statement hang in the air around us, anticipating his reply but dreading it all the same. "What I don't understand is why you were ignoring me in the first place, had I done something wrong?" His tone was soft but clipped with hurt. I didn't know how to fully explain why I was ignoring him; in all honesty I didn't even know why I was ignoring him, it was his friend I should have been worried about. So I lied to him, for the second time. "There's a lot going on at home right now and I was just so wrapped up in my own little world that I didn't even think to involve you, and I feel bad about that. Then finding your sister in the wood, shot! Would it surprise you if I wasn't a little shocked?" He hiccupped a laugh "but I'm here now, I want to apologise. I want to make things better." He looked at me his expression puzzled as though I was the mystery box he was trying to solve, in reality it was him who was the puzzle, I was drowning in unknown waters, if only he could throw a lifeline that would pull me back to understanding. "Are you done ignoring me then, can we be friends?" He smiled, silent laughter in his eyes. I stuck my hand out, he took hold of it, and just like the day he first talked to me only a week ago I shook it "friends."

Cole

I was running, this time I was running for myself. After talking to Rain about her mother last night I decided I needed to clear my head. My paws were silent upon the ground, not a leaf ruffled. It was light and I was a wolf. I knew by the position of the sun that it was late morning therefore I had about five minutes before I lost grasp of my wolf. Five minutes of freedom. The forest sang to me, compelling me to vanish into its depth. Its song had become more tempting every day.

I heard the crunching of leaves a moment too late to hide myself. Stood in front of me was Lily. Her eyes locking me into an unbreakable gaze. She spoke her voice wavering telling me she was more afraid than her face was telling me. "It's you."

Lily

The wolf kept my steady gaze, my heart began to beat so hard in my chest it actually hurt. He looked exactly the same. Stormy grey fur matched with piercing blue eyes. His very presence should have scared me, every instinct in my body screamed at me that he was dangerous, that I should have been running for the hills. However, his gentle eyes told me he wouldn't hurt me. His giant skull nodded to me, telling me he understood what I was saying. A strange sensation erupted in my chest tugging me closer to the wolf. My feet began to take my body forward even though I hadn't told them to. The wolf just looked at me, not moving. I was now close enough to smell the scent of the woods on his fur; he bent his giant body towards me so our foreheads could touch as my knees folded themselves down as I knelt on the floor. The fur on his forehead was short and bristly, tickling me ever so slightly. A shock than ran through me making me shiver, then my senses disappeared, exposing me to a vision I had never seen before.

I stood within a golden circle. The golden dust it had been drawn with glowed like the stars on a clear winter's night. People gathered around the circle hands intertwined with their neighbours. I came to realise that I wasn't alone in the circle; I had a companion, a boy. His hand was warm in mine as he held on tightly, his knuckles white. He was tall with dark spiky hair eyes bluer than the summer's sky. A lady with a willowy figure stepped out of the shadows. Her dress imprinted with gems the same colour as the gold dust spread upon the floor. She was strangely beautiful, her smile illuminated the darkness. The crowd fell silent as she approached; she reached a hand to me. "Lily are you ready to remember?"

I gasped and fell backwards; the wolf rushed to my side pressing his head against mine, checking if I was okay. "Did you see what I saw?" The wolf looked at me and nodded. Amelia's voice slid into my mind *you are a dream breaker, you dream about Ever, it's all real.* I shook her out of my head. "Are you a werewolf, do werewolves even exist?" The wolfs still eyes suddenly became alarmed, I had my answer. "I won't tell anyone, your secrets safe with me. It's not like anyone would believe me anyways." His body then began to shake and rip apart, I quickly stood on shaky feet. Fear clinging to me as I watched his paws turn into fingers, fur turn into human skin, and his wolfish face turn back into a human one.

Cole

It hurt, hurt a lot actually to shift back into a human, it was more painful as I was going against an alpha's command. *No matter what don't ever shift in front of someone that isn't pack!* Lily quickly tore of her jacket and carefully placed it over my nearly fully shifted body, she stepped away. Her alarmed eyes stayed with me as I completed transition. Her fast heartbeat the only sound I could hear. I wrapped the jacket firmly around me, still sat on the damp forest floor, I looked at her. Realization dawned on her. "It's you, the boy that was with Reeve!" I nodded. She slowly crept nearer to sit by me a small smile playing on her lips. "Do you speak?" I laughed out loud, for what seemed like the first time in forever. She had a nice voice. "Yes I speak" her smile became a shade brighter when I replied. "What's your name, I'm Lily?" She formally stuck her hand out to shake; it struck me as old fashioned and odd, I shook it anyway. "Cole." "Nice to properly meet you Cole." I smiled back at her, it was hard not to she radiated such energy. "And you, it's hard to believe the last time I saw you, you were just a little girl." Though it was obvious that she had grown up in the six years I had been away, her face still held the childlike expression she had worn on that day. Her laugh was soft and made my stomach twist. "I could say the same about you, I never knew what you really looked like just your…wolf" she gulped down her confusion before carrying on, it was always hard for humans to accept the truth of who we were, she was doing incredibly well Dean had once told me that Delia hadn't taken it so easily when she eventually found out. "I looked for you after that day, but I never found you." My heart skipped a beat, she looked for me?

"I was moving away that day, dad decided it was time to move on after he found out you had seen me." I didn't know if that was the real reason we had moved away. We moved to different places that had alerted trouble, but all the places we had been had been reasonably quiet. I would never question my father on this that definitely would get me a black eye. "But you came back?"

"Yes, well this is our home, this is where we've always belonged." We sat in silence for a moment before she answered. "Is there more of you here?" Her curiosity burnt into me like a hot iron.

"Yes, but I can't tell you about them, I've already broken the law by showing myself to you, my dad will kill me if you found out anything else!" And I meant literally kill me.

"Then why did you show me?" I looked at her properly taking in her sweet appearance and calm demeanour. "Your different, you could see me when nobody else could."

Lily

I looked at Cole closely as he told me why he had shown me his true identity. I studied his features finding similarities to his wolf self and human one, he had the same icy blue eyes and inky black hair that highlighted his grey pelt. His wolf instincts still on overdrive as he sat in his human skin. His voice carried over the slight breeze to my ears. "Your different, you could see me when nobody else could." Amelia's words rang in my head again, does Cole know, does he know I'm not human, is that what he meant? We sat in silence as I processed his words, I was in total and utter comfort in his presence. It irked me, why wasn't I afraid? Deep inside me something knew he was dangerous, yet I knew he wouldn't hurt me. I was bombarded with conflicting emotions. Should I stay and learn about the world Cole belonged to, the world I belonged to? Or leave and pretend the conversation with Amelia never happened. I knew my heart had made its decision, my mind still swam with the possibilities of both options. He waited patiently as though he knew the war I was wading through. "I should get home" my voice barley a whisper. "I'll walk you out of the wood" he answered as he quickly scanned the trees.
"You don't have to" I looked at him, he returned my gaze, longing drifting into his icy blue irises.
"I want to."

Cole

I stood before she could answer me, wrapping the jacket around my middle. "I'm going to shift but I'm not that strong so I'll have to make myself scarce when were at the edge." She nodded her eyes going round when she realised she would have to watch me shift again. I slowly let in a breath and welcomed the dull ache of the change. Heat spread across my body as it changed forms.

We walked in silence, well it's not like I could talk anyway. She intrigued me as she scanned the forest for impending danger. What got me the most was the knowledge that she couldn't be human, she could see my wolf form therefore making her not Mortalis, but what was she? I would've know if she was another wolf or Lamia my body would be able to sense it. She looked normal so she couldn't be one of the fey, who was she? My heart thudded loudly held captive in my chest, I wanted her to like me, to understand me. Never had I ever experienced this before. I have lived many places, seen many people, never had anyone caught my eye like she had. My very soul reached out to her, if only hers would do the same.

Lily

We neared the entrance to the wood. He stayed behind me and waited as I walked to the very edge, I had made up my mind. I turned to look at him, his body trembling again. "Will I see you again?" His wolf eyes stared at me, his giant grey head nodded. Then just like that, he disappeared. I knew getting to know him would be dangerous, for us both. That I was finally accepting the part of me that wasn't so human. Yet, I couldn't stay away. His image had been imprinted in my heart from the very first moment that I saw him, and with every passing day since then, I found myself falling.

Cole

I glumly returned home in my human skin, after losing grasp of my wolf within seconds of leaving Lily at the boundary line. The cold air bit into my bare skin causing goose bumps to appear, shivers shook my body. I hoped nobody was home. Nobody to question where I had been, who I had been with, the obvious question would be why had I been in my wolf skin when it was light? Walking onto our large open back garden, that mum had yet to work on I noticed Rain waiting for me on the decking. Covering her eyes with her hand she threw me a towel. Stretching my hearing out I didn't detect movement inside the house. Mum and Skyla would be out in the village trying to find mum a job, dad would be out on the boundary lines with Hector and Dean making sure the shield was still intact. The boundary lines were the shield between our world and the human one, our whole supernatural community was hidden in the depths of the woods. The woods stretch further out sometimes it felt like it never ended. We had an invisible shield around our world, a physical barrier that humans cannot pass through, we lived outside of the shield. We were the community's protectors therefore it was our responsibility to keep the community and humans safe.

"Who were you with?" Rain asked still covering her face. Wrapping the towel firmly round me I sat by her. "Nobody." Opening her eyes she looked at me.
"Liar" she didn't say anything else for a while and I didn't answer her. Both caught in our own thoughts. It had been six years since I saw Lily, now she knew who I was, knew what I was. And yet, she still wanted to see me again. I couldn't help but let hope consume me. "Can you tell me about this world you belong to, my father never shared his secrets." I looked at her curious face, why would she like to learn about Ever? Her innocence and imperviousness protects her from the dangers that are unknown to her. "What do you want to know?" She didn't even hesitate. "Everything."

I told Rain to give me a minute to change, it also gave me a moment to process what she wanted to know, was I ready to accept the world I belonged to? Returning outside I nodded towards the woods. "Let's walk and I'll explain on the way, I want to show you something." Standing quickly from her perch on the deck we began to walk.

Deeper we went into the wood, trees surrounding us. "Our world and the human one are split by what we call boundary lines. It's an invisible shield that keeps humans out, it's located deep inside the forest. We live outside the shield because we're the community's protectors. The human village outside the forest is called Evergreen, the world inside the shield is called

Ever." I stopped, waiting for Rain to catch up with me. "So what's the forest called?" She asked, slightly breathless.

"The forest doesn't have a name technically, we just call it the gateway." Her eye brow furrowed as the information sunk in. "What's this community like?" I took a deep breath and began to walk again, keeping my gaze on the treacherous forest, wondering if the tree would betray my secrets. "I've only been inside the shield a few times, I moved around a lot, the two other families that are in our pack looked after the forest while we were gone. Anyway the community as I remember it wasn't anything special, looked very human. It's split into five villages, each for different creatures." She stopped suddenly. "Creatures?" I turned to look at her, fear painted her features. I laughed her obliviousness was quite humorous. "You didn't think we were the only monsters did you?" She simply shrugged her shoulders at me.

"Well one of the villages is called Keila that's where the sagae live."

"Sagae?" Right that meant she didn't understand the language either. "Sagae are witches. Keila is supposed to be very pretty but enclosed, witches like to live close together as their power is stronger in a group. The next village is called Kovu that's where the Nereides live, Nereides means Mermaid. There's about three large lakes in Kovu therefore it's the best place for them, there's also a small stream that leads to the ocean, but many of them don't use it as the ocean isn't protected like the land is." I paused to glance at her stunned expression.

"Mermaids, witches" I nodded.

"That's not all. The other two villages are called Keva and Kolga that's where the Praedictas fatales live, that means fairies, nobody really knows what that land looks like only a chosen few have ever entered and most of the time they don't remember the experience to recall any detail. Then there's the Lamia which means vampires, they got the worst land that Ever has, very dark and desolate not much life exist there. Then again vampires are dead so their land kind of represents them in a weird metaphorical sense."

"Wait vampires exist?" We both stopped to check our surroundings, the sun had moved in the sky telling me it was around lunch time. "Yes vampires exist, as our natural enemies of course they exist, there has to be balance. Lastly the town in Ever that's where the shadows live." Before I could add anything else my senses caught a scent, the smell of blood and death began to suffocate my senses. Seems like my natural enemies had come out to play. I held my breath.

The dark clouds rumbled above us, blocking the light from the sun. The trees turned dark, the wood I once thought was my friend became my foe as the rain started to fall. Shadows darted amongst the trees. I could feel my wolf clawing at my skin, begging to be released. But I couldn't. I wasn't strong enough in this darkening afternoon, the sun hadn't set. "Rain get behind me." She stiffly moved to stand behind me, I could feel her trembling. Fear rolled off her into me. Two shadows emerged from the distance, one male the other female. Their transparent skin seemed to glow as they approached us, my heart thumped loudly in my chest. The man had dark hair like myself, the girl a golden halo of curls, both had the coal black eyes that came with being a vampire. Black like their souls. The man spoke they were only a few feet from us now. "Well, well, well look who we have here Luna." The women smiled at the man with an evil tint in her dark eyes.

"I don't know Levi who do we have here?" The man began to laugh, his laugh was loud and hollow in the empty wood. "I believe we've caught the Alphas son, what a prize." The women cackled alongside him. "Aww and his human girlfriend is with him too" she added. I could hear Rains heartbeat pick up from behind me. They stared at us for a moment before Levi spoke. "What are you doing out here little wolf, a little far from your pack?" He scanned the forest as though he was checking the pack weren't near. "It's none of your business why I'm out here, it is my business to ask what you're doing out here, while the sun is still in the sky." Before I could even comprehend my next thought Levi was directly in front of me, his sharp fangs slipping out of his mouth as he snarled at me. "You have no authority to ask me that question little wolf, your barley a protector, I don't care who your father is, try being cocky again with me I'll rip you to pieces!" I stared blankly at him, my father had taught me to be a protector feel fear on the inside not on the out, don't show your opponent that you're afraid. "You forget your promise Levi, you're not allowed out here." The vamp hissed at me and lunged for me his fangs snapping. Before I could react I felt his weight leave me. I watched in horror as Rain forced Levi back, punching him over and over again in his abdomen he didn't move he was too strong especially compared to Rains human strength. Letting my wolf instincts flow I raced towards them and knocked him down forcing Rain back behind me. I managed to get my hand around his neck about to break it when I heard Rain scream. Pushing Levi away from me hard, he flew into a tree. Knocked out. The bark splintering with his impact. I turned to Rain. Luna held her limply in her arms as she sucked her blood from her neck. I knew what I had to do.

I shifted so quickly that when I pounced my muscles were still changing. Knocking Rain out of the way I clawed and ripped my claws at Luna. Her screams filled the forest, I could smell blood in my nostrils, driving my wolf further. Biting into Lunas neck I felt her try and push me of, but it was too late for her as I ripped her head off. Her body went limp beneath me. Looking towards where I had thrown Levi I saw no body, he must have ran off. Quickly shifting back I ran towards Rain. Her small body was crumpled on the ground, blood seeped from the holes in her neck. Placing pressure I tried to wake her, but she lay motionless. Carefully hoisting her into my arms I ran with her, back the way we had come.

Lily

"Remember what?" I asked the lady as she approached the golden circle. Looking towards the boy who held my hand I came to realise it was Cole, he squeezed my hand comforting me. "Remember who you are Lily." The people who had surrounded the circle disappeared including Cole.

Instead I stood facing a castle. It was old fashioned, the walls crumbling. The sapphire flags from the towers flapped in the wind. I blinked. Suddenly I was in a room. I could feel the warmth of the fire blazing from the corner, the room was a dull grey stone, a weird patterned logo that twisted the words Umbra hung on the walls. Two golden and red velvet chairs stood in the centre of the room. A man sat in one of them. He was young, pale and fair. His blue gaze held thoughts deeper than the ocean that roared from outside. He looked troubled. A women entered the room and bowed at the man. She wore a white nurse's dress with a matching apron. Her grey streaked hair tied tightly back. Blood smothered her white apron. Her voice was quiet "your majesty it's a girl!" The man stood quickly from his throne, his deep burgundy cloak clouded around him, his once worried eyes shone with joy. "Let me see her." The women nodded and bowed at him before retreating. The man paced until she returned with a small bundle in her arms. She bowed once more at the man before placing the bundle in the man's waiting arms "your daughter your majesty." The man's eyes brimmed with tears at her stared down at his sleeping

*daughter, her blonde wisps of hair stuck to her forehead as he kissed them
"my little Lily."*

Cole

When we made it to our garden I started shouting, shouting for mum, for
dad for anyone. Dad, Dean and Hector rushed out from our house, they
must have just got home. Dad reached us first. Checking me over before
looking at Rain, I let Dean take her from me as he rushed her inside telling
Hector to go and get Delia, and something about some painkillers in the
bathroom cabinet. Leaving me naked outside with dad. He looked at me,
really looked at me. Fear etched in his eyes, he was worried. "Are you
okay?" Concerned filled his tone. Confused I just nodded. Then, for the
first time in six years, he hugged me. He gripped me tightly as though I
was about to disappear into thin air. "We found that girl vamp when we
were coming back, we could smell you had been there. But then we saw
all the blood so we raced home. We thought we had lost you." His voice
began to crack. He let me go and I noticed he was crying. "Cole I've done
things in the past that I regret, I've hurt you and I can't ever forgive myself
for those things. I get angry and lash out. But thinking that you were dead
snapped me out of everything. I saw who I was and hated it. I'm sorry I
know you can never forgive me but I promise I'll be a proper father
again." And with that he turned and walked into the house. Leaving me
alone and confused.

It felt like I had stood and contemplated things for forever, that's when
Reeve found me. He tossed me some shorts, waiting for me to pull them
on before speaking. "Your dad just called me and told me to enrol you
into school." Looking up I saw him smiling, shock kept the words that
were jumbled in my mind from spilling out. "First day tomorrow here's
your uniform, dads bringing some books over later when he comes to
collect mum, are you okay?" I sat down on the deck and nodded at him.
This was all too much to take in; seeing Lily, Rain nearly dying, killing a
vampire, my dad, going to school. I felt like I was going to faint. Reeve
took a seat next to me sensing something I hadn't said. "Do you want to
talk about whatever has you in a twist?" I shook my head it was too

complicated to explain. "Ok well you know where I am if you need me, I'll see you tomorrow. Bright and early!" He smiled at me and left.

Two weeks ago I moved back here, hoping things would be different. For a while nothing had changed, but then Rain appeared, I met Lily, Rain nearly died, my dad wanted to be my dad again. Now everything has changed.

Lily

I had always hated Mondays. The fact that the weekend was over was bad enough, let alone the classes that awaited me. Walking into the maths block was one of the most depressing moments of my existence. Flanking me, as we walked into class was Sky and Lexi, Mr Parker was already writing equations on the board. We split ways as we weren't allowed to sit in class together anymore, apparently we were a distraction to the rest of the students. It's not my fault that Lexi laughs loud, so loud it makes the floor shake, and that her long legs stick out from under the table. Tripping up those who dared walk past. Taking my seat at the back of the class I smiled at Emily the girl who shared the back row with me. She was nice with curly blonde hair and dark eyes, she ran like I did so we had that In common, not much else. Mr Parker cleared his throat to get our attention, knowing he was just going to tell us what we were doing for the lesson, I looked down beginning to doodle in my book.

"Class this is our new student Cole Star." Looking up abruptly I saw Cole standing at the front of the class sporting the ugly green school uniform. I could see that every girl had started to pay attention now, their interest irritated me. What the hell was he doing here? "Cole take a seat next to Lily at the back." My heart stopped. Cole began walking towards me his icy blue eyes locked onto me, a small smile playing on his lips. Taking the seat on the opposite side of me he began pulling out his exercise book. I whispered to him. "What are you doing here?" He laughed softly. "I'm here to learn like you." He didn't look at me instead his gaze was locked on the equations Mr Parker was drawing on the board, my attention should have been too, but it wasn't. I took the time to study him while he was occupied with something else. His inky black hair was spiked, but I noticed it curled around his ears and the back of his neck. His icy blue eyes had layers of blue in them not just a solid colour, his skin was pale under the fluorescent lights. He began to chuckle under his breath, I noticed he had a dimple in his cheek too. "Will you stop staring at me I'm trying to listen here?" I blushed and turned my attention onto Mr Parker too.

After the lesson had finished I waited for Cole to come out of the room, he was taking his time to talk to Mr Parker. "Are you coming?" Lexi shouted from down the corridor. She only ever had one volume and that was loud.

"I'll catch you up." Lexi frowned before nodding and disappearing into the crowd. Five minutes later Cole walked out of the classroom, smiling when he saw me. "So when do you come to school?" He frowned for a moment as we began to walk towards the yard for break.

"Since my dad decided home-schooling was no longer an option." I nodded at his answer, but something in his tone told me that he was hiding something.

As the day went on I realised me and Cole shared the same classes, apart from English. Lexi was in his English. "Do you know the new boy Cole?" She blurted out as we waited in the queue for lunch. I looked across the dining hall to find Cole sitting with Reeve and his collection of friends. "Yeah I knew him before he came here." Technically that wasn't a lie. She beamed at me.

 "He's in my English will you...introduce us?" I nearly dropped my food, did she like him?

"You want me to introduce you to him?" We sat down at our table that stood near the long window that looked out at the yard. The usual occupants sat around us, Sky, Ella, Sean and Luke. Our group of friends was small but perfect. "Well...he's cute." I looked at Lexi her eyes hidden behind darkened shades, her face glowed with promise. "Sure I'll introduce you." Smiling at me she began to dig into her food, I however, no longer had an appetite. "Lily you okay?" I snapped out of my irrational jealous haze to see Sean talking to me. "Yeah I'm just not hungry." Sean could've been a good looking guy if he hadn't been a friend. He had short blonde hair with brown eyes, tanned skin from playing sport all summer and a smile that could light up a room. Many girls have tried to date him but he cared too much for sport to date. Luke was the geek in our group, he had dark hair with freckles and small wire framed glasses. He however dated Ella a small ginger haired girl with huge green eyes. At first we all found it weird that two of our friends were dating, but we came to accept it, they were cute together.

The end of the day finally came for the rest of the students, I however, still had an hour here to train. Championships were two weeks away. Mr Light wasn't there when I arrived so I started stretching knowing he would be here soon. I nearly jumped out of my skin when someone tapped me on the shoulder. "Whoa!" Reeve stepped back his hands held high laughing. I placed my hand over my speeding heart and smiled "god Reeve you nearly gave me a heart attack!" He laughed. Over the past few days we had grown closer, texting every day and speaking in between classes. "Sorry, I just wanted to say hi I didn't get to see you today I was a little preoccupied." I smiled at him and waved it away. "Don't need to apologise you could've just text me."
"I prefer talking like this." I turned away from him before he could see me blush.
"Lily start lapping!" Mr Light shouted as he walked towards us, I huffed turning to look at Reeve with an apologetic smile. "You've got to train, text me when you get home." I smiled and nodded. He stepped towards me so he was directly in front of me, he paused then brushed a kiss on my forehead before turning and leaving. Mr Light simply looked at me. Blushing and my heart skipping a beat I began to do my laps.

Cole

I felt different. A good different. I felt like I was finally me, the person I've always wanted to be, the normal me. I felt like I was in a dream. Returning home after a day of school finding mum in the kitchen cooking dinner, Skyla in the living room watching cartoons on the television. The most satisfying feeling consumed me when I realised this was finally my life.

School had been everything I had expected it to be, but better. It gave me the chance to talk to Lily, get to know her, finally. Quickly changing out of my uniform I went to check on Rain. The dimly lit room made her normally tanned skin look ashen. She lay immobile. The only sound was her slow breath and barely audible heartbeat. She hadn't woken up. "She's lost a lot of blood but she's healing, slowly." Turning I found my father in the doorway, still in shock from what he had revealed yesterday. I didn't know how to react to him anymore, sensing my discomfort he spoke. "Listen I know I've not been a good father in the past, that I hurt you and your mother. But please let me make it up to you, I don't ever want you to be afraid of me, ever again! Please forgive me." He looked down as emotion weighed on his shoulders. Surprising myself and him I took the few steps that separated us and hugged him, tightly. I could smell the salt of his tears as he let them fall freely, his sins trailing down his face. Stepping back he patted my shoulder with a slight smile before leaving. Turning back to Rain I moved a curl of her face before turning to leave, about to take a step a warm hand gripped my wrist.

Lily

The house was dark and empty when I returned home from training. Letting myself in I turned on all the lights, finding comfort in the now illuminated rooms. Knowing mum had taken dad to a hospital appointment and had dropped Leah of at her ballet classes the worry that had begun building up inside of me diminished slightly. Where was Leo? Pulling my phone out of my back pocket I dialled his number. The irritating sound of Leo's ringtone filled the empty silence of the house, heart pounding I followed the sound as it guided me up the stairs. The noise brought me to Leo's room his door cracked open ever so slightly. Fumbling I switched on the bedroom light.

Silently creeping into his room I found nothing. "Boo!" Dropping my phone I let out a mighty scream that even surprised me. Closing my eyes I let fear overwhelm me. Warm hands gripped my arms "Lily it's me Leo." Peeling back my eyes lids I looked into my brothers amused eyes. Anger kicked my fear out of my body. Letting me go as though he sensed my anger he began to laugh. "It was supposed to be a joke, lighten up a little." Still staring at him I shouted.
"Well I didn't find it funny you scared me half to death, I thought something had happened to you, I thought someone was going to kill me!" He immediately stopped laughing his serious expression returning. "Lily what's going on?" Picking up my phone I turned to leave, but he stopped me. "Nothing my dreams have me a little on the edge that's all."

Turning me around so he could look me in the face, worry etched onto his face now. "I'm sorry, do you want to talk about it?" I shook my head at him. "Don't worry nothing I can't handle but no more jokes like that." He smiled holding his pinkie finger up to me like we used to do when we were kids "I promise." Smiling back I shook his pinkie with my own.

Returning to my room I couldn't shake the unnerving feeling that I was being watched.

Cole

Rain kept her grip on me as she gasped for breath, her eyes bloodshot. Delia was by her side nursing her, yet she kept her reddened gaze on me. The room was full, mum, dad, Dean and Hector all stood and watched Rain writhe in pain. "What's wrong with her?" I asked Delia as she rubbed Rains back, soothing her. "I think she has an infection, but I don't know where." Delia was a nurse at the local hospital, she was Rains only hope. "I think we need to take her to a hospital?" I said.
"No!" They all answered, looking to Delia she added the details I was missing.
"She has werewolf blood, if she goes to a hospital their bound to find something in her blood, an abnormality. We have to protect the pack." Looking at Rain I watched her fever consume her, her heart beat which was slow only an hour ago beat rapidly in her chest. "Cole...you...never got to...finish telling me...about Ever!" Rain gasped between heavy breaths. Mum looked at me.
"You told her about Ever?" Her worry latched onto me, dad spoke up.
"He has done nothing wrong she would have learned about Ever sooner or later, Cole finish your story the rest of us should leave, let Rain rest." Nodding everybody left following dad, Delia waited behind a moment "call me if she gets worse." Nodding at her I watched her leave before looking back at Rain.

Her tired eyes looked at me. Waiting. "Where bout's in the story did I get to?" Her heavy breathing stopped for a moment before she answered voice cracking "you...were talking about...shadows."
"Shadows is the nickname we give to the royals of Ever." She swallowed hard before answering.
"Royals?"

"Yes Ever had a King and Queen."

"Had?" Looking past her to the window I noticed it had become dark. The night sky was a jigsaw of clouds, no moon to set the world alight.

"The Queen died about sixteen years ago, she was giving birth and she just died. The only royals that are left is the King, his mother, brother and his wife."

"What...about the...baby?" I looked at Rain her eyes began brimming with tears, I didn't understand why the story upset her. "Nobody knows". Rain looked at me with pain filled eyes, she turned away from me, away from the story. Blocking my words out. It occurred to me that the story was sad, a women died giving birth to a child only for the child to disappear anyway. A huge swell of emotion burned inside of me, leaving the room I decided I needed the release of the wolf. I had been right all along I wasn't ready to accept the world I belonged to.

Lily

The man looked down at the baby smiling, love and adoration shone in his brilliant blue irises. The baby shared his gaze and his fair hair, she was beautiful and angelic as she held onto to his finger with her tiny hand. "Brother." A man called from the doorway sharing the same handsome looks as the man by the cradle only a shade darker. The new man wore fitted leather trousers and a worn black top, his emerald cloak fitted around his shoulders. The man's gaze left the child's and looked towards the man. "Lucas you have news?" The man, Lucas looked at the man as though he was in pain.

"It is true, he is here. I won't let anything happen to you or my new niece. I promised our father that I would always protect you. Losing Alana was devastating I won't allow you to be childless too." The man managed a small smile in the direction of Lucas. But it was forced. "Thank you brother." Picking up the child from where she lay in the cradle he held her in his arms. The golden sunlight that trailed from the window made the blonde strands of her hair glow. "I won't let anything hurt you, my little Lily" the man whispered as he kissed the child's head.

Gasping I sat up straight, heart pounding. Two nights I had dreamt of the same man, the same child. Looking around I found myself not in a castle but in my room. I had slept. The clock read 3:15am. Where had the rest of the night gone? Leah's familiar shape lay in her bed, soundless and asleep. When had she come home? The dream felt so real, I felt the love the man shared for his child as though it was my own. Never had my dreams been so real. The girl her name was Lily. Somewhere in the back of my mind this all made sense. But here, right now, nothing made sense.

Cole

Lily looked tired and pale as she took a seat next to me in history. Human history had always intrigued me, but her shadowed eyes and strained smile caught my attention more. "Are you okay, you look tired?" Rubbing her eyes and yawning she replied.
"Bad dream." A girl sat behind us tapped Lily on the shoulder. She was small her dark hair hung in ringlets around her face. She was strange with a baby blue eye and a chocolate one. "Lily have you heard from Lexi?" Lily turned to face the girl giving me the chance to study her like she had studied me the day before. For the first time I noticed that her hair was a mixture of light blonde and gold which curled loosely at the ends. She was pale but not sickly pale, the best thing about her was her eyes. They were an endless blue that shone brighter with her smile. She was beautiful. Sensing my eyes on her Lily faced me, a slight blush crept onto her cheeks. "Will you stop staring at me I'm trying to concentrate?" We laughed and turned our attention to the front of the class.

At break I sat with Reeve and his friends. His friends were all popular and incredible at sport, I however was the oddity in the group. His friends were nice and polite, who gladly made me feel welcome here. "So Cole do you know this Lily that Reeves obsessed with?" One of Reeves friends asked I think his name was Joe. The way Joe was smiling when he said Lily's name made me want to punch him in the face. "Yeah I've known her a while why?" That caught Reeves attention who was previously silently texting away on his phone. "You know Lily, since when?" His jealous frown made me want to laugh, but also cower away from him. "I knew her before I moved away, I didn't know she was the same person you were talking about." I answered truthfully. Reeve nodded his frown still in place. Joe began to laugh.
"Aww Reeve are you scared of a little competition?" This time it was my turn to frown.
"There's no competition, I'm not interested in Lily like that." I lied. Reeve looked at me as though he knew I was lying, I shrugged my shoulders at him. "Well guys I'm going to class see you at lunch." I stood to leave and

began walking to the double doors into the English block. Reeve quickly caught up with me, my lie probably bugging him more than it should. "Ignore Joe he likes to make everything a big deal." Pulling the door open I flicked my gaze to him. "I'm not bothered but clearly you are." Reeve stopped walking, ignoring the annoyed shouts from students trying to pass by. "Be honest with me Cole do you like Lily?" He looked at me with sad eyes. Reeve was like my brother and if that meant ignoring my growing feelings for Lily then that's what I'll do. Pack came first hands down, yeah Lily was important to me, but so was Reeve. I couldn't lose him. "No Reeve we're just friends." Reeve took a long breath before smiling, lightly punching me in the arm he said "see you at lunch." He left leaving me in the empty corridor.

Lily

The willowy woman waited patiently for me, as she sat on a moss smothered bolder, her golden curls illuminating the darkness. Her beauty radiated light around her like a halo. She was an angel shining in the shrouding darkness. Her pale eyes were kind, but something about them screamed danger. Why was I here? "Lily have you figured it out yet?" Her mouth didn't move, yet I heard her voice. "I'm in your head Lily." Her voice again only this time I felt it, her voice in my head, an unwelcome visitor. "Who are you?" I asked out loud my voice wavering the fear that had suddenly built up inside me. "The question you should be asking is, who are you?" She stood up, poised gracefully as she smiled at me. "Who am I?" The lady turned softly away from me and began walking, I tried to follow but my feet wouldn't move. "That's what you're trying to find out." Her voice followed me as I woke.

"Lily, Lily wake up!" Sky's voice was urgent yet distant. I was alone. The darkness that had surrounded me was suffocating. I began to panic, my heart stuttered in my chest. I couldn't breathe. I swallowed oxygen in but I didn't stop the fire burning inside of me. I was so tired. Then suddenly I was reborn, ripped from the darkness and brought back to the land of the living.

A cold hand held mine, another stroked my face gently. I was no longer in the darkness, but the school corridor. Sky above me speaking to me, my senses were muffled, her words silent. The fire had followed me, searing my veins. I screamed. "Help someone help me!" Sky screamed as tears ran down her face. I tried to speak, the fire held onto my throat in a death grip. Another hand held me now, warmer. I struggled against their hold the fire only getting hotter with their touch. What was wrong with me? The owner of the hand spoke to me. "Lily, Lily look at me!" Reeves voice was firm and alarmed as he held my hand tightly. I tried to look at him, but it was too painful. I lay immobile.

Then hundreds of voices were talking to me. Some I recognised, Reeve, Sky, Lexi, Cole, now Leo too. I could hear him swearing at someone to do something to help. I could hear the sound of an ambulance as it neared. I tried to open my eyes. I screamed. Then everything disappeared.

Cole

I watched. Watched as Lily writhed in pain on the corridor floor. Never speaking, only long agonised screams that pierced into your very soul. I watched. There was nothing anyone could do, nobody knew what was wrong with her. Reeve sat by her head holding her hand, he was speaking to her, she didn't respond. By now the crowd was large, each person trying to speak to her, each getting the same response as I did, a scream. I watched. Watched as she cried silent tears, watched her face contort in pain. It was like watching Rain all over again, but worse. Because in a weird hurtful way I could feel her pain as though it was my own.

I could hear the sirens of the ambulance as it neared. The crowd began to scatter as teachers forced them back. But I stayed. Reeve and Sky held both of her hands. A boy who was older than me who must have been Lily's older brother from the way he screamed at a teacher to help stood back. His eyes filled with pain. The door opened admitting two paramedics who raced to Lily's side, forcing Reeve and Sky to let go. I watched as they carefully guided her body onto a gurney, I watched her leave attached to an oxygen mask, I watched as the paramedics got her into the ambulance with her brother. I watched as that ambulance drove away in hurried succession. I watched her leave, not knowing if she was going to be okay.

I walked Reeve home. Normally he would walk with his friends, me I would walk alone. Not today. He needed me, and I him. We walked in silence both of us thinking about the same thing. Lily. Reeve looked tired under the afternoon light, worry etched his features, I probably looked the same. "Do you think she will be okay?" He asked when we made it to the outside of his house, the sun was slowly ducking behind the trees, the day turning cooler. "I don't know, I hope so." Reeve let out a giant sigh, the sigh was a mixture of different emotions, fear, confusion, anger, maybe a hint of jealousy too. Today had been a long day. I sat by him. "I've never seen anything like it, I didn't know what to do Cole, I could sense she was in pain but..." he stopped. It was obvious to me now, more obvious than it was before that Reeve did care deeply for Lily. It was strange, they hadn't been talking for long. Then again wasn't it the same for me? "I know, but she's in the best place at the moment. I'm sure the hospital will know what's wrong with her." I hoped he believed what I was saying, even if I didn't. I didn't know if Reeve knew that Lily couldn't be human, but if I offered that information he would ask how I would know, and I would have to tell him that she had seen me as a wolf. Tell him I broke the law. "She looked tired maybe she's training too hard again." Reeve let the statement hang in the air, I knew he didn't believe what he said. He was merely convincing himself that there was a logical reason for Lily's illness.

The door cracked open from behind us making us both jump. It was Carmen who squeezed herself through the doorway. Carmen was thirteen and was home schooled. Due to the fact that when she was younger she was bullied for being different. She didn't look unusual, in fact she was quite pretty, petite light blonde and brown hair, a nice smile. There was just something about her that the other kids didn't like. Maybe it was the way her eyes dilate all the time as she struggles to tame her wolf. Or the fact that every time she was near you were filled with an instant state of calm. Reeves parents couldn't stand another day of her coming home and crying for hours, so she was home schooled. Though it was better than before I knew she didn't enjoy it. Like me and my sister she was lonely, starved of friendship from others her age. Carmen lightly pushed me and Reeve apart so she was sat in the middle. Taking one of my hands from my lap she held it in her own, she did the same to Reeve. She must have sensed our anxiety from inside, I knew I could sense my own. She was helping us, calming us. "Would you like to share what has you both so worked up?" Her voice was soft and light. Reeve looked down before answering his sister.

"Lily." Lily had saved Carmen's life only a week ago and the two had formed an odd friendship, anxiety now rolled off her too. "What happened to Lily?" She swallowed.

"We found her collapsed on the floor, she was screaming out in pain, her skin was boiling hot. We had to call the ambulance." Reeve never looked at either of us as he spoke, instead kept his eyes on the darkening wood. "Is she going to be okay?" Her question was left unanswered as neither of us knew the answer. The three of us sat in comfortable silence, growing up together we were all close, we were pack. Together we watched the sun descend beneath the trees, and the sky turn from blue to the amber and violet hues of sunset.

Lily

The fire burned within me. Scorching flames flickering beneath my skin.

Cole

Two days ago Lily was rushed to hospital after collapsing at school, a ferocious fever consumed her every breath. I hadn't heard from her, neither had Reeve. Her brother wasn't at school, there was nobody to ask. Her friends hadn't heard anything either, her friend Sky, who was in my history class told me that she tried to visit her at the hospital, but they wouldn't let her in. I felt like I had gone back six years, back when I didn't know her, back when I thought she didn't exist.

Lily

The fire was dormant, for now. I awoke to the clinging smell of disinfectant, crème walls and a scratchy hospital gown. Bolting up straight I took in my surroundings. The room was quiet basic, cream walls, metal beds, beeping machines. It looked like I was the only occupant of the room, which made me feel slightly relieved. Before I could comprehend another thought, my mother walked through the door. Her face lit up when she saw I had awoken, her hug was hard and urgent. Sitting back she stroked my hair, tears made her hazel eyes glassy. "You're awake." I nodded against her hand, still not sure exactly what happened to me. "What happened to me?" My voice surprised me by being strong. Mum let go of my face and took my hand instead. "You had a fever, the doctor couldn't tell us why you had a fever just that you had one. You collapsed at school, you've been out for two days, we were so worried." Her voice cracked. I swell of guilt bubbled inside of me, she had dad to worry about not me. "I'm sorry mum." She took me back into her arms and rubbed my back like she used to when I was younger. "It's not your fault Lily, none of this is your fault." I couldn't help but think she wasn't just talking about my fever.

Cole

After being at school for a full week now weekends became boring. Reeve was at football practice with the boys from his group, I couldn't really say 'our' group because it wasn't. They weren't my friends they were acquaintances, they were someone who would help point me in the right direction of a classroom if I washed up in their area sometime. I thought about joining the team, but I was worried. As a werewolf our speed, strength and senses were all enhanced even in our human forms. As the alpha's son my let's call them 'powers' were a lot stronger than Reeves. He has it easier, he could tone it down. But me, I couldn't. Joining any form of sporting club wasn't an option, but I wanted it. Then again it would only get worse when you fully became a protector, when you received your family crest on your arm and your wolf became a part of your everyday life. Your senses would be like a wolf all the time even in your human skin. Feeling lonely I walked round to the Moon's house, hoping Jett was in. Rain had woken up fever free a few days ago, she was still weak but found comfort in my little sister Skyla.

The Moon's house was the smallest building on the complex of wood where we lived. Though it was small it was the better looking house on the outside. The walls weren't crumbling for a start. I knocked on the door waiting for someone to answer. I heard crashing and fumbling, and maybe a few swear words before the door was tugged forcefully open. Hector stood before me, his once anxious expression formed an easy smile when he saw me. "Cole come in come in!" Stepping inside my senses were suddenly ambushed with the sweet aroma of chocolate chip cookies. Lila must have been baking again. My empty stomach rumbled. "Hungry? Come into the kitchen Lila was just preparing lunch" Hector laughed and gently pulled me into the kitchen. Lila was Hector's wife, like my mother and Reeves's mother she was human. However, unlike my own mother Lila can sure as hell cook!

The kitchen's platinum white tiles glittered as the afternoon sun shone in through the open window admitting a gust of autumn air. "Cole how nice to see you" Lila smiled when she spotted me making my way into the kitchen, her subtle French accent was as pleasant as the breeze. "Nice to see you too Lila it's been a while." Last time I had seen Lila I had been moving away. I hadn't had chance to come over here with everything that had been going on. Lila hadn't change from the last time that I had seen her. She still had the same sandy blonde hair and aluminous green eyes that matched her sons. "It sure has kid, you staying for lunch?" The question was really rhetorical, she knew I would be staying for lunch. "Sure, where's Jett?"
"I'm right here" he answered as he swept into the kitchen kissing his mum on the cheek before taking a chair next to me. Unlike his mother, Jett had changed since the last time I had seen him. His hair had grown longer and lighter, it was almost the same sandy blonde as his mothers. His face had changed, aged, grown older. His eyes were the same, which made me feel slightly relieved. I felt sudden longing for the nine year old boy I had left behind, with his cute chubby cheeks and mischievous spikes. Jett caught me staring at him and smiled. "Not seen me in six years, don't tell me you didn't think I was going to change?" He laughed at me. I hit him playfully in the shoulder before digging into whatever Lila had cooked up for us. "Dad told me you've started school. How you finding it?" It's not the question I thought he'd ask.
"Schools fine, great actually I've just got a lot to catch up on."
"Bet Lily will help you with that" his statement made me nearly choke on my chicken enchilada.

"What!" He turned to face me with a serious face, well as much of a serious face a fifteen year old can manage. "Reeve told me you knew her before he did and that you both have classes together so I thought as you were friends she could help you catch up." Oh he wasn't thinking anything else. Phew.

"Besides I know you like her so you won't mind spending time with her even if it is studying" now I did choke on my food. He patted me roughly on the back. "What are you on about?"

"I'm saying I know you like Lily from the way you nearly choked on your food before when I mentioned her, I'm not stupid. Just do me a favour. Don't fall in love with her!" Now I looked at him with a serious face, well as much of a serious face a 'sixteen' year old can muster. "Don't worry I'm not going to fall in love with her." Jett visibly relaxed and began biting into his enchilada. "Good because I'm not going to let some girl swoop in and rip apart you and your best friend, I won't tell Reeve you like her I don't think that would go down very well. So your secret is safe with me." He patted my shoulder and carried on eating. Me, however had lost his appetite.

"Thanks Jett, that means a lot." Hector shuffled back into the kitchen Lila on his arm. They were both smiling. Lila and Hectors relationship seemed to never die they were always happy and never argued. "It was love at first sight" he would tell us, then Lila would smile and wink before kissing her husband on the lips. I wanted a love like theirs one day. "So Cole you gave us quite a scare the other day" Hectors voice was fatherly and caring.

"Well when I left I never intended to kill a vampire now did I" a gasp sounded next to me, Jett was suddenly excited.

"You killed a vamp and didn't come and tell me!" I looked guiltily towards him.

"Sorry Jett a lot happened between then, I was just trying to catch my breath." He smiled at me the same innocent smile that has always been present on his face. "Don't worry about it, next time I'll kick your arse if you don't come to tell me!" We all began to laugh, Lila came up behind her son and hugged him. "You will not kick Coles 'arse' you will kick his behind no swearing in this house" she looked towards her husband and son "even mild swearing." I laughed along with them in their easy chatter that I missed so much.

I returned home later that evening. The day had become dark and empty. There was no moon tonight to light up the night sky. Walking inside I heard people laughing in the living room. Laughter? Stepping into the living room I saw my family sat around the fire, a game of monopoly in front of them. Skyla sat on my father's knee giggling as he tickled her. Mum sat with Rain who was currently handing her money from the box. Rain still looked drained but she also looked happy. Her maroon gaze found me. "Cole come play monopoly your dads such a cheater!" She laughed at my dad as he pulled a face. "I do not cheat, I'm simply better at buying the correct places than you." They both laughed. Mum held her hand to me, I took it and sat down. Skyla scrambled from dads knee to sit on me instead. "I'll help you win I know dads tricks" she giggled in my ear. Dad and mum were laughing hard "hey sky you can't tell him all my secrets." She smiled sweetly at him with her big innocent eyes "sure I can."

The night went quickly and soon people began to fall asleep, exhausted from laughing over and over again. But I was wide awake. Skyla helped me win two games, my victory still rang in my veins. I smiled. I finally knew what true happiness felt like. It was this night, this laughter, this moment. I finally felt content.

Lily

Hospitals were fine, until you were alone. Night had fallen on the hospital. Condemning its occupants to sleep and dream. Yet, I was awake. My room was empty of the living. Myself not included. The only indication of life was the flickering fluorescent light which hung on the ceiling in the vacant corridor. I obviously knew there were others sharing the hospital with me, but the night had captured their voices. My fever which had burned me inside out was resting, dormant. For now anyway. I stood. This hospital was built for people who were ill or...dead. At this very moment I was neither of those things. My body suddenly felt obliged to leave even though I hadn't yet been discharged. I began to quietly fumble around for the clothes I knew mum had left for me when she had visited earlier this evening. If I was leaving I wasn't about to go round wearing my pyjamas. Changed, I tiptoed down the hallway. Adrenalin sizzling in my veins instead of my dreadful fever. This was the second time I had sunk out. The first being my house, now a hospital. I felt my rebellious mind twitch under that concept. I smiled. The double doors were the only indication that the endless hallway did in fact end somewhere. I had made it out of my room and down the corridor without being detected. Small voices entered the hall behind me. Quickly turning down a narrower corridor I hid myself behind a wall. The voices slowly faded away as they moved further away from me. I waited a few seconds before slipping back onto the main hallway. The exit was directly in front of me. The urge to leave became too much and I sprinted out of the door. Freedom within my grasp.

After escaping into the night from the hospital, the adrenalin began to fade, fear taking its place. If it had been daytime I would have known exactly where to go to get home. At night the world looked different. I debated whether to go back into the hotel of the ill and dead, but a slight rustle behind me stopped me in my tracks.

From the tree line that stopped a few metres from the hospital a figure emerged. The man's face was hidden by the shadows. I could tell he was very pale, almost transparent. His hair was darker than the night sky. Stepping into the car parks lights I saw his face. He was good looking in a raw kind of way, and the way he confidently strolled towards me told me he knew exactly how good looking his face was. Jerk. His coal black eyes burned into me with his intense gaze. I watched him carefully progress towards me. "Can you see me little girl?" Fear clung onto my vocal cords, I nodded. His dark eye brows rose to his hairline. He looked surprised then he composed his features into a smirk. "What are you?" He called. Then suddenly he was directly in front of my face, invading my personal space. Sniffing me? I trembled with fear. He definitely wasn't human, but if he was his parents should have taught him some manners. "You smell human, yet you can see me?" He spoke to me. Finding my voice I managed to stutter out. "What are you?" The man smirked at me maliciously. "Your worst nightmare!" He lunged at me.

Cole

I was just falling to sleep when Dean Skies rushed into the house shouting for my father. "James Lamia attack at the hospital, we've got to move now!" Dad who had been groggy with sleep seemed suddenly awake. "Let's move!" I raced after them to where Hector had been waiting. "I'm coming with you" I spoke before they could turn and leave. Dad spun round clutching my shoulders. "No son, I've nearly lost you to a vampire once I'm not letting that happen again." He turned to go, I shouted after him. "How will I become a protector if you won't even let me protect?" Dad let worry etch his face, Dean took him by the shoulder looking at me. "He's right James how will they learn?" Dad sighed a loaded sigh before nodding at me, but looked grim. "Ok fine, stick close the Lamia aren't normally alone, keep your wits about you. All of you shift now!" The order ripped through us forcing our bodies to shift. Adrenalin pumped through me but fear made sure she still clung to my heart, as I plunged into the night.

Lily

I ran. My heart crashed against my chest, pleading to escape. I was blind in this eerie darkness. The crunching of my feet over the leaves drowned out my attackers approach. My breath was stolen from me as my advancer tackled me to the ground. I screamed. The man pinned me to the ground I tried to escape his hold but he was too strong. Pointed fangs slipped from his lips as he snarled at me. His dark black eyes blazing at me as he laughed, enjoying my fear. "You're a little fighter." His breath smelled of blood, which made me want to gag. Then, I was no longer alone. Bodies surrounded me and the man. The man pulled me up and held me against his body his arm wrapped tightly around my neck. His icy skin chilling me down to the bone. Four wolves stood in front of us. One of the wolves was a dusty brown his neighbour was white with grey patches. The wolf closest to me was pure black his growl was louder than the others. From the way the others flanked him I guessed him to be the natural leader. The last wolf was stood back from the others his intense blue gaze was on me the whole time. Cole. Hope flooded my senses. "You want her, come get her!" The man growled at the wolves whose answer was snapping their jaws at him. The black wolf growled loudly then pounced onto the man the other wolves not far behind him. The man had lost his grip on me letting me stumble out of the way. I fell to the ground, the wet forest floor scratching at my bare skin on my arms and face. Cole came to me placing himself protectively in front of me as he kept his gaze on the fight. He nudged me with his humongous head, checking if I was alright. The man had managed to knock out the white wolf who lay stiffly on the ground a small whimper falling from his muzzle. The others were too preoccupied to help him, I heard Cole whine. His eyes swimming with longing to help. "Go Cole check if he's okay, I'll stay by you." Cole looked back at me and nodded. We made it over to the wolf his breathing slow. Cole nudged him and whined but he lay unresponsive. I sat by the wolf making sure I kept my eye on the fight that lay ahead. Suddenly I felt compelled to reach out and brush his ivory fur. I reached out with my hand. I had barely touched the wolf before he jerked awake, his eyes on me. He looked to Cole then to the fight. His gaze then found me again and something in his eyes suggested he was in awe of me. I pushed him back down before he could stand. "You're hurt you can't fight." The wolf looked to the fight then back to me. Remembering I'm not supposed to know about Cole I spoke "your friend can take your place" I jerked my head at Cole who stood still. He nodded to the wolf before dashing to the other two wolves' aid. The wolf just stared at me with wonder. And I stared back. He seemed different compared to the others. He was smaller, nimbler. The way he watched and fought wasn't aggressive, merely necessary. He reminded me of what I felt when I felt Carmen that day. Calm.

Before I knew it the others had joined us, each staring at me as though I was some sort of god. Well everyone except Cole who just stared at the others with confusion. I looked behind them to see that the man had vanished. No evidence that his presence was even here, apart from the red hand marks around my wrists, and small bruises dotting my side from where I had thrown myself out of the way. The black wolf stared at Cole I watched their silent conversation before Cole nodded. He came to stand behind me and nudged me forward. He wanted me to leave. I began walking he made sure he was stood beside me the whole time. I looked back to the others but like the man they too had disappeared. The sky had begun to turn purple and pink the sun just rising beneath the tree line. Sun rise. The wood opened to us like a door and I found myself at the entry just a few streets from my house. I looked back at Cole but he was gone. He had vanished as quietly as he had come. I was alone. I stepped out of the wood back into reality. I made my way home.

Cole

The sun had nearly fully risen by the time I got home. When I got inside I found the living room full to the brim. Dean and his wife Delia, Hector and Lila and my mum and dad were all sat hunched together, whispering. When they saw me they stopped. All of them looking displeased. They knew. Somehow they had figured out that Lily knew about me. "Cole come in" my father spoke using his alpha tone, I was never getting away with this. I sat. They all stared at me. "Do you know the girl we just saved?" I looked to my father he didn't look angry, just disappointed. Which in fact was worst. God I've only just got him back don't let this take him away again. I nodded before speaking. "She goes to my school her names Lily." Everyone gasped. Hector spoke "it can't be can it?" Dean looked at him before answering. "When I first met her I never really thought anything of it but now." I looked between them both confused. My mum just clutched my father's hand. "Is it true James, have we found her after all these years?" My father looked suddenly tired the night must be catching up on him. He stroked my mother's hand gently. "Yes Sophie I think we have." The adults then burst into laughter and smiles, but I sit here confused. "Will someone tell me what's going on?" My father laughed as he hugged me "all in good time son, all in good time."

Lily

I had a lot of explaining to do the next morning. Mum had woken up worried after receiving a phone call that I hadn't spent the night in my hospital bed. The worry quickly turned into anger when she found me about to knock on the door at four in the morning. "What the hell were you thinking?" She had shouted before pushing me up the stairs to my room telling me we would talk about it later. Leah who was fast asleep didn't even stir when I gently kissed her on the cheek. I missed sharing a room with her weirdly. Laying in my bed I was far from sleep too worked up about what had happened. Who was that man? Why did he want to kill me? Would I be dead if Cole and the others hadn't showed up when they did? Where was Cole now? The questions ran through my head like a mantra. Tomorrow I was going to find the answers before this new reality that I had newly been introduced to me drove me to insanity.

Cole

Sunday was a drag. I was alone in the house. Dad and the others had left early to go into Ever for a secret meeting. I was to stay behind and care for Rain and Skyla while mum was at work. I thought Rain was old enough to look after herself, then again I didn't even know how old she was. Jett and Reeve had all had their friends to hang around with, so I couldn't ask them over to keep me company. Therefore I went seeking for my own company. I found Rain in my sister's room, mum had bought paint to decorate our rooms yesterday, which was a clear indication that we were staying here. Rain stood in my mother's borrowed clothes, they clung loosely to her small structure. She had grown weaker as the days past, no longer controlled by a fever, but still controlled by the illness that claimed her body. A paintbrush in her hand carefully applying baby pink to the walls. My sister stood next to her, slapping paint messily onto the walls. She watched Rain in the corner of her eye, trying to mimic the careful brush strokes she applied to the walls.

"Are you going to help Cole or are you just going to stand there?" Rain turned to face me a smile playing on her lips. I shrugged but grabbed a paintbrush anyways. I really needed to paint my room, the dull walls were officially depressing me. "How's Lily, is she okay now?" I pondered on the question. A few days ago I knew nothing of Lily's situation, then last night happened. "I don't really know." Rain stopped painting to look at me "are you okay?" I smiled at her not sure how to answer. I was okay, but I was also worried. The pack was keeping a secret from me, about Lily. I felt so out of the loop. You would have thought that by being a wolf they would confide in me about things, but obviously I wasn't that trustworthy. "I'm okay" I answered. She nodded at my answer even though I knew she didn't believe it. "Can I ask you a question?" She didn't look at me when she nodded, instead her eyes focused as she began to paint delicate butterflies onto the walls in a dark endless blue. "How old are you?" From the way her lips tugged slightly at the edge I knew she didn't think that was the question I wanted to ask. ! ? Fifteen my birthday is the first of June, my dad used to say that's why my eyes were so bright when I used to smile. Because I was born at the start of summer and held that warmth and promise inside of me." She sniffed slightly before she carried on. "I don't think it really applies to me anymore." Skyla laid her paintbrush on top of the tub carefully before taking Rain's hand in her small one. She smiled carefully up at her. "Mummy used to tell me that you never really lose what you've always had." Rain smiled back, and I could be mistaken but I swear I saw a little of that light her father used to talk about twinkle in her eyes.

Lily

I was grounded. I had been allowed to text everyone that I was okay and home, but for the rest of the weekend I stayed home. In bed. Friends tried to pop over to say hi, but mum never let them over the threshold. She was still angry at me for sneaking out of the hospital. Leo smiled at me but never talked, he too was disappointed that I snuck out, Leah was my life line she kept me straying from boredom and insanity. I stayed in our room with her playing with her dolls and doll houses. It was Sunday night when mum decided she wanted to break her silence. I was getting ready for bed when she appeared at the door. "Are you going to school tomorrow?" I turned to face her. She already wore her sapphire silk pyjamas, with matching slippers. Her ginger curls hung loosely around her face. I felt uncomfortable, this was the second time I had seen her in her pyjamas in the past week, her normal smartness seemed to be wearing off. "Yes." She smiled then her expression turned serious. "When was the last time you had a dream?" Frowning I turned away from her, pulling the covers from my head, I didn't want her to see my face as I lied. "When you heard me scream, you let me have the day of school." I heard her loud relieved breath leave her body before she answered me, "ok, sleep well." I didn't look back until I heard the door close behind her.

Dawn broke behind the trees, the sun glowing a harsh yellow. I stood facing my house. The living room light shined through the window to where I was standing. Through the window I saw my family sharing the sofa, all laughing at the TV. My mother and father sat close, Leo sat hugging Leah. My father looked normal, healthy. No tubes to help him breathe. A voice started behind me "you don't belong here Lily." I quickly turned. There stood on the street was the man I had been dreaming about. The fair haired man with no name. His burgundy cloak had aged along with his face. "Who are you?" I asked. The man walked towards me stretching a shaking hand. Compelled I reached for him. When our hands touched a sharp jolt raced up my arms searing my soul. "Remember me little Lily."

Cole

I found myself alone Monday morning. It was first period and my history class was desolate. Mr Wright, a professor in history and philosophy sat typing away at his desk. He was a smart looking man with perfectly combed dark hair and studious looking jam jar glasses. He looked young, yet his soul was old from what I could tell. He looked to me as I walked in, probably intrigued by my confused expression. "Ah Cole what can I do for you?" I looked at him as he typed away on his laptop. "I have history now I was wondering where the rest of the class is." Mr Wright began to chuckle under his breath. "It's the year elevens trip today, did nobody tell you...well obviously not. Well it doesn't matter not all the year elevens were going anyway." He amazed me in a way I couldn't comprehend. He spoke so fluently it was as though he spoke a completely different language. He carried on as though I had answered him. "well you can stay with me if you would like, you seem very intrigued in history normally, care to join me as I ponder on the reasoning why the world had to have two major global wars, before they realised that we were becoming monsters?" He smiled politely at me. I had to admit his proclamation was poking my interest. His view on humans being monsters was quiet correct in thinking, if only he knew the real horrors and wars the world had endured. He would then come to the conclusion that humans weren't the only true monsters out there. I sat down at a desk in front of him, he stood beaming at me before placing a lined piece of paper on my desk. "I would very much like to know your views on this particular subject. Using the facts you have learnt in the classes you have attended since you started here I would like you to answer this question. 'Are humans as a species truly monsters, or is it like Darwin's theory of natural selection, are there only a chosen few who have it in them to become monsters'? I waited patiently for him to finish, thinking his question wasn't really a history question at all. "Sir I don't quite understand, becoming a monster isn't about natural selection. It's about who you are on the inside. Evil isn't for a selected few, it's a choice." Mr Wright smiled widely at me, his smile was a pleasant one until it was directed to you personally. He had the kind of smile that made you either feel like the smartest person in the world, or the stupidest. I wasn't quite sure which of those I was feeling under his smile, intimidated might be a good start. "Your right Cole evil is merely a choice, and you've severely impressed me with your understanding. You are the first student to realise that evil is a choice not something that has been given by inheritance or events. However, many would argue this statement because life puts you in situations that can change you forever, it's in these situations where your darkest secrets come to life and you discover a you, you never thought existed." I looked down at the blank page, to me that represented life, just a blank sheet waiting for events to be added to it. "I think it's all based upon the philosophy you live by each day. Some live life as though they could die any moment, others live as though they've lived a million times over. If you believe that situations change you then I agree but the situations shouldn't make you evil. In life you love and lose that's the way of life but even after those situations you should still have enough humanity to pull you back to the light." Mr Wright looked as though he might burst with excitement. "Cole, never in my twenty years of teaching have I met a person with a true understanding of the world as you. There is something about you that screams something I don't understand, and I can't help but be in utter amazement. Do you have any idea what you would like to do when you're older?" At first I was too shocked to answer him, he couldn't possibly understand how deeply I understand the world. I was an outsider constantly looking in. I had become extremely observant. Half of what I had spoken about probably wasn't even about this world. "I don't know yet sir, I was waiting to see what grades I would get at the end." Mr Wright was about to add something when someone walked through the classroom door.

Lily

It took me about ten seconds to realise I should have stayed at home. Today was the year elevens trip into town, school had took pity on us after a tiresome mock exam week, which I had conveniently missed since I was in the hospital. Begrudgingly I slowly made my way to my first period class. History. The classroom was like most of the schools classrooms; old and small with a minority of windows on one side. Pushing the door open I found that the room wasn't empty. Mr Wright stood at the front with a beaming smile stretching across his ageless face, and Cole sat directly in front of him smiling back slightly. I let the door slide close behind me.

Mr Wrights gaze flicked to me, his expression visibly changing to one of sympathy. Great. Cole turning quickly in his seat to see me smiled lazily at me. "Lily school wasn't expecting you back today, everything okay?" I carefully took the seat next to Cole neither of them looked away from me as though I might disappear if they did. "I'm better, being home was driving me insane." Mr Wright smiled at me before he began to rummage around on his desk. I flicked my gaze to Cole. He looked tired. "Are you okay?" I asked. He began to laugh quietly.
"Aren't I the one that's supposed to be asking that question?" I smiled at him before I began to pull my books out of my bag. "I'm fine, grounded but fine." He shook his head at me but kept his smile in place. "Shouldn't sneak out of hospitals then." I was about to ask how he knew that I had snuck out, when I remembered he and the others had come to save me that night. The past two nights I've managed to keep the attack out of my mind. Now, it all came flooding back. "Well lesson learned."

We spent the rest of the lesson answering Mr Wrights strange question, in the end I wrote that I had no idea why people were the way they were which was true, I didn't even know who I was. Cole however seemed to write a very opinionated essay which he refused to let me read. The end of the school day came as swiftly as it had come. Cole wasn't in my last period which meant I couldn't talk to him, I was itching to ask about the other night. How did they know I was in danger, did the rest of the pack know I knew who Cole was, and most importantly who was that man and why did he try to kill me?

Lost in thought I found myself in the middle of the forest, directly in front of Reeves house to be more precise. Next thing I knew I was knocking on the door how the hell did I get here? Luckily Carmen answered with a friendly smile and tightening hug. She pulled me inside and had me in her room before I could even say hello. Her room was decorated exactly how I would decorate mine at home. The walls were a teal colour with one white wall which had a heart engraved upon it, looking closer I came to realise that the heart was made up of photos. Some were scenery, most were with her parents and Reeve, there was even a few with Cole and another boy who I recognised to be Jett Moon who was in the year below. She had a single bed with white covers and turquoise pillows a few teddy bears had managed to keep their place on the end of the bed. Mine had long ago been stuffed in the attic somewhere. Carmen stood quietly by the door. Watching me as I scanned her room. She nervously fiddled with a ring on her finger. "Your ring it's pretty". Looking at her ring she carefully pulled it off and offered it me in her palm. Picking it out of her hand I examined it. It was a simple silver band with a silver ball. In the ball half of it was covered in tiny gems to represent a crescent moon. The other side was covered in tiny yellow topaz with tiny strands swirling away from the centre. She came to stand by me "it represents the sun and moon, the yellow side with the swirls around it is the sun, and the other side is the moon it's made up of tiny moonstones." Carefully placing it back into her waiting hand I looked out the window. That ring obviously meant a lot to her. "It's nice to see you well again Lily" she said quietly as though I might snap at her for mentioning that I was ill. Sitting on her bed I sighed a loaded sigh. I was so tired. The dream from the night before had clung to me all day. The dreams were becoming more cryptic each night, and I desperately wished I had someone to talk to. I wanted to visit Amelia but mum would suspect something if I did. "It's nice to be better." "Carmen who was at the door?" Delia asked as she pushed open Carmen's bedroom door. She wore her navy blue scrubs which meant she had been to work or was going to work. "Oh it's you Lily dear, how you are feeling?" She came in to give me a gentle hug, her worry screaming at me. "I'm better now thanks for asking." She nodded at my response but kept her eyes on me a little longer than necessary. "You going to work mum?" Carmen asked her mother as she pulled drawers open looking for something. Delia stood straightening herself "yes I'm going now, I've left a pizza for you and Reeve for when he comes back. Dad said he will be back in an hour, will you be okay on your own until then?" Delia looked over to her daughter whose attention was on a box she had found not her mother's worried expression. "She will be okay I'll stay with her until her dad comes home." I offered with a small smile. Delia looked gratefully towards me "thank you Lily, well I better go see you in the morning." She left kissing Carmen on the head.

Carmen waited for the front door to close before speaking "I don't need a babysitter you know?" She laughed. I shrugged at her smiling for real this time "you never know." She carried on giggling before taking a seat next to me. The box still in her hand. The box was nothing special it was small black velvet with a slight dusting of dust. She handed it to me. "I made you this, when the boys came back to tell me you had to go to hospital I wanted to give you a get well present. I tried taking it to the hospital but they wouldn't let me in, so I'm giving it to you now." I smiled at her, it was so sweet of her to do this, nobody else had. Then again I hadn't really expected anyone to. "You shouldn't have." She laughed slightly.

"Just open it already!" I laughed along with her. Slowly lifting the lid of the box I found a delicate silver flower charm attached to a silver chain, the detail on the petals was incredible, and it was un -mistakably a Lily. "You made this, it's beautiful?" Carmen smiled shyly.

"My grandmother taught me how, I already had the Lily I just had to find the stone, I asked Reeve what month you were born so I could use your birthstone. You were born in September so it has a sapphire."

"Carmen its beautiful thank you!"

"You're welcome. Here put it on." The Lily looked fragile as I looked at it with a mirror once we had managed to get it on. It was one of the most beautiful gifts anyone has given to me.

I stayed with Carmen until Dean returned home, I couldn't stay longer I felt a dream tugging at me. It was dark therefore they wouldn't let me walk about the forest on my own, which in actual fact I was grateful for as they both accompanied me out of the woods back onto lighted streets. I waved goodbye to them but my mind was already drifting somewhere else.

He chased. I ran. If he caught me I would be dead, but if he didn't then he would.

Cole

She faced me. Her smile, her laugh, her everything. She was the lifeline to my continuous wandering. If she cut the rope; I would be lost.

I woke gasping for air. My heart stammered in my chest. The dream clinging to my skin, burying itself into my memories. It had felt so real, the hope the love for a girl I didn't even know yet. Her face was always clouded from me. I desperately wanted to know what was hidden beneath the haze. What was her face like? Did I already know her? I suddenly remembered why I normally found things to do at night, why I normally didn't sleep. The dreams had always haunted me from as long as I could remember. The dreams I had thought had long ago vanished when I was ten, granting me the freedom to sleep soundlessly. Until now. The dreams plagued me rendering me with a constant fatigued body, I was lost, and I had no one to tell that maybe just maybe I was losing myself in a fit of incoherent dreams.

Lily

Everything seemed to have gone back to normal by Tuesday. My parents seemed to have forgiven me for running away from the hospital, even Leo seemed normal again. School was the same, people seemed to have forgotten my screaming episode and went back to ignoring my existence...well not everybody. My friends had become more wary of me now, concerned for my well-being. Sky and Lexi never left my side unless we were in class. Sean and Luke became my bodyguards, not too close to me to be annoying but not far enough to make me see what exactly they were doing. Ella was the only one who hadn't changed. She carelessly chatted away to me about her nails and her new job and how Luke was taking her to the cinema tomorrow to celebrate her birthday, I tried not to laugh. Though she had become boring I was thankful she hadn't changed, she was the only reminder of how everything used to be, before everyone found me screaming in pain on the cold corridor floor. An echo of that pain appeared in the pit of my stomach, a subtle reminder that things weren't entirely back to normal.

Reeve found me at lunch. I was alone in Mrs Smith's classroom catching up on some work that I had missed in the week I was staying at the hotel of the ill and dead. He took the seat next to me and began pulling books out of his bag, laughing I asked "what are you doing?" He smiled carefully at me. "I saw you studying here alone and thought you needed some company, besides I have history homework due in tomorrow and have no time to do it tonight." I shrugged at him.

"Then stay be my guest, but I want you to know this is not voluntary work, I was made to stay here and catch up!" He laughed along with me, as he began writing.

"Dad wanted me to say thanks to you for staying with Carmen while he was still out, mum and dad don't like leaving her on her own you know especially at night." I looked at him but he carried on writing. I don't blame them I wouldn't like to leave someone in the middle of the forest at night on their own, even in the day the forest still frightened me. "It's ok I like spending time with Carmen, she's nice and calm." Reeve laughed something about my words had humoured him, I wanted to know but didn't pry.

For the rest of dinner we sat in easy silence or talked about unimportant things. He made me feel alive which I hadn't felt since the day I collapsed. He made me forget about my dreams, the man that tried to kill me, the wolves and Cole. Something inside of me told me I didn't want to forget about Cole, then the other part of me told me that my attention should have been on the boy sat right next to me, who cared for me, who made me smile, who wasn't a secret that I had to try to figure out. Reeve agreed to call me after he had finished football practice later that evening. I left the classroom with a smile brightening up my face.

Cole

It was obvious that I was way over my head here. I had let killing my first vamp and accompanying my first hunt to cloud my better judgment. After school had finished and I was home basking in the comfort of a free TV for once, dad finds me to ask for a favour. Not any kind of favour, a favour that had me going all the way into the woods, all the way into Ever to speak to Prince Lucas. Well maybe not speak to him directly, merely handing him a message from my father. Letting this renewed confidence take over I gladly agreed. That was my first mistake; I stood in Ever town square, Rain at my side, nerves and anxiety dancing across my skin.

Ever was a beautiful community hidden in the depths of the woods. The village was quaint and old fashioned as though it hadn't moved on since medieval times. The people who lived in the village still dressed in old attire, formal dress and cloaks to block out the cold. I felt as though I had stepped into the past, seeing the world in a whole different light. Rain was mesmerised by everything, the people, the buildings, the vast scenery. My eyes were on the solid crumbling structure that represented Evelyn Castle, the sapphire flags flapping in the wind. I could smell the brininess of the sea and hear the crashing of its waves upon the beach. "Do Mermaids live in that ocean?" Rain pointed towards the beach where boats swayed against the tide.

"No back in the old days before Ever had a royal family and the community was split into different sections, witches would hunt the Mers that lived in the ocean. See Mermaids blood is incredibly valuable because it has magic, so witches would hunt them down to use their blood in their spells to make them more potent. Humans would hunt them too for their tears, a Mermaids tears can heal any wound or illness. Then there were the Vampires who just hunted them for sport, like they do for everything. When the Shadows came around they gave the Mers the lakes of Kovu so they would be safe from harm, only the Shadows can go into the different lands." Rain had kept her attention on me the whole time, still intrigued to find out more about Ever.

"So you couldn't enter Kovu or the other places then unless you was that specific creature?"

"Exactly!" Seems she was catching on fast.

Finally we reached the castle. The entrance was a narrow opening wooden bridge that led to the golden and silver engraved door with the symbol of the shadows intertwined in the paint work. "What does Umbra mean?" Rain asked as she read the words in the middle of the symbol. I smiled at her and watched servants hang little white Lilies on the bridge. "It means Shadows." She laughed and began walking over the bridge leaving me trailing behind her. "That makes sense." I didn't know if she was being sarcastic or not. Inside the castle was cold, the stone was a dark grey but the castle was illuminated by countless candles and crystal chandeliers. Red carpets with golden embroidery walked the corridors and lined the spiralling stair cases. The windows were wide and bright emitting the suns glow and the smell of sea salt. "Can I help you?" A woman had appeared next to Rain making her jump out of her skin, gripping her heart she smiled at the woman. She was elderly with grey streaked hair tied back in a bun, a white nurse's outfit with matching apron were her uniform. "Yes my name is Cole Star, my father is James Star I'm here to deliver message to Prince Lucas." The woman beamed at me, then looked to Rain, waiting. Rain blinked at her before giving her name "I'm with him my name is Rain Cloud." Rain cringed away from the woman after giving her name. The woman laughed politely before nodding us towards the corridor to our right. "My name is Gwen I am the head servant here, master Lucas isn't here today but you may deliver the message to his wife, or would you prefer the king?" She stopped then glancing back to us, waiting, again. I didn't know what the message was, maybe it isn't important enough to go to the king. Gwen spoke up "we shall give it to the king all things from your father get reported to him anyways, please follow me."

Gwen led us down a long corridor. We were then told to wait outside the solid oak door that led into the throne room. Gwen entered alone. The corridor wasn't empty of faces, in fact generations of royals stared back at me through their golden frames. Paintings had always given me the creeps. My eyes found our current king, he was younger in this painting no older than twenty. His fair hair was as lights as his smile, a woman held his arm in the painting looking as angelic as he. This must have been Queen Alana, she was striking with golden curls and grey stormy eyes. "Is that the queen?" Rain looked sadly at the painting.
"Yeah that's Queen Alana, I remember mum telling me that she was an amazing queen, so genuine and full of compassion and love for her people." Rain carried on looking at her.
"It's sad that her daughter was never given the chance to live and share those traits don't you think?" I nodded agreeing with her. The door suddenly opened, and Gwen stepped out smiling at each of us "the king is ready to see you now."

Lily

I was pleasantly surprised when I arrived home after school. For three reasons, reason number one being that Leah had decided that she didn't want to see me trip over her Barbie's anymore and packed all of them away so that our bedroom looked like a bedroom again. She had only done this because Barbie had unfortunately become headless, and Ken was in a fatal accident that meant his legs were no longer attached to his body. The second reason was that when I walked into the kitchen I found I pot simmering on the stove releasing an irresistible smell that made my empty stomach clench, why couldn't I smell burning? The third reason was that sat in my living room chatting away to my father was Lexi.

She beamed at me brightly as I walked through the door and kissed my dad on the cheek. "There you are Lily I was just waiting for you." She quickly stood dragging me out of the room by the hand, my dad calling carefully after us "not too late girls it is a school night." Lexi laughed carefully and called back loudly "sure thing Mr Found!" Before I knew it Lexi had me out of the door and back onto the street. "What's going on, you kidnapping me or something?" She laughed loudly at me, pulling me down the road.

"Yes I am, I convinced your parents to let me and Sky take you out for some fun since you've been a little gloomy lately." Smiling I wriggled out of her grasp but kept pace with her increasing speed.

"So you had to kidnap me the one night mum decides to make something edible?" Lexi laughed and twirled on the road, she had so much energy it was unreal.

"Yeah sorry about that, but tonight was the only night we could get everyone together." Handing me a piece of gum I asked "everyone?" Skipping now Lexi entered the details I was missing.

"Oh you know, Luke, Sean Ella…Reeve." She ran when she said the last name leaving my bewildered mind to come to the concept of what she was saying. I ran after her. "You invited Reeve?" Slowing down she heaved in a breath, Lexi and running had a mutual relationship, which meant she only ran in P.E when Mr Light threatened detention for lack of participation, or if she saw Ian Somerhalder walking on by. "Yes I invited Reeve, it's about time you two saw each other out of school. I would have invited his hot friend Cole but I didn't have his number so…he's obviously not coming." Linking arms we made our way down the road to where Sky lurked patiently. Her shy smile and cautious hug made me realise I hadn't been a good friend recently, too absorbed in my own problems I had forgotten about the ones who care about me. Smiling I linked arms with both of them as they giggled, Lexi began to sing loudly and even though we couldn't sing we joined in along with her.

Cole

The throne room was darker than the corridors. No candles had been lit, no chandeliers dangled from the ceiling. There was only a window, with an extraordinary view of the roaring ocean. We were silent as we entered too afraid to use our voices. The king was sat comfortably in his throne which was directly in front of us, as he heard our footsteps he looked up, his blue irises were nearly as icy as my own, yet they held a warmth that should have melted away the remnants of coldness. He smiled politely at us as we came to a standstill. He stood and spoke carefully to the servants that were making themselves look busy "leave us please." Bowing or curtsying they left silently closing the oak door behind them. The kings gaze found me again, "you have a message for me I am told." Nodding quickly I nervously approach him to put the envelope in his waiting hand, his kind smile was the only thing holding me together. "You do look like your father boy, I reckon you'll be a mighty protector when you're ready." Smiling slightly I answered in a shaky voice "thank you your majesty" I stepped back to join Rains side again, the king's gaze following me as I did. "Are you the Omega of the protector pack?" His question was directed at Rain who looked petrified as she answered "no your majesty I am a friend of Coles, I'm not a wolf." The king looked surprised at that for some reason, yet he didn't press any further. His attention was drawn back to the envelope. Sitting back in his throne he opened it with careful fingers. Scanning the rushed scrawl his once sincere eyes began to shine with undeniable joy and hope. He stood quickly shouting "Gwen Gwen come quickly!" The old lady rushed through the door, alarm written all over her face. "What is wrong your majesty?" The king ushered her over with a hopeful hand "come read this!" Gwen quickly moved herself to stand by the king to read the outstretched letter. Once read her face melted into the same expression as the kings, joy. The king grabbed me by the hand then and shook it graciously "thank you my boy this is the news I have been waiting for, for fifteen years!" Shocked and confused I just smiled at him waiting for him to tell me what the hell was going on. "Tell your father thank you, tell him to go ahead with his plan, tell him it is time Ever welcomed their long lost princess back!" I looked to Rain who stared at me back with the same confused question swimming in our minds. What the hell just happened?

Lily

People aren't joking when they say time flies when you're having fun. The night disappeared quickly, filled with laughter. Sky and Lexi took me to the small café in the middle of the village where we found something to eat before meeting up with the others at the bowling alley. I could tell that Reeve was uncomfortable, he didn't know my friends. Taking pity on him I stuck by him most of the night, which I have to admit was okay with me. I became the joke of the night as everyone came to the conclusion that I was rubbish at bowling, in the end I convinced them to let me have the barrier up so I wouldn't have to watch another ball not hit any pins. I swear a five year old was laughing at me as she easily scored a strike. To our utter dismay the clock struck ten and we realised our fun had to end. Saying goodbye to everyone I began to walk out towards the street where it wasn't so dark. "Lily, wait!" Turning around I found Reeve jogging towards me. I stopped and waited for him to catch up. "Can I walk you home, I don't like the idea of you out here on your own at night?" I laughed at him and started to walk again, he kept up with me easily. "Believe me I can take care of myself." He laughed quietly then looked at me.
"Humour me."

The night swept away the light, not even the moon was present in the sky to paint the streets in its iridescence. Reeve stuck close by me as we walked, which was both comforting and uncomfortable. A boy had never walked me home before, and I was oddly touched by the concept that he wanted to make sure I made it home safely. The living room light was still shining by the time that we reached my house. "So this is where you live?" Reeve scanned the twin houses before settling on my scarlet door. I nodded. He turned back to me something flickering in his eyes that I didn't recognise. "Well I better go, see you at school." I nodded shyly not sure how to reply. Reeve took a step closer to me. The smell of his aftershave filled my senses. "Good night Lily" he whispered quietly before placing gently a kiss on my cheek, leaving shivers to claim my body. I smiled and blushed, he returned my smile before turning to walk home. I watched him disappear down the street before opening my door and stepping back into reality.

Cole

I didn't sleep that night, too afraid of the dreams that would plague me.
Instead I found myself walking. I didn't know where I was going exactly
only that I was to keep going. I wasn't alone. Rain and Reeve accompanied
me. Rain was with me as she felt as though she had slept for an eternity
and needed to live in the real world for a while, and Reeve because he
was on the night shift tonight. "How long you been out tonight Reeve?"
Rain asked. I had finally introduced them to one another, both seemed
intrigued to find out more about each another, as both of them have only
lived on the few details I had shared about one another. Reeve politely
answered Rain's question. "Since half ten, I don't really need to be out still
but I might as well stay with you both".
"Thought you was supposed to be out here at nine?" I questioned
knowing this is the time I have to be out here every Sunday night. I knew
because I was the Alpha's son that the pack regarded my chores more
important but still. Reeve surprised me by blushing slightly, his heartbeat
speeding a little bit, which either indicated to me he was recalling a fond
memory or...he was lying. "Well Lily's friends invited me out with them for
a night out, they thought Lily needed a fun night so we stayed a bit late
and I walked her home." A pang of jealousy his me in the gut, why hadn't I
been invited? Then again I shouldn't really be surprised, I was friends with
Lily, not the others. Rain filled in my silence. "How's it going with you two
anyways?" Reeve smiled at her "I think were good, she seems to be
warming to me." They both laughed but I didn't join them. I had promised
Jett I wouldn't let a girl come between the two of us but I hadn't realised
at the time how hard that promise would be to keep. I should get over it
really Lily obviously liked Reeve, and why shouldn't she? Compared to me
Reeve was the straight A student with a shining personality, where as I
was some messed up kid who can't even sleep at night. I had let my hope
in finding Lily cloud my judgment. Never had it occurred to me that Lily
would find someone else, yet now it made sense. Three weeks ago she
didn't even know I existed. Now she did and she still picked my best
friend. I would be lying if I didn't admit that it hurt a little bit.

Rain and Reeve chatted mindlessly to one another while I walked on brooding. I had come to the decision that I shouldn't try with Lily I should wait for her to come to me. I needed to stop putting my heart on my sleeve and keep it in the cage within my chest. Then maybe she will realise that she should be with me.

Lily

Championships came quicker than expected. I found myself barely eating anything early Friday morning, too nervous to keep my toast down. "Lily you have to eat something or you won't have any energy to run." Mum managed to say whilst fritting in and out of rooms. I silently agreed with her even though my stomach didn't. Leo came to join me his eyes concerned as he looked at my toast that had been torn apart but not eaten. "Mum's right Lil you should eat something."
"I am" and to prove a point I took a bite out of the toast and felt it slide down my throat into my empty stomach which clenched with nerves.
"Lily we have to leave now take that with you!" Mum shouted from the door. My whole family had decided to come and support me. Mum had called into school to get Leah and Leo permission to be out of school so they could watch, and mum had got permission from the hospital to take dad out for the day. They evidently said it would be a good idea for him to be out. Which I was glad about, if he hadn't been there in the stands watching I don't think I could do it. There's never once been a competition that he hadn't been there, it's only now that I realise I had taken his cheery attendance for granted. I should have been more thankful.

We piled into Mum's small blue car, which always felt like it was going to break down any minute. A text from my friends kept my strained smile on my face. My phone dinged once more emitting another text expecting it to be Lexi carrying on her conversation I looked and was mildly surprised to find it was from Reeve. Last night, his kiss on my cheek lingered in my mind as I opened the text. 'Good luck Lily, I know you will be great! Can I see you later?' my strained smile turned real. I texted back thank you and that I would text him when I get home to see when we can meet. He agreed. Leo turned to me in his seat something glimmering in his eyes "who put a smile on your face?" I laughed shakily which only reminded me of my nerves. Was I ready? Had being in the hospital affected my chances? I guess there was only one way to find out.

Cole

Lily wasn't at school, but that was because she was competing in championships. It was all around school everyone was talking about her. The school seemed to have forgotten her episode on the corridor instead they talked about how amazing of a runner she is and that they hope she places today. I sat with Reeve at lunch not listening to his friend's mindless talk about the girls in their year, Reeve didn't appear to be listening either. He was distracted I could tell, his gaze was locked on the window but his mind was faraway. I felt a tap on my shoulder, turning around I found one of Lily's friends by my shoulder. She was tall really tall, she smiled shyly at me but I couldn't see her eyes which were hidden beneath black tinted sunglasses, If I could then I would have been able to tell whether her shyness was authentic or not. "Hi Lily didn't get the chance to introduce us properly I'm Lexi." Her smile was big and I couldn't help but to return it. I stood nodding my head to the other side of the hall so I didn't have to talk in front of Reeves friends. She followed me. "Sorry they're just too loud I'm Cole by the way." She laughed it was loud but pleasant.
"I know Lily told me about you." Panic beginning to rise, sensing my distress she carried on "nothing weird just your name and that she knew you before you started here." Panic over. I began to laugh. She filled in the silence "I was wondering...actually we was wondering if you would like to sit with us. Sean one of the guys in our group thought you should hang around with some people in the same classes as you, he'd be happy to introduce you to the others in our group." I was oddly touched by this, it felt as though somewhere in the week and a half I've attended here I had

become a part of the school community. "That would be great I'll just grab my stuff." She nodded enthusiastically and followed me to get my stuff. Reeve didn't even look up at me to engaged in his phone, his friends wouldn't miss me they thought I was just someone that tagged along. And I was, I wanted real friends, a group where I didn't feel alone even when I was in the company of others, I wanted to belong.

Lexi led me over to the table where she normally sat, I sat by her and a boy with short blonde spiky hair. The boy held a hand out to me with a polite smile, "hi I'm Sean you're Cole right?" I shook his hand and nodded with a smile. I realised I was actually quite shy, well with people I didn't know. He smiled back at me and began pointing at the other occupants of the table "that's Luke the other guy around here." Luke was a nerdy looking guy with dark hair and a huge amount of freckles, next to him was a bright green eyed ginger girl who Sean named Ella. "Then obviously you know Lexi she's the big mouth around here" they all began to laugh and Lexi swatted him playfully on the arm. "And lastly there's Sky." I had met Sky before, a small girl with masses of black hair and unusual eyes, for that factor I felt more comfortable around her. I knew what it was like to not be so normal. I smiled politely at them all. After the introductions were over they all began their own conversations. Sean turned to me engaging me in a conversation on the school's football team and how I should try out. He was on all the sports teams and told me everything about them. At the end of lunch the whole 'gang' gave me their numbers telling me to text them, they didn't give me a chance to say I didn't have a mobile before they had left. Lexi waited saying she had the next class with me so we could walk together. Belonging felt like such a big part of being normal, being here. And finally I felt like I had found it.

Lily

The arena where the championships were being held had to be bigger than the whole of Ever Green. The arena was packed full of people some of them competitors but most were spectators. I found Mr Light amongst them, chatting away to a man with a severe rounded belly. When he saw me he ushered me over with a very urgent hand. "Lily I would like you to meet Mr Robert Johnson he's here to find some new talent for his national team!" I shook Mr Johnson's outstretched hand, it was sweaty. "Nice to meet you Lily your coach here has been talking non-stop about you, I can't wait to see how you run." He laughed but it sounded like he was choking. "Can't wait to run, excuse me I have to go and get my numbers." I left the two behind to carry on their conversation. The rest of my family had left me to go and find a seat in the stands. The queue for the numbers was long, and I stood alone. The rest of the athletes had their team mates around to talk to but I was from a team of one. A girl bumped into my shoulder. "Oh sorry." The girl beamed at me she had the complexion of dark coffee and her hair was only a shade darker, tied back in tight plait that ran down her spine. "Your Lily right, I'm Nadia they say you're the one to watch on this track." I turned around fully so my attention was on her. "They've talked about me?" She nodded rapidly her energy evident.

"Yeah rumour has it you can run the 100 in less than thirteen seconds, I mean that's rapid!" I laughed along with her. She carried on our conversation which I was thankful for. She told me who to look out for and who wouldn't be a problem. Before I knew it I had my number stuck on my track uniform and I was stood at the starting line. The past few months of intense training had finally got me here, all of that hard work was for this very moment.

My nerves clung to me but my adrenalin pushed them away. I had to forget that I hadn't trained since the day I went to the hospital, forget that my chances of placing was more than unlikely forget that everyone in the arena was watching me right now. The starter came to stand on the side line. The orange gun in her hand. "On your marks..." I began to crouch down. "Set" I lifted up to stand on my toes. I saw the starter raise her arm her finger on the trigger. Pop! I hadn't really raced against anyone else due to being a one woman team. I ran as fast as I could, the fact that I was against others only made me try harder. As I ran I could feel every muscle in my body working, contracting. Keeping me moving forward. I could hear the sound of our thunderous feet against the track, feel the anticipation of the spectators that surrounded us. My heart beat faster. I sped across the finish line, the timers taking my time. The other racers came to stand by me each of us out of breath and shaking from the adrenalin rush. We all looked to the placing board where our times and places would be shown. One by one names began to appear. I held my breath 'third place...Kacey Williams' the crowd began to roar with applause. 'Second place Nadia Jenkins' Nadia looked over to me with huge smile I mouthed congrats to her she replied with a smile then looked to the board. 'First place... Lily Found'! I felt like my breathing had stopped completely. People were gathered around me saying congratulations. Nadia held my arm guiding me to the medal podium. But I felt faraway from this moment.

A man helped me to stand on the middle podium. Nadia and the girl who placed third stood by my sides. Three officials handed us each a bouquet of flowers, mine were white roses. Their potent scent should have been enough to bring me back, yet I still wandered on through limbo. The official shook my hand with a care free smile which I returned. The man that I had met earlier Mr Johnson was the one who got to give me my medal. I bowed my head to him so he could carefully put the medal around my neck. He beamed at me and shook my hand "well done Lily we will talk when the photos are over." I let him go turning my attention to the thousands of faces waiting for me to smile.

Finally I was allowed to leave the stands to see my family. My mum enveloped me in a crushing hug that Leo Leah and dad joined. All of them laughing and saying congratulations. Mr Light made his way over to me, he patted me awkwardly on the shoulder but had a huge smile on his face. "I'm so happy for you Lily, you did it!" I laughed.
"Yeah but I couldn't do it without you coach" he laughed and I swear I saw him blush a little.
"Come on kid let's see what Mr Johnson has to say." Smiling back at my family I allowed him to pull me away, ready to face my future.

We got home late that night. Turns out if you win your race you're expected to stick around the whole night. My face ached from where I've had to keep a smile in place for countless photos. The ride home was quiet. Dad was fast asleep in the front seat of the car, Leah was the same except her legs were stretched across Leo. I texted Reeve telling him that I was sorry that we got home late and that I would meet him tomorrow. He gladly agreed along with his congratulations.

At home I went straight to bed, hopefully I would be too physically and mentally drained to dream, unfortunately I was wrong...

I knew I was in the castle from the colouring of the stone walls, the crimson carpets, and the sound of the crashing waves against the shore. The man from my previous dreams was here sharing the room with me. He looked younger somehow, eyes brighter with youth. A woman was here too. She was beautifully angelic as she stood by the window her stormy grey eyes focused on the turquoise waves and the ivory surf. Her long golden curls shined in the slow sunset. "Alana" the man spoke. The woman turned her smile was sweet and shy. The man moved towards Alana both his hands stretching towards her. She stepped forward placing her porcelain hands into his, her smile never faltering. Slowly the man bent down to one knee. Alana's face began to radiate with joy and surprise. Locking her gaze into his the man asked "Alana will you marry me?" She too bent down to kiss the man softly on his lips before answering "yes."

Cole

Saturday morning Jett accompanied me into town after convincing his mother that he needed new clothes and that the market street in the middle of the village just won't cut it anymore. Lila decided she too needed some things in town, really she was coming to keep an eye on Jett apparently he had been known to attract trouble. He just laughed and shrugged. The town was outrageously crowded nothing like the streets of Ever Green. Mum had given me some money to buy a mobile saying that if I wanted to blend in at school I would definitely need to become part of the mobile phone and internet generation. I agreed, how was I supposed to keep up with my friends if I can't text them.

We left Lila near the culinary shop where she had spotted some colourful knives that she thought would go perfectly in the kitchen, Jett just rolled his eyes before walking away "might as well leave now she will be in there hours." I just laughed and jogged to catch up with his speedy pace. We found a desolate phone shop that sold second hand phones, I knew the phone was old and crappy but it did its use. I added everyone's numbers into its brain including Jetts and Reeves before texting everyone my number. Jett then dragged me to a shop that sold designer clothes at knock off prices, telling me these labels were clearly not real. "Nobody needs to know these aren't real right?" Jett asked whilst holding up a navy polo shirt with a golden embodied horse and jockey on. "Sure." Jett dragged me around town for about three hours before Lila found us again, weighed down by at least six bags. "Ready to go you two?" Nodding we made our way towards the car park. Suddenly my body began to sense we weren't alone. My wolf scratching the surface. Looking across the street I saw a familiar figure with coal black eyes that matched his hair. Levi. He smiled arrogantly at me before stepping on to the street from the shadows. He stepped in front of a woman who couldn't be any older than me, she talked carelessly on her phone oblivious to what was in front of her. Levi then grasped her by the arms. The girl stopped talking puzzled by the pressure on her arms and her inability to walk forward. Levi looked at me then black eyes on blue. His face curved into a malevolent smile. Before I could do anything Levi moved his hand to the girl's neck and snapped it. Her body fell to the floor, dead weight upon the pavement. He looked back at me "this is just the beginning." He called before disappearing into the crowd. I heard voices around me then. Lila's accent piercing the bubble that had surrounded me. "Cole we have to go, come on move!" Her urgent voice brought me back. She looked at me then, and then to the woman's body on the pavement. I let her guide me to the car.

Noticing Jett had gone stark white, his normally joyous face had turned sombre. I clasped his shoulder "it will be alright." He looked at me. His eyes looking more childlike by the minute. "Will it?"

Lily

It was all over the news. A woman in her early twenties was just walking along the pavement after spending her afternoon shopping when she dropped dead without warning. Her death was impossible. Her death was caused by a broken neck but there had been nobody around to break it. Police were puzzled. But I wasn't. I knew that woman didn't just die, she was murdered. There would be no justice because her killer couldn't be seen. Every day I learned more about Ever whether it was intentional or not. I needed to know more, I needed to know what this all meant to me, but most of all, I wanted to know how to get the dreams to stop. I think it's time to visit Amelia again, and I knew exactly who needed to be with me.

Cole

My first phone call was an unknown number. I was already wary of everything since the incident that happened earlier. Lila had brought me home and told me to talk to my father, who listened carefully before going to warn the rest of the pack. The ringtone was annoying and urgent. I cautiously answered it "hello?" There was a pause before a reply.

"Is this Cole?" It was a woman's voice, vaguely familiar.

"Yes who's this?" There was a release of breath before she began to speak again.

"Good Cole its Lily I... I need your help." Lily?

"Are you okay, is there something wrong?" I let worry slip into my tone.

"Oh no nothing wrong, I just need your help with something. Can you meet me somewhere?" I paused, my silent promise to myself lingered in my head, I promised myself to let her come to me. I smiled slightly. "Yes."

Lily

Cole agreed to meet me at the entrance of the wood, saying it was safer if I stayed on the street rather than enter alone. I looked down at what I was wearing suddenly nervous, faded black converse with faded ripped jeans. God it's just Cole I reminded myself whilst tugging at a loose strand on my jeans. I basically looked a mess with my hair pulled carelessly up into a bun, I heard a sudden snap from behind me. Heart racing I spun on my advancer. Cole stopped when he saw me, and raised his hands with an amused expression. "Whoa Lily chill it's just me" he laughed as he came to stand by me. I felt suddenly safer. We began walking before I answered "sorry, do you really blame me for being a little bit jumpy lately?" He stayed beside me matching his stride with mine with ease. I could tell from his face that he was remembering the other night. "I get it. Where are we going anyways?" Crossing the road, I looked at my surroundings, wondering which was the best way to get to Amelia's. "We're going to visit my great grandma, she has dementia." He frowned for a moment before his face cleared again. "So why do you need me?" We passed the silent meadows that borders the street just behind the estate Amelia lives on. "There some things you need to know about me Cole, things that I haven't told anyone before. But I need you to promise me something first." He looked at me then stopped. "What's going on Lily?" I stopped walking too. "Promise me that whatever I tell you, you can't tell anyone else. If I tell you then only you, my brother and my grandma know." He stared at me for a while before speaking. "I promise not to tell." I began to walk inhaling a deep breath, he followed.

Cole

She talked. I listened. She confessed her biggest secret, told me about her dreams. Told me that she was afraid to fall asleep, afraid she might not wake up again. She was like me. The dreams the way they plague her every night, was like me. She stopped when we reached a dilapidated house with ivy strung walls. "Please don't think differently of me Cole." Her face had changed. Something in her expression made me want to reach out and hug her. But I couldn't. That went against the rules I had set for myself. She had to come to me. "Lily I'm a werewolf if you don't treat me differently because of that factor this certainly won't change my opinion on you." She smiled slightly before reaching forward and rapped on the door.

The door took a while to swing open. When it did an elderly lady answered the door with a cautious smile. Even though it was evident that she was in her late seventies, something about her screamed youth. She let us in with a brief hello. Slamming the door and locking it before ushering us into her petite kitchen. We seated ourselves around her small oak table. Lily pulled out a small chocolate bar from her jacket pocket and handed it to Amelia, who ripped into it with pure passion. Lily snuck a glance at me and mouthed "don't ask." Amelia finally sat down at the table with us. "Can I ask why you decided to bring a wolf with you today Lily?" My hackles immediately began to rise, tension welling up inside of me. Too close. "How do you know about me?" She grimaced at me as though I was some sort of nuisance. "I can sense you." Lily just looked at me in utter bewilderment. "What do you mean you can sense him?" The old lady stood them making herself busy by moving things from one side to another. "It's one of the quirks that comes with being a Dream Breaker, you can sense the supernatural." Lily followed her with her eyes around the room. "What else can we do?" Amelia stopped moving then. "You're not ready to know yet Lily, when the time's right I will tell you but for now

I think it's best if you leave." Lily stood and slowly moved towards her "Amelia please." She begged. Amelia turned on Lily then eyes fierce her voice firmer than it was before. "No Lily you need to leave, you need to stop digging, if you stop digging they won't find you and you'll be safe. Go now both of you!" Before either of us can say anything Amelia had us out of the house and the door was slamming in our faces. "She said stop digging and they won't find me, who's looking for me Cole?" I had no idea.

I left Lily at the edge of her road. Both of us were too worked up about the conversation with Amelia to even detect that we were being followed. I watched Lily walk into the safety of the house before turning into the depths of the woods. As soon as I was alone my skin began to prickle in warning, my instincts sensing that there was something about to catch up with me. I was then suddenly thrown to the ground a force hitting me from behind. Standing back up I saw what had hit me. A wolf stood in front of me growling furiously. The wolf's dark brown eyes that matched his coat told me exactly who the wolf was, unease began to stir up inside of me. Reeve. He continued to stare me down. "What's your problem?" Snarling slightly he shifted, I turned and stripped of my plain green polo and threw it at him. He huffed which was an indication I could turn around. He did not look happy. "What were you doing with Lily?" Jealousy did not look good on him. Jetts words rang in my head "I don't want some girl to come between you two." So I lied very carefully so he wouldn't sense it. "I took some papers to her that the teachers gave me so she can catch up on the work she missed." He stared at me for a while making sure I wasn't lying. After a long while he took a relieved breath and an apologetic smile stretched across his face. "Sorry Cole." I shrugged at him already feeling guilty for lying to him. "It's alright, you wanna run?" He nodded at me and quickly shifted back into a wolf. I followed, I hadn't shifted since the night me and the pack found Lily, the wolf felt brand new.

We ran. Darting in and out amongst the trees. We started slow then gradually became faster. When we were younger and things used to be simpler. Me, Reeve, Jett and Carmen would all run the boundary lines as fast as we could, racing each other. Me and Reeve would always draw. We hadn't raced since the day I left. I felt a weird sense of nostalgia out here, letting the autumn breeze beat at my fur as I ran, Reeve matching his stride to mine in perfect harmony. Reeve was my brother in so many ways and I knew then, in this moment that I couldn't do anything to hurt him. It was then I made a new set of rules for myself. I wouldn't chase Lily, if she came to me for help I would help her. But I wouldn't fall in love with her.

Lily

I stared at my medal that hung on the wall by my bed. It's where all the medals, trophies, certificates from my previous accomplishments were hung. Yet the one I had just obtained stood out more than the others. I had competed in championships before, when I was younger but this one felt different, I felt different. I shouldn't have been able to even place let alone come first, I hadn't been training. I felt like I had cheated somehow, but that was impossible.

I woke this morning hoping I would find some answers about who I was. Instead I got an answer and about a billion more questions. Amelia's response to Cole, to everything had been strange. I knew she had all the answers to my questions, yet I didn't know if she was willing to give them to me. I had to find a new way of finding answers, but how? Most importantly from who?

The angelic woman whose name I had learned to be Alana sat quietly at a window seat gently stroking her rounded belly, a secret smile lighting up her face. The sunset was a beautiful picture behind her, painting the ocean in shimmers. Her voice was soft as she began to sing a song I didn't recognize. The language wasn't English. The pale haired man lurked at the edge of the door, hand raised to knock on the open door, but stopped. Instead he listened to her voice as it moved around the room. He smiled a little before turning to leave. Her voice stopped him "you could always sing with me?" He laughed a little before stepping into the room. "I won't sing but I'll listen." He came and sat by her, she took one of his hands and placed it over her stomach, her voice began to echo through the room once more. The baby kicked. The man smiled.

Cole

Monday came too fast and I found myself back in the classroom, maths of all places. I hadn't slept last night, Sundays were the days I found myself on duty in the woods, even though I was sleep deprived I was grateful that I hadn't slept, I couldn't take anymore dreams. The classroom was loud enough to block out my thoughts. A chair squeaked next to me as Lily sat down looking equally as tired as me. She smiled briefly before turning away and started to pull her books out of her bag. "Hey are you okay?" She sighed, a very loaded sigh. Before turning her tired gaze to me. "Not really I had a dream last night, so I didn't get much sleep."
"Would you like to talk about it?" She rubbed her eyes then turned to watch sir write our instructions on the board. "No, not yet, I'm not ready to talk about my dreams."
"Ok well you know where I am if you do need to talk." She nodded but her attention was somewhere far away.

At lunch I found myself being dragged to football try outs with Sean. He had been on the team since starting here, so had Reeve. Mr Light was the coach for everything in this school. He was an older man with a tanned face and grey streaked hair. There was only two other people trying out this term the rest were already on the team. Coach got us to team up so we could do some skills Sean decided we were to be partners, I was happy that he hadn't decided to leave me. We had been doing skills for about ten minutes before I realised that we were being watched. The whole school seemed to be sitting on the banking watching us train, soaking up the little sunlight that the day offered.

I was just about to pass the ball to Sean when all my senses suddenly... disappeared.

We ran together, just me and her. She held my hand tightly; her grasp urgent. I felt the world fading in the distance, she was weak, I was strong. If she fell, I would pick her up again.

"Cole, Cole can you hear me?" Reeves voice was fierce and urgent by me. I could hear other voices too. All trying to reach me. But I wasn't lost, was I? Another voice entered the darkness with me. "Cole can you hear me?" Lily's voice was the light, and I grasped on it as it pulled me back to reality. I opened my eyes blinded by the sunlight. Lily was bent down next to me her tired expression looked worse with worry. My voice was steady when I spoke "what happened?" Sean crouched down next to her so he could look at me, "you just passed out." Mr Light helped me to my feet, his grasp strong on my arm. "Do you need to sit down son?" He asked me as we made our way inside, Sean, Lily and Reeve on our tail. "I think I'm alright." The nurse got me to sit down on the bed anyways and made herself busy checking my temperature. Mr Light left to tend to other matters, ushering Lily, Reeve and Sean away. "Well Cole you have a choice if you're feeling better I think you can stay to finish the day, if you're not feeling well then we will call your parents and you can go home." I thought about what she said, there wasn't anything medically wrong with me. Seems like even if I avoid sleeping the dreams will still catch up with me in the day. "I'm fine, I'll stay."

Lily

I had a very ugly sense of Deja vu when Cole hit the floor at football practice. The way he just passed out was familiar and had me re-thinking everything I knew about him. He was a werewolf I knew that for definite, but what else was there? There was so many things I didn't know about him. The familiarities between our tired expressions and lack of sleep became more evident. Did he dream? Was he a dreamer like me, or was I just reading into things too much because I desperately longed for someone I could talk to about this, someone who could understand rather than Amelia? I decided instead of just coming out with the question I would give him the opportunity to tell me.

It was last period. Physics was always a drag. Cole sat on the row next me casually chatting away to Sean and Luke who sat either side of him. Lexi was sat by me, mindlessly chewing away at a newly replaced stick of gum which she always carried with her. Her bored expression became confused as Miss Jenkins a middle aged woman who had never been in a long term relationship, we only knew this because last year she decided to have a breakdown in class, after a date had gone wrong. She stood by the white board as she tried to catch her student's attention, which was impossible. It was last period of the day, and it was physics. Lexi turned to me her bored expression disappearing. "So are you planning on talking to me this lesson or do I have to sit in silence?" Her face contorted in a woeful expression at the idea of sitting in silence she adjusted her sunglasses. I still can't understand how she still gets away with wearing them inside. I laughed. "Ok what do you want to talk about?" She huffed "anything, as long as it's not physics." We both laughed which caught the boy's attention. All three of them looked over at us. Sean spoke up "you two okay?" Lexi frowned at him before answering him "why wouldn't we be okay Sean?" Sean had the decency to look slightly afraid, Lexi can become very prickly at times and when she does you have to become very cautious. "Nothing I was just thinking you never laugh in physics, I'm pretty sure I've only ever seen you cry in this classroom." We all laughed apart from Lexi. She just stared at Sean with an icy expression, if her eyes had been open for view I'm pretty sure Sean would have been frozen into a statue. Sean had been joking with her but she didn't take it that way. In fact she completely flipped. "Well you're now going to see me walk out of this classroom." Her voice was calm. Lexi effortlessly picked up her stuff and swept out of the classroom, too swift for Miss Jenkins to do anything. She was gone. Sean, Luke and Cole's eyes were on the door that was swinging shut, they looked at me. I looked back. An unasked question hung in the air around us. "What was that?"

When school was finished I tried calling Lexi, her phone went straight to voicemail 'hey this is Lexi if I love you, you can leave a message, if not call someone else'! I didn't leave a message. Sky found me as I walked out of school, I stopped to wait for her to catch up. She looked even more fragile and helpless than normal. "Have you heard from her?" She asked as she got to my side, we began to walk. "No have you?" She shook her head. Sky hated fights, or people being angry. She was as dainty as a fairy and as fragile as a porcelain doll. Even though nobody had argued, she would still hurt for Lexi who had been clearly bothered about something. "Would you like to come to mine, my phones at home we can try her again?" She looked at me her mismatched eyes pleading and innocent. I nodded.

Sky's house was a lot larger than mine. She lived on an estate where the elderly and rich all lived. Her parents were both successful lawyers, therefore having the money to spoil their daughter and younger brother Noah with everything they could possibly want. Although my mother was a doctor unlike Sky's parents we weren't rich, mum only worked three days a week now and all the money she earned went to paying for the bills, food and dad's treatment.

Noah, Sky's younger brother looked a lot like her. They had the same pale translucent skin, dark hair and careful smile. Noah was as sweet as a twelve year old can be. We stepped onto Sky's long paved drive way, and past two immaculate silver cars. The house was remarkably clean and looked unlived in. the marble floors and stairs gleamed as I entered. The house was filled with a lot of glass and marble. There were three floors, the first and second floors were modernised in marble and magnolia walls. The third floor homed Noah and Sky's rooms which were decorated to their tastes. Sky led me up to her room which was the far room on the third floor. It was all pastel pinks and greens with white flowers. I would have liked the room if it hadn't had green. I sat on her bed whilst Sky fetched her phone from her ivory dressing table. She dialled Lexis number. It rang one, twice, three times…four. A crackle rang through the line before Lexis voice rang out clear "can't you guys leave me alone for at least an hour. Stop ringing me I don't want to talk!" Then the line went dead. Sky who looked as though she might burst in tears at any moment stared at the phone in her hand. "Don't be angry." Sky whispered still looking at the phone. I looked at her confused, unease bit at my stomach. "Why would I be angry?" She looked at me tears began to stream down her face. "You'll see."

Cole

Rain had slowly begun to get better, then her condition just deteriorated. She was fine one moment, then she wasn't. It was the same as the time she had got bitten by Luna. Her body would shut down then would be returned in a furious fever. I sat with her as she lay in bed, keeping a cold flannel on her head. Delia had been over to check her then left to get some medicine. Mum took Skyla out as she was becoming worried for Rain's welfare. That left dad who lurked in the corner, something in his expression was hard to read. But I knew he needed to say something, from the way he nervously tapped his foot up and down. "Just say what you need to say before you make a hole in the floor." Dad looked down to where his foot tapped and stopped it, as though he had just noticed what he was doing. He sighed. "Cole I don't know how to save her." I looked at him. His eyes didn't hold his usual reverence, his mouth set in a glum line. I couldn't answer straight away I had to let his statement sink in. He had allowed her to come here in hope of finding a cure for her to be untimely death, to find out there was no cure at all. Anger bubble inside of me and I came to realise I wasn't angry for myself, but for her. "What do you mean you don't know how to save her?"

Dad sucked in a breath before he answered. "I don't know how to save her because I don't even know what's wrong with her." I stood from the bed and began to pace out my anxiety.

Dad's eyes followed my every step. "We can't just let her die." Dad stood quickly and grabbed my shoulders gently stopping my pacing. His eyes level on mine, blue on blue. "Do you care about her?" Not the question I was expecting. In actual fact I hadn't anticipated a question from dad at all. Dad added some clarity to his question "I mean do you feel something for her?" I thought about his question. Rain had become a part of the family, I cared for her like I cared for my sister Skyla, but I had the sense he wasn't hinting at that. "I care for her the same way I care for my sister." Dad looked slightly relived. "So you haven't made a bond?" His questioning made more sense now. The bond dad was asking about was a feeling us were wolves get when we meet our mate. When we meet we create a bond to one another. You can have more than one bond dad had told me, but in the end your wolf will decide. It was weird really. But if I had made a bond with Rain it made dads job of saving her a lot more difficult, see when a bond is created a part of your soul intertwines with the other and if that person dies, you can die too. If I had bonded with Rain and dad can't save her, I might have lost my life too. I realised I hadn't answered him, I felt his anxiety roll of him in waves. "No we didn't bond." He breathed again and hugged me hard against his chest. "That's a relief I can't lose you Cole." I remembered a time when I wouldn't have believed him, yet in this moment. His arms crushing me to him. I couldn't help but believe him.

End of part one.

I desire the things which will destroy me in the end.
Sylvia Plath.

Reeve

I found Cole on the decking after finishing my patrol of the boundary lines. He was sad under the dark sky. Purple shadows circled his eyes making his already pale complexion, paler. I had been worried about him since the incident at football practice. Being the alpha's son he was a lot stronger than me, which means passing out was unheard of. He was so out of it that he didn't even twitch as I came and sat by him. For as long as I could remember me and Cole had always shared everything with each other, no matter how stupid it was it would have been said. Then Cole left. For the six years he was gone I relied on letters or postcards to remind me he still existed. He was my brother in so many ways, and I missed him when he was gone. We all did. The day I got the letter telling me he was coming home is a day I can remember with ease. I had been at football practice soaking in the September sun as I kicked the ball around the pitch. I remember walking home with Toby and Peter the only two on the team that lived near the woods. I remember walking into the house a letter waiting on the counter, Cole's familiar scrawl on some paper. It read *I'm coming home.* I remember feeling happy that my best friend was coming back.

Then he was home and I saw what looked like my best friend, but wasn't. Instead of seeing a lively boy I saw an empty man. His secrets locked away somewhere only he could find. I remember making myself a deal that day 'I would bring back the boy I once knew'. Stepping back into the present letting the past fade away. I looked at Cole and realised I had been selfish. I shouldn't try to change him, I should just accept him. The boy next to me looked tired and broken. "How's Rain?" I asked. Cole blinked into the night, his mind far away. "Bad, your mums helping her." His voice was dead.
"Maybe you should get some sleep." Cole took a long intake of breath.
"I can't." I knew I should have stopped but I couldn't help it.
"Why not?" Cole turned and looked at me. Face to face he looked worse. His eyes were red and blotchy, the circles more prominent. His skin sallow. His face looked like Lily's when she fainted in class at the start of the year. Cole cleared his throat. "I can't because I'm afraid." His voice quivered slightly telling me he was being deadly serious. Softly I asked "sacred of what?" Cole took a breath. His eyes moving to find the wood instead of my face. "That if I go to sleep, I might not wake up again."

Lily

I ran as fast as I could. My breath hitching in my chest. The world was dark and empty. My attacker chasing me tried to grab me. "You can run, but I will always catch you." The voice was dead in my ear. The attacker's arms had found me. They snared me in their grasp. His voice was in my ear, snarling "are you ready to die?" I screamed.

I woke with a start, still screaming. My heart beating too fast in my chest. I looked around but didn't recognise my surroundings. Someone's hand was on me. I looked over to find Sky's worried face. "Why...why am I here?" Sky looked at me as though I was mental. She carefully turned on her bedside lamp, illuminating the room in peach light. "You stayed the night, you said you were too tired to walk home so I called your mum and she said you could stay." I rubbed my eyes roughly hoping my memory would come along with every rub. "I don't remember." Sky rubbed her eyes too. And pulled her long black hair back into a ponytail, her face looked younger. "Are you okay do you want me to call your mum?" We both looked at her alarm clock on the bedside table 4:30am. I shook my head "I'm fine I just had a bad dream, besides it's too early to call mum." Sky nodded her head as though she was convincing herself of something. "Ok well let's get some sleep we will see how you are in the morning." The last thing I remember is Sky explaining to me that Lexi had told her she was thinking about dropping out of school. She had been worrying that I would be angry at her for not telling me Lexi's secret, but I was far from mad. I was confused about Lexi's behaviour. I nodded and laid back down, hoping for a few hours of dreamless sleep. Sky turned off the light and laid back down beside me. I knew she didn't go back to sleep.

Cole

I knew telling Reeve about my dreams was a bad idea but right now I needed someone. He decided to stay with me. He laid on the floor, me on my bed. Mum and Dad didn't ask why he was staying. Actually I think they were relieved the two of us were becoming close again. I knew they had noticed the distance between the two of us. From Reeves easy careful breathing I knew he wasn't asleep. "What are you thinking about?" I had discovered that talking became easier when you couldn't see someone's face. "I was thinking about the time when you climbed that tree to prove a point." I laughed.
"Yeah then I fell out of it and broke my arm, it was painful but my point had been proven." We both laughed. The day he had remembered was

back in the summer when I was eight and he had also been eight. That summer had been a good one, full of water fights, races, long nights around a camp fire, our parents laughing. The point I had been trying to make was that I would be a better protector than him because I was more courageous. He had said "ok then climb that tree to the top and we will see just how brave you are." Of course I had climbed it. Then fallen out of it.

I let my memories fade. "Sometimes I wish we could go back to those days." I heard Reeve turn over in his make shift bed. "Sometimes I do too."

Lily

The next day was same as the day before, and the day before that. The same circle of pretending that everything was fine still wafted around us. Lexi had missed the past three days of school and had ignored all our attempts to find out what was wrong. Sky pretended that my dreams and short term amnesia hadn't happened. There was a weird air surrounding Cole too, he was hiding from me. We hadn't spoken since the day he collapsed at practice. I didn't know how to approach the subject, surely if he dreamed too he would have told me when I told him. Again the part where I didn't know much about him came into play, would he tell me or did I have to ask?

My opportunity came about Friday morning as I sat by Cole in History. He looked like death warmed up as he gaze scanned the board. "Hey are you okay?" I whispered as the class quietened down. Cole appeared not to have heard me. I repeated my question a little louder. Cole finally replied. "No not really, look Lily I have to tell you something, but not here okay." I nodded to him I suddenly felt alarmed. Before I could say anything else Mrs Elliot the head teacher came into the classroom. "Sorry to interrupt your lesson but can I borrow Cole Star please." Sir nodded and Cole stood stiffly from his chair looking like he was a rabbit caught in the headlights. "Follow me Cole." Mrs Elliot said as she began walking out of the classroom. Cole ducked down quickly to whisper in my ear "meet me after school, in the clearing where you found Carmen." Then he was gone.

The day went slowly as though it was intentionally being annoying. I spent my breaks with my friends who were ignoring the fact that Lexi had walked past our table and sat down at a table on her own without even a glance towards us. What was wrong with her? Reeve sat with me at the end of lunch for a while where he joined into our mindless banter. He quickly kissed my forehead goodbye before walking with his friends to class leaving me blushing slightly. When school finished I rushed out of the entrance doors to catch up to Lexi. She was walking briskly through the crowd, I managed to grab her bag and pull her to a stop. "Hey what's wrong with you?" Lexi turned around her face was thunderous, her eyes cold. She wasn't wearing her sun glasses which made her face oddly naked her eyes seemed darker than before. Her voice was hard and defensive "nothing." I raised my eyebrows slightly. "Well it doesn't seem like nothing, first you storm out of class, then you ignore our calls, you don't sit with us, you don't talk to us. That doesn't seem like nothing Lexi." Lexi just stood there watching me with a bored expression, I went on. "We're your friends Lex don't push us away?" Lexi pulled her bag from my grasp and turned away from me, her voice was low but I still heard her "Then I think it's about time you took a hint." Then, she walked away from me.

I knew I was late meeting Cole due to catching up with Lexi. The sun had moved in the darkening sky as I made my way into the woods, hoping I would be able to find my way back to the clearing. Last time I had Carmen's scream to guide the way, now there was only silence. I didn't have to worry as my feet seemed to remember their way as they guided me through the trees to the clearing. Cole stood in the middle of the clearing facing away from me. The landscape hadn't changed since the last time I had been there. The still existent grass was bronze instead of green, and the trees that boarded had begun to shed their autumn leaves. Cole was dark against the light scenery he must have had time to change as he was in a black t-shirt and dark jeans. The crunch of leaves sounded my approach he turned. Somehow he looked even more tired here where he was exposed to the elements. His smile was small as I moved towards him. "Thanks for meeting me." I stopped just a few metres away from him. "Why out here?" Cole looked around at the nature that surrounded us. "This is the only place I don't feel watched." A shiver crept up my spine with sly stealth. I knew what he meant. I felt watched everywhere I went these days, but here in this clearing I felt free of gazes. "What do you need to tell me?" He sighed before folding in his legs and sitting down on the floor. He stared up at me with his piercing blue eyes, waiting for me to join him on the floor. I obliged. "Do you remember when you told me about your dreams?" I nodded at him "well, I have them too, before you say anything I was going to tell you then but I didn't know how. I thought I lost my dreams when I was ten, then suddenly they came back and there worse than before." His voice sounded pained as he spoke. "I wanted to tell you and then when you told me even more so, especially when I discovered similarities between us how we both seemed to lose our dreams and now there back with vengeance, how we both were tired all the time, and the fact that we both fainted. I don't know about you but I've never fainted in my life until football practice the other day." His words tumbled out in a rush and it became evident that he had been holding onto this for a while now. "There's one more similarity." Cole looked at me with raised eyes brows "we both lost our dreams when we were ten, the same day we saw each other for the first time." By the look on his face it was obvious that Cole hadn't yet thought of that. "What does this all mean?" He asked. It was a question I had asked myself plenty of times. I thought maybe Cole would have had more answers as he was from this world we were all a part of, obviously I was wrong. We both were as oblivious as the other. "I think we need to get Amelia to talk." Cole nodded like he was agreeing to me. Then he stood held a hand to me to help me up. "Then let's go, better now than never."

Cole

I felt lighter now that I had finally told Lily about my dreams. I now had her and Reeve who I could turn to. The two of us made our way to Lily's grandmothers. Last time she had seen us she hadn't been very warm and welcoming, but something inside of me told me she was just protecting us. The old lady was like Lily and me from what Lily had informed me as we walked. Like us she dreamed. This meant that it was likely she knew more about this stuff than us and right now we needed answers. The door was unlocked when we got there which immediately put both of us on edge "she always locks the door" Lily whispered. Nodding I pushed her behind me. "Stay close to me, I'll go in first." My wolf instinctively took over my senses. We entered quietly. Inside the house was as neat as it was the last time we had been here. The only difference was the smell of burning cake which did a good job of covering up the potent scent of wolf. My wolf ripped at my insides wanting to escape but I kept my human skin on. We found Amelia in the kitchen trying to ice the cake she had burnt. "Amelia?" Lily spoke carefully. The old lady jumped slightly before turning to face us, a smile stretching across her face easily. "Lily, Cole come in come in, I just baked cake." Lily looked at me as though Amelia had gone mad but took a seat at the table, I took the chair closest to the door. I strained my smell to detect the smell of wolf again but I had lost it in the scent of chocolate and vanilla icing. "What can I do for you both aren't you supposed to be in school?" Amelia carried on icing her cake as though it was the most important thing ever. Lily answered her. "School finished about an hour ago and we came for a chat." Amelia let out a slight laugh that wavered a tiny bit. "You mean you came to interrogate me."

Amelia brought three slices of cake over to the table and placed one in front of each of us. I spoke up "we don't want to interrogate you, we just want some answers." Amelia stared at me as though she was searching for something, she looked away obviously not finding whatever she was looking for. "What do you want to know?" Lily looked taken back but quickly composed herself. "Why did I lose my dreams?" Amelia began eating her cake, her eyes told me she was thinking. "I'm not actually sure all I know is that I lost mine when I met a man, his name was Jack he was a very nice man actually I just saw him one day and he bumped into me and got talking." Lily leaned forward.
"Do you mean Grandpa Jack?" Amelia stopped eating and looked at Lily. "Yes my dreams disappeared when I met your great grandfather, but like I said they came back eventually." Lily carried on, determination to achieve something was written all over her face.
"When did they come back?" Amelia pushed her half eaten cake away from her. She clasped her hands into her lap and began to twiddle a dull gold wedding band on her finger. "Well I said my dreams disappeared when I met Jack, see that was the last time I saw him, for a while anyways.

I found him two years later he had just moved back here with his family. After that my dreams came back." Lily sat back thinking, I decided it was my turn to ask a question.

"Did your dreams get worse when they came back?" Amelia turned her attention onto me, with her gaze on me I felt as though I was being assessed. "Yes they were dreadful but after a while they settled down again, now I only dream once a month." Then suddenly her gaze became foggy her smile slipped from her face. Amelia had forgotten. Lily hugged her goodbye saying that she would be back for a visit soon. Amelia waved at us through the window, her smile strained. When we were out of sight I turned to Lily. "There was a wolf in that house."

"What do you mean?" She stared at me clearly alarmed.

"I mean when I walked in I smelt a wolf except I couldn't detect it fully because of the scent of the cake."

"What should we do?" I shrugged.

"We keep an eye on her."

Lily

Time flew then. Cole had kept his promise and we regularly went to check Amelia was okay. I began to knuckle down on school work before I had another detention, and before I knew it, it was the last day of school, breaking up for the Christmas holidays. The past few months had vanished into thin air. Where had time gone? Me and Cole were no nearer to knowing what was going on with the dreams, in fact we were no closer to anything. Christmas was always my favourite time of the year, the snow, the decorations, the food and of course the presents. I still hadn't made that much progress with Lexi, she still sat with us in class and talked but at break and on holidays she was silent. Sean and Luke were both away for Christmas with their families, going abroad somewhere. Ella and Sky were still here to make sure I didn't go crazy, and of course there was Reeve. Over the past few months our relationship had grown we saw each other most days after school, depending on when we both had training. We both seemed comfortable in each other's company, yet he still hasn't kissed me. I didn't let myself worry over it though, if he didn't want to kiss me then that's fine with me, well I'd pretend it was fine anyway.

Presently I found myself in my last detention of this term, my maths teacher wasn't happy that I hadn't handed in any homework's from this year, therefore I had to make up for it now. Great everyone loves a bit of trigonometry. I looked at the clock 13:00 still another half hour until lunch finished. I huffed and slumped in my chair. "Wow you look so happy" I looked up to see Cole grinning at me from the doorway. "That is because I am having the time of my life!" I laughed along with him. He took a seat next to me. "So what you up to this holiday?" I sighed.

"Eating, eating and probably more eating I might see Ella and Sky in-between all the eating, what about you." He laughed.

"Well the first week I'm in Ever to celebrate Christmas, Reeve will be there too but we will be back for New Year's." The thought of not seeing Reeve and Cole at Christmas just put a downer on my already bleak day. Cole carried on ignoring my disappointed expression "I'm hoping I'll find some answers in Ever about all this, I was wondering if you would come one day and we can research." The prospect of finding out some answers was compelling but the thought of going into Ever where all the monsters live made the idea a lot less compelling. "I thinks it's best if you go on your own, I'll be too chicken to talk to anyone." Cole stood up and laughed. "Well I would be with you, but it's up to you give us a call if you change your mind, have a nice Christmas Lil, I'll tell Reeve you looked disappointed not to see his beautiful face on Christmas morning." I laughed and waved him goodbye "have a nice Christmas too Cole, just remember those who take the mick out of others get Coal in their stockings!" Cole laughed and called as he walked away. "How do you think I got my name?"

Cole

The house had become seriously festive when I returned home from school. The Christmas tree stood tall by the fire filling the space with the sharp scent of wood smoke and pine. The tree was bare apart from its foliage. It was mums tradition to have us all together to decorate the tree, which meant the tree would have to wait a while longer to be dressed as dad wasn't home yet. The rest of the house however, had been doused in tinsel, ornaments and makeshift snowflakes. Mum and Skyla had made gingerbread men earlier which Rain had helped ice.

Rain had been here for four months now and finally looked content within our family. Her health kept us on our toes, but it wouldn't be home without her now. The past four months have flown by; school, friends, football had made me forget how much time had actually passed. People aren't lying when they say 'time flies when you're having fun'. The day after tomorrow we would leave for Ever to spend Christmas day at the castle. We didn't normally do this but this year the pack had been invited by the king himself, how could we refuse? It seemed like only seconds ago that I and Rain were at the castle, handing over the letter to the king from my father. That was the day we found out the long lost princess had been found. Maybe I would get to meet her. What was she like? Where has she been all this time? Why did people rumour her to be dead? My thoughts were then interrupted by Rain as she walked in "Cole we're going over to Hector's house for dinner, and we're leaving now. Your mum, dad and Skyla are already there." She waited patiently for me to move.
"Why?" Rain smiled brightly as me.
"It's a surprise."

It was obvious when I walked through the door what was happening. Rain walked in from behind me and flicked on the light switch. "Surprise!" The crowd sang as they sprang up from wherever they had been hiding. Jett shouted "happy birthday Cole!" I laughed then, still shocked. They hadn't tried to surprise me on my birthday in a long time. The crowd gathered around to hug me individually each saying happy birthday to me. Then I caught the scents of a crowd of people I hadn't been expecting to see here tonight. Sean, Luke, Ella, Sky, Lily even Lexi all stood in the centre of the room. Beaming at me. They all sang together "happy birthday Cole!" Then they all gathered around me in a crushing group hug that made us all laugh hard. As they squeezed I managed to ask "what are you guys doing here." Releasing me Sean spoke up hitting me gently on the shoulder "we weren't about to miss your birthday now were we, even though you didn't mention it." Luke pushed him out of the way, Sean pretended to look hurt but his wide smile gave him away. "Good thing Reeve told us wasn't it, here this is from all of us." Luke pushed a large parcel into my hands along with a card. I smiled at him before carefully unfolding the wrapping paper. Inside was a box, the box contained a brand new pair of football boots which were a bright shade of green. I looked up and Lexi spoke "we thought it was time you had your own pair, I hope you like the colour Reeve said green was your favourite." They all looked at me eagerly waiting for my approval. My heart warmed. I smiled at each and every one of them "I love them." There was a massive sigh of relief from all of them. Our laughter was interrupted by a tap on my shoulder. It was my father who had a very bright smile on his face "happy birthday son!"

"Thanks dad, oh erm dad these are my friends Sean, Luke, Ella, Sky, Lexi and Lily" I said gesturing to each of them "guys this is my dad." My dad nodded to each of them his gaze lingering slightly longer on Lily than the rest "nice to meet you all, please call me James."

The rest if the night disappeared in a flash. I opened presents, hugged people, said thank you, blew out my candles on my cake. At the end of the night I found myself alone sitting on my decking everyone was leaving and saying goodbye to one another. Someone sat by me. "I've decided that if you're going to find some answers in Ever then I should at least try to find some answers here." Lily talked fast but quietly. Her gaze never leaving the wood. "That seems fair." I added. "Lily you ready to leave?" Reeve called from across the lawn where he was waiting with Carmen. It was those two's patrol tonight. She nodded at him and stood "I do hope you have a nice Christmas Cole and I hope you've had a nice birthday." I watched her leave wanting to say something to her but I couldn't find the words.

Lily

The throne room looked different from what I could remember. Instead of a bare dull room I saw a roaring fire with tinsel and candles. A large dark table stood in the middle with three red cushioned chairs. The table bore a feast that could feed a thousand men, turkey, beef, and pork. The pale man from my previous dreams sat at the head of the table, Lucas his dark haired brother sat at his left tucking into a turkey leg. On his right sat a woman I hadn't seen before. She was small brittle looking. Her hair was silver like her eyes, her skin aged. The pale man spoke up "mother what seems to be troubling you?" The lady smiled sadly at the other side of the table.

"That there should be at least two other people here sharing this meal."
The pale man looked startled for a moment before composing himself.
"My daughter is still alive and maybe one day she will be here at this
table, but for now let us be thankful that there is still people eating at this
table." The woman stayed silent.

I found myself at Sky's house the next morning. It was Christmas Eve which meant I'd probably not see her again until Boxing Day. Her house had been elaborately decorated. Her mum answered the door. "Lily it's so good to see you I'm glad to see you back in good health." Mrs Sara Wilson was always impeccably dressed in a pencil skirt with matching blazer, her hair pulled tightly in a slick bun. It was Sara that had blessed her children with the pale complexion and dark hair. She let me in and guided me into their spacious beige marbled kitchen where Sky was baking cookies. "Hey Lily" she called over her shoulder. I took a seat at the breakfast bar where Noah was busy drawing. I looked over to see a very detailed picture of the kitchen. "Wow Noah that's amazing!" Noah looked at me and blushed slightly. "Thanks."
"So Sky what are we doing today?" Sky quickly placed the cookies in the oven, washed her hands and faced me. She had a splash of flour on her face. "We're going to see Sean and Luke before they go on holiday, which means we will see Ella because she will be with Luke." She laughed at that.
"What about Lexi?" The problem with Lex was this 'she didn't want to see us, period'. She had turned up yesterday for Cole's birthday, spoke when she had been spoken to, wished Cole a happy birthday then left. Sky looked away for a moment probably to compose herself. "Well we can go round her house just to say hi." I nodded. Sky ran upstairs to quickly change. "So where are you two off to?" Sara asked as she breezed into the kitchen her blackberry locked in her hand. "We're going to see the boys before they leave." She nodded then turned her attention on her son. "Noah stop drawing." Then she left the room. Sky walked back in slightly out of breath. Noah didn't look up as he began to pack away his pencils, then he screwed up his drawing and threw it in the bin as he walked out of the room. "Why doesn't your mum want him drawing, he's clearly talented." Sky checked her cookies as she spoke. "Because they say that artist don't make any money and it's not the life they want for their son, they want him to be a dentist or something just as fancy."

"But what does Noah want?" Sky sighed took out the cookies and placed them in a neat stack on a plate. "I don't know he won't talk to me but I'm sure he wants what every child wants right, to make their parents happy."

Reeve

I was packing my bag when Carmen walked through the door without knocking! She laughed when she saw my face. "What are you doing?" I resumed packing my stuff to indicate what I was in fact doing, hoping she might get my polite hint and leave. Obviously not. "Are you going to see Lily today?" Carmen stood twiddling her ring on her finger. The ring was our families crest. Aunt Lila gave it to her on her tenth birthday, she had said she was tired of waiting for Carmen to be old enough to wear it. Dad and Lila were brother and sister. However Lila wasn't biologically his sibling. My grandparents adopted her when she was thirteen when they visited France for a holiday, instead of a carefree break from their only child they found an abandoned girl who couldn't remember her name. My grandparents had always been remarkable people. They took in this lost broken girl and made her whole again with love and affection. They created a safety net around her which was family. And she rewarded them with the same love and affection, and the acceptance of what they were. Even if the weight of the family crest was too much for her. Dad didn't have any other siblings until Lila and even now he was extremely protective over her.

"Yeah I'm going to see her later she's saying goodbye to Sean and Luke at the moment." She sat down on the edge of my bed looking pensive. "Do you know how mum and dad met?" I did actually I remember dad telling me about it once. Back when I first wanted to know how wolves bonded with others. When he was fifteen his parents moved him and Lila here. They had moved around a lot for the past couple of years due to problems that the shadows wanted grandfather to fix. James and Hector were already residence here and best friends. Dad had found comfort in both of them knowing that they were werewolves too. It was during this time the three families came together and decided to become a large pack. The Stars were put in charge, James's father had been a kind and fair Alpha from what dad had told me, he died long before I was born.

It had only been a week since they moved in when Hector and Lila spotted each other and instantly bonded with one another. Dad had said he was furious, dad and Hector ended up fighting but James pulled him away made him see reason. He was just walking away when he saw her. By her I mean my mum. She was walking away from him with a group of friends, laughing smiling. He felt the tingled promise of the bond, and he desperately waited for her to look up and see him, but she didn't. "It took him a while didn't it?" Carmen laughed.

"Yeah from what I heard dad got so impatient of her not seeing him he just stood up in the middle of biology and shouted her name." Ah yes my father ever so stylish couldn't wait for his beloved to look at him, instead made a complete fool out of himself in a classroom full of his peers. Who were just as confused as her? But then she finally saw him and everything that didn't make sense about the situation finally did. "Why do you ask anyways?" Carmen stood to look out of the window. Snow had begun to fall painting the world in a glistening shade of ivory. "I was just thinking that we seem to only bond with humans right but why is that?" She asked a good question, I didn't know why we always bonded with humans but we did, it's just the way things had always been. "Do you miss them?" "Who?" I asked whilst adding my phone charger to my case, hoping the castle had some sort of electricity but not counting on it. "Our grandparents, it doesn't feel like Christmas without them." She answered sadly still looking out of the window. As remarkable as my grandparents were, they weren't remarkable enough to outwit death. Like James and Hector's mothers my grandmother died of human causes. Whereas my grandfather like the rest died fighting for what he believed in. Ridding the human world of vampires, and other dark creatures that plagued our world. Carmen was right it didn't feel like Christmas without them. Without my grandmothers warm arms hugging me tight, or my grandfather's booming laugh as he laughed at the jokes inside of the Christmas crackers. "You're right it doesn't."

Lily

After saying goodbye to the boys and exchanging gifts and cards me and Sky headed towards Lexi's house. She lived only a road away from me which was only another road away from Sean's. As you can probably see Ever Green isn't the largest place you will ever see. Lexi's house was like mine, small and joined together with its twins. We knocked on the door. There was always someone home, no matter what time of day it was there was always someone home. But today the house remained silent, empty. Sky peeped through the window that looked into the living room, there was nobody there. We rang the house phone and nobody ventured to answer it. We were about to leave when we suddenly heard voices from around the back. Looking at one another we nodded and silently made our way around to the garden, making sure our footsteps were silent upon the ground.

At the very corner of Lexi's back garden where a tyre swing used to be before we pulled it down a few months back stood Lexi. Except she wasn't alone. Stood directly in front of her was the man I had nightmares about, the man that chased me and tried to kill me the night I snuck out of the hotel of the ill and dead. He looked paler under the faint sun, snowflakes kissed his pale skin as they gently began to fall. "Get me the information Lexi or your friends get it!" Lexi surprised me by keeping her voice level, no hint of fear present. "I will get you nothing and you will not hurt my friends!" The man smiled. It was one of the smiles that you instantly knew something bad was going to happen. "I'll let you sleep on it before you decide to disobey me, if I were you I would take my offer, or you know who will die first." He snarled at her before disappearing completely. Lexi stood there as though she was in a trance. We approached her. She snapped out of her daze when she saw us, her stunned face turned angry. "Were you guys spying on me?" We both took a step back as though Lexi's anger had physically punched us in the gut. Sky spoke up "no we just got here, what wrong with you?" Lexi shook her head and her face changed into an anxious one. "Doesn't matter what are you doing here?" Sky handed over a present and card, I did the same pretending I wasn't still in shock over what I had just heard and the fact the Sky just lied for the first time. "Oh...thanks." Sky smiled hooked her arm with mine "it's okay anyway we have to go Lily's got to see Reeve and I have to go and give my gift to Cole, see you later." Sky pulled me out of the back garden leaving Lexi literally speechless as she watched us leave.

When we were safely on the street away from prying ears I pulled Sky to a stop "What the hell was that, you just lied?" Sky stopped.
"Well I couldn't tell her that we were spying on her now could I, and if we stayed I would have told her the truth which would have made her hate

us more than she does now." She finally took a breath. "What the hell is going on with her, who is that man?" I let her question hang in the air between us. I couldn't tell her that I knew the man and that he had tried to kill me once. "Look Sky I have no idea what's going on with Lexi or that man, but that doesn't matter what matters is that Lexi's in some sort of danger, we all are. If she doesn't hand over this information then one of us is going to get hurt!" We started to walk, but we stayed close.
"So what are we going to do?"
"We find answers."

Cole

I was nearly packed when my phone started to ring in its annoying obnoxious tone. "Hello." There was a pause then a voice came through the phone "Cole, its Lily I need your help can we meet?" I looked at the clock. Dad, mum and Skyla had already left, me and Rain were supposed to leave in an hour. "Yes but it will have to be quick."

Knowing I wouldn't be able to leave the house without Rain having to know where I was going I decided to take her with me. It was time she met Lily, I had told Rain all about her which I hoped Lily wouldn't take offensively, but I needed someone to vent to about her. Maybe it was time to tell Rain about my dreams too. Rain was happy to come. We met Lily in the same place I had met her before, at the edge of the wood just a street away from her house. She smiled when she saw me but it faltered when she saw Rain. "Lily I would like you to meet my friend Rain, Rain this is Lily." Rain stuck her hand out to Lily who took it.
"Nice to finally meet you, I've heard a lot about you." Lily gave me a look I couldn't quite decipher.
"What's the problem Lil?" Lily closed her eyes and took a long breath before explaining the whole exchange between Lexi and the dark haired man. "We don't know what he wants and Lexi doesn't know that we know." Scratching my head I managed.
"I think it's best if she doesn't know that we know, and the man that you're referring to who attacked you all those months ago, his names Levi he's the son of a very powerful Lamia."

"Lamia?" She questioned. Rain spoke for the first time since the conversation started.

"It means Vampire." A look of horror spread across Lily's face, I could smell her fear as though it was spiralling around me. "That's not possible". Rain placed a hand on Lily's shoulder and spoke carefully. "It's possible believe me, before I came to live with Cole I didn't believe in all this, in Ever but it's all real Lily and yeah it's scary, but life's Scary." Lily smiled gratefully at Rain who removed her hand from her shoulder. "So what should be do about Lexi?"

"I have no idea, just keep an eye on her I'll warn my dad about it when I see him later he will need to know if he's threatening people." Rain poked me in the arm and pointed to the sky. It had become a stormy grey colour which meant the snowstorm was coming and it was getting late. "Lily we have to go but be safe okay, I know you want answers but if it puts you in danger then it's not worth it, I'll be back in a week, have you seen Reeve?" She shook her head "then I'll tell him to call you, have a nice Christmas." I began to leave but she called me back.

"Sky said she forgot to give you her present last night so I said I'd bring it, I'll see you when you get back have a nice Christmas both of you." She waved goodbye and disappeared on the street.

I watched her disappear around the corner before opening Sky's present carefully, Rain was stood close to me. the present was a stuffed animal, not just any animal but a stormy grey wolf with piercing blue eyes, and stuck on its pelt was a sticky note it read 'I know what you are'. My stomach dropped.

Reeve

Cole was late. Which was strange because he was usually very punctual. We had the rest of the night and tomorrow morning to spend all together as a pack, one big giant family. Then tomorrow evening we would join the king, his brother and their mother for Christmas dinner. I hadn't met the king or Prince Lucas, but the kings mother Primrose I had met. I had only been five but I could remember clearly the warm welcoming lady with silvery hair. I hoped time had not aged her of her warmth. The castle was huge and consisted of fourteen flours, one of those floors had been granted to us. There was eight bedrooms which would be divided between us all. Adults would get their own, kids would probably have to share. I'm a werewolf but I wouldn't lie and say this castle didn't give me the creeps, so... I would make Cole or Jett share a room with me.

The day had been long, as we all eagerly anticipated Christmas morning. I hadn't been able to see Lily either, both of us had too much on to spare the time to see one another. Though she did call, and promised to see me the moment I got home. I missed her already. Over the past four months we have grown closer, there was no longer awkwardness around us whenever we spoke. Our relationship was easy, yet I still hadn't kissed her. I couldn't, not yet; I needed to be sure that she felt the same way as I did. Maybe if we had bonded everything would be easier. The bond wasn't one sided, it went both ways. Unlike my parents and Cole's and Jett's parents I didn't just look at Lily and instantly bond with her. My wolf wanted it but there was something in her that stopped it. When I spoke to dad he told me it happens when the one you want to bond with has feelings for another, whether they know it themselves or not. When we first started talking it drove me mad, kept me awake at night. Who was this person that had captured her feelings when I couldn't? Dad told me to be patient that people's feelings change all the time. And over time I began to see what he meant. We still hadn't bonded but the link between us had grown stronger. Though our link was strong it wasn't complete. Did I already know this person who kept my girls heart in his hands? Cole was still late.

Cole

Nobody asked where we had been, Rain never mentioned it either. We all simply shared the rest of the night together in peaceful harmony. We laughed, played games and eventually worn ourselves out enough to sleep. Skyla would share a room with Rain who kindly asked Carmen to join. Earning a thankful smile from Reeve, I knew he worried about Carmen more than his parents did. He wanted her to be close to others as well as the family. To have friends of her own. Jett insisted on having his own room which was fine that meant us boys could all have our own rooms. I was just settling into bed when a knock sounded on my door "Yeah?" The door creaked open emitting Reeve. His face spoke his anxiousness even if his voice didn't. "Can I stay in here, the castle gives me the creeps?" Laughing at him I threw a cushion at his face, which he caught on reaction. "Sure as long as you don't starfish like Jett does, he's a nightmare." The room was very basic and simple. A double bed, a white wardrobe, beige walls and a double panelled window. Reeve lay beside me not speaking for a moment. His eyebrows were furrowed in a way I recognised as deep thought. I knew better not to interrupt his thought stream. When we were younger he could be thinking for minutes or hours, but when he was done he always had the greatest plan ever, or the smartest response. But the way he lay thinking tonight told me something was bothering him and it wasn't just some witty come back to my starfish joke. "Do you remember when I asked you if you like Lily?" His voice was different than before, guarded. There was little distance between us which meant if I lied he would be able to tell. From the way you shifted your body uncomfortably when you lied, or as my heart rate increased. Smart kid. "Yes." I answered carefully keeping my breathing under control.

"Were you telling the truth?" Something in his voice betrayed him, he had been thinking on this for a while now which meant by allowing him to share a room with me had been a trap, and I had willing walked into it. "No." His breathing stopped for a second then carried on in its normal succession. "Why did you lie?" I couldn't look at him, because if I did I knew everything I felt would just pour out of me. Then he would be broken.

"Because I didn't want to." It wasn't a lie, when I found out that Reeve liked Lily I tried to stop my growing feelings for her but our similarities had brought us closer. I didn't want to hurt him.

"Does she like you?" I didn't know how Lily felt, I had to always guess when it came to her. But I did know how she felt about Reeve. "She likes you Reeve." Reeve turned to look at me. His eyes gave away the internal pain he was in even if his face didn't. "That's not what I asked." Looking up at the ceiling I tried to think of an answer. But I couldn't. "I don't know." Reeve rolled over on his side so his back was too me. "Goodnight Cole." I closed my eyes pushing this conversation far away from me "night." But neither of us went to sleep.

Lily

Snowflakes floated gracefully around me, mesmerizing me in their winter beauty. I was alone. The naked trees were shadows against the greying sky, their branches stretching for the sunlight that had been stolen by winter's late arrival. Everything was quiet, the only sound was my breath as I exhaled watching the swirls of breath twirl away from me. I knew I was being watched from the prickle at the back of my neck, the sense I wasn't entirely alone. Snow always did have the power to make landscapes look larger than they really were, an illusion made from ivory powder. If the distance was far, or seem far I knew it was time to run, my thoughts 'I hope this illusion isn't real'.

When I woke I was cold. Chills ran through my bones. I wasn't in the warmth and comfort of my bed as I thought I was, I was outside. Dawn hadn't yet broke which meant the sky was still dark. I looked around. The bottoms of my pyjama bottoms were soaked as were my slippers, my thin grey t-shirt wasn't doing a very good job of keeping me warm either. When I began to recognise where I was I let dread and a tinge of fear settle in the pit of my stomach. I was in Lexi's back garden; standing in the same place as Lexi was whilst speaking to Levi. What the hell am I doing here? Taking a step towards the gate that led to the front of the house I was stopped by the garden light switching on, dousing me in golden light and telling the owners of the house that someone was in their back garden. I stood still too cold and afraid to move a muscle. I heard the lock on the back door sound and I was too slow to not be seen by whoever was letting themselves out.

I froze my back to them. "Lily?" Sighing with relief I turned around to find that it was Lexi who had come to my rescue. She didn't say anything just stared at me for the majority of two seconds before quickly enveloping me into a hug, I was thankful. "God your freezing come on we'll get you warmed up." Lexi took my frozen hand into her cold one and walked me inside where the heating was on high. We managed to creep past her parents' bedroom without a sound. Inside her room she gave me a pair of socks and slippers and her white fluffy dressing gown to put on. Her room wasn't like Sky's it consisted of two white walls and one black one which was covered in art, band posters and photos of us. There were clothes scattered around the room like a tornado had just torn through. Lexi sat by me on the bed. "What the hell were you thinking walking all the way over here in the middle of the night, in the freaking snow?" Her voice was loud even in whisper. Well I wasn't about to go on about my dreams and how sometimes I sleep walk, or can't remember parts of the night. "Ermmm I have no idea, I couldn't sleep...so I went for a walk and I just...ended up here."

"Well you could of got hypothermia next time you can't sleep go and watch a boring movie like I don't know something from the old days." She smiled and I got a glimpse of my old friend who would sit by me in physics and make the lesson go fast or trip over in P.E just to make it look like she was injured so she wouldn't have to do it. "Sorry." She looked down and her face turned sad, I wanted to comfort her but I didn't know what was going on. "You don't have to be sorry, look its three o clock in the morning, we better get you home in your bed before your mum wakes up and finds that you're gone. I can guarantee that you won't get a visit from Father Christmas." She stood up pulled on some boots and handed me her snow boots which she used when her family went on skiing holidays, she pulled two puffy coats from her wardrobe and handed me one before pulling herself into the other. "What are you doing?" She zipped herself up pulled me from the bed and checked if the coast was clear. "Taking you home."

This is the fourth time this year I have snuck out of somewhere if we're including sneaking out of my own house to get to Lexi's even if I did it unconsciously. Apparently Lexi's parents were real heavy sleepers which came in handy as Lexi was very noisy as she moved about the house finding the door keys, she would never make it as a burglar. The temperature had dropped even more since I had been in Lexi's house. "Looks like it's going to be a white Christmas after all." She said as we made our way down the street trying to be quiet so we wouldn't disturb the neighbours. I listened to the slight crunch my footsteps made as they made contact with the porcelain snow. "Look earlier when you and Sky came over I over reacted. There's a lot going on right now and I know I haven't been a good friend to all of you...I just want you to know I'm getting there, I'm trying to sort all this mess out and then things can go back to normal. What I'm trying to say is...will you bear with me?" She looked at me sadly.

"Yes Lexi but what's going on you can tell me?" She stopped and I noticed that we were in front of my house, how did we get here so fast? "I can't tell you just trust me okay, everything I'm doing is to protect you, all of you just know that okay. Merry Christmas Lil." She handed me a small parcel then left, quickly walking down the street leaving me alone here on the pavement. I opened the parcel carefully inside was a plain silver box, opening it up I found a delicate handmade dream catcher it was silver and gold, blue and green gems hung from it with beautiful white feathers. There was a note at the bottom of the box. 'I know you have bad dreams, I hope this stops you from wandering' love Lexi. She knew?

Cole

Christmas came with its easy excitement. Skyla had awoken everyone at the crack of dawn to tell us Santa had been and had brought snow with him. She was right, Ever had a sugar coating of snow and the sky was the dull grey that promised more. One of the spare rooms had been converted into a living room where a fire crackled and a sweet smelling Christmas tree stood bearing presents beneath its leaves. We all crowded into the room hugging and wishing a merry Christmas. Skyla grabbed my hand and pulled me down next to the tree pushing a present towards me "this one is for you Cole." Her giddiness was contagious, her smile radiated in the room. Inside the box she had handed me was a medal. The medal was gold and had a boss with the emblem of the shadows. I looked to dad who had mum stuck to his side, both of them looked proudly at me dad spoke up "congratulations son you finally made it, you're a protector!" I laughed, no way!
"You're joking." Mum laughed at me.
"No he's not you killed a vampire Cole which means you're ready we just had to wait to get the medal, now it's official, look at your arm." I looked at my arm and patterned along my fore arm was the words *Nos qouque stellarum* in black italic writing at the end was a star. Dad, Hector and Dean held out their arms and the same writing tattooed their skin, except the ending was different. For Hector it said *Luna* and for Dean it said

caelem. Dad spoke "we keep the stars." Dean smiled "we keep the sky." I looked to Hector he rolled his eyes and laughed as he carried on "we keep the moon." Mum came and sat by me rubbing the writing "you now have the family tattoo which means your now a protector." I looked at everyone then, my little sister looked at me in awe, Rain looked as though she might die of excitement, Jett just grinned but Reeve, I didn't recognise the look on his face. Anger?

The rest of the morning went swiftly. Reeve talked to everyone else but me, and everyone else ignored it as though nothing happened. I asked questions about what being a protector meant, which all the men were happy to answer. They explained that by killing a vampire you're wolfs true instinct is released which enables you to become a protector. When my father had learned that I had killed Luna he notified the King, who made the medal for me which contains the last step, by touching the metal the tattoo was then transferred onto my skin. Branding me a protector forever. When it was time to get ready for dinner we all vacated to our separate rooms. Reeve was in my room waiting for me. "I always thought it would be me to become a protector first." I waited by the door just in case he decided to jump me or something. "I'm sorry Reeve." Reeve looked at me for the first time in the past few hours. "Don't be none of this is your fault." And with that he stood and left leaving his sullen mood behind to infect me.

Lily

Christmas morning was always an event in this house. Mum and Dad didn't know about my little midnight stroll last night, they didn't even ask why I woke up in a puffy coat and snow boots. Leah being the youngest was obviously the most excited as she ripped into her presents, screaming when she realised she had been bought the new doll she wanted. Dad sat back in his favourite chair just smiling away as though he was the happiest he's ever been. Mum was obviously her normal self, dressed perfectly and fretting about the kitchen hoping she won't burn the turkey. (The second year in a row). Both sets of grandparents were coming over later for dinner. Mum didn't have any brothers and sisters, she was an only child. Dad however had a brother who I've never met. Uncle Zac had been estranged from his family from the moment he turned eighteen; tired of always coming second in his parents affections he decided to have nothing to do with them, or his straight A student of a brother who his parents both doted on. He wasn't a bad uncle, he sent birthday cards, Christmas cards blessing us with some notes inside, and he even managed to pick up the phone every few months to check that his brother's condition hadn't worsened. Mum had told me that uncle Zac had in fact called the day after I was admitted to hospital to check that his niece was okay. For these reasons I came to the conclusion that uncle Zac wasn't a bad man. That he did care for his family even if he did keep us an arm's length away, even though he couldn't forgive his parents for their lack of love towards him.

When the excitement of opening presents had toned down and Leah had vacated upstairs to introduce her new doll to her older ones I stayed to sit with dad. Leo had been given an hour by mum to go and visit his girlfriend while she slaved in the kitchen, refusing my help. Dad's last hospital appointment had confirmed that his cancer had spread to a different part of his body, mum had been the one to tell us, we hadn't told Leah. "Dad are you scared?" Dad looked at me from his chair and smiled slightly at me, he patted his knee. "I think I'm too big to come and sit on your knee."

"You'll never be too big." Standing I went to sit carefully on his knee, I was worried I might crush his frail body, but if I was heavy he didn't complain, he merely put his arms around me and put his chin on top of my head. "What do I have to be afraid of?" We've had this conversation before only a few months ago. "Of dying." He sighed, I felt his chest move up and down as he did.
"I'm not afraid of dying Lil, I'm afraid to leave you all here alone. I'm afraid that when I'm gone you might forget me." I didn't realise I was crying until I began to taste salt on my lips.
"We could never forget you, you never forget those who you love and daddy I love you lots." I hadn't called him daddy since I was eight, since I came to the conclusion I wasn't getting to old to call him daddy. His arms tightened around me and his voice wasn't as strong as it was before. I had never seen my father cry but I felt this was close enough, this only made the tears fall harder. "I love you baby girl and I will always be with you."

Cole

I felt like I was going to a wedding. All the women were dressed in their best dresses and high heels, shiny necklaces and dangly earrings. Whereas the men were in proper shirts and trousers, pressed ties and polished shoes. I don't think I've ever worn a tie before in my life. My tie was baby blue which matched Rain's baby blue dress. Jett's canary yellow tie matched my sister's pixie dress. I began to see a pattern, all the men's ties matched one of the girl's dresses, apart from Reeve. Reeve sidled up to me his good humour back "maybe my tie matches the princess's dress." Laughing at him I said "no I bet your tie matches the king's mothers dress." Reeve mocked horror. Laughing we waited in the corridor outside the throne room where me and Rain had waited for Gwen to come and collect us. We both stared at the paintings "I think I only recognise the latest one." I agreed with Reeve the other faces had no identities to me, they were the unknown past that I hadn't be bothered to learn. Gwen entered through the entrance doors. She curtseyed before speaking "I will seat you now the king and his family will enter after you." Spreading the doors wide Gwen led us through.

The room had changed since I had last been here. The throne had been moved and had been replaced by a long stretching table with numerous ruby cushioned seats. The table had a number of golden candelabras the flames flickering as we moved. The ocean was silent behind us, I saw snowflakes fall gracefully. The two heads of the table were left vacant along with the seat to the right of them. Gwen then told us to take a seat where we wanted. I sat in the middle with Reeve and Rain on either side of me. An announcer came to the door and stamped his foot before opening the door "Ladies and Gentlemen I announce to you Prince Lucas and his wife Lady Dia." The double doors swung open and in stepped the prince and his wife. The prince looked like his brother only he wasn't fair, he had all the same features but darker. His wife was a long slender woman. Her skin was sallow and the shadows under her eyes were stark. Her dark hair only made her look paler, she smiled carefully. We all stood and waited for Lucas to take his seat at one of the ends of the table and his wife to sit at his side. The announcer stamped his foot once again. "Introducing Pace Umbra king of Ever and the Duchess of Ever Mrs Primrose." The announcer pulled open the double doors. The king's mother walked beside her son with her arm looped with his. The king hadn't change since I had seen him the last time. I had never met Mrs

Primrose, though I heard she was a wonderful lady. Like I had thought Primroses emerald dress matched Reeves Emerald tie, he looked at me and smiled ruefully. The king took his seat and Primrose took hers which was evidently next to Reeve. It was tradition in Ever that the women would wear something to match the man they were out with, I'm pretty sure Reeve wasn't happy about the tradition being thrust upon him now, she was a little old for him. The king smiled kindly at Gwen "you may bring out the starters Gwen."

 Gwen began barking orders at the servants that were loitering around the room. The king laughed "excuse Gwen she likes things to be in order. I would like to say now that I have all of your attention is to thank you for joining me and my family here on this joyous day. But most importantly I would like to thank you James and your men for keeping the boundaries of Ever safe and secure and giving me the hope that one day my daughter may get to sit around this table with me." Everyone clapped graciously. My dad smiled and asked.
"My I speak your majesty?" The king smiled and nodded. My father's voice changed to the one he always used when speaking to us when we had done something that had please him. "Firstly I would like to thank you your majesty, and your family for having my family here today to share this wonderful holiday. I would also like to thank my pack for it would not be possible to keep Ever safe without them. And lastly, I would like to congratulate my son, who's finally become a protector, you make me proud everyday son and I hope you will keep doing that for the rest of your life." He sat down and everyone clapped Jett whooped but his mother silenced him with her frown. The starter came and silenced everyone as they ate, I didn't know what it was but it tasted amazing. The king was speaking to my father who was sat at his other side. "Now that your son is a protector are you going to tell him the truth or are you thinking about keeping it to yourself a little longer?" My dad thought for a while, I knew I shouldn't be eavesdropping but I wanted to know what secret he was hiding. "If you don't mind your majesty I thought you could tell him, you have more of an understanding than I, and I think he would be more likely to believe you over me." The king frowned. "Why wouldn't he believe you?" My dad's face became calmer almost emotionless. "We haven't had an amazing relationship for the past few years so he might be still wary about things I say." The king looked as though he was trying to figure out what had made us so distant. "Very well James if you want me

to speak to him then a will, but what are you going to do if he doesn't believe what I tell him?"

"Something tells me he will believe you." The king looked deeply at my father.

"Is there something you want to tell me?" My dad's face turned kind and smiley again.

"No your majesty." The king nodded. The rest of the meal was a delicious as the starter. Lucas and his wife sat in silence the whole time. And as soon as dessert had finished they excused themselves and left. The king and Mrs Primrose didn't comment on their silence. I felt as though something had happened before they had entered the room, and they had brought their attitudes with them. The king stood making me forget my train of thought "it has been a real pleasure to share this meal with you, but I must excuse myself I have come to realise that as I get older the more early I need to go to bed, so with that in mind I must retire for the night. I would like to see you Cole if you don't mind before you leave for the town tomorrow, I will have Gwen come and collect you. Good night everyone." We all said goodnight and watched him leave his burgundy cloak flowing after him. "Now that my sons have gone I think it time we take out the brandy, anyone like to join me?" The men agreed eagerly and Primrose led them down the hall to where they kept the brandy leaving the women and children.

Lila spoke to me "make sure you dress smart tomorrow Cole you wouldn't want to insult the king." If I hadn't heard my fathers and the kings conversation I would have been worried about why the king wanted to see me, but now that I knew I was just anxious to know what my father had been keeping from me all this time. It had come to my attention that since the king announced he wanted to see me that mum hadn't looked at me. Primrose came back through the door "children I think it is time you all went to bed you have a busy few days ahead, ladies please join me in the other room." The ladies made their way to the other room. Rain and Carmen took a hold of Skyla it was the first time I noticed that Carmen wasn't wearing a dress, I stopped her. "I didn't have a dress so mum told me to wear these." She tugged at her dark jeans and flimsy white top. I thought it strange that she didn't have a dress, even Rain had a dress and she had only come with the clothes on her back when she arrived at our home. I didn't let it bother me, although it did clearly go against tradition. Perhaps it was symbolic that even though Carmen was a wolf and a part of the pack, she wasn't like us. Reeve and I were just leaving when Primrose grabbed hold of both of our hands, she was awfully strong for an elderly woman. "When my son is finished speaking to you Cole I would like you too to come and see me." With that she let us go and left the room gracefully.

Lily

Mum didn't burn the turkey, actually she didn't burn anything. Both sets of grandparents had turned up blessing us with hugs and kisses and even more presents, and congratulated me on winning my race at championships. The whole event was warm and wonderful, but the chat with my dad still lingered. It made me so sad that he thought we would forget him when he was gone, how could I? He was my dad I could never forget him, ever! Eventually it was time for everyone to leave. Leah had been put to bed and Leo and dad were playing on Leo's knew game on the Xbox. Mum came and sat by me, she was smiling but her smile was sad. "Are you okay?" She sniffed and put her arm around me, I tucked myself under her chin. "I was just remembering that one Christmas before Leah was born, it was just like this them too playing on a game and you tucked up on here on the sofa watching. It just makes me sad when I realise how much time has passed. I don't want you to grow up I want you to all stay the same." I hugged mum tight.
"We will always be the same, and we will always be with you." I felt as though this Christmas had been an emotional one. That was before the dream came...

The sea roared in the night as the man made his way down the beach. The lights from the castle lit his path as he carefully maneuverers over sand and stone. The moon was bright and edged towards the horizon, the stars twinkled and reflected in his pale eyes. He was smiling. The past few dreams of the man had been either from the past or present, in the present he was always sad, but now something had made him smile. He stopped by an opening to a cave, he put his hand on the crumbling stone as he did the cave began to rumble and collapse creating a doorway. He made his way inside, it was dark and dimly lit by candles. A man waited at the door at the end of the corridor "your majesty I wasn't expecting you?" The king smiled. "I didn't know I was coming." The guard stepped aside and opened the door. The room was like the corridor only lit by candles. Inside was a stone coffin, the man made his way towards it. There was writing engraved on the lid 'in loving memory of Alana Lily Greys, a devoted wife and loving Queen' at the end was a detailed pattern of a Lily. The man went down on his knees and gently placed his hands on the lid. "We've found her Alana, our daughter she's safe and I'll bring her home and I will tell her everything. I wish you were here, my world turned dark when you left but maybe I've found the light. I need your wisdom Alana I don't even know where to start." I watched a man who was filled with so much heartache cry silently as though if he made a sound he would wake the dead.

Cole

The morning brought Gwen to my door and Lily to my phone. It was around seven o clock when my mobile rang. Reeve had slept in Jett's room last night so he wasn't there when I answered the phone to Lily "hello?"
"Cole?"
"Yeah Lily this is me what's up?" She paused.
"Did you dream last night?" I paused.
"No did you?"
"Yes." Confused I asked.
"Is that what you want to talk about?" Another pause from her.
"Yes, it was about a man, he went to visit his dead wife's grave to tell her that they had found there lost daughter." Her story rang clear with familiarity. She was dreaming about the king and Queen Alana, and the lost princess. "And?" She sighed.
"And nothing it freaked me out because this isn't the only time I've dreamed about them and I was wondering if you did too?" Thinking about it, I hadn't. I dreamt about a girl whose face was hidden from me. "No I've never dreamt about them."
"Do you know who they are?" Collecting my thoughts I answered.
"Yes..." there was a knock at the door telling me Gwen had come in search for me.
"Sorry Lil I have to go I'll call you later." I hung up before she could answer and went to the door. Gwen stood there patiently in her usual attire.

"Good morning you have five minutes to make yourself presentable and I will take you to the king, then I will take you and your friend to Mrs Primrose." I stood frozen. She wafted her hands at me "chop chop lad I don't have all day." Running back inside the room I made myself look 'presentable' though my spiky hair wouldn't go flat. Gwen was waiting for me outside the door, she flashed a quick smile at me before gesturing down the hall and that I should follow.

She guided me down the now familiar corridor that led to the throne room. The portraits watched me as I passed them and the entrance to the throne room. "You are to meet the king in his private chambers." Gwen spoke into the echoing corridor. The king's quarters were unfortunately at the other end of the castle, which meant a long cold trek through the grey corridors. When we eventually got there Gwen made herself scarce, with the only instruction to knock on the door. I knocked clearly twice on the door, nerves suddenly making an arrival. The door swung open and the king stood tall at the other side, he smiled kindly. "Please come in Cole and take a seat." The king's room was like the rest of the castle grey walled, cold and old fashioned with a mahogany table stretching out in the middle of the room, with a matching chair at either end. I took the seat nearest the door. The king sat opposite. "I guess you must be wondering why I asked you here, am I right?" I was too nervous to use my voice, so I nodded. The king crossed his pale hands in front of him. "Well Cole your sixteen which means I believe you're ready to be told who you really are." Crossing my arms so the king wouldn't see my hands shaking I asked "what do you mean?" The king stood and walked over to the window which wasn't far from the table we sat at. His eyes held a storm like the ocean roared furiously. "You're not just any old wolf Cole, your special." The king paused to let his words sink in. but his words barley brushed the surface. I knew I wasn't just any old wolf; I knew that every night my mind was filled with dreams, and I knew that these dreams meant something. "I know about your dreams Cole." The king turned to look at me full on.
"Is this what you wanted to talk to me about your majesty?" The king seated himself once again and ringed his hands. He was clearly nervous about something. "No Cole I am the only one who knows about your dreams, your family have no idea, and I would appreciate if you didn't tell them." Looking down at the table I realised there was a fairly large scratch in the middle. "Why not?" The king held me in place with his icy gaze.

"Because you are the only one who can help my daughter, this is why I wanted you to come." If he wanted to discuss my ability to dream and my family didn't know, what had my father been talking about. Keeping his gaze with my own icy irises, I spoke "I thought you knew where your daughter was your majesty?" The king finally let his gaze fall and his voice was strained with emotion. "No, your father only wrote of a sighting of her. Which means she will need your help to return." The king obviously saw something in my expression that made him elaborate. "My daughter had been hunted from the moment she was born. My sister in law Dia, who you met last night is a witch. She created a spell that would protect my daughter from harm. She created a spell that only a person with the gift of dreaming would be able to find her. Which means those who do not possess the gift wouldn't be able to find her or harm her. Her enemies could walk past her in the street and not be able to do anything, unless they had the gift." Riddling out his words I asked.

"Then how do the pack know about her?" The king smiled slightly.

"Because as you well know, your pack is special, its strong that's why Dia added the wolves to her spell, so one day they would be able to protect her if they ever crossed paths."

"Why did she pick the gift of dreaming? Why not something that would link her to you so you could find her?" The king's gaze found mine again, his face had lost its easy smile.

"Because I'm being watched, I would have led my enemies straight to her, and she picked that gift because it's incredibly rare, and because my daughter also possess this gift." My breath caught for a moment, unease settled into my stomach. "What did you say your daughter's name was again your majesty?" The king looked at me his smile returning, a sparkle began gleaming in his eye as he proudly said "Lily."

Reeve

Cole was silent as he accompanied me and Gwen to Mrs Primrose's chambers. He had previously had a meeting with the king, which I knew without a doubt was the key to his unease and silence. There was something about him that had changed. Not only could I know detect the unmistakable power of the protector on him, but anxiety. An emotion prohibited to protectors. Something was wrong. The past few days had been tense between us which left me in no proper position to ask what was bothering him. Gwen quickly led us into the room where the king's mother awaited us. When we reached the room Gwen hastily pushed us both inside and closed the door quickly as she vacated.

Mrs Primrose stood waiting for us to enter patiently. "Good morning boys, I'll make it quick. Cole you're a protector and Reeve you are not, therefore your first mission is to become one." Anxiety now claimed my body too. Cole spoke up, his face emotionless. "What are you saying mi 'lady?" Mrs Primrose looked me dead in the eye before turning to look out of the window, diffusing some of the tension coiling inside of me. "He must kill a vampire of course, and I know just the bloodsucker for you." I looked At Cole who carried on looking emotionless. There was no way I was ready to kill a Vamp. I knew when Cole killed Luna he was far from ready. "Who did you have in mind?" She smiled rather maliciously before answering something dangerous in her ageing face. "Levi."

I had to jog to catch up with Cole as we left Mrs Primrose's chambers. I could no longer sense any emotion on him what so ever. Being a protector allowed you to have more control over your body. It made your senses heightened as though you were seeing the world through your wolf, but wearing human skin. It also allowed you to have control over your emotions. You only had to feel when you wanted to feel, or feel those emotions that you want to be felt. Right now it seemed Cole didn't want to feel anything. "Are you okay?" Cole stopped. We were at the main door that led to the bridge into Ever. "Why wouldn't I be?" I looked at him. He looked like he always did but something in his expression made him foreign to me. "You seem weird that's all." He huffed then turned to walk out the door, not waiting for me to follow, but he knew I would anyway. He spoke. "You shouldn't be worrying about me anyway, worry about the fact that Primrose had literally put you on a suicide mission." He was right, why couldn't she have picked another vamp, someone a little less dangerous. "Why do you reckon she wants him dead?" We were in the middle of town by now and it seemed that even Boxing Day sales made an appearance here, as people walked cladded in cloaks and fur to shop among the markets. "I don't know, maybe because the shadows have always had a problem with his father and want to make an example, though I wish for your sake she had picked someone easier. Not only is

Levi old and evil he has immense power, some say even stronger than his fathers." This was definitely not making me feel any better. Levi was the son of Seth the evil murderous leader of the Lamia. Seth had been known to have a sort of power, but nobody knew what that power was exactly. If his son was more powerful than him, then I was definitely dead. "So what are we going to do?" We stopped and turned around to look at the way we had come. Evelyn castle stood tall and stark against the greying cloud. "I have an idea, it doesn't quite follow Primroses plans but I think it might help us later." I looked at him, he no longer looked emotionless, but his expression wasn't good either. "What's the plan?" He smiled. "First we need another vampire."

Lily

I spent Boxing Day with Sky and her family. A few years back we had created a tradition that me, Sky and Lexi would spend Boxing Day together as the majority of these holidays are spent with family. But Boxing Day had always been our day. This year we were one short. I didn't tell Sky that I had wandered to Lexi's house in the middle of the night, that she found me, got me warm and then walked me home. I hadn't even told Cole who was the closest thing I had right now to the answers I had long been waiting for. I hoped he was finding some answers in Ever, because there was no luck here. The day went fast as we watched classic Disney films wrapped in blankets and stuffing our faces with popcorn. When I left later that night I decided I wasn't yet ready to go home. I decided I nice walk might ease my troubling mind.

 The woods looked softer with a powdering of snow, I felt more at peace as I walked in its tranquillity. The snow sparkled under the crescent moons light. I hadn't walked very far when I realised I was being followed. My follower's steps were muffled in the snow but still detectable. I quickly bent down and grabbed a fallen branch that was nearly thicker than my arm, I spun on my advancer. A woman held her hands up to me, slight fear and disbelief clouded her dark eyes. She was tall and slender, she had porcelain skin and dark hair. Her emerald cloak clung to her and she looked at me. Her clothes were old fashioned as though she had lived long ago and had only just found her way again. "I didn't mean to startle you dear one, only to see if my eyes were deceiving me." Her voice was strangely familiar, as though I had heard her once before.

"Who are you?" The woman smiled at me gently before stepping closer. "Who I am is not important right now, dear one. For you are in danger! I must ask you to leave these woods and never enter again alone, for these woods hide many horrors in which you are not ready to accept yet." When her hand touch my arm I thought it would be cold but it was strangely warm, she gently tugged my sleeve pulling me back the way I had come. "Do I know you?" The woman smiled sadly as we progressed out of the woods, onto the lightened streets. "Yes, I am a piece of your forgotten past dear one, now you must go and never come back." She pushed me forward. "Wait I need answers please!" She looked at me sadly. Before slowly stepping into the woods again. "I can only tell you to listen to your dreams, for all will become clear, until we meet again dear one." And like that she was gone.

Cole

I felt different. Yesterday I had been too in shock to notice the difference in me. The subtle changes that were happening inside my body. I sat beside Reeve as we awaited the rest to come out of the castle. Ever looked pretty in its ivory coating. The old fashioned buildings looked less worn away, the oceans voice was slow and steady; unlike Reeves heart, which battered against his chest. Primrose hadn't made his life any easier. She had literally put him on a suicide mission. Levi was severely lethal. The least the old lady could have done was ask him to take out one of his many guards. I actually thought she liked Reeve. But I had a plan. If Reeve killed another Vamp, he would become a protector, which meant he would be a lot stronger than he is now. It might give him a chance if he had to go against Levi. The worse part was we didn't even know why we were going after Levi. Why us? He wouldn't be alone in this mission. Primrose hadn't said he had to go it solo, so I knew I would be the one to help him. We couldn't tell our parents they would surely stop us. The time of them constantly babying us was over! I am a protector now, and the first person I was going to protect was Reeve. Then I had my own mission to be getting on with.

Lily

After my strange encounter with the woman in the wood, I thought it more urgent to find out the answers me and Cole had been searching for. There was only one person that knew anything and that was Amelia, it was getting her to share those secrets which was the problem. Sometimes her memory failed her, but most of the time it was her being down right stubborn. Maybe that's where I get it from. But first of all I wanted to know exactly what Lexi knew about me. Finding her was the easy part, it was getting her to talk to me which was the problem. It seemed two of the people closest to me, didn't like sharing their secrets with me anymore, realising this made my heart hurt just a little. I decide I would just walk past Lexi's to see if anyone was in, if there wasn't then I could just carry on walking, if there was I could just say I was just passing and might as well say hi. It felt weird to walk back to Lexi's knowing only two days ago I had walked there unconsciously in my sleep.

The house was quiet when I walked past, which was unusual. Normally you would hear Lexi's music thumping through the walls and her out of tune screech as she sang along to the chorus. Not today, the house stayed silent. Balling up some courage I went to knock on the door only to find it was already opening. Lexi's mother had always looked like she belonged in the city. With her dyed blonde curls and chocolate eyes that matched the leather boots she was wearing. Her makeup was always done in a way you would expect to see actresses as they stepped onto the red carpet. But not today. As she walked out of the door I noticed her hair wasn't evenly curled, and her coal black eyeliner was smudged to make her resemble a panda. "Lily what are you doing here?" I didn't know if it was a city thing but Lexi's mother always managed to hide her common accent, replaced with easy, but annoying snootiness. "I was wondering if Lexi was here." Her eyes flicked to the door that was still hanging open before she bent down close to me. "Tell me Lily, is something wrong, should I be worrying, is she doing drugs is she...?" I stopped her before she could say anything else. I couldn't tell her the truth about her daughter's withdrawal from us because I didn't want her to get into trouble, and I couldn't exactly say "no Mrs White your daughters not doing drugs," just hanging round a psychotic vampire that tried to kill me once! So I lied, which was becoming a sort of habit nowadays.

"I don't believe there's anything to worry about, she's fine at school." Mrs White raised an eyebrow at me as though she didn't quite believe me. Before she could say anything else. Lexi appeared at the door. "Lily I was just about to call you, come in" before I could speak Lexi had grabbed my arm and pulled me inside. "I thought you were going out?" Her mum looked at me then to Lexi before grabbing her car keys and saying "yes, I'll be home in an hour." Before she could say anything else though, Lexi had already shut the door in her face. "Let's go to my room."

Lexi had tidied her room since the last time I had been here. There was no longer clothes doting the floor, or an unkempt bed. "Why is your mum so stressed about you?" Lexi made herself busy by tiding up her dressing table. I had never seen so many hair products for someone that has short hair like Lexi. "Same reason you and Sky are." I took of my coat it was too hot to keep on I threw it across her bed, I stood and crossed my arms against my chest. "Are you going to start telling me something I want to know?" Lexi stopped tiding and came to stand in front of me, adopting the same pose. "You don't want to know any of it." Rolling my eyes at her I answered.
"Try me." Lexi huffed as though she had been defeated, but she hadn't, not yet.
"The man you and Sky saw me with, his names Levi. I met him a few months ago at this party thing for my parents. At first I thought he was interested in me so we started seeing each other. We had hung out a couple of times before he started asking questions, about you, about Sky about everyone. He would get really angry if I didn't tell him, he would threaten to hurt me or you or my family, so I kept talking." By now both I and Lexi had found refuge sitting on her bed, I let the tears fall down her face, keeping my attention on her story. "One night he came to me and he was fuming, said he had been attacked by some people because he tried talking to you. I asked him why he was so obsessed with knowing you, he said you were special, that you had some sort of power that he needed. He wants to use me to get to you Lily but I won't let it happen. He's evil and I can see it now, he's...a vampire." When her sobs began to rack her body I let her find comfort in my embrace. "I know what he is Lex, he didn't try to talk to me, he tried to kill me." Lexi sniffed, I could feel her salty tears stain my jumper but I didn't mind. "I know." Pushing her back so I could look at her I saw something I didn't like in her eyes. "What do you mean you know?" She stopped crying and looked me dead in the eye.

"I know he tried to kill you, because I told him where to find you." I felt my heart stutter in my chest. I felt like I was falling. The last thing I saw was Lexi lung forward towards me, then everything went black.

Cole

I knew something was wrong with Lily. From the cold shudder that ran across my body, and the slight sad ache I got in my heart. I didn't know how I knew I was sensing Lily, I just knew. Before I could even comprehend another thought my body had shifted into its wolf form. It was a good job that I was out walking on my own, or else there would have been a lot of questions, and I would have to tell someone where I was going. My paws took me out of Ever and through the shield back into the woods I knew better than anyone. I let my senses drive me without even thinking. Though I did start to worry when my path started taking me out of the woods, onto unsheltered streets. I kept low in the shadows so nobody would see me. My senses drew me to a cluster of houses. A light was on in one of the bedrooms, the familiar scent of perfume that Lily always wore hung in the air, along with her distress. Heart pounding I shifted just enough to open the door and let myself inside. The rest of the house was dark and empty. The light from the bedroom upstairs glowed dimly. Using my stealth I made my way up the stairs silently, my focus on the voices that were in the room.

"Why am I tied up, why did you attack me!" Lily exclaimed, her fear ripped into me.
"He wants you Lily, and when he wants something he gets it." Lexi's voice was almost unrecognisable. I could only detect Lily's thumping heartbeat, which under normal circumstances would mean there was only one person in the room. As this wasn't any normal circumstance, I hazard a guess that Lexi wasn't exactly human anymore. "So you're working for him now, why he's evil!" Lexi laughed in a malicious way, I could hear her moving around the room.
"I owe him you see. He made me, made me strong and invincible whereas before I was weak and feeble, but not anymore!" I heard her snarl and I knew from Lily's scream Lexi had shown her fangs. I decided it was time to

show myself, stepping into the room I felt two sets of eyes pierce into me. Lily's heart began to slow down as I glanced at her, she looked slightly relieved. Lexi however looked livid. "What are you doing here you mangy mutt, get out of my house!" I decided I would show her my fangs too, she took a step back, her ebony eyes started to look frightened. She turned to Lily. "Looks like I'm not the only one keeping secrets." Not taking my eyes of Lexi I bit at the ties holding Lily and released her, she stood up, I placed myself protectively in front of her. "I don't know what you mean." Lexi laughed but kept glaring at me.

"I think you do, not only did you not share that you're a dream breaker, but you know of the existence of werewolves." She pulled a revolted look as she spoke the word werewolf, I growled but Lily placed a calming hand on my head. "How do you know I'm a dream breaker, and I didn't know about the werewolves until the night Levi attacked me." Lexi didn't seem convinced of Lily's lie. "I knew you were a dream breaker because the night Levi attacked you, he knew you wasn't human, and when the werewolves appeared he figured it out. Werewolves wouldn't have come in aid of just anybody, he knew you were special. So we put our heads together, your symptoms of tiredness, fainting, sleep walking it wasn't hard to figure out." Lily lifted her head defiantly.

"So what that I am, you didn't tell me you were…" Lily choked I knew she didn't want to accept that her best friend was now a vampire. Lexi laughed viciously. "What…a vampire." Lily nodded. "Well maybe if you had paid attention you would have noticed sooner." Lexi lifted her right arm and pulled up her sleeve revealing the same black italic writing of my own tattoo. *Mortalitate ad immortalitatem.* "Mortality to immortality" she spoke proudly. Lily just stared at the tattoo as though if she looked at it long enough it would disappear. "How long?" Her voice was quiet but strong. Lexi looked at her hard "since the day I walked out of physics."

Lily

Lexi was a vampire. Lexi was a vampire. Lexi was a vampire. I hoped maybe if I said it enough times it might just sink in. my best friend was a vampire. She helped another vampire try and kill me. She played me, tied me up. She was a monster. Then suddenly I became emotionless. I didn't care for the memories we shared, I didn't care that for the past few years she had been like a sister to me. All I cared about was getting me and Cole out of here without getting hurt, but if that meant hurting Lexi to do it, then so be it. She had chosen the side she wanted to be on. She was a vampire, a blood sucking vampire and I didn't want anything to do with her. Poking Cole in his side I glanced at the door hoping he would get my hint, he nodded slightly. Standing fully in front of me he pushed me towards the door growling at Lexi as he did. Lexi watched him with distrust and a tinge of fear which made me oddly happy for some reason. "I'm warning you now Lily, Levi won't give up. He wants you dead." Keeping my eyes steady on her I asked myself how did I not know? Looking at Lexi I now saw the resemblance between her and Levi. Her coal black eyes, her transparent skin, her moody and defiant expression. She was no longer happy go lucky Lexi, no she was a monster. "And are you going to help him?" We didn't wait for an answer, Cole had managed to get us both to the door and we ran down the stairs and out the door, but it didn't matter. Lexi didn't try to follow.

The day had turned dark as we made our way onto the streets. Cole nudged me towards the woods and tugged at my jacket. Following his hint I removed my jacket and handed it to him. He grabbed hold of the jacket with his teeth and trotted into the security of the shadows. A few moments later he emerged in his human form, my jacket wrapped around his middle, I made my way towards him. His face was so sincere and comforting. He opened his arms to me as best as he could. I didn't know how much I needed a hug until Coles warm arms were wrapped around me. His scent filled my senses, he smelled of pine. He rubbed my back comfortingly. I felt cold when he finally let go of me. My heart stuttered a little bit. It was an odd feeling. How could two people make me feel this way? I asked myself. We sat down in the shadows. We didn't talk for what felt like an eternity. Cole broke the silence. "I'm sorry Lily." I couldn't look at him, I kept my gaze on the road in front of us. Thinking of what it must look like to a passer-by two kids hiding in the woods. "How did I not know, how did you not know?" Cole sighed it was long and loaded.
"Because you didn't want to see it Lily, you wanted to believe in the old Lexi. And me, I should have known, but I haven't been a protector long, so my senses wouldn't have been able to detect her yet, as she's still so young." His words were intriguing, not been a protector long, did that mean something more. I inquired him about it. "It means I'm an official

pack member, I can accompany hunts, my wolf is a lot stronger, and I'm a lot stronger." I thought it weird. He had always seemed strong to me, how could you possibly be stronger? I looked at the tattoo that patterned his arm, the same ink as Lexi's but different words. "What does your tattoo mean?" Cole rubbed his hand over the words and looked at me. "It says we keep the stars, it's my family's crest. Humans can't see it." I decided to change the subject then, not liking the fact that both of my friends had tattoos that could only be seen by the supernatural, and that branded them as the supernatural. "How come you weren't a protector before?" I looked at Cole then, he was looking at the ground. His expression guarded. "I hadn't killed a vampire before." From his tone I knew he didn't regret killing this vampire, but something also told me he had no choice. "What happened?" Cole sighed another loaded sigh and explained the story about Levi and Luna's attack. How she had nearly killed Rain, how he had no choice. When he had finished he looked awfully vulnerable. I don't know what made me do it, maybe because we had become close, and he was the only person who truly knew me inside and out, or the fact that he had just saved me when I thought my best friend, the vampire might kill me. I reached my hand to his face and turned it towards me, leaning forward I gently placed my lips onto his startled ones. A weird spark erupted when our lips touched, sending shivers down both our spines. Pulling back I saw Cole looking at me in a way that made me want to smile forever. He smiled at me, a smile I had never seen before, and his eyes were twinkling with something that I didn't recognise. But it only lasted a moment, the spark dimed the smile slipped from his face and he spoke. "We can't tell Reeve."

Cole

For a moment, I actually thought we had bonded. When our lips had touched and the spark had flickered between us I actually thought we might bond. The hope and want was burning inside my veins. Then it vanished when I remembered that we couldn't bond, not yet. Because her heart belonged to someone else too. Reeve. My best friend. My brother. I had said to myself that Lily had to come to me, and she had. But why did it hurt me so much when she did. I knew loving her was wrong but I could no longer help it. I had promised Jett not to let a girl come between us, but now it was too late. I had done the one thing I vowed never to do. I fell in love with Lily. And so had Reeve. Only one of us could be with her, which meant it would be her choice. The problem was that she loved us both.

Lily looked away from me, something in her expression was unreadable. "I should get home." Her voice was soft and devoid of any emotion. Nodding I started to stand but she placed her hand on my shoulder. "No you stay here, you already risked being seen when you came to rescue me, which I never thanked you for, so thank you." She still didn't look at me.
"You're welcome." Lily stood up and looked down at me.
"How did you know I was in trouble anyway?" Standing up I looked at her at eye level. She kept her eyes to the ground but I pulled her chin up so she was looking at me. "I don't know what it was, I just had a feeling you were in danger. And before I knew it I had shifted and the same tug I got six years ago when I first saw you brought me to you earlier." Lily stared at me hard in the eye for a moment before dropping her gaze and stepping back from me. "I'll see you in four days then." Nodding at her she turned and began walking out of the shadows. Shifting quickly I caught up with her, her jacket in my mouth. Nudging her hand with my head. Lily stopped took the jacket from my mouth and bent down to me. She stroked my head "you need to get back before your family realises your gone. I'll be alright getting home. Thank you for saving me." Before I could even comprehend another thought she moved closer and kissed me on the head before standing quickly. "I know" she said "don't tell Reeve."

Reeve

We spent our remaining time in Ever in the town. Getting to know the locals and the castle. Cole and I spent most of our time planning our secret mission for Mrs Primrose. Choosing which vampire I should hunt before we attempted to kill Levi. Cole had been kind of edgy the past few days, spending his spare time alone. I could only guess it was to do with becoming a protector. Dad had mentioned that when he had first become a protector he found it hard to adjust to all his senses being more heightened than usual, especially his emotions.

It was our last night here. We were staying at a lodge in the middle of town right by the sea. The adults were sat in the dining area enjoying a rare drink with each other. The kids decided they wanted to go and check out the beach, since the snow had stopped yesterday. Carmen said "we might as well see it while we're here, we don't know when we will be back." She was right, when would we be back? Cole carried Skyla on his shoulders and Rain and Carmen held hands and skipped down the hill towards the beach, Jett was already in the surf splashing the girls when they came close. I kept pace with Cole. The beach was tranquil and beautiful under the moonlit sky. The waves crashed loudly against the shore, the surf spreading along the sand. Skyla squealed. "Let me down Cole." Laughing he pulled her down from his shoulders and let her run to Carmen and Rain who were playing in the surf. Cole was smiling as he watched the girls splash one another. "Are you ready to go home?" I asked. Keeping his gaze on the girls he answered.

"Yeah Sean's party's going to be great." Recalling the blonde boy in Lily's group, I remembered him inviting me to his new year's party on the rare occasion we actually spoke to one another. "Oh yeah I forgot about that." "I have a vampire you can kill." The way he just dropped it into the conversation shocked me, and it took me a while to process what he was saying. "Who?" Cole began walking towards the sea and I followed. He splashed Skyla who squealed loudly and tried to splash him back. "Lexi." I stared at him. He was busy joining in the water fight. "Lexi's a vampire?" Cole stopped.

"Yeah and she's working for Levi." I didn't want to ask how he knew all of this, because I had no right to question a protector so I just asked. "But Lexi's Lily's best friend." Cole picked up his sister and spun her around to make her giggle even louder, putting her back down we both watched her laugh dizzily as she fell on her bottom in the water. "Lily doesn't know you're a werewolf so how would she know any better?"

"But it wouldn't be right." Cole turned to me directly. Here standing in the surf with the dark sky against him and his dangerous expression I no longer knew him. Suddenly he became a stranger to me. "If you won't kill her, then I will."

Lily

The lady with the willowy figure emerged from the mist. Her golden curls illuminated the darkness that pressed in around us. "You're nearly there Lily." She seemed both close and faraway as she spoke. "I don't understand." My voice echoed into the night. The beautiful lady smiled, it was radiant. "You've nearly figured out who you are." Trying to step closer I noticed I couldn't move, stuck to the ground where I stood. "No I haven't, I don't know who I am." The lady smiled once again, her expression resembled pity, but something told me that this lady didn't pity others, she didn't feel anything at all. "Yes you have, you're just not listening."

Cole

"You remember what I've asked of you?" The king asked me. I was back in his private chambers, sitting in the same place as before. "Yes your majesty." The king didn't smile when he looked at me. There was years of pain and heartache shining at me through his eyes. "Good because you're the only person who can help me now Cole, bring my daughter home."

Lily

I found myself at Sky's house early New Year's Eve. We decided to get ready for Sean's part here as Sky's house was closer to his than mine, I was also staying the night at Sky's after the party had finished. Leo and his friends were having their own party down near the woods which meant mum Leah and dad were left at the house for their own celebration. With everything going on the selfish part of me needed tonight. An escape from the dreams, an escape from being me. The party started at eight which meant we had an hour to get ready. Which was fine, I wasn't one of those girls who needed an hour just to put some lip gloss on. I was seated at Sky's old fashioned ivory dressing table. Sky was busy standing behind me making my long straggly hair into perfect curls with her curling wand. Sky was already done. She had pulled her masses of curling black hair up in to a winding bun with a plait wrapped around it to expose her pale face. Her makeup was natural and pretty. "Do you think Lexi will show up?" Obviously I hadn't told Sky that our best friend was now an immortal bloodsucker, who was in league with another blood sucker that had tried to kill me. "I have no idea, probably not." Sky was a fragile soul and it hurt me to see her hurt over someone that didn't deserve her hurt. There was a part of me that wanted so badly to tell Sky what was going on. So she could see and make judgment of Lexi herself. Then there was the other part of me that didn't want her to know, because I knew it would be far safer for her not to. Sky switched of the curling wand ran her fingers through my hair then smiled happily. "Your hairs done, time for your makeup." Smiling and rolling my eyes at her I turned the chair to face her. "Okay but just natural like yours okay." She smiled at me as she began brushing something soft onto my face. "Are Cole and Reeve coming?" She spoke as the brush tickled my cheeks.

"Yeah there both coming."

"Should be interesting then." Opening my eyes to look at her I let my face cloud into confusion.

"What's that supposed to mean?" Sky laughed slightly before standing to get her mascara from the side. "Well it's interesting that it's so obvious that both of them like you and that you like both of them." I was too shocked to speak. Was I that transparent? Sky came and sat in front of me, her face was sweet as always. "Why didn't you tell me?" I knew she was trying extremely hard to keep the hurt out of her voice, but I detected it anyway. "Because I didn't know how I felt." I looked down. Sky took my hand from my lap and squeezed it gently. "I get it, but if you want my opinion I think Reeve is better for you than Cole?" Looking up Sky's face had turned hard and serious. "What makes you say that?"

"Just trust me. Cole is real nice and everything but there's something dangerous under the surface and I don't want you to get caught up in that." Her words burned into me. There was a hidden meaning under her words 'there's something dangerous under the surface'. It wasn't possible was it? She couldn't possibly know Coles secret. Could she?

We didn't talk about Cole or Reeve for the rest of the time we had to get ready. Instead we talked about what we thought Ella might show up in. last time Sean had a party she showed up in a dress that could only be resembled to a mouldy green lampshade. Her eccentric style had always made her a sort of laughing stock of the group, however Ella's confidence was endless therefore she didn't care what we thought, she just wore it

anyway. It must be nice to be like that, so confident in your own skin. Looking at myself in the mirror I didn't recognise my reflection. Looking back at me with the same sapphire blue eyes as my own was a small slender girl, with long perfect golden curls, natural looking makeup and a pale knee length white dress with a golden belt. Next to me was Sky. With her delicate up do and dark puffy dress with silver embroidery. She smiled "we're like Ying and Yang, but I don't know which colours which." We both giggled. Looking at the alarm clock on the bedside table told us we had five minutes to get to Sean's, which was easy. Ever Green was not a big place. We walked down the stairs where Noah was waiting in the kitchen, his drawing pad was out again. "Where's mum and dad?" Sky asked as she carefully pulled on her ballerina pumps. Noah didn't look up from his drawing when he answered "there upstairs with some wine their watching some movie so I'm staying down here." Sky frowned.
"But its New Year's Eve you should go be with them." From what I could remember. Sky's parents had always been there for their kids when it was the important stuff, such as hospital appointments and football practice. But when it came to spending quality time with their kids they seemed to not think that was as important as working away on their blackberry's or too wrapped up in their own problems. "Well you're not spending time with them, you're going to a party!" I knew Noah's tone had caught Sky of guard. Noah was never one to be angry at anyone. "You could come with us." Sky offered as she came and stood by her brother, looking at what he was drawing. Noah smiled slightly but kept his gaze on the paper. "Nah it's alright, I think I'll just finish this, but thanks. Have fun at the party." Sky frowned at the drawing before nodding to him "thanks lets go Lil."

We were walking along the street towards Sean's the night had grown chilly but the party was inside so we didn't bother to bring a jacket. "Is he going to be okay?" Sky hated talking about her family. I knew she didn't like the way her family made Noah feel but she never said anything to her parents. But that was Sky, she never wanted to upset the balance of things, even if it meant making her life better. "Yeah he will be okay, he'll probably go up just before midnight." We didn't talk the rest of the way. Instead we let the nights silence cleanse us. When we arrived at Sean's we saw the whole house was lit up with fairy lights and disco balls. Smiling sky grabbed hold of my hand and pulled me towards the door "come on let's just have some fun."

Cole

We were finally back from Ever. It was definitely nice to be home, but a part of me wanted to go back to the land where all the answers were. My room seemed unfamiliar to me as I hadn't been here in a week. The walls were no longer an odd shade of cream but a dark navy blue. There still wasn't much furniture in here. Just my bed, a dresser where my second hand TV stood. I was looking in my mirror which hung on the wall by the door. I stood glaring at my reflection. There was a knock at the door and Rain entered. She smiled at me before closing the door behind her and stepping inside. "Why do you look so angry?" Laughing I sat on my bed. "Because my hair is a mess!" Rain laughed loudly and came to stand in front of me a brush from my dresser in her hand. "You're such a girl! Here let me help." I let her brush out the gel that I'd put in to try and calm the spikes and curls. "I didn't know you had curly hair." Huffing I answered. "That's because I try to keep it straight." Stepping away from me and placing the brush back where she found it she pointed to the mirror. "Well I think you look fine." Staring at my reflection I saw my natural hair, slight spikes and curls. For once it didn't look to bad. "Is that what you're wearing?" She spoke as she indicated my clothing with a swish of her hand. Looking down at my faded jeans and green polo I nodded with a raised eyebrow. "Oh god help me, sit. How long have we got?" Looking at my watch which was one of my presents from Christmas I saw that it was half past seven. "We have twenty minutes before Reeve comes to pick me up." Nodding she started going through my clothes. "Good because it might take a while to make you look presentable, you're like a walking fashion disaster!" I laughed sarcastically at her.
"Well thanks, because I'm sure that wasn't supposed to hurt my feelings." Smiling at me with a glint in her eye she turned to look back my clothes. There was another knock at the door.

Smiling to myself I shouted to the closed door "is that someone else who wants to insult me?" The door opened and mum stepped in smiling. "I would never insult you." Laughing at her I said.
"Yes you would." She smiled at me and came to sit by me watching Rain frown at my clothes as she riffled through them. "What's she doing?" Rain

stood up with a pair of dark navy jeans. She chucked them at me and smiled at my mum. "I'm helping him look presentable put them on!" Grabbing the jeans I went to the bathroom to put them on. I returned to the bathroom to see both women awaiting me. Rain smiled "that's better now put that top on!" She ordered as she threw a black polo in my direction. Stripping of my other top I replaced it with the new one. Mum smiled "yes definitely better, well done Rain I didn't know it was possible to make him look smart." Laughing lightly I spoke to her "I thought you said you would never insult me." Standing she quickly hugged me straightening my shirt she said "and I still won't." The doorbell rang and mum left to answer it. Rain came and stood by me she squeezed my arm slightly. "Go and have fun, tell me how it goes." She winked at me before leaving. It wasn't until I was stepping out of the house with Reeve did I figure out what she meant.

Lily

Inside the music was so loud that I could feel the vibrations of it through the floor into my feet. We immediately found Sean, Luke and Ella who were in the kitchen collecting a drink. It looked like Sean had invited the whole school, it wouldn't surprise me if he had, sometimes he liked to go a little overboard. Sean hugged each of us and smiled brightly. Both he and Luke glowed with a tan from their holiday. Ella clung to Luke's arm, her face didn't hold her usual happiness but a sad sullen expression. Luke didn't look to happy either, though he to like Sean hugged each of us. Maybe he and Ella had been fighting. Sean handed me and Sky a plastic cup with a bright coloured liquid inside. "Let's have some fun yeah, where's Cole?"
"Why I'm here, did you miss me?" Cole and Reeve had just entered the kitchen. Cole smiled brightly at Sean his arms spread wide with a smirk of his face. Sean gladly went along with the tirade he smiled and ran to him. "Why of course I missed you." We all laughed at them, they released each other and fist bumped. "Maybe you need a holiday Cole we're going to have to start calling you Casper!" Cole thumped him on the arm and laughed. "Well that's because you're incredibly tanned, it almost looks fake, what did you really use. Moroccan sunset?" Sean actually looked scared for a moment as he checked out his arms, then he caught on that

Cole was just joking he shoved him back. "Very funny, come on get a drink, hey Reeve." Sean dragged Cole to the counter to collect a drink and Reeve made his way to me. He smiled shyly "hi." Smiling back I said "hey." Not being able to figure out anything original to say. Taking the drink Sean offered him he took a sip and winced. "What's this?" All of us started to laugh apart from Cole and Reeve who were not used to Sean's homemade punch. Luke spoke up. "You really don't want to know what's in there, but I can guarantee you one thing. You won't need a lot of it to get drunk." We all laughed again remembering the last time we had a party. Luke had only had one glass of punch before he was gone, the rest of us weren't far behind him. I believe we found both he and Sean asleep on the bottom of the lawn with balloon animal hats stuck to their heads once. A girl came in to the kitchen and sidled up to Sean. I recognised her as Jasmine a skinny blonde girl in my English class. "Are you coming babe?" All six of us turned to stare at Sean who had gone bright red in the face. Grimacing at all of us he spoke his voice slightly more nervous than before. "Erm yeah guys this is my girlfriend Jasmine, Jaz this is Luke, Ella, Sky, Reeve, Cole and of course you know Lily." Jasmine smiled at all of us politely. Cole was grinning broadly at Sean who mumbled to him "I'll tell you later." Cole laughed loudly before pushing Sean away "sure you will, go and have fun with your girlfriend." Sean laughed and pulled Jasmine away with her hand. Sky interrupted the sudden silence with her uncontrollable laughter. I turned to her "what are you laughing at?" She stopped laughing to look at all of us. Her pale face was flushed with laughter. "That Sean has a girlfriend" we all laughed, she was right it was pretty funny, and unexpected. Cole spoke up glancing at his watch "well guys its nine o clock on the dot which means we have three hours to get ourselves drunk everyone in." He placed his cup of punch in the middle waiting for us. Sky surprised me by placing hers in too "I'll drink to that." Shaking his head Luke followed suit, which meant Ella added hers too. Knowing I would regret it in the morning I placed mine in to, we all turned to look at Reeve who looked slightly startled. Sighing he too placed his cup into the middle. "Here's to forgetting about the past, the present and the future. Let's just be thankful if we can remember tonight. Happy New Year everyone." We all mumbled Happy New Year to one another before downing our drinks. I felt a little light headed afterwards. We heard Sean shout from the living room as he cranked up the music even louder "everybody dance!" Squealing Sky took hold of my hand and Ella's and tugged us into the crowded living room to dance.

Cole

Reeve and Luke stayed with me in the kitchen. We each had got another drink and were watching the girls dance. Lily looked amazing tonight, after what happened between us I tried to keep my gaze of her. Sky still had me slightly worried, she knew I was a werewolf after all. But tonight I wasn't going to worry about any of that. Tonight I was going to forget the past, the present and the future and just have fun. Luke still looked glum which I thought was odd, he and Ella were always quite cheerful. "Something going on Luke?" Luke was staring into his drink.
"Yeah me and Ella are basically over, but I don't know how to tell her." He began swirling his drink around in his cup. "You need to tell her though, it's better to get it over with rather than stringing her along." Reeve spoke his words of wisdom. I turned to look at Reeve who looked serious, he looked at me too. I raised my eyebrow at him. "What I'm just saying." Turning away I placed my drink on the kitchen counter. "Well I'm not standing here to watch all the fun, if you don't want to join me then stay here." I left them gawking after me and went to join the girls on what was left of the overcrowded living room floor.

All three of them smiled as me as I joined their circle. They weren't really dancing just swaying from side to side. Which was okay with me, as I couldn't dance at all. Ella spoke over the music. "Are the others coming to join?" She nodded her head in the direction of Reeve and Luke who were still both looking glum by the kitchen table. Laughing I answered "no, there to busy moping." Sky frowned then shouted into the circle "well we're having none of that, we promised to forget the past, the present and future and just be thankful if we remember this night in the morning. Therefore they need to have fun." All three of us laughed as she stormed out of the living room and grabbed Reeve and Luke by the hands, and pulled them towards the dance floor. Surprisingly they didn't object. I looked to Lily who had made it her mission to keep her eyes of both me and Reeve. She was evidently in the middle of both of us. Reeve ducked his head to whisper in her ear, though the music was thumping loudly around us and he was whispering, with my enhanced hearing I could still hear him. "You look very pretty tonight." Lily looked up and smiled sweetly, a blush crept along her cheeks. His words made me want to strangle him. "Thanks, you don't look to bad yourself." He smiled brightly at her and grabbed her hand. He spun her under his arms and they began dancing clumsily, but they were too busy laughing to notice that they looked like a bunch of love drunk idiots. It was just making me angry. Sky saved me by grabbing my hand and spinning herself under my arm. Luke and Ella had begun dancing together, both looked happier than they did at the start of the night. Perhaps they weren't over just yet. "You look angry." Sky didn't shout, but I knew she knew I could hear her. "I'm not, I'm actually extremely happy." Swinging our arms from side to side she kept her head low as she answered. "Liar, I know Reeve being with Lily bothers you." I didn't answer her. She seemed to know an awful lot about me. I couldn't figure out if that scared me yet. She carried on as though I had answered. "Even if you're not glad she's with Reeve I am ..." I was about to protest when she stopped me. "No wait, let me finish." Sighing I nodded and let her carry on. "Because Reeve is different from you Cole, he's not like you. He won't hurt her but you will." Her voice full of conviction pierced into my heart making it bleed just a little bit. I let her hands go and stepped back. "How do you know I would hurt her and Reeve wouldn't?" She looked at me. Her blue and brown eyes were innocent and pleading for me to understand. "Because you're a...werewolf and he's not." I was too shocked that she had just come out with it, humans tend to be a bit scared to admit the truth. I also found it a bit ironic how she thought I was dangerous because I was a werewolf and she thought Reeve was the good guy because he apparently wasn't. I stepped closer to her letting a little bit of anger slip into my tone "you don't know anything!" Summing up all the courage and anger she had she also stepped closer, and looked slightly intimidating. "I know more than you think Cole Star, I'm not stupid!" She backed away from me. "Cole there's something I need to tell you..." I knew she was about to tell me something important from the way her face turned back into her vulnerable state. But she was interrupted by Ella who grabbed a hold of her hand and pulled us into a huge dancing circle. Time flew then, we were all lost in the beat of the music and the laughter around us.

We came back to reality eventually. Sean who stood up on the sofa, he had turned the music down and was shouting so we could hear him. "Well you beautiful intoxicated lot it's ten to twelve so I want your drunk butts outside on the garden where the party continues, we have an ten minutes to midnight so enjoy, get drunk and look out for the fireworks!" Whooping everyone followed his lead and went outside where the bushes had been dressed in elaborate fairy lights and a disco ball was hanging from a window. The music had been cranked up loud again. I looked for Sky but in the move she had disappeared, just like the past few hours.

Lily

We decided to go for a walk. We had lost Cole and the others in the move outside so Reeve had suggested to go for a walk since it was way more crowded in the garden than it had been inside. Sean's punch had definitely dulled my senses a little bit. Reeve looked as though he hadn't drank anything at all, I was suddenly envious of him for being immune to alcohol. He held my hand tightly as though he was afraid I might fall of something. Then again I was thankful because I thought that was entirely possible. Sean's house like most of the houses near the north end of Ever Green had their gardens boarded by the forest. Sean's garden had always been our most popular haunt when we were kids. Me, Sky, Sean, Luke and Ella all used to come down here when we were six to race paper boats down the stream about two minutes from his garden. It was there where we found ourselves now. The stream had grown into a river and now had a wooden bridge built across it. "Have you ever been here?" I asked sitting down on the banking. I watched pebbles move along with the flow of water. "No I haven't been this far north of the woods. Where I live we tend to stay near the south side." He sat down beside me.
"We would come here all the time as kids. Sean had come up with the idea that we should race boats on the stream. Well the best we could do was paper boat. For the record I always won." He smiled at me. "Sure you did."
"I did, but don't ask Sean okay because he will obviously say that I was lying and that he always won." He laughed then took my hand in his. He looked so serious as he looked up to the sky. The sky was perfectly clear tonight, with an elaborate crescent moon. The stars sparkled independently against the dark sky. He stood up and pulled me up with him. We stood under the moons iridescence, enjoying the silence. Then the silence was pierced by voices shouting; ten, nine, eight, seven, six, five, four, three, two, one…Happy New Year! Reeve turned to me, he placed his hands on each side of my face and pulled me close to his "Happy New Year Lily" he whispered then he placed his lips on to mine. Kissing him back I waited for the same spark to erupt between us like it had done when I kissed Cole for the first time, but it never came. Pulling back I smiled slightly "Happy New Year Reeve." He looked as though he

was about to kiss me again when we heard the snap of a twig breaking. Turning towards it I saw Cole. He looked at me then to Reeve before taking in a long breath, exhaling he turned on his heel and fled. I wanted to follow.

"You know he loves you don't you?" When Reeve spoke I waited for something in his voice to tell me he hated the fact that Cole did, but there was nothing. Looking at him I saw his face was strangely emotionless. "And you love him too." It wasn't a question, it was a statement. All this time I thought I had managed to at least keep it from him, but I even failed at that. "I hope you know that I...love...you too." Reeve smiled slightly but it didn't quite reach his eyes.
"Maybe, but you love him more." I stepped towards him but he backed away.
"Reeve, I'm sorry." He looked at me directly. He was such a caring and kind person, and it hurt so much to look at him now and know that I was hurting him. Just because I couldn't control my feelings. "Lily, you can't choose who you fall in love with in this world. I've only ever wanted you to be happy and I thought maybe I was the person that could make that happen, but I was wrong. I've known for a while how Cole felt and like a true brother he tried to stop his feelings for you, but I already knew that he wouldn't be able to. I'm just glad you let me love you." Closing the distance between us I hugged him, thankfully he hugged me back. I let some tears escape from my eyes. "I am sorry Reeve, I never wanted to hurt you." Pulling back from me he smiled, and brushed my tears away. Leaning in he kissed my head, then let me go. "It's okay, now do me a favour, go and find him."
"What?" Laughing uneasily he pushed me in the direction of the party. "Go and find Cole and tell him how you feel."
"Why are you being so nice, if this situation was in reverse … "he cut me off before I could finish.
"If the situation was in reverse you would understand. Cole is like my brother, and recently I feel as though he's losing himself but when he's with you, he's normal."

Cole

I was looking for Sky when the crowd began counting down the seconds to midnight. I had just entered the sheltering of the woods when I heard a voice "Happy New Year Lily." Coming to a stop and directly in front of me standing beside the river, with the moonlight dancing over them was Reeve and Lily. I watched Reeve lean in and kiss Lily; and to my utter dismay I watched her kiss him back. She pulled back and spoke "Happy New Year Reeve." Knowing I definitely didn't want to see this I started to retreat, unfortunately my foot had found a twig and it snapped. Both of them turned sharply towards me. I didn't wait for either of them to speak, I quickly turned on my heel and walked away, anger simmering just under the surface. I knew I needed to get out of here, my wolf was clawing up inside of me.

I had made it down the street near the opening to the woods when I heard footsteps progressing towards me at a run. Turning around I saw Lily, she slowed down and walked towards me. "Cole I..."I held up my hand before she could apologise.
"Please don't say sorry, you're with Reeve I get it. What we had was nothing I get it, so please let's not do this." She huffed at me and put her hands on her hips.
"No I wasn't going to apologise, which means you can't run away from me." Turning fully to face her I asked "then what are you doing out here?" She started walking towards me again and didn't stop until she was directly in front of me. "Reeve told me to come and stop you. Because he knows how you feel about me. And he knows how I feel about you." My heart began to crash against my chest "how you feel about me?" I gulped down my sudden nerves. She suddenly looked to the floor staring at the pavement. "I love him Cole" my heart began to slow down with disappointment. Then her dark blue eyes were bearing into me, searing my soul with their earnest. "But...I love you more." Smiling bigger than I've ever smiled before I pulled her to me and kissed her, she immediately kissed me back. Pulling back after a moment I kept her head in my hands. She smiled up at me sweetly "I love you too." Grinning she stood on her tiptoes and stole a kiss from my lips.

Reeve

I had finally found the guts to kiss her. Yet in doing so I also found out how she truly felt. I knew there was a part of her that loved me, and that made me want to shout with happiness. But in kissing her I knew that there was a bigger part of her that loved Cole. I loved her I knew that. But Cole meant more to me, I didn't want to lose him as a friend, as a brother. He was pack, and that overrode everything I might have felt for Lily. In life you love and lose that's what Cole had always told me; and he was right I had loved, now it was my time to lose, and I was okay with that. Lily and Cole deserved each other. I had made up my mind about what my next step would be. I knew I couldn't tell anyone, but I had to tell him. I didn't want him to think that if I left it was because of him, because it's not. I'm leaving for me, there something I have to do, and I have to do it alone. I just hoped he would understand.

Cole

We had a few days left of the Christmas holidays before we had to return to school. I hadn't spoken to Reeve since New Year's Eve but I had spoken to Carmen. Carmen had come on boundary control instead of Reeve with me Thursday morning. I raised an eyebrow when she stepped off the porch. "He's not avoiding you Cole, he said he just needs some time." Nodding at her we began to walk into the depth of the wood. "Are you angry at me?" Carmen shook her head at me and smiled slightly. "No I could never be mad at you Cole and neither can Reeve. Besides I always knew she was going to be with you anyway." Laughing I said.
"And how did you know that." Her smile slipped from her face for a moment then she quickly replaced it. "I don't know I just had a feeling." I knew if I inquired about it she wouldn't tell me so I didn't waste my breath. Instead we walked. Since I became a protector dad had allowed the younger members of the pack be more involved in the packs duty, such as checking the boundary lines. He was still cautious about if there ever was a Lamia attack, but I knew he was loosening the reins a little bit. "Has Jett spoken to you?" I hadn't seen Jett since we came back from Ever. Not because I was avoiding him, I had been a little preoccupied to go and visit. "No why?" She giggled a little bit, it wasn't an annoying sound, but it wasn't entirely unpleasant either. "Because he's annoyed you haven't gone to spill the beans about Lily yet." Grimacing a little bit I remembered the last time I hadn't told him something. Then again why did he want to know he was the one that had told me not to fall in love

with her? "I hope he does realise it's a delicate subject right now." She nodded and started checking the circle rocks. The rocks she was checking were known as the perimeter. They were huge boulders placed in a perfect circle. They had been blessed with the shadows magic to keep the shield around the forest intact. "He does know, that's probably why he wants to talk." She was checking the middle boulder with great scrutiny. There was four boulders surrounding the middle boulder. The outer ones represented the four villages of Ever each of them were engraved with the logo of each of the creatures. The middle one represented Ever itself, that boulder was engraved with the shadows logo.

Carmen stepped back from the rocks "I know I looked like I knew what I was doing, but I actually have no idea." Laughing I came to stand by her. "You have to check if the engravings are still intact or else the magic doesn't work." Nodding she began her examination of the rocks again. I had been staring at the shadows mark for what felt like forever when Carmen spoke up. "Hey Cole what's up with the Lamia marking?" Moving towards where she was stood I bent down to look at the marking. The marking were supposed to be patterned into the rock with gold italic writing, but unlike the rest the Lamia marking looked starkly different. Instead of gold the writing had turned dark and black as though it had been attempted to be burned off. "This isn't normal, we need to get back and tell dad. I think someone's tried to tamper with it." Carmen looked at me she looked slightly startled "but who would do that?"
"I have a pretty good idea."

Lily

Sky had forgiven me for choosing to be with the slightly more dangerous boy Cole instead of staying with Reeve. She did huff about it for a while saying that I would have been better with Reeve but in the end she accepted it as a true friend. When I thought about it I knew what she was saying was right. Yes I probably would have been better off with Reeve, because he was caring and safe and not a member of the supernatural. But maybe I didn't care maybe I liked being with someone that was slightly dangerous who could offer me an adventure. Reeve had been right you don't choose who you fall in love with in this world.

Cole and I had spent our New Year's Day with our parents. We had spoken over the phone for a while but he had to get some sleep, he had to be up early in the morning to do something for the pack, I was to see him later though. Knowing I didn't want to just spend my time waiting for him inside I decided to go and visit Amelia. I walked quickly to her house the cold breeze following my every footstep. Knocking on the dilapidated door I awaited her answer. It took her a few moments to pull the door open, when she saw me she smiled brightly and beckoned me inside.

I always loved Amelia's house at Christmas. It was always traditionally dressed in wreaths and old fashioned Christian ornaments. Her Christmas tree stood tall and green in the middle of the living room with ruby red and gaudy gold Christmas stars, with matching tinsel. She led me into the kitchen where the same tinsel from the tree hung limply around the window. "I have your present in here Lily if you want it, I knew you would be around so you can take Leo's and Leah's with you when you go home." I sat at the table and she handed me a small box with an emerald green bow tied around it. "Thank you, did you like your present?" Amelia smiled and lifted the silver diamond necklace we had bought her for Christmas. "Yes I do thank you, now open!" She sat down opposite me and waited apprehensively for me to open up the gift. Untying the tie around the middle I opened up the box. There laid amongst the velvet cushion was a shiny silver band with a beautiful azure stone planted in the middle, if you look closer the stone was made up of layers of blue, going darker as it gets towards the middle. "It's known as a dream stone." Slipping the bracelet onto my wrist I noticed it was oddly light. "It's beautiful, thank you." Amelia smiled at me. "You're welcome just promise me that you will never take it off." Closing the box back up and placing it into my bag I asked. "What's a dream stone?" Amelia seemed to come into focus more, it seemed as though she was firmly in the room whereas normally she seemed to drift off into different places. "A dream stone is incredibly rare. That one was mine but I don't need it anymore. It allows the wearer to recall dreams that they've had before since they began wearing it. It also allows you to show others your dreams too, you simply rub the stone and the dreams appear in front of you. I'm giving it to you so you can better understand your dreams, I know your finding it hard. But if you take it off the power of your dreams can land into someone else's hands, which is dangerous for you, therefore you must not take it off! Only you can take it of Lily, nobody can pull it off you." I listened intently; maybe I had been wrong about Amelia, maybe she did want to share her secrets after all. "There's something else, you can wipe the stone of your previous dreams. If there's a particular dream you don't want to revisit then you can get rid of it, by thinking of the dream and wishing it away, you will know if it has worked because the stone will glow red. I haven't deleted my dreams from this stone." Shocked I just stared at her with disbelief she smiled slyly. "I used to share my dreams with you once, now that's what I'm doing again. Maybe my dreams will help you figure yours out."

"Can I ask a question?" She nodded but reluctantly.

"Why did I collapse all those months ago, why can't I recall certain nights, why did I feel like I was burning from the inside out?" She patted my hand sympathetically.

"Because you weren't listening then. Your gift was trying to do its own thing but you weren't allowing it, so it made your life hard. It seems that when things get tough pain is trigger for understanding." Suddenly she stood up, she stood up so quickly she knocked the chair over, alarm was written all over her face. "Lily you need to go now!" Stepping towards her I spoke.

"What's going on?" Panic gripped her features, she was then pulling me towards the back door, I could hear banging from the front door

"Amelia?" Slowly opening the back door so it wouldn't make a sound she motioned me out "shhh Lily be quiet, now listen, go through the wood till you reach the stream on the northern side of the forest, then get to the road. Go as fast as you can and don't look back!" She pushed me through the door.

"But what about you?" There was a sudden bang and I heard wood splintering.

"Don't worry about me, now go run now!" She carefully pulled the door closed, I got to the sheltering of the wood and saw her cautiously enter the hall, but her ear splitting scream would always haunt me. Then I ran, ran faster than I've ever ran before.

Cole

Dad called a pack meeting when me and Carmen returned from the perimeter. It was weird to get used to the fact that I now was able to attend these meetings. The pack members filed into our living room. Dean and Hector stood by the window with dad and Reeve and Jett took the sofa. Each of them were looking at me and Carmen, waiting for us to speak. My dad spoke up. "Cole, Carmen would you like to tell us what you found at the perimeter this afternoon." Nodding at my father I stepped forward and began to speak. I used my protector power to lock away my emotions so my nerves wouldn't show. "Yes, well it was Carmen who noticed it actually. From what we can tell all of the markings are intact apart from one. The Lamia mark looked dark and looked as though someone had burned it off. If the logo has been tampered with it would make sense why we keep having more and more Lamia attacks, as their no longer stuck in one place." The pack murmured in agreement. "So what are we going to do James?" Asked Dean. Dad looked out of the window for a moment before turning to all of us. "Well firstly we have to inform the king that one of the stones is no longer apart of the shield. Until it's repaired the only thing we can do is try to control the vampire situation."

"And how do you plan on doing that three of us aren't even protectors yet. There's four of you and about a thousand of them." Reeve didn't normally speak up against my father. The men seemed shocked, Dean looked as though he wanted to tell his son off, and apologise to dad. "Your right Reeve, so what do you propose to do?" This was dad's favourite and best weapon. He would never ask you what to do unless he had found a solution to the question already.

"You make the rest of us protectors." The men didn't seemed fazed by what Reeve said, however Carmen looked as though she might throw up and Jett stood up, heat spreading to his face. "Some of us are not ready to become a protector, you go and kill a vamp if you want but keep me out of it!" Hector placed a comforting hand onto his sons shoulder.

"Calm down son nobody's forcing you to do anything." Jett sat back down but carried on glaring at Reeve who was doing a good job at ignoring him. Instead his eyes were on my father challenging him to tell him he was wrong. "Maybe your right Reeve maybe it is time for you to for fill your destiny." Carmen stood up and looked at my father and her brother. "Are you really willing to put our lives in danger just to become protectors?" My dad smiled at her slightly whereas Reeve kept his eyes on my father. "You've always known you would become a protector one day Carmen, so why not make today that day?" Dean came to stand by his daughter who stepped back to soak up his comfort. "You can't actually be serious James, Carmen and Jett are definitely not ready their fifteen, Cole wasn't even ready he just had no choice." My dad folded his arms across his chest and looked calmly at Dean. "And what about Reeve?" Dean looked over to his son who sat grumpily at the sofa glaring at the floor. "He's not ready either." Laughing slightly Reeve stood up and for the first time in two days I saw him properly. He looked tired and defeated, but there was determination in his eyes. If became evident that he had been thinking on the lines of this conversation for a while. He had just needed the right situation to have it, and that was obviously now. "How would you know what I'm ready for?" Dean looked taken back. Carmen and Reeve had never been ones to talk back to adults, yet both of them seemed to have forgotten that. "Because I'm your father, and I know what's best for you." Reeve shook his head and smiled dangerously.

"No you think you know what's best for me. I'm done with you and mum babying me all the time. I'm done with this pack deciding what's best for me and what's not. I'm done with being told what to do. I deserve my own free will don't I, or are you going to take that too?" All of us stared at him with disbelief. Apart from my father who stared at him as though he was finally seeing him for the first time. "What do you want then Reeve, here's your free will take it?" Reeve carried on looking at my father intently. "I wish to leave... for a while."

"Leave?" We all spoke in unison. Apart from my father who smiled slightly.

"How long for?" My father asked.

"Dad you can't be serious?" I spoke finally entering the conversation. Dad looked at me and nodded. "He asked for his own free will so I'm giving it to him." We all stared at him in disbelief.

"Give me two months." My father considered it for a moment before nodding at him.

"Fine you can have two months, but then you must return. The sooner you learn what your free will has cost, the better." Reeve finally smiled. "Thank you." And with that he walked out the door. Carmen quickly ran after him Dean not far behind her. Hector spoke up for the first time since comforting his son. "I hope you know what you're doing James." My dad turned and smiled at me, I didn't return his smile. Frowning at me he turned to Hector "I always know what I'm doing."

Lily

I ran as fast as I could through the thick forest. The woods near Amelia's were a lot thicker and denser than the forest near my house. I kept running. I could feel the soft earth underneath my feet. Feel the fresh air enter my lungs. When I stopped I found myself in the clearing where I had once waited for Cole. It was also the same clearing I found Carmen naked and bleeding. Now I faced my worst fear. Stood in the middle of the clearing was Lexi. She smiled malevolently at me. "I did warn you."

"Yes you did my dear, yes you did." The second voice came from behind me. It was male and I knew straight away without looking who the voice belonged to. Levi came and stood next me. This close I could feel the iciness of his skin. "So we meet again Lily, the last time we met weren't the best of situations, wouldn't you say." Determined to not show fear I clenched my teeth.

"You could say that. I don't normally meet new people by trying to rip their throats out, I mean what's the point of meeting them if you're just going to kill them?" Levi laughed sharply. He moved so fast that I tried not to freak when his face was directly in front of yours. "You're quite right. You seem determined not to show your fear little Princess" he reached out with his cold hand and brushed a lock of hair away from my face. "Your determination is wasted today, I am not here to kill you." I stepped back so I didn't have to be so close to him.

"Then what are you here for, I'm pretty sure you're not here for general chit chat." He smiled at me, it was cold but slightly friendlier than the smile Lexi had delivered. "Your right princess, I'm not here for what did you call it 'general chit chat', I'm here so you can deliver a message for me. Tell your little mutt of a boyfriend that the perimeter is the least of his worries." Standing straight and lifting my head high I smiled dimly. "Why can't you do it yourself?" Levi narrowed his eyes at me before smiling. "Well I can, but I don't know if I'll be able to control myself see your little boyfriend killed a good friend of mine, which means I might not deliver the message, I might just return the favour. My heart suddenly jumped into my throat. My sudden spike in emotion made Levi laugh. "And there it is, I know you'll deliver the message because you wouldn't want to risk your sweet little wolfs life, we will meet again little princess. This is far from over." And like smoke they both had vanished.

Cole

I had just vacated into my bedroom when my obnoxious phone started ringing. Lily's number glowed on my screen. "Hello."

"Hey you got a minute?" Frowning to myself as I looked in the mirror as I answered.

"Yeah what's up?" Lily began explaining her visit with Amelia, and her gift of the dream stone and its amazing properties. She then explained about the intruder and how she Amelia made her run and leave her behind. She finally got to the bit where she had seen Lexi and Levi in the clearing. "He told me to tell you the perimeter was the least of your worries and that this is far from over." I was really starting to hate on this guy. Not only was he stalking my girlfriend with his newly turned vampire who happened to Lily's ex best friend, he was also making my life as a protector extremely hard. "What does this even mean?" I knew Lily was worried but this really was my burden the bare. "Don't worry about it, it's to do with the pack, so we should leave it to the pack to sort it out." I heard her sigh slightly which made me want to reach inside of the phone and hug her. "Okay, there was something else he kept calling me princess and I'm pretty sure it wasn't some cute pet name." Laughing slightly to diffuse the tension inside of me I didn't know how to answer. If Levi was calling Lily Princess, it meant that he knew what she was, and the only way for her enemies to find her was if they possessed the same gift as us. Levi had a power that was stronger than his fathers but nobody knew exactly what that power had been. But I think I've just figured it out. It would explain everything. Levi was a dream breaker like me and Lily. That's how he found her that day in the forest, and that's what's got the king so worried. "Cole?" Realising that I hadn't answered her I had to come up quickly with an answer. "Maybe it was just a cute pet name."

"Eww I hope not." We laughed together. We carried on our conversation for another hour, speaking about pointless stuff. And all the while, the tension that had wrapped itself firmly around me slowly unravel and vanished like magic.

Reeve

I reached my house quickly after leaving Cole's. I knew Carmen and dad were hot on my tail so I ran upstairs and locked myself into my room. The lock wouldn't stop dad coming in if he wanted to or Carmen for that matter, but all I heard was the front door open and shut. Nobody attempted coming up the stairs. They were giving me space. I pulled a duffle bag out from underneath my bed. The bag was filled with money, supplies, spare clothes and blankets. James had done the one thing I thought he would never do, he let me have my free will. He had given me two months. Two months to get out of this place, to see some of the places Cole's seen, solve some of the world's problems along the way. My duffle had been packed for a few weeks now. I had always known I was leaving, but it wasn't for forever. Lily had been the one keeping me here. Now she wasn't which meant I really was free. Leaving my mobile phone on my bed I pulled the bag onto my shoulder and unlocked my door. I took the stairs one at a time.

Mum, dad and Carmen were all waiting for me when I descended the stairs. Both mum and Carmen looked as though they had been crying, and dad looked like he wasn't far from cracking. "I'm not trying to hurt you." Mum smiled at me slightly but the tears streaming down her face were kind of ruining the effect. "We know." I could feel my own emotions welling up inside of me, but I would not crack. "This is just something I need to do." Dad was the first one to hug me. He hugged me hard and kissed my head before releasing me, tears brimmed his eyes. "I hope you find what you're looking for son." Nodding at him I accepted the squeezing hug of my sister.
"There's always another way to be free you know." Smiling at her I nodded.
"I know but this is my type of freedom." Mum was the last to hug me. She hugged me tight and for a moment I thought she might never let go, she did, but very reluctantly. "I love you Reeve, just come home soon okay."

Stepping out of the house I felt freer than I've ever done before. Even more free than wearing my wolf skin running the boundary lines with my pack at my sides. I felt free because for once I've made a decision for me, I felt free because I no longer had to rely on anyone else, all I had to do was rely on me. It was the most liberating feeling I've ever felt. I waved goodbye to my family, but I knew there was another member I had to say goodbye to.

Cole

After speaking to Lily and not wanting to stay in the house I decided to go and sit on the deck. The last time I had been out here had been my birthday. It seemed such a long time ago now, yet in reality it wasn't. The sun had begun its slow departure behind the trees and the sky was painted in a minority of colours. "Are you always sitting on the deck?" Swinging my head to the side I saw Reeve approaching a bag swung across his shoulder. I stood quickly. "You're really leaving?" Smiling sadly he nodded and dropped his bag by the deck and came to stand by me. "It's just something I have to do." Sighing we both took a seat back on the deck.

"Why do you have to go alone, maybe I should come with you." Reeve shook his head at me but there was a slight smile on his face. "No I need to be alone. I'm tired of relying on other people, I'm tired of being told what to do. I just want to be free, even for a moment. And your dads given me that. I'll be back Cole I was never going to be gone forever." I ducked my head. It had been so much easier when it had been me who was leaving. "What are you going to do about school?" He laughed slightly. "Dads making up some excuse for me, I'll be fine. I mean I've been at school for like six years you've been there five months and you're doing just fine, so I'm not worried."

"What about Primroses mission?" Reeve sighed heavily before answering me.

"For now it's postponed but I keep my promises, when I come back then we will do something about it, but for now she can wait." Keeping my eyes to the ground I asked.

"Why do you have to go?"

"Because most of the time you have to be alone and free to finally discover who you are, and I want to know who I am Cole. I always thought I knew but in reality I don't." He sighed shakily and it came to my attention that this goodbye was hard for him to. "Just do me a favour okay, look after Lily and watch out for Carmen for me we all know what she can be like." He stood up and swung his bag across his shoulder. I stood and bumped his outstretched fist, but it felt wrong I smiled and hugged him tight catching him of guard he laughed along with me "I'll look after them." Smiling he closed his eyes and inhaled slowly, when he re-opened his eyes and exhaled I saw the excitement in his eyes. "See you in two months."

"Two months." He smiled one last time before striding away into the forest, the sun disappearing just as he did.

Carmen

My brother was gone. I watched him leave, but I knew he was coming back. It wasn't a goodbye, not really. He had left a rope for us, and if we tugged hard enough on it he would come back. No matter how much we might want to pull the rope, we knew we couldn't. In two months his rope would run out and he would have to return home; so until then, I will wait. And hope that his free will had been worth it.

End of part two

Home is not where you are born; home is where all your attempts to escape cease.
Naguib Mahfouz.

Lily

It was late when Cole came to visit me. It was the first time he had been to my house, I suddenly realised. His face was sullen and tired when I pulled open the door. Quickly I pulled him inside and wrapped my arms protectively around him. Ensuring that he only felt my comfort and love for him. I shivered when his cold skin met mine, he was freezing. His skin felt like it was made out of ice. "Are you okay?" Cole rested his chin on top of my shoulder before shrugging his shoulders. "What's going on Cole?" His sigh was full of ripped emotion as he let it escape from his body.

"Reeve's gone." Blood suddenly running cold I clutched him closer. "I don't understand." He pushed me gently away so he could see my face. His own eyes were so sad that it brought tears to my own. "He's been wanting to leave for a while now, but you were the only thing holding him back. He hasn't seen the world like I have, and he desperately wants to at least glimpse at it once. If he hadn't gone now, then he never would have. He would always be stuck here, dreaming of something else." Although Cole had clearly stated that Reeve had been wanting to depart for a while now. I couldn't help but feel kind of responsible for his abrupt exit.

Cole must have sensed my wavelength as he placed his hands on either side of my face so he could look me directly in the eye, where tears began breaking down my defences. "This is not your fault, Reeve has always been a...butterfly. Slowly changing into something greater and then finally finding the courage to open up his wings and fly away." Wiping away the tears that I could no longer hold back with his thumb he smiled sadly at me. "But he's also our friend which means that his wings will guide him home again." Kissing me on my forehead he smiled and brushed my cheeks once more. "Now none of that he would say that he's not worth your tears." Smiling I reached up to plant a quick kiss on his lips when a cough sounded from behind us. Dam so close.

To my utter dismay and embarrassment my whole family stood congregated in the hallway; smiling brightly at us, well nearly everyone. Dad whose face looked as though it had been carved out of stone spoke first "well Lily would you like to introduce your friend here or do you want to kiss him first?" Blushing I turned to face my family smiling sheepishly.

"Mum dad, Leo Leah this is Cole, Cole this is my family." Cole smiled at each of them and even stepped forward to shake my father's hand. Brave man. Mum spoke up as she ushered us all into the kitchen as it was the biggest room in the house. "Is he a boyfriend, or just a friend?" Cole grinned at her as he clung to my hand. "Boyfriend, I hope?" Smiling up at him I nodded my head, he returned my smile and kissed me gently on the head. Leah squealed loudly and ran and hugged him around the middle. "Lily's never brought a boy home before!" Cole who also had a younger sibling tolerated her hug and patted her back. "Good to know." Laughing I abandoned his side and went to stand next to the two formidable men that stood watching. I stood in the middle of them both and watched Cole talk kindly to my mother and sister.

It was important to me that they got along. I placed a hand on each of their arms and squeezed slightly. "You know you two could be a little less hostile you know, I like him and I want him to like you too. So smile and pretend you don't want to punch him in the face." Leo smirked slightly. "I don't want to punch him in the face." Dad laughed slightly and not in a humorous way.
"Speak for yourself. I just nearly saw him kiss my daughter in my hallway. I would like nothing more than to punch him in the face." Smiling I hit him gently in the stomach which he faked injury, to humour me. He laughed when he saw my determined face. "Fine I'll be nice, I'll just punch him in my head." Laughing I hugged him tightly which he returned with gusto. "If it helps."

Cole

I could picture someone like Lily growing up here in this home. Even though I knew her true identity I couldn't help but forget that she wasn't biological of this family. I watched the way her and her siblings interacted, the way little Leah hung on her every word as though it was a sacred text she needed to remember. Or the way she and Leo only had to look at each other and know what the other was thinking. Then there was the fierce protectiveness of her father which I sensed when I shook his hand earlier. The way he shook with too much grip. The bond between them was truly touching and I wondered if she hadn't been taken away, whether she would have shared the same relationship with the king.

They didn't question me on why I had visited so late. Instead, they asked where I had been, what cities, countries had I seen. They made me feel so at ease here that I almost forgot that I was a werewolf. They dulled me into a kind of false reality where I was just a boy, dating a girl. That we were normal, that we were human. Like me Lily hadn't yet got round to telling me about her family, we were just getting to know each other first. But I learned a lot tonight. I knew Lily's father was ill before he even told me. We were on our own as we sat in the comfortable living room. Lily had to help her mother get Leah to bed but she was putting up quite a battle, Leo had vacated to his room after his mobile rang, a girls voice on the other end. Her father was sat reclined comfortably in a brown leather seat. He looked exhausted, yet managed to keep a front up. He was either trying to impress me or intimidate me. However it had neither effect, all I felt was sorry for him. "I'm sick Cole, really sick." Sometimes it took me by surprise how blunt people become so close to death, yet, from the tone of his voice I knew he was sharing this information for a purpose rather than sympathy. He didn't seem like the man to seek that from strangers. I leaned forward to indicate that I was listening, and that he should continue. "Are you okay?" I knew his answer before he even thought it, of course he wasn't, he was dying. He gulped and smiled slightly at me. "No, I haven't been okay for a while now, and I'll never be okay again." He looked me straight in the eye, and for once I didn't feel uncomfortable or intimidated by another's gaze. My wolf respected him for some reason. It was a strange feeling but I was grateful. I wanted him to like me. "I want to ask you for a favour."
"What can I do for you...sir?" He rubbed his hands down his face hoping to sweep away the vulnerability that I knew was building up inside of him. "Please call me Sam. I know from what I've seen tonight that you make her happy Cole, and I like that, and I like you." He swallowed before continuing his voice dipping in and out of his emotions. "I don't know when, but I know someday soon that I will pass over. When I die Cole I want you to be there for her. I want you to be the anchor that will save her from drifting into a sea of grief, because she will, because I know her. She has a loving soul, and once she's hurt she falls and I don't want that to happen. I don't want her to forget me, I just want her to live. Will you do this for me, will you help save her when the unavertable comes?" At first I was too shocked to even comprehend a thought. Emotion even started to

swell up inside of me and I thought I had complete control over my emotions. He kept his gaze on me, his eyes slightly watered. "Yes Sam, I promise."

It was around midnight when I got home from Lily's. The house was dark as I let myself in. Stretching my hearing out I detected the slumbering bodies of my sister and father. With my sight I detected my mother's silhouette waiting patiently in the living room for me. She looked younger and fragile as she sat crossed legged on the cream cushions of the sofa, the moonlight draping over her like a dressing gown. Her ebony hair was free and curling, her wary emerald eyes were on me. "Where have you been?" Her voice was quiet so she wouldn't awaken those who were sleeping. "I was just out, I didn't think it would be a problem." She stood up quickly and stared me down. She was the only human I knew that had the power to intimidate me and my wolf. Even though she was at least a foot shorter than me, her accusing glare made me smaller. "You are joking right! We thought you had disappeared with Reeve. You wasn't answering your phone, nobody had seen you. We were worried!" Before she could concoct another argument I pulled her to me and folded her into a hug. Diffusing some of the anger that was burning up inside of her. "I'm sorry I should have thought." She wrapped her arms around me reminding me of Leah's bear hug just a few hours before. It had been a long day. "I can't bare the thought of losing you Cole. Don't do that to me again, please." Pushing her carefully away I looked down at my mother's hurt, tear stained face. I vowed to myself that I would never be the cause of that face ever again. "I won't I promise." I said for the second time tonight.

Lily

Its time Lily. Come find me.

I woke with a start sweat trickled down my spine and danced across my brow. My heart beat fast inside my chest. I hadn't dreamed of anything. I was in a dreamless heaven when on intruder invaded my mind with her voice. *Its time Lily. Come find me.* Was it a warning, a suggestion? The better question was who was it? The voice seemed familiar somehow, as though the woman had spoken to me many times. Then I figured it out. The voice belonged to the lady in the wood. The slim lady that talked in riddles. But she wasn't real, was she? How could I find her, I didn't know her? Amelia's bracelet seemed to burn against my wrist. She hadn't deleted her dreams because there was something she wanted me to see. Taking a deep breath I closed my eyes. I placed my hand on top of the bracelet, focusing I spoke on instinct "reveal." The bracelet began to vibrate against my touch, I was then transported into a world of conflicting images. The images were fast and fleeting. Focusing I discovered that the images contained Amelia as a child, a teenager as an adult. These were her dreams. *Lily focus now, think of something specific. The dream before the night she lost them.* The images stopped moving. Then one picture began moving towards me. Before it was in front of me it turned into a small white glowing ball, it was the most beautiful thing I had ever seen. Sparkling against the dark background of my subconscious, as it drew closer I could hear the faint sound of laughter and birdsong, of peace. Suddenly the memory forced itself into my chest, then everything...went dark.

The forest looked different as I walked in amongst the naked branches. Winter had stripped them of its vibrant colours leaving them pale and worthless. The wood seemed younger in this time, and maybe it was. The dream kept me walking, kept me pressing on as though the key was somewhere to be discovered. I heard a laugh from behind me and turned just in time to see a girl run past me, laughing as a boy made an attempt to catch her. From their clothing I knew time had gone backwards. Slowing the girl let the boy catch her. She was pretty and blonde. This must have been Amelia when she was younger. The man was tall with thick dark curls and a charming smile. "Jack do you really have to go?" The man stopped smiling and pulled Amelia to him, he brushed her tears away with a careful hand, just like Cole had done for me. "I won't be gone forever, I'll come back for you." Amelia's tears didn't waver as she sank into Jack's hug.

"But I am nothing without you." Pushing her away he grabbed her face and looked her directly in the eye, she wasn't scared of the fire that burned inside his eyes, like I would have been. "You are not nothing Amelia, you are everything to me. Because of you I've found happiness and acceptance, for someone like me that's not easy." Smiling sadly up at him she placed her hands on his. "But what about the bond, won't it break if you go?" Smiling Jack placed a quick kiss on her startled lips. "No sweetheart, once a bond is made it can never be broken. No matter how far I go, not matter how many oceans are between us, you will be mine, and I yours." Smiling she let him go. "Forever." Smiling at her with love and adoration he replied.
"Forever."

Suddenly I was transported back to reality. Though I had asked for a dream, I got a memory. She was in love with a man called Jack I already knew that. The man must have been my great Grandfather who I had only met once before he died. A sweet man who still liked to treat his wife. Amelia had begun forgetting things when he passed, doctors say the cause was traumatic stress due to the fact that it had been Amelia who had discovered her husband's dead body. My conclusion was heartbreak. Nobody wants to remember a life they had with someone so special when that special someone is gone. I didn't know much of Amelia's past only from what mum told me. Her and Jack had only two children my grandmother Jocelyn and another daughter Alice. My grandmother had a normal loving upbringing and left her home at the age of eighteen where she fell in love with my grandfather Charlie, or Charles but from what he told me not even his mother called him that. Whereas Alice who was notorious for stirring up trouble and had constant battles with her parents left her home at the unexpected age of fourteen. Mum said nobody knew where she went, that Amelia and Jack spent years trying to locate her. And to this day her whereabouts is still a mystery.

Rubbing my hand over the tranquil stone I was consumed with its calming effects. Tomorrow I would seek out Amelia only to check if she was alright. Then I would empty the stone of all its secrets and hopefully reveal some of the answers that I've been waiting for. But for now, I will let the calming sensations of the stone dull me into a hopefully dreamless sleep.

I woke the next morning feeling amazingly fresh. For the first time in months I had slept soundly. I skimmed the light blue rock on my wrist gingerly. I could do this, see a dream of Amelia's instead of my own. Checking the clock on my bedside table I found that it was nine o clock in the morning, leaving me an hour before I had to get out of bed. I had decided to go see Amelia around eleven when she was most lucid. Closing my eyes once more I folded my palm across the cool stone and felt it begin to vibrate across my skin. Maybe she hadn't just hidden her dreams in the stone. *Day she first met Jack.* Like before the flickering images came to a standstill, and her memory formed into a glimmering ball that sprang into my chest, then I was pulled down into the abyss.

I recognised my school almost immediately. The structure hadn't changed only its students. People I didn't recognise walked across the quad in the same hideous uniform they still forced upon us. I spotted Amelia straight away. She walked confidently across the lawn. Her luminous blonde hair spiralled in the wind, and she kept her light eyes on her destination. A girl called her name from behind her. Spinning around to greet the girl she found Jack standing behind her. Tall and brooding. Their eyes met for the first time. Something flickered across their faces, and some invisible tug pulled them together. She wasn't afraid or conflicted as Jack brushed her cheek with his thumb, and smiled charmingly down at her. "It's you."
Returning his smile she answered.
"It's me."

Waking again I checked the clock to see that another hour had passed. It hadn't felt like I had been in the memory that long. Tumbling out of bed I grabbed something to wear. Downstairs Leah played with the new toys she had been given for Christmas and dad sat watching his favourite programme. Mum sat slumped at the kitchen table, forehead creasing as she skim read the bills that surrounded her. "Are you okay?" Mum jumped slightly, blinked then smiled falsely as she placed the letter facing down on the table. "Yes, where are you off to?" Frowning at her I went to the fridge to pull out the juice. "Seeing Sky then Cole later probably, where's Leo?" Mum rubbed her hands up and down her jeans to ease some of the stress stirring up inside her. "Gone to see Maria. Will you be back for dinner you could bring Cole, lovely boy?" Mum stood quickly and dropped the mug of tea that had gone cold by her. Getting a cloth I nudged her out of the way to clean up the liquid and move the shards of pottery. "Mum you're obviously not okay." She sunk back into her chair defeated. Head in her hands. "No your right I'm not. I'm just a bit stressed right now." Placing my hands on her arms to draw away her own hands from her face I looked at her. "Me and Leo can help you know." She sniffed away the tears she struggled now a days to keep from falling. "No you don't need to, in a couple of months Leo will be at university and you'll be doing whatever, and I will have figured out a way to pay all these dam bills." Grimacing slightly I guessed money was the issue right now. "I can get a job and help, just until dad gets better." We both knew in reality dad wasn't getting any better, but the lie reassured us both. "You shouldn't have to do that though darling. I am your mother I should be helping you not the other way around." I stood and kissed her on the head, before hugging her. "Sometimes kids have to help their parents, besides I want to help." Kissing my hair she released me, her face strained with emotion. "You're a good girl, now go have fun!" I laughed at her before doing as I was told. "Sure thing." I closed the front door behind me, but not before I heard my mother's agonizing sigh.

Cole

It was the last day of the holidays before we went back to school. I found myself hanging out with Luke and Sean. They had called to ask if I wanted to go to town with them, no girls invited. I had walked to Sean's where his brother waited to take us in the car. After parking in the already overcrowded city he headed off telling us to be back at the car for four or he would leave without us. "He wouldn't actually" Sean reassured us as we watched his brother walk the opposite way. Sean mirrored his older brother in the looks department. However when it came to personalities they were complete opposites. Where Sean was warm and bubbly, Daniel was cold and quiet. We walked past the street where only a few weeks ago a woman was murdered by Levi, the police were still looking for a more accurate reason for her untimely and unexplainable death.

"So where are we going?" I asked as we walked past a small café that was hidden tightly on the street. "Well its Jaz's birthday and its Luke and Ella's however long they've been together anniversary." Luke smiled sarcastically at Sean who dodged out of the way of his impending stomach punch. "We've been together a year!" Sean put his hands in the air and mouthed "oooh."

"So we're here to shop for girls, so why didn't we bring one?" Sean thought a moment before replying. "Well we couldn't bring Jaz or Ella for obvious reasons. And we didn't invite Lily because we plan on talking about her, which means we couldn't just invite Sky because the others would have suspected something." Luke looked admirably up at his friend.

"Good logic!" Bowing at Luke he smiled.

"Why thank you, I'm here all week." Sean's commotion was giving the other customers something to complain about as they brushed past us with annoyance. "Why are you planning on talking about Lily?" We entered a jewellery shop with expensive price tags. Luke decided it was time to unleash his own logic. "Well considering we were all under the impression that Lily was with Reeve, only to see you two kiss on the street on New Year's Eve, we couldn't help but be interested." Luke and Sean laughed. Well I should have known that they would want to know what the story was. Sean and Luke faced me and gave me both of theirs attention. Luke was smiling and Sean just looked stupid as he raised an eyebrow at me. "Well...I guess she was with Reeve, but she had feelings for both of us. So on New Year's Reeve asked Lily to choose and she um...chose me." There was obvious factors that I couldn't tell such as that she knew I was a werewolf and that we were both Dream Breakers and that she had kissed me first the night I had saved her from her ex vampire best friend. Sean clapped me on the shoulder, he was still smiling "we kind of guessed you had a thing for each other, but as long as you're both happy putting up with one another then everything's all good." Luke nodded in agreement. If only they knew that everything was far from all good. "Thanks guys that means a lot." We then turned back to the jewellery. Sean's smiled slipped from his face as he gulped. "Maybe we should have risked it, we should have brought Sky." Luke didn't look any better. Laughing I guided them over to a woman who worked here to ask for some crucial advice.

Lily

I didn't knock when I arrived at Amelia's. Instead I let myself in using the spare key she hid under the slab that was lose near the front door. The house was quiet, unlike Cole I couldn't pick up the same smells as he could. Instead I only smelt the lavender incense she burned to lull her to sleep. The house was immaculate apart from the muddy paw prints that patterned her cream carpets. Heart pounding I entered her living room. At first nothing seemed unusual. The TV played an old movie I had watched many times here when Amelia used to babysit after school before mum finished work. The furniture was still in its pristine condition. Then slumped in an odd way in her favourite chair was Amelia. She looked as though she was asleep, but no person slept like that. Cautiously I moved myself towards her. I watched her chest rise and fall which gave me hope, she was still breathing. Her skin was ice cold as I nudged her with a hand to wake her. I had barely touched her when her eyes shot open. "Alana is that you?" Why did that name seem so familiar? "No Amelia, its Lily." "Lily" she whispered at me. Her hand moved towards me and she touched my face, her eyes were intent on me. "You look an awful like someone I used to know." Taking her hand from my face I held it in my own. "Are you okay can you sit?" Bobbing her head she began to move her body. As she lifted her head from the pillow I noticed something more alarming than her flashback. Blood stained where she had lain. Moving fast I reached out and noticed a bite mark in her neck, the area was red and swollen. Blood still dripped from the area. It was new, it couldn't be more than a day old. "What happened?" Amelia moved her hand to place it over the cut on her neck. She frowned. "I don't remember." Years of first aid classes began to kick in. Grabbing the bobble I always held on my wrist I tied Amelia's straggly grey curls out of the way so nothing was on the cut. Telling her not to not move I got a bowl of warm water and a clean cloth. Kneeling in front of her I carefully cleaned the cut and the blood that dripped from it. "Thank you, you were always so kind. So like her you know." Keeping my attention on the cut I questioned.

"Like who?" Amelia's voice was soft and I noticed the person she talked about she held a lot of affection for. "Alana, she was a girl I knew once. Looked and acted a lot like you do. She was very kind and compassionate. She got the crown prince of Ever to fall in love with her, I knew she would be great." Then it clicked. The name Alana seemed so familiar because I had dreamt of her in the past, her and the king or the crown prince. "How did you know her?" I slowly placed a plaster on the cut and sat back to look at Amelia. She stared off in to the distance, living in some other time. She was smiling but her eyes were sad. "My Jack new the prince, we were visiting him one night when Alana arrived from some far country. He asked me to look after her. She was quite distraught. Her father had been killed on their journey here. We stayed at the palace for a few months she let me take care of her." So Amelia knew Alana before the prince married her.

"Did you keep in touch?" Amelia looked down at me and smiled. She looked younger for some reason. "Yes we went to their wedding a few months later. I was also there when she found out she was pregnant." Swallowing I asked the question that had plagued me since I started having the dreams, and the moment Levi called me princess. But there was also something else. The more I thought about it the more obvious it became...I looked like neither of my parents, I had just chosen to ignore it. "Am I adopted?" Amelia's smile faltered and the sadness in her eyes deepened. "I guess you figured it out then?" Standing I started to pace the floor, hoping its rhythm would ease the growing anxiety that was coiled up inside of me. "How?" She closed her eyes and breathed heavily. When she opened them again she had composed her features. "Even before Alana died giving birth the king knew his child was in danger. When she died he got to keep the child until her first birthday. On that day he intrusted me and Jack to find her a home where she would be safe, where she couldn't be found. Your parents were a normal loving couple who already had Leo and wanted another. We told them the child was important and needed to be loved, they knew nothing of her past, or of any gift." Huffing I glared at her.

"Why do you keep referring to a child or her when we both know it's me, I'm the girl that disappeared. I'm the princess that everyone has been looking for." Tears spilled from both of our eyes, she reached for me and I let her take my hands into hers. Hoping she would give me some comfort. "Yes you are Princess Lily Ever, and yes you have been lost but not anymore. You have been discovered by your love, by your people and unfortunately your enemies."

"Tell me what that means, please I need answers I have to make sense of all this." I didn't bother to wipe away the tears as they fell carelessly down my cheeks. My whole life has been one big lie. My gift is what makes me wanted by the supernatural. My real mother was dead...because of me. "You were first discovered when you were ten years old on the side of the road where the wood borders." Blinking I saw she was looking very intently at me.

"The day I met Cole." She squeezed my hands in hers.

"Yes the day you discovered your love. Six years later you were discovered by someone in your dreams."

"The lady who talks in riddles." She squeezed tighter.

"Yes she is a part of Ever, therefore she is your people, and then a few months ago you were attacked by a man." Catching on where she was going I squeezed her hand too. "Levi."

"Your enemy." It began to make sense now. It was a pattern and it all started the day I accidently came across Cole when coming home from school. "Are you saying that if I hadn't seen Cole that day none of this would have happened, I would have been normal?"

"No you just would never have figured out why you weren't normal. You would have always felt as if you weren't even if you didn't dream." I slid down to the floor my hands still in her wrinkled ones. The truth was starting to weigh me down. "How does Cole link into all this?" She slid off her chair and knelt in front of me. I suddenly got a picture of what she would have looked like when she had children. When they were upset I could see her adopting the same pose, so she was on the same level as them. "He's your love Lily, each wolf has a mate and you're his, have you bonded yet?" Confused I looked into her clear irises, so much pain in such a little space.

"What do you mean?"

"I mean do you feel compelled to be near him, do you seek comfort in him, do you miss him when he's not around, when you looked at one another when you met again did you feel a searing pain in your chest?"

"No but I do love him if that's what you mean?" She leaned forward and looked directly into my eyes. She looked confused at first but then it cleared. "Makes sense now, you're in love with another too so your ignoring what is already there, but soon you will see." I let Reeves name slip from my mouth. I didn't love him in the same way that I loved Cole, but there was still something there. When you love someone it doesn't just disappear. Amelia leant back and pulled me to my feet. And for the first time since I was at least nine she hugged me. I was surrounded by the comforting smell of lavender. "I think it best that you don't dig too hard for the bond, it can be a fickle and dangerous thing, especially with exposure to your enemies."

"Why?" I whispered into her shoulder, her curls were escaping the band, they tickled my face.

"Because once you've bonded you will be linked forever, you will never love another person the same way. In some cases depending on how deep the bond is, if one of you dies so can the other." Pulling away I

noticed more tears spilling from her eyes. "How do you know so much about the wolves?" She rubbed my arms and smiled sadly.
"Because my Jack was one."

Cole

I got home around five from town. The boys had decided on necklaces for their girls, but decided not to acknowledge the price tags that came with them. Opening my front door I heard laughter from the kitchen, very familiar laughter. Entering the kitchen I found my mother, Skyla and Lily all laughing with one another. Skyla was the first to spot me. "Cole look who came to see you." Lily smiled a blush creeping onto her cheeks. My parents knew of her real identity. "Sorry I thought you would be home." I moved closer to her and smiled.
"It's okay it was just a surprise." Mum laughed and squeezed me on the shoulder.
"A very nice surprise I'd say, come on Skyla let's leave them be, you will stay for dinner won't you Lily, James would find it a shame if you left without telling you at least one embarrassing story about Cole." Lily laughed whereas I grimaced.
"That would be great, though I have to say he will have to think of a good one to top the one you just told me." Swinging round to my mother who was literally crying from her laughter, she winked at me. "You said you would never insult me!" She stopped laughing for a moment to hug me quickly. "And I didn't I just humiliated you a tiny bit, I'll call you when dinners ready." Glaring as she left the kitchen I pulled Lily outside onto the decking.

The winter evening wasn't cold as we stepped out of the house onto the decking. The landscape was dark and peaceful as we sat. "It's beautiful out here."
"Me, Reeve, Carmen and Jett used to spend a lot of time out here when we were kids. What story did she tell you by the way just so I can amend

what she said because most of it won't be true?" Lily chuckled beside me. "Something about you running around with her tights of your head." "Dam." She looked at me thinking I had hurt myself. "What?" I smiled at her concern.

"Dam I can't amend that story, unfortunately it's true." She giggled with me.

"So what do I owe the pleasure of your visit, not that I don't appreciate seeing that pretty face of yours?" She stopped giggling. Her expression became hard and emotionless.

"I went to see Amelia today, at first I intended to ask her about the dream I had when I touched the dream stone, but that isn't exactly what happened." My protector sense switched itself on, detecting the emotions she had tried to lock away. "What happened?" She turned to face me full on. "She was attacked, there were paw prints on the floor but her neck had been bitten. When I woke her up she thought I was Alana. She explained to me who she was and how she knew her. Cole she told me that I'm adopted." The tears started to fall and her voice was faltering. I pulled her to me and let her bury her face in my chest. Her sadness was so strong that I could feel it in my own heart. Her whole life was just one big fat complicated lie. "I'm sorry Lily." She sniffed.

"She told me that I'm the lost princess." Knowing I would regret it but knowing she would only be more hurt if she found out that I knew and hadn't told her I answered. "I know." She pulled quickly away from me, I felt cold when she did. "What do you mean you know?" I closed my eyes for a second and prayed she wouldn't be too angry at me. "I found out when I was in Ever the king told me." She didn't speak for a second but when she did her voice was dead and flat.

"Why didn't you tell me?" I reached for her but she moved away, I tried not to let the hurt trail into my voice. "Because he didn't want me to, he wanted me to find a way to bring you back to him, he wanted to be the one to explain." She looked down at the floor, I saw tears slide from her cheeks to the wooden slats she sat upon. "I can't...I'm not ready. I'm not this person I'm just Lily." Reaching forward I lifted her chin so she was looking at me, the hurt in her eyes pierced into me like a knife in the chest. "You're not just Lily. Before you knew the truth you weren't just Lily. You were an amazing girl with an amazing talent for running. You were a girl that is loved by many. And you're a girl who puts people before herself, a girl that dreams about a world that shouldn't exists. That's not just anybody Lily. But it is you." She smiled slightly.

"I don't know who I am anymore, I don't know who my family is, or my friends. My parents lied to me about where I'm from. Lexi's a vampire and I think Sky knows more about you than you think, and Reeve's gone...and." So she had caught onto Sky too had she, good to know? "Not many people know who they are Lily, at least now you know the truth and you can decide what you want to do with that truth. And your family lied to protect you. As for everything else, I guess their trying to discovering who they are too". She looked at me.

"And what about you, you didn't tell me the truth either!" Sighing I took her hand and held it to my chest. "I didn't tell you because I couldn't, I couldn't betray my king's word but I understand that you're mad. Please forgive me though." She leant forward and kissed me, I could taste her tears on my lips. "I forgive you but no more lies okay, we can't build a relationship on lies. For once I just want to be able to talk and laugh with someone knowing they are on the same page as me. I've hated feeling alone in this." I nodded in agreement and pulled her back into a hug. "Lily Cole dinners ready!" My mother's voiced pierced the sadness between us.

"Coming!" I shouted back. Standing I pulled Lily to her feet and brushed the tears from her face. Leaning down I kissed her quickly. "You will be okay." She smiled and let me lead her inside.

Lily

Cole led me inside to his awaiting family. Rain and Skyla were already seated at the faded wooden table that stood in the middle of the kitchen. Rain stood and hugged me, it was soft and comforting, she smelled like cinnamon. "Good to see you again Lily" she smiled. Smiling back I said "you too." Skyla stood up on her chair and pointed to the one next to her. "Lily sit next to me!" Cole frowned at his little sister as he placed a plate in front of each of us.

"I thought I normally sit next to you?" Skyla smiled sweetly back at her brother. The resemblance between them was undeniable. "Well now I want Lily so go sit next to Rain." Cole just rolled his eyes at me as I took a seat. "I think I will take my lady's other side if that's alright with you Skyla." Her response was to stick her tongue out at him. Rain laughed "Big brother has officially been demoted to the loser in the family". Cole looked up to Rain and smiled wickedly.

"Bite me". Cole's mum came over to the table with a steaming pot of something that smelt divine. "I hope you like chicken casserole if not I can make you something else."

"It's alright Mrs Star chicken casseroles fine." She smiled brightly at me as she spooned the food onto each of our plates. "Please call me Sophie." Cole smiled at each of us when he took the seat next to me. "Honey I'm home!" A voice called from the hallway. I was the only one who didn't laugh. "We're in here and before you say something like you normally would we have a guest." Cole's father rounded the corner and placed a kiss on his wife's head before scanning the table to see who she had been referring to. His gaze found mine, there was a split second where his face was expressionless then he smiled at me. "Ah I see Lily isn't it nice to see you again." Swallowing down my sudden nerves and unease under his stare I smiled back. "And you Mr Star." Taking the last seat at the table he chuckled. "I haven't been called Mr Star since I was at school, please call me James."

We tucked into our food and I listened to the conversations that went on. James explained his day was boring as he and Hector were out checking the boundary lines (whatever they were). I found it odd that they spoke about wolf business around me. Wasn't I not meant to know? I decided if James was going to openly talk about his pack I might as well ask a question that had been nagging at me since I left Amelia's. "Mr Star, I mean James may I ask you a question?" Smiling at me James placed his hands together and leaned forward a little bit, Cole stopped eating. "Yes my dear go ahead." Putting down my knife and fork I sat on my hands to stop them from shaking. I didn't know what it was about James that rubbed me the wrong way. "I was wondering if you knew a man called Jack...Jack Cloud." Cole and Rain both choked. Cole didn't look at me instead he took a swig of his drink. Rain however kept her maroon eyes on me, then moved them to James. Cole's father didn't let anything slip into his expression. "Yes he was the last wolf from the Cloud line there are only three families left now. Mine, the Moons and the Skies." My turn to choke.

"Sorry but did you just say the Skies as in Reeve and Carmen Skies?" James returned the smile to his face, as though he took happiness in revealing secrets. "Yes I did, I'm surprised you didn't know actually seen as you knew about Cole." Cole took one of my hands and held it tight, he glanced at me quickly. I wasn't the only one that was uneasy. "Lily does know about me but I didn't tell her about the rest of the pack." James pushed his plate away and looked at his son as though he was transparent. "Well it's good to know there are some laws you won't break." Sophie looked up sharply and stared down her husband. Brave woman. "James, not now." But James was on a roll, there was no reigning him in now. "I'm also guessing she knows her true identity then, I knew when the king decided to fill you in you would tell her. It's bad enough that you break the wolf laws but to break your king's word." Cole stood quickly pulling me up with him. Anger and power rippled beneath the surface. He stared angrily down at his father, who only looked up calmly. "Yes I broke some of the rules but I never told Lily the truth. My loyalty to the king means something to me whether you believe me or not. Lily didn't come here to be attacked she came to get to know you, but instead you've made a perfectly good meal awkward. We're leaving, tonight's my night shift so don't expect me to come home." Cole dragged me out of the kitchen, I waved sadly at the girls who looked sad as they watched us leave. James's face never changed.

Outside Cole let go of me and began to pace. I reached for him but he stepped back. His eyes were wild and frantic. The animal was trying to get lose. It was perhaps in this moment I finally realised how animal Cole truly was, that he must fight every single day of his life to seem almost normal. "No stay there, I need to control." His voice was strained as he fought for control. Pushing away the fear that bubbled under the surface I closed the distance between us. Grabbing his face I kissed him forcefully as though acting on my own instincts. He immediately relaxed and kissed me back. Pulling away but keeping hold of his face I smiled. "Are you okay now?" He stroked my face gently and smiled down at me. "Yes thank you." He kissed the end of my nose before stepping back. "I'm sorry about my dad." I took hold of his hand and we began walking towards then end of the wood. "It's alright, I've learnt to expect the unexpected." He shook his head in agitation.

"You shouldn't have to, I wanted you to like my family like I like yours."
Smiling into the dark stretching wood I squeezed his hand. "You like my
family." Swinging our arms between us he began to smile. "Yes there
amazing, your sister she reminds me a lot of Skyla." I liked that he liked
my family. "Anyway I do like your family, your mum and sister are
amazing and Rain's great to. And your dads okay I think he's just worried
about you." Cole pulled a face that indicated he didn't agree. "I don't
make excuses for my father." We stopped walking and I noticed we had
already made it back to the street. "Do you want to come back to mine?"
Cole glanced back into the woods his expression unreadable. "Nah I need
to get out on patrol Jett will get moody if I leave him on his own for too
long." Nodding at him I let go of his hand.
"I can't believe Carmen, Reeve and Jett are wolves too you would have
thought I would have at least worked it out. I mean I found Carmen in the
wood naked, then again I didn't really know about wolves then, but
Reeve, I thought I would at least know when it came to him." Before I
could say anything else Cole had silenced me with a kiss. "Do you want me
to walk you home or will you be alright?" Stepping back I smiled.
"I'll be fine, I need the time to get my thoughts together anyway."
"Okay I guess I'll see you tomorrow?" I nodded and began to walk onto
the lit streets. Turning around I found that he had already disappeared.

Cole

Shifting quickly I found my release in my wolf. Tearing into the woods I
left all worries behind. All that mattered was the ground beneath my feet
and the growing distance between me and my father. Thinking about him
only angered me more. Before I knew it I was near the shield between this
world and the next. I didn't know my intention was to go to Ever until I
had passed under the shield into the town. Still running I ran to castle
Evelyn. I didn't know what I was going to do I just needed someone to
vent to. Gwen seemed like a good solution she looked like the type of
woman who had an opinion on everything, hoping my father was one of
them I ran to the front door. It was there I encountered a problem, I
couldn't just turn up naked. I mean these people were royalty, well maybe

not Gwen but she was at least a lady. The front door to the castle opened and Gwen stood in its entrance. Spotting me she smiled kindly. Bending down she patted me on the head as though I was a common dog. "Come Cole the king said you would be arriving." Confused I followed her inside.

The castle was warm and cosy. The fires blazing along the corridors. Gwen led me into the throne room where the king awaited me. Trotting inside the king smiled down at me, like Gwen he patted me on the head. It was quite patronising actually, I hope they realise I'm not actually a dog. "Gwen grab a cloak for him would you, he can't speak while he's in this form, all we will hear is his bark." Gwen hurried out and returned nearly a second later with a thick sapphire cloak that was basically like a dressing gown. Moving towards me she placed the gown around me so I could shift. Shifting quickly, I stood and tugged the cloak tightly around me. Gwen bowed and closed the door behind her as she left. The king carried on smiling at me as he took a seat at his throne. "If you don't mind me asking how you knew I was coming your majesty." The king smiled at me, he suddenly didn't look as old and sad as before. "A guard reported that a wolf was running through Ever, so I hazard a guess that it was you, as you're the only one of your pack that is how do I put it, bold enough to go gallivanting through my streets." That made me smile, I was different from my pack, not like my father. "I'm guessing you came for a reason Cole, or did you just need to let of some steam?"
"A bit of both your majesty." The king stood and went to the table at the far corner where food and drink was spread. Using a golden jug he poured water into two matching goblets. He handed one to me. "Thank you, your majesty." The water was cool and refreshing as I swallowed.
"Please call me Pace while we are on our own, there is no need for formality when you are doing so much for me." Nodding I took another sip before placing it back on the table.
"There's something I need to tell you, about Lily." Pace placed his goblet down to and looked at me eagerly. "She knows who she is, her grandmother Amelia told her." The king looked shocked for a moment but then a fond smile appeared on his face. "Amelia Cloud, a lovely woman her husband was a good friend and advisor of mine back when I was just the crown prince. Amelia and Jack were the ones in charge of getting Lily away all those years ago, the last time I had heard from her was when my father and Jack died."
"Were Jack and your father close too." The king laughed.

"Yes they were best friends I guess you could say, the day my father died was the same day Jack died. My father died from an illness of some sort he had been sick for a while but our healers could do nothing for him, Jack died saving a group of Mortalis from Seth." The mention of Levi's father made my teeth clench. He was one of the most malicious evil vampires there was, apart from his son that is. "Amelia was close to my wife before she died, they were too very important people to me, to Ever. I guess getting her to come to me will be hard. I'm guessing she's angry and confused." Nodding he sighed. "I see well all I can ask is that you try."

"Your majesty, I was wondering if you knew anything of Jacks children?" Moving some papers around the table the king thought for a moment before answering. "They had two girls I believe Jocelyn who was in all means of the word a perfectly normal child. Then there was Alice, always had trouble with her but were devastated when she disappeared. We still don't know where she went." The Alice I remembered was sweet and kind not troublesome. Then again I had only known her a few days. "The girl I first came here with Rain, well she's Alice's daughter." The king stopped moving. He was completely speechless. "Are you sure?" I nodded at him. "Yes she has the family locket. I met Alice once I was only little when she came to my father to inform him that Jack had died." The king frowned. "Strange that your father never mentioned this, even stranger to know that Alice is still alive." It was truly not my father's day today not only was I annoyed with him, but now the king. "Cole you need to take Rain to see Amelia. Maybe Amelia can use Rain to track her." Nodding I turned to leave. But stopped when the king asked a question that caught me off guard. "Do you love my daughter?" Turning around the king just looked at me. Looked at me as though I was normal, that I wasn't about to sprout fur and gain two extra legs. "Yes...yes I do." The king smiled brightly. " I wouldn't pick anyone better for her."

Lily

My father and mother were alone when I entered the house. Both sat comfortably on the sofa, their hands intertwined between them. Leah must have been in bed, and Leo in his room. They looked happy, content. Whereas I was the unpredictable storm, controllable but destructible. I decided to sit in front of the TV on the floor which forced them both to look at me as I made them spill the truth. Smiling dad turned off the TV.

They both looked at me bewildered. I decided I had cried too many times today, therefore I locked my emotions tightly away. "I think there's something you need to tell me." Looking at one another in confusion they faced me. My father swished his hand in the air "Like what?" Keeping my gaze steady on them, I finally found the courage to confront them. "Like the fact that I'm adopted." My mother gasped loudly, I watched my father's expression not change, but his free hand clenched tightly in a fist. "How did you find out?" His voice had an undertone of anger. "Does it matter how I found out. What matters is that you both lied to me, why didn't you tell me the truth?" To my utter horror I watched tears fall down my mother's cheeks. She had been a wall for the past three years since dad found out about his cancer, but now. She finally cracked, shards of stone began to crumble. "We didn't know the truth to tell you." Anger bubbled inside of me. The past week has been an emotional roller coaster, from loving Reeve, to choosing Cole, to being threatened by Levi and Lexi, to Amelia's words and Cole's father, this was the last thing I needed. "Then for once in my life tell me the truth what do you know?"

Mum let go of my father's hand and tried to embrace me, but I didn't let her. No not yet. I needed the truth. Sighing shakily she didn't try to grab me again, instead she moved towards the fireplace where an old iron case stood. Crouching down she opened it and revealed an envelope that had aged with time. Closing the box again she handed it to me. The letter was addressed to me. "When Amelia and Jack came to us all those years ago, they made us promise to look after you. They said you were special, and that you needed to be loved and guided. And when the time was right to give you this letter. We've never opened it, but it's yours." I stared down at the envelope hoping it contained something worthwhile, some truth that I could consume and believe. My father stood and placed his hand on his wife's shoulder. His face was still composed but his eyes held the turmoil I knew he was really feeling. "They didn't tell us anything other than that, nothing of where you came from, or who you were other than your name. We took you in because we wanted another child and wasn't sure if it was going to happen. But no matter what that letter says you need to know that we do love you, and you will always be our daughter, nothing can change that." Stepping closer to the door I looked at them both. For so long they had been everything I had ever known and I knew the hurt I was feeling was mostly to do with the fact I had been lied to not just by them but everyone I loved, Cole and Amelia included. I knew I was leaving even before I had stepped foot into the house. "I'm sorry." Before they could stop me, I escaped leaving everything I had ever known behind.

I technically had nowhere to go. I couldn't go to my friends because they didn't know what was going on. And even if Sky did I didn't want to drag her into this. I couldn't go to Cole in fear of seeing his father again, and I couldn't go to Amelia. If I was truly a threat I wouldn't drag her down with me. I quickly made my way back into the woods. My feet knew the path off by heart now and I found my way to Reeve's illuminated house in record speed. If I couldn't speak to Cole or even Reeve, realising in that moment how much I wanted to talk to him. Then I would speak to Carmen. I knocked quietly, knowing they were wolves too made me have the confidence that they would have heard it. Carmen was the one to answer, she looked tired but her face brightened when she saw me. "Lily come in come in!" Stepping into the warmth I noticed she was in her pyjamas.
"Sorry I didn't mean to intrude." Smiling she took my hand and dragged me upstairs.
"Don't worry about it, what's wrong I know somethings wrong?" Sitting in her tranquil room and presence I suddenly felt a whole lot better.
"Carmen I know you're a wolf, and I know you know that I'm the lost Princess." Carmen came to sit by me on the bed, her face calm and still held a smile. "I won't ask how you found out, I'm just sorry that you did. You should know not all of us know. Only the protectors and I knew who you really were." Pulling the necklace she gave me I ran my fingers over its petals. "Why don't Reeve and Jett know?" Moving towards her wardrobe she began rummaging through her clothes. "Because they aren't protectors, I only know because I'm seen as special in the pack." I pulled my hair from its bobble releasing some of the pressure building in my head, I felt tired and drained. "Because you're the only girl." She smiled as she turned to face me "something like that, here try these on they should fit." The soft blush pink pyjamas fell onto my lap. "What for?" Carmen folded her arms across her chest and smiled slightly. "Well you can't sleep in jeans. I'll get dad to make us some hot chocolate he always does it better than me. I'm not letting you go home you're staying and I'm taking care of you." I smiled gratefully at her. Before anything else could be said Dean walked past the door and doubled back when he saw me. "Lily good to see you, what's going on?" The likeness between Dean and his children was stark, I felt like I was looking into the mirror of time when

I looked at Dean, I pictured that's what Reeve would look like years later. "We are having an emergency sleep over which means your hot chocolate skills are needed in immediate action!" Dean laughed and ruffled his daughter's hair. "As you wish boss, and Lily are you okay do you need me to call anyone?" Not unless you knew someone that could turn back time so I could re-do my life, or find a way to change myself so I could be normal. "No I'm fine thank you." He smiled and made his way down the stairs. Carmen pulled me up from the bed and pushed me into the bathroom. "Go and get changed, the envelope will still be there when you're done." I had been clinging to the envelope the whole time hoping it had something that would make sense inside.

"Do you think I should open it?" Placing a spare tooth brush in my hand she pushed me into the platinum tiled bathroom. "Not until you ready." "And if I'm not?" Closing the door behind her I heard her answer through the door.

"Then there's always tomorrow."

Cole

Dawn broke through the trees painting the landscape in its colourful embrace. The naked branches reached towards the sun in hope that the light would return its features to them. I watched the early morning mist swirl and collapse under the weight of the sun's rays. It would have been cold if I hadn't been in fur. Jett sat hunched next to me, groggy with sleep. I nipped his side making him jump and yelp. He growled at me with frustration, I nodded my head in the direction of home telling him it was good to leave. We walked home too tired to run. Our paws were silent as we made our way through crunching leaves. We reached the tree where we had hidden our clothes last night and shifted. Dressed we both stretched and yawned. It was around seven in the morning, no time to sleep. "I hate night watches in the winter, in the summer the sun rises earlier so we can at least get a couple hours of sleep before school!" I silently disagreed. Night watches used to be one of my favourite activities, due to the need to be awake. Sleep had never been one of my favourite things to do. We reached the cluster of houses and split ways, Jett gave me a quick wave before jogging lethargically into his house. "Cole."

Turning to the sound of my name I saw Dean make his way out of his house. I hadn't spoken to Dean properly since the day Reeve left. "Morning." He smiled at me and made his way over, concern blanketing his face. "Are you okay?" Smiling at him I wanted to laugh at his fatherly concern.

"Yes." He didn't seem convinced.

"I was wondering if you could do me a favour." Shifting on to a different foot I raised an eyebrow at him. "It would mean breaking a rule." Defying my father, definitely in. "Go on" I smiled. Glancing at my house then to his he stepped closer and bent close to my ear. "I need you to find a way to keep Reeve from coming back." Frowning I looked at him.

"Why?"

"Recently I've sensed something changing, perhaps a threat coming and with the vamps acting the way they have been I would prefer if Reeve wasn't here, you know to keep him safe if I could find a way to keep Carmen away too I would."

"How can I help?"

"Only the son of the Alpha has enough power to overturn an order, it's what bugs James the most about you because you will be the only true threat to his power, send a letter to Reeve telling him not to come home, he can and will listen to you". And with that he turned on his heel returning to his house not realising that perhaps he had given me the answer to one of the biggest questions I have ever had, why my father treated me the way he did? Because I was more powerful than him.

Lily

I woke the next morning to unfamiliar light and soft pink pyjamas clinging to me. Looking over to my side I saw Carmen still sleeping soundly. Her room was even more tranquil with the blinds drawn forbidding sunlight to stream in. looking at the clock that hung ahead of me I saw that it was in fact eight in the morning. I had half an hour to get to school before I was officially late, before Mr Porter the stern receptionist who loved making disappointing phone call to parents about their children's behaviour, would call up my own parents to inform them of my absence. Still I didn't move. School seemed stupid now compared to everything I had just learnt. It was mundane and human above all else and this factor made it surprisingly unbearable. I had gone to bed wishing time would just go back and place me in a life that was normal. Now however, I had accepted that I was abnormal, and decided I didn't want to be any other way. Carmen stirred in her sleep, her light brown eyes awakening. "Morning." I whispered as she sat up in her bed. She smiled lazily back at me. "You seem better this morning." She watched me as I got out of bed and made my way towards the pile of clothes I had been wearing the night before. Picking them up I smiled brightly at her "so what are we doing today?" Frowning quizzically at me she answered me. "Don't you have school?" I shrugged at her.

"Yeah but I'm not going so you'll just have to put up with my presence a little longer." I could still hear her laugh as I walked into the bathroom to get changed.

Cole

Lily wasn't at school. I felt lonely as I sat down in history. The chair she normally occupied by me sat empty and cold. Was she okay? Was she ill? Had she fallen out with her parents? All these questions ran through my mind as I attempted the exam question we had been given. The whole class sat in silent concentration, which only made my thoughts louder. There was a light tap on my shoulder. Turning around I found Sky leaning forward so she could speak to me. Her face mirrored my own. "Where's Lily?" Her voice was awfully quite, but she knew I could hear her anyway. "Your guess is better than mine. I saw her yesterday and she seemed fine." Sky frowned slightly. When she looked back at me her eyes were frantic and alarmed, which only made my protector senses go off. "I called Lily's house this morning when I didn't see her in form. Emily that's Lily's mum said that they had got into a fight last night and Lily had walked out and hadn't come back. Nobody's seen her. She got all worried because she thought that she was with me, but I thought she was with you!" My heart began hammering against my chest. Looking around to make sure we weren't disturbing the others I answered. "I haven't seen her since last night. If she's not with me and she's not with you, then where is she?" Sky shook her head, just as confused and worried as me. I quickly stood up attracting most of the class's attention including Mr Wright. "Cole is there something wrong?" Swinging my attention on to my teacher I fixed him with the most pathetic smile I could managed. "Sorry sir it's just I don't feel too good, could I go and see the nurse I feel a bit faint." Mr Wright looked at me with sincere concern and smiled sympathetically at me. "Of course Cole, take someone with you just in case." Students looked eagerly at me to choose them just so they could get out of class for a few minutes. "Sky will come." Not giving her a chance to disagree I walked weakly out of the classroom, leaving her trailing behind.

She gently closed the classroom door behind her. "What are you doing?" Increasing my pace down the halls I located the easiest exit. Nudging her towards the door I carried on "we are going to find Lily, I found this exit when I first started here, it leads to the short path into the woods that's where we are going to start." She looked at me startled. She stopped just as we got to the door.
"If I have to break about a dozen school rules to do this then you at least need to do something for me." Keeping my gaze on her I raised an eyebrow.
"What do you want?" She inhaled a long breath and released it once again.
"Tell me who you are Cole."

Lily

Carmen decided it was time I started learning about Ever "you are the Princess of it so you should at least know what you're the Princess of" she said as we ate breakfast quickly. Winter was in full swing as we stepped out into the wood. Its chilly wind whipped at me as we began to walk, pulling my coat around me tighter to trap in some heat we pressed on. Carmen pointed out the markings for the boundary lines that kept the shield between the human world and Ever intact. She explained what the huge engraved boulders in the middle of the wood were for. I caressed my hand over the middle boulder with the engraving for the shadows. A weird spiralling pattern that had the word Umbra intertwined within it. The gold glimmered in the December sunlight. "So my real father he is the king?" Carmen was looking at the boulder that had the word Lupus on as she spoke, her voice was soft and warm. "Yes he's been king since he was eighteen. Took over when his father died. His mother's still alive. She's a nice lady you will love her, always had a soft spot for Reeve." She smiled ruefully at me. My heart begin to ache slightly.

"What's her name?" Carmen moved to the next boulder that was engraved with the word Lamia, unlike the others it wasn't patterned in gold but a burnt charcoal black. "She's called Primrose, she and the king's brother Lucas are the only Royals left. Lucas and his wife Dia never had children." So I only had four real relatives left, what about Alana's family? Carmen glanced at me as we moved to the next boulder with the word Nereides patterned in gold onto the rock. "You're thinking about Alana's family aren't you?" I nodded at her but kept my gaze on the rock. "Nobody knows of Alana's family except the king so when you meet him you can ask." I stepped away from the boulders and turned my back on Carmen. I let my gaze dance over the bare branches and rest of the cloudy horizon. "I haven't decided if I am going to meet him yet."

I heard Carmen approached me carefully as though I was some kind of wild animal. "Why wouldn't you want to meet him?" I sighed and let the emotion I had been locking away seep into it, hopefully diffusing some of the tension that was built up inside of me. "Because I don't know him." Carmen patted my arm and suddenly felt calm and peaceful.

"How do you do that?" Carmen laughed and released me, still her calming touch had made my emotions pack their bags and vacate my body, leaving me at ease. "When I said I was special to the pack it's not because I am the only girl, it because I'm an Omega" I was about to ask what that was when she raised her hand to me. "If you shush I will explain it to you" I laughed and told her to carry on. "An Omega had the gift of calming, when people are feeling anxious or anger I can diffuse those emotions by drawing them from their body and leaving them with a calming effect. I don't always have to touch you sometimes I can visualise and do it but it takes longer. If you're really angry I only have to touch you and all of that anger will be gone."

"Did your parents know that you were going to be an Omega?" Carmen laughed as we made our way towards hers again. "Yes dad sensed it when I was born, that's how I got my name, ironic huh?" I smiled at her. Everything started making sense again, just before we stepped back into her house Carmen stopped me. "I know you don't want to meet the king because you don't know him. But this is your chance to know him, he's

the only one who can give you the answers that you seek so desperately."
I silently agreed with her.

Stepping into the house I found Dean looking startled as he stared down a
rather familiar man. The man was tall and handsome with dark features
and a billowing emerald cloak. The man's dark brown eyes found me and
he smiled at me. "Hello little niece, I am your uncle...Uncle Lucas."

I looked up at my uncle's face looking for something familiar in his
expression that I would find in my own. My uncle smiled at me patiently,
waiting for me to speak. But I couldn't, my voice had become trapped
inside of me. Dean looked at me and smiled slightly "Carmen why don't
we make some drinks and give Lily sometime to speak to her uncle."
Carmen looked as though she didn't want to leave my side but followed
her father's suggestion and grudgingly made her way into the kitchen,
with Dean on her tail. Lucas swished his hand at me and indicated to me
to take the seat opposite him as he sat on the Skies sofa as though it was
his own. "Why are you here?" I finally managed as I sat carefully on the
leather sofa, very much aware that my uncle's gaze hadn't left me as I did.
He was a stern looking man, but there was a fierce friendliness in his
expression that I recognised, as I saw it often in my own reflection. "My
wife informed me she had seen you, you are very much like your mother
you know." So that was who the dark haired lady was.
"I remember she never told me who she was." Dean and Carmen returned
with tea and biscuits. Carmen sat by me keeping a calming hand on my
shoulder, Dean stayed standing. "You are all clearly wondering why I am
here after keeping our distance for all these years, but now that you have
been discovered it is my duty to bring you home." Dean came around the
chair and stood protectively behind me. "Shouldn't it be her decision
when she goes home? She doesn't know about Ever yet she doesn't truly
understand who she is." Lucas watched Dean patiently, but from the set
of his jaw I knew it annoyed him that Dean was speaking against him. "Lily
doesn't have a choice, she will learn about herself and Ever when she
returns." I stood up and placed myself next to Dean. "I don't have a
choice, I thought everyone had a choice!" Lucas stood up and
straightened his cloak, he looked at me levelly. "I apologise I didn't mean
it like that. I just hoped you would have been more eager to return
home." He came and stood in front of me. Placing a hand inside his cloak
he pulled out a small silver box and handed it to me. "Your father wanted

me to give this to you. He also wanted me to tell you that only open the letter that your parents gave you when you're ready, and not before then." He smiled down at me before placing his gaze on Dean and Carmen. "Thank you for your hospitality Mr Skies I shall see you tomorrow for our annual meeting." Then he swept out of the house his emerald cloak floating behind him.

Dean frowned at his front door for while "he's the only royal that I've know that thinks he's better than everyone else." I sat back down on the sofa the package still in my hands. Carmen came and sat by me "what is it?" I shrugged as I carefully opened the lid. There was a note on top of the tissue paper, the paper was aged and wrinkled. Carefully opening I read the letter.

To my dearest Lily,

I planned on giving this to you in person when you turned sixteen. I know now that I cannot. I didn't know your life was in danger until you were a few days from being born into this world. Your mother Alana had fallen ill while still pregnant with you, and I knew that I would lose her too. I just hadn't anticipated it to be in death. The year I got to keep you was the best and most heart-breaking year of my life. You were so little and precious to me but I knew soon you would have to go. I cannot explain in a letter why your life had to be so difficult, why you had to go away. If you're reading this then you have been discovered by your love, your people and your enemy. It means it is time for your return but I only wish that you return on your own accord. If you choose never to return, to keep your back turned on Ever then I won't blame you. I only ask that you always wear the gift I have given you, because it will ensure your safety. It was your mothers, she said that if you were ever lost, then to hold it and it will guide you home again. No matter what you choose, you will always be my daughter and I love you no matter what, my little Lily. With hope, your father, Pace Ever.

So he was allowing me to choose, my father seemed like a decent person. I also felt some relief because of this. Even though he didn't know me he was still being a father, and Alana didn't die because of me, she was already ill. Removing the delicate tissue paper from the box it revealed a long aged necklace with a glowing red ruby hanging like flames on the chain. Pulling it out of the box I heard Dean gasp slightly from behind me. "What is it?" Dean came from around the back of the chair so he was facing me he reached out and touched the stone surface before quickly pulling his hand away hissing, as though he had been burned. "It's incredibly rare, it's called the heart of fire, if the wearer is wearing it those who want to do them harm will be burnt if they tried to harm them whilst wearing the stone." Frowning at the necklace I placed it around my neck, it felt heavy against my chest, but radiated a weird warmth through me. "Did it burn you?" Dean smiled at me and sat down on the sofa where Lucas had occupied. "It doesn't like supernatural creatures such as myself." Carmen looked worriedly between me and her dad and I knew there was something she wanted to share. "Spit it out Carmen!"

"I thought the heart of fire was only associated with the myth of the Guardians?"
"What are Guardians?" Dean rubbed his forehead with his hand, it seemed the day had been a stressful one on him. "The Guardians are the protectors and rulers of the earth and sky. They have ancient magic which gives them the power to command every living and supernatural thing on this earth. In the legend it was said that once upon a time an angel came down to earth to bargain with the Earth queen for a life she had condemned. In doing so he fell in love with her. So in the end they ended up having a child. Well this child was born of the heavens and earth which meant he was very powerful. The earth queen wanted the child to live on earth but the angel wanted the child to live in heaven. Then we're not sure what happened, but the child grew up and became a guardian that protected heaven and earth." Intrigued I pressed him some more.
"So why is this stone associated with them?" He sighed and lent back on the sofa, arms spread on the back of the seat. "Well that stone was supposed to be the gift that the man who created the guardians gave to his daughter to protect her, from what the legend says the stone was supposed to be passed down daughter to daughter." If what Dean was saying was true how did Alana get hold of the stone?

Cole

My feet began slipping on the slick damp ground. The rain had made the outskirts of the forest a treacherous place and I knew Sky was struggling to keep up with me. Turning around I saw Sky's wet matted hair and mud stained clothes, she did not look happy. Looking at my phone I found that it was half twelve we had been traipsing through the woods for hours and still no Lily. "Sky I don't think she's here." But Sky didn't answer me. Turning around I saw that she was staring at something to the left of her. The mist and slight rain meant her vision wouldn't be as good as mine, but from the look on her face I knew she saw Lexi as clearly as I did. I moved to stand next to her, I could feel her trembles even though we weren't touching. Lexi smirked at us. I blinked then she was there, in front of our faces. Sky gave a little whimper, her gaze however didn't falter.

 "Well look who we have here then, a filthy mutt and an ex best friend!" Placing myself in front of Sky I stared down Lexi, she wasn't old enough to intimidate me just yet. "What are you doing here Lexi, Levi got tired of you already?" Lexi snarled at me and allowed her prominent fangs to slip from her lips, Sky went still behind me. "Don't think you can talk to me like that mutt, I'll rip you to pieces. But as you asked I came here for Sky actually." Sky peaked around my shoulder slowly looking at Lexi as if she had never known her. "What do you want with me?" Lexi stepped back a little and her fangs retreated back into her mouth. She almost looked normal. The rain made her transparent skin even more so and her dark eyes had grown darker. "I want you to choose the right side Sky, there's a war brewing and I don't want you to be caught in this mess." Sky stepped in front of me this time and stared down Lexi with fierce anger. "What about you're other friends!" Lexi laughed a hollow laugh. She had changed so much in the space of a few months, I can still remember the loud bubbly girl who I spoke to in English, now I only saw the shell of that girl, as she trembled in maliciousness. "You were the only one that ever understood me, before this happened. Ella only hung out with us because of Luke and Luke only hung out with us because of Sean, and Sean I don't know about Sean and don't get me started on Lily!" Sky crossed her arms across her chest and glared at Lexi. "What about Lily?" Lexi laughed loudly and folded her legs in and sat on the wet ground, not bothered that the rain and floor were soaking her head to toe. "Lily, well she was always so perfect, so talented. Everyone wanted to be her, to be with her. I mean look at her now. She has everything! Then look at me what do I have?" Sky's face faltered as she listened to Lexi's pathetic story. "You had everything too Lex, you had friends, a family, you were going to dance to perform. But now you traded it all in for what you've become now, a monster! You had so much faith in me but that faith is misplaced. I cannot save you when you don't want to save yourself!" Lexi looked up to Sky who hadn't moved an inch since she moved in front of me. I watched Lexi let a single tear fall from her eye before catching it in her palm. She stared at that single tear for a minute before throwing it to the ground. Blink, she was gone. And Sky fell helplessly against me.

Lily

Carmen and Dean allowed me some time on my own. I was sat on their front deck, letting the winter wind wipe away my thoughts. A few months ago I would have appreciated all the new things I was learning, but now I was just confused and freaked out. "Lily?" I looked up to see a very muddy and rumpled Cole and not far behind him a far worse Sky. I stood and smiled at the both of them. "What happened to you two?" Sky stormed past Cole to reach me. She pointed an angry finger in my direction to match her expression and shouted. "Well we thought you was missing as you didn't tell either of us where you were. So we called your parents and they informed me that you never returned home last night. So this idiot came up with a bright idea to go trekking through the woods after a rainstorm, only to find out you was here the whole time!" I stepped back. Her outburst had caught me by surprise. Normally Sky was quite calm and collected, but obviously not today. "Look I'm sorry I left my phone at home so I couldn't call." Sky glared at me and slumped herself onto the deck; running her fingers through her matted hair. "Well I think you could have found a way!" Cole just stared at us both in shock. It was as though he couldn't quite believe that I was really here, or that Sky had shouted at me. "I'm going to get a shower." Cole didn't say anything else. He just turned on his heel and headed towards his house, slamming the front door shut behind him. "He's angry at me isn't he?" Sky gave me a look as though she thought I was stupid. "Well wouldn't you be. If he hadn't called you to tell you he had walked out of his house and not coming to school, and then to find out you went to your ex's house instead of his." I hadn't thought of that.

I had only wanted to get away from my parents, I would have gone to Cole but the likely hood of running into his father had kept me away. "Come on let's get you home so you can shower." Sky didn't move however, she stayed seated. "I can't go home, Mr evil receptionist would have called my parents to tell me I left school premises without permission, they're going to kill me." I looked down at Sky and saw her worried eyes stare out into the wood. Her matted muddy hair clung around her face, her clothes were wet and filthy. "Fine then I will have to face my own parents, I'm not letting you freeze anymore." Pulling her up I began leading her into the woods back to my house. "Why did you go to Reeves, why didn't you go to Cole's or mine?" I knew she had wanted to ask that question. But I couldn't explain the answer. "I knew Cole was out and I didn't want to drag you into this mess." Sky stopped walking and pulled her hand from my grip.

"Listen Lily I know what Cole is, I know about Lexi! Which means you can tell me things, you don't have to be alone in this."

"How did you find out?" Sky smiled slightly and moved her hair out of her eyes, her blue one was glistening more than the darker one. "A few weeks ago I was walking home from my nanas when I saw an erratic dog running wild about the streets. I thought it was a stray so I followed it and it led me to Lexi's house. When it got to the door I watched the dog transform into a human, into Cole. And Lexi after that weird encounter in her garden with that man I started following her. It was just before school broke up for Christmas. I followed her into the woods, when she stopped that man was there again except he wasn't alone, a girl was there she looked kind of funny then before I knew it, Lexi bit her in the neck…and drank her…blood." Sky began to cry and I folded her into my embrace. She had witnessed this all on her own and not told a soul, I admired her strength. "Let's get you home, and I'll tell you about me."

Cole

I stood under the spray of the hot shower, listening to my own thoughts. Of all the places she could have gone, why Reeve's? Why hadn't she come to me? I knew there was a part of her heart I hadn't yet been able to capture because it belonged to my best friend, but she said she loved me more, so why hadn't she come? There was a slight knock on the door "Cole is that you?" Rain's voice vibrated through the door to my ears. "Yeah one second." Turning off the shower I stepped out and wrapped a towel around me before opening the bathroom to see Rain waiting for me. Today she had her curls piled on top of her head, with black ripped jeggings and a faded oversized top, paint dotted her clothing. She saw me looking and smiled slightly "I'm painting the spare room, your dad said it was mine and to do what I like with it." I moved into my room to grab some clothes before she spoke again. "School rang to say you had left the grounds without permission, I was the only one here so I pretended to be your mum. I said that you felt ill and I gave you permission to come home. The dude on the phone wasn't impressed but asks you to return as soon as you're well again." I swung round to look at her. She stood in the middle of my door way a satisfied smile playing on her lips. "You're welcome."

"Thank you." She smiled and left to her room where the smell of fresh paint was most potent.

Changing quickly I followed her to her room. She had painted the walls in a light mauve colour, but had patterned it with detailed ivory flowers and intertwining olive stems with matching leaves. "This is amazing" Rain looked around at the painted walls and merely shrugged her shoulders. She was clearly very talented. "I have something to tell you." Rain stopped painting for a moment, then very carefully placed her brush down and sat herself on the floor so her full attention was on me. "Do you know how when you first came here you told me about your mother?" Rain nodded face intrigued and confused. "Well I found out something…Lily's great grandmother Amelia is your mums mum." Rain didn't speak for a while just stared blankly into space.

"So she's my grandmother?"

"Yes." She began fiddling with the locket around her neck. The way she carefully did it informed me that it was fragile and she had been told to be careful with it. "Can I meet her?" I came and sat myself down in front of her. She looked more innocent and younger than she did before. Her vulnerability made me want to reach out and hug her. "Yes but we need Lily first we can't just turn up at Amelia's without Lily." Rain looked at me.

She reminded me of the flowers she had painted upon her violet walls, fragile and pale, waiting for the vicious wind to tear them up from their roots. "Then ask her, because I don't know how long I've got left."

Lily

Nobody was home when me and Sky reached it. Leo and Leah would still be at school, and mum and dad were at some sort of appointment for dad's health management, I only knew this from the appointment time plastered on a note on the fridge. While she was in the shower I changed into to clean clothes and packed a small bag. It wasn't time for me to come home just yet. Sky came out drying her hair in a towel, looking better now she was dry, and in borrowed clothes of mine. She came and sat on the bed where I was playing with the glowing red pendent. "So you're really this lost princess, you're really adopted?" I nodded and before I knew it Sky had wrapped me in a warm hug and tears were streaming down my face. She smelled like my coconut shampoo not her usual strawberry scent. "It's okay Lil, I'll help you get through this." Her words were comforting but how could she help? How could she possibly begin to understand the situation I was in? "Sky can I stay with you tonight, I just need to figure somethings out first." Sky squeezed me before she let go, she nodded but she looked slightly worried. "Leave a note to tell them you're okay and where you are." Right, my parents. They would be worried about me even though they could have avoided all of this if they had just been honest with me, then again I don't blame them. They didn't know enough to tell me the truth and I wouldn't have believed them anyway. "Okay let's go."

Sky's parents were still at work when we arrived at hers which gave her the sneaky opportunity to delete the accusing message the school had left on their answering machine. We were just settling into her room when we heard footsteps making their way up the stairs on the Sky's floor. Sky looked at her alarm clock that red half past one, two early for her family to be returning. The footsteps stopped outside of her door, we could see the faint shadow of shoes from the small gap under the door. Heart beating fast I grabbed Sky's hand and dragged her around the corner so the wardrobe was guarding us. Hiding we heard the turn of the door handle as the person entered. Sky gasped but quickly placed her hand over her mouth. Grabbing whatever was closest to me, I stepped away from the wardrobe about to hit the person in the head with the lamp as my chosen weapon, when quick as a flash a pale hand shot out and caught my wrist. Looking up at my attacker I saw Cole's highly amused face. "So your bright idea was to hit me over the head with a lamp?" His face was serious but his eyes was laughing.

"Well next time don't break into someone's house, and at least announce yourself, Sky you can come out its just Cole." Sky shakily moved from the wardrobe to come and stand next to me, she gave Cole a slight smile. "Technically I didn't break in as the door was open." He sat down at Sky's ivory dressing table and was looking at both of us, waiting. "Next time knock you gave me a heart attack!" Sky finally spoke, Cole smiled and nodded his head at her.

We both took refuge on her bed so we could see Cole who looked like he was going to burst with something. "Are you going to tell us whatever you have to tell us Cole, or are you just going to let yourself implode?" Cole smirked at me before speaking.

"Well when I went home Rain was there so I was speaking to her, and to make a long story short she wants to meet Amelia." I frowned at him, so did Sky.

"Why does she want to meet my great grandmother?" Cole looked uneasy for a moment.

"Because Amelia is her grandmother."

Cole

I remembered how only a few weeks ago how desperate me and Lily were for answers, and now we had them but the secrets seemed to just keep spilling out. Lily was silent in a complete state of shock. It seemed some secrets were harder to hear, never mind comprehend. Sky was the one who broke the silence. "So this Rain is the granddaughter of Lily's great grandmother who isn't really her grandmother?" I nodded at her.

"But my grandmother Jocelyn never had a daughter other than my mother." Lily looked at me with a furrowed expression, so I filled in the blanks. "Yeah but Amelia had Alice. Alice is Rain's mother and I know this because I've met her before." Lily looked shocked and slightly wary. "But Alice went missing years ago. And if that was true she would have had to be at least in her late forties when she had Rain." I stood up and began to pace. None of this made sense. I recalled the image of Alice. A smiling young woman, a woman who could look no older than twenty. "She definitely wasn't in her late forties when I met her and that was only what fifteen years ago." Sky had been watching me pace while Lily kept her confused expression on the cream carpet. "So how is that possible?" Lily stood up and looked at us both.

"It isn't possible Amelia had Alice when she was twenty, Alice disappeared when she was fourteen. That was nearly forty years ago. How old is Rain? Recalling the numerous times we had spoken I recalled her once telling me she was two years younger than me. "She's fifteen."

"That would have made Alice forty one when you saw her." Sky did the math a lot quicker than I did. Lily was looking at me intently, her fingers twirling the flower pendent around her neck. "She definitely didn't look forty one either she looked no older than twenty." Sky turned to look at Lily.

"How old was Amelia when she had Jocelyn?"

"She was sixteen when she had my grandma and my grandma was eighteen when she had my mum, but my grandmother doesn't look her age but she is old if you know what I mean." Both me and Sky nodded at her, I knew what she was getting at. "So what are the options, what could she be?" Resuming my pacing I thought hard about the variety of supernatural characteristics there was and if they linked to anything. "Well rule out vampire, one she didn't have the pale skin and black eyes but she was pregnant so she has to be alive." Lily and Sky sat back down both looked unsure and agitated. "Could she be a wolf like you?" Sky questioned.

"No I would have been able to sense her if she was but even if she was a wolf she would still have looked her age we're not immortal. She was definitely not a faerie or a mermaid so that leaves a witch or Custos." Both of them looked at me blankly. Sometimes I forget that they don't know the language. "Custos is the name given to those who protect the Triple Binding." Sky gave me an annoyed look. "If we didn't know what Custos meant were not going to know what the Triple Binding is either." Smiling at her I answered.

"I was just going to explain. The Triple Binding is a binding contract made between earth, heaven and the Guardians." Lily suddenly look very much alert. Her eyes never left mine. "The Guardians were first created by a man who was the child of heaven and earth, it's a long story but the man and his followers created a balance between the supernatural and the humans. They have the power to command every supernatural being, every human on this earth." Lily suddenly sprang to her feet. She quickly pulled out a huge ruby sized amulet that was blazing with flames I moved towards her but she stopped me. "Don't it burns those who are supernatural."

"But it's burning you!" But it wasn't. She held the stone in her hands and the tawny flames spiralled off the stone, kissing her pale fingers but leaving no burn behind. "I think it wants to show us something." Sky was watching fascinated.

"What is it?" But Lily didn't have time to answer before the stone seared a blistering red and shot orange flames into each of our chests. I felt the warm flames engulf me, swallowing me until I could see nothing but the flames. I felt myself falling, and I knew the other two were falling right Behind me.

Lily

I opened my eyes and watched as the orange flames sizzled away leaving no trace that I had been on fire. The three of us stood upon a growing mountain. The scene was serene and beautiful. We were so high up that I felt if I reached my hand up I would be able to touch the turquoise sky. We were surrounded by more mountains the same size as the one we stood upon each capped with a sprinkle of snow.

We weren't alone on the mountain. A woman sat straight upon a throne made of the same coloured earth as the mountain. She wore a bronze coloured gown with garnet coloured stones scattered along the bottom. Her brown eyes were guarded as she watched the rocky steps that led down the mountain side. Her crown looked as though it was made up of twisted vines with a few green leaves poking out at the end. She twirled a piece of her dark brown locks around her finger as she waited. She made no acknowledgement that she could see us. Cole and Sky were staring at her when I whispered. "I think we're in a memory." They looked like they wanted to say something but was interrupted by another figure stepping into the scene.

A man had climbed the steps onto the mountain top where we were stood. He was dressed in dark ebony clothes with a golden cloak wrapped around his strong body. His hair was dark but his eyes were the bluest eyes I had ever seen. When he was just a few steps from the stone throne he bowed to the woman. "Serena it's always a pleasure to see your lovely face again." The women smiled slightly at the man and bowed her head in respect to him. "Likewise Cameron, how is my son?" Sky and Cole looked at me as though I knew what was going on, I merely shrugged and placed my gaze back on the scene. Cameron smiled back at Serena before answering "I'm sure he is well, I haven't seen much of him due to his wanders but his feet always bring him home eventually." Serena gave a sad smile.

Suddenly the sky began to move and crack open, the earth under our feet began to shake. Serena and Cameron watched the sky as is split apart and spat out another man who landed beside me, making my heart jump into my mouth. Unlike Cameron this man was dressed in elaborate silver clothes with a matching cloak. He did not wear a crown, but from his clothes and the way he walked I knew he was royal too. Opening his eyes he smiled at the two and walked towards them. Like his clothes his eyes were an elaborate shade of silver turning a dark grey at the edges. This time the woman stood from her throne and curtseyed to the man as he made his way over. Cameron bowed his head. "Serena, Cameron it's been a while." Serena smiled more brightly at this man than she had at Cameron. "Yes too long Silas." Silas returned her smile before pulling out a silver piece of paper with a white quill. "I am the ruler of heaven, you the queen of earth and where is my son to represent the Guardians?" Cameron looked uneasy for a minute before composing his features. "He is on his travels your majesty he told me to come here and collect the binding." Silas didn't smile at him but carried on his speech. "On this day we create the Triple Binding a contract that allows for the child of all three to come forth and shatter the curse put to us Serena to keep us trapped in our human forms, and allows for our son to not choose his real nature". Serena looked anxious for a moment.
"What happens to us when they pledge themselves to rule?" Cameron placed a comforting hand on her arm. "You will be free to return home." Cameron was the first to take hold of the quill and sign his name, then

Silas and lastly Serena. After she had signed her name the paper began to glow then Cameron took hold of it. "The Custos will take good care of this until the time comes." Silas smiled before closing his eyes once again and letting the sky swallow him whole. Serena watched as Cameron progressed back down the steps of the mountain. She slumped herself back onto her throne. "I still fear I'll have to wait hundreds of years before I can return home and even then" she paused to look longingly down the mountain "my son will not join me." I watched a single tear fall from her eyes, before my body was once again engulfed by flames.

We were no longer on the mountain but back in Sky's bedroom and the pendent back around my neck. Dormant once again. "What the hell just happened?" Cole was the first to speak. Sky just sat on her bed too shocked to even ask questions. "This pendent belonged to the first daughter of the guardians, which means it's probably got loads of secrets and memories stored inside. So it showed us one."
"It showed us what the Triple Binding was. It was an agreement. But what I don't get is why do they need someone to set them free and where is this home they want to return to so bad?" Sky shook her head then looked at us both. "I think we need to prioritise. Let's deal with Rain and Alice first then maybe we can figure out this Triple Binding stuff, agreed?" Both me and Cole nodded in union. It was comforting to know someone had a plan. Cole glanced at his watch.
"I need to go but I think we need Rain to see Amelia tomorrow. Rain's anxious about how much time she has left. So can we see Amelia tomorrow?"
"If you two go I'll cover for you at school." I turned to look at Sky. My soft loving best friend who never lies to anybody. I felt like I was somehow corrupting her. "Are you sure." She nodded. Cole smiled gratefully at her and told me to meet him at the edge of the wood at eight. Then he was gone as quietly as he had come. Sky fell back on her bed and rubbed the stress lines from her head. I followed suit. "I think were in need of ice cream and some classic films don't you?" I laughed at her "I couldn't agree more." I was in some serious need for some normalcy.

Cole

I was walking back through the wood lost in the memory I had just witnessed when I heard it. At first I wasn't sure what I had heard, then, the sound came again. It was a small whimper, a cry. I followed it keeping my steps silent. I couldn't even hear the sound of my heart beating against my chest, but I could feel it, as though it was anxious to escape the cage that keeps it protected. I turned to the right where the whimpering was the loudest. I found myself at one of my old childhood haunts. It was known as moonlight creak. There was a small river that ran through the wood and connected to a small stream on the north side of the forest. The river circled an island where a huge oak tree stood tall and strong. It was on the bark of this tree where my name was engraved along with Carmen's, Jetts and Reeve's. There was some initials that we didn't recognise but they were a lot older and worn than ours. The cries were coming from behind the tree.

I rounded the corner and felt my stomach drop to my feet. There propped up against the tree was my little sister. Her small body was curled inwards to dull the obvious pain she was in. I reached for her. She turned towards me and when she did I felt the pain that she was in like I had just been stabbed in the heart. Her pale eyes were full of tears and her long black hair was messy from the wind, but that couldn't hide the large bloody gash that stretched across her cheek and eye. "Skyla what happened!" My voice shook as I folded her into a hug. She was shaking against me. I picked her up and carried her home. She still didn't speak to me. Instead she kept her arms locked around my neck and face buried in my shoulder.

Rain was the only one who was home. She took Skyla from me and sat her on the kitchen side so I could locate the first aid kit. When I came back Rain had calmed her down so she was no longer crying. "Where's mum wasn't she looking after her." Rain took the disinfectant and cotton wool from me and turned to my sister. "This is going to sting a little bit okay" her voice was soft and calming. "And I have no idea Cole I was taking a nap." Skyla flinched when she placed the soaked cotton wool onto her face, but she didn't make a noise. "Skyla what happened to you?" Her voice was still soft as she spoke. Skyla looked up at me. Her face so innocent it made me want to cry. "I don't know...mummy was with me...then." Her tears began to fall again and my heart broke along with her. "I looked for her but I couldn't find her. Then I heard a noise...I ran but I fell then I don't remember how I got to the tree...all I knew was that my face hurt." I moved to hug her and she squeezed me back. Her story didn't make much sense, but it still left an uneasy feeling surrounding me. Where was mum? I felt a gentle hand on my arm and looked up to see Rain who looked sympathetically at me. "Why don't you try to call her while I put her a plaster on." I nodded at her and let go of Skyla and reached for my phone. That's when I noticed the muddy paw prints that led out onto the deck. Following them I noticed there was also blood staining the deck. I sniffed but couldn't find a scent. I dialled mums number, one ring...two ring...three...four... "Cole" More alert "Mum!" There was a pause then the line went dead in my hand.

Lily

My moment of normalcy didn't last very long. The phone call from Cole had me packing up the few things I had brought to Sky's with me and making my way back through the woods. When he answered the door my heart actually broke. He looked so sad and tired. I just hugged him and hoped I could comfort him. His sister had been attacked and his mother was missing. The pack was out doing the perimeter lines which left Rain and Cole to deal with everything on their own. Skyla was sat on the kitchen side when I entered. Her scraggy teddy bear was tucked under her chin and her thumb was in her mouth. If I hadn't seen the bandage covering the left side of her face I would have thought that she was okay. "I think we need to call someone" Rain said into the silence. Cole picked up Skyla and sat her on his knee. She fell against him closing her eye and falling softly to sleep. "Nobody's answering their phones." Rain looked fragile as she shook with anger. Her oversized clothes that clung to her thin body didn't help her case either. She had changed from the first time I had met her. She looked physically weaker but her eyes held a strength I hadn't seen before. It was almost admirable. Then a thought occurred to me. I didn't know if I was ready to talk to her yet but if it would help Skyla then it was worth it. "We could call my mum she's a doctor she would know what to do." Cole looked at me as though he could read that if it hadn't been important then I wouldn't have suggest it. He nodded at me. I quickly dialled my mother's number and took a breath it rang for a while and for a split second I thought she might not answer. "Lily is that you?" I sighed a heavy sigh.

"Yeah it's me."

"Are you coming home, I think we need to talk?" I closed my eyes for a moment, processing what she was saying. "I need your help, Cole's sister has been hurt and nobody's answering their phones." She immediately went into doctor mode asking about how deep the cut was and if it was infected or anything. She agreed to come to us. Cole gave her directions to his house and true to her word she arrived ten minutes later.

She was dressed in her normal attire, smart crème blouse and dark tailored trousers. Her red hair held back in a tight bun. She knelt down to Skyla who was now awake and still on Cole's lap. My mum gave her a warm and gentle smile as she carefully removed the bandage. She then examined the gash intently for a moment before she stepped back and smiled at Skyla. She pulled a lolly from her pocket and handed it to her. It was the same thing she used to do for me and Leo whenever we were hurt. She finally spoke looking at all three of us. "She's lucky that the scratch got just above her eye. You did well by cleaning it but it will need stitches as it's quite deep." Cole just nodded at her. Mum did the stitches quickly so Skyla wouldn't have to be sat still so long. She winced a few times but other than that she didn't indicate she was in any pain. When finished mum washed her hands then faced Cole again. "Keep it clean it should heal over a few weeks, in three weeks call me and I'll come remove them." Cole nodded and thanked her, grateful for her help and the fact she didn't ask what had happened. She smiled back at him then she faced me. "Lily I would like a moment with you please." She walked onto the decking and waited for me to follow.

She slid the door closed behind her not realising a door wouldn't stop Cole hearing her words. "I would like it very much if you came home so I and your father could talk to you about this. I don't know where you've been staying and I know you haven't been to school. Your priorities shouldn't change because of this Lily, you still belong at home and at school." I waited for her to finish patiently before I spoke. "I'm staying with Sky tonight and I haven't forgotten about school I'm just figuring some stuff out first." She placed her hands on her hips and looked at me sternly as though I was five again and refusing to go to bed. "Despite everything I am still your mother so if I tell you, you need to come home then you come home!" I stepped off the deck, and closed my eyes. I hated hurting her despite the lies but if I didn't she would carry on. I couldn't go home not yet. I firstly needed to understand where I stand and who I am and I couldn't do that at home. "I don't want to come home...I don't want to be with you." Her gasp was almost heart-breaking and the tears that brimmed her eyes nearly had me running towards her and apologising. She breathed deeply and composed herself. "I guess I understand. I hope you change your mind." She turned on her heel and walked back inside. I heard her say her goodbyes to Cole, Rain and Skyla before the front door closed signalling her departure. I let myself sink to the ground, knees to my chest and cry till I had nothing left inside of me.

Cole

I could hear her cries from inside. Each time a new tear fell my heart broke into a million pieces. I handed Skyla to Rain who took her into the living room to watch cartoons. I slid open the sliding deck door and went and sat down by Lily. She was no longer crying. She didn't look at me when I sat by her, instead she kept her bloodshot eyes on the wood, a strange longing swimming in her irises. I put my arm around her and she sank into me. Both needing one another's comfort. It was a while before either of us spoke, the sun had begun its descent and the moon began to rise in the sky. "I remember when I was six and me and Sky used to pretend we were these Princesses from a faraway land where magic existed." I squeezed her tighter as she carried on.
"I guess it's every little girls dream to become a princess and have magic. It was my dream once, so why does my reality still feel dreamlike?" I didn't know the answer, but I don't think she was expecting me to answer. We stayed like that; until the sky turned dark and cloudy.

"Cole, Lily are you out there?" My father's voice was unusually soft as he called us. He came outside and sat by me. His face was taut and anxious. "Cole please tell me you know what's going on?" My father had never looked vulnerable in his life, yet here in this moment he looked as though all his defences had been defeated. "You probably know more than I do."

He kept his pale eyes on the floor his voice different than normal. "I have the pack out looking for your mother, Rain's with Skyla. This wasn't supposed to happen this is why we have a shield, to protect us!" He was working himself into a state. I let go of Lily and grabbed hold of my father, and hugged him tight. It only took a second for him to wrap his arms around me and return my hug. "We'll go look too, you should stay with Skyla. She's strong but not that strong." It was Lily who had spoken, shocking both me and my father. We stepped back from one another, my father fixed Lily with a slight smile. "It's not safe out there for you, I can't ask you to do that." Lily took hold of my hand, and for once it seemed she was the strong one. "It's a good thing you're not asking then, we will find her, come on Cole." She dragged me back through the house so she could pick up her coat and scarf, then we was back out the door heading into the middle of the forest. "My father's right you know, it's not safe." Lily smiled brightly at me before scanning her surroundings.
"Good thing I have you to keep me safe then isn't it." I laughed slightly despite the situation we was in. Then together, hand in hand. We stumbled into the night looking for my mother.

Lily

The pack and I looked all night but still no sign of Sophie. She had vanished like the morning mist, leaving no trail behind that she was even here, apart from muddy paw prints and blood without a scent. First it was Amelia now it was Sophie. It seemed not even the wolves were safe now. The mysteries kept piling up from Carmen being shot, to the woman dying in the middle of the street, to Amelia's attack and now to Sophie's disappearance. We had agreed only a few hours ago to figure one thing out at a time. Now even that seemed impossible.

Cole

We looked all night, through the dark and cold. Despite her trembling hands and blue lips Lily pressed on, refusing to go back until we had searched the whole forest. When we found no trace, I lost all hope I had been clinging onto. My mum was human. She was emotionally strong, but she was no match to some of the monsters out there. We returned home as the sun rose in the sky. Dad and the rest of the pack left for Ever to consult the king. I was so tired but my worry kept me wide awake.

Rain came into the kitchen and made me and Lily sit down on the chairs that surrounded the table. She handed each of us a steaming cup of coffee and a warm plate full of eggs and bacon. She took a seat too, but didn't eat. "Skyla's still in bed, eat up you've both been out all night." Both of us picked up our forks and picked at the food, neither of us really hungry. Rain looked at each of us "I know we were planning on seeing Amelia today, and I understand it might not be possible under the circumstances." I looked at her and she stopped talking.
"You can still go to Amelia's, Lily will take you. It's my responsibility to be with my pack and my family not you two." Both of them looked sharply at me. Rain looked very much taken back. Since she had been here she had become one of the family, and then I just made it clear that she wasn't. "Rain I'm sorry I didn't mean anything by it." But it was too late. I could see the hurt written all over her face. "Its fine Cole I understand. Lily I would like to change before we go is that alright?" When Lily nodded, Rain smiled at her and vacated the room quickly. I kept my gaze on the food she had made me making me feel even more terrible. I heard Lily move to put her plate on the side. Then she came to me bent down and kissed me on the head. Then she left. Leaving me feeling even worse.

Lily

Day broke through the greying clouds as I stepped out of Cole's house. My feet felt heavy as I stepped onto the forest floor, which crunched beneath my soles. I knew Cole was hurting inside and I really didn't know how to comfort him, but he shouldn't have taken it out on Rain. All she had done was make a suggestion. I heard the door close behind me as Rain came and stood by my side. She wore baggy grey jeans, faded converse and an oversized white top, her dark curls pulled back into a ponytail to expose her tired skinny face. I looked down at what I was wearing. Dark ripped muddy jeans, my long blue jacket had holes in the sleeves and my hair was a windswept mess. Great. Rain smiled at me "should we go?" She offered her arm, and without thinking I took it, and lead the way through the wood.

Cole

My mother's warm hand held my face as she looked worriedly down at me. "Cole wake up!" But I wasn't asleep was I? We were in a dark room, damp grey walls surrounded me. Chains enveloped her ankles and wrist, cuts traced her arms. Yet she wasn't scared, she didn't show that she was hurt. "Mum where are we?" My mum smiled and kissed me on the head. She stepped back from me then. "You've always been special Cole, but you are only half of the equation. You need her to find me, your gifts are stronger together." My vision suddenly went blurry and her profile started to vanish. "Wait don't leave me, tell me where you are!"
"You and Lily Cole, it's always been you too." Then like my vision she vanished, and I woke up.

Lily

"Lily you didn't listen to me!" I was no longer in the wood with Rain, but in a room full of darkness. The willowy lady standing closer to me than she had ever done before. She looked angry. "What do you mean?" She huffed in my face, revealing the scent of her breath, damp leaves and a forgotten summer. "I asked you to come to me, yet you have not graced me with your presence!" Her pretty face was contorted in annoyance. "Maybe you should have told me where I can find you." She looked dead in my eye, a small dangerous, yet beautiful smile slid onto her face. "I will give you a clue, but for a price." What could she possibly want from me? I guess there was only one way to find out. "What do you want?" Her smile was so bright it nearly blinded me. She was then suddenly by my ear, whispering. "I only ask for you to give me your word that one day when I need your help, you will give it to me." I breathed in deeply.

"I promise." She laughed then. It was a soft laugh that tickled my hearing. Then for the first time, she took hold of my hand. I was then filled with warmth and wisdom as she began to speak. "The stone you bare on your wrist, and the stone you wear around your neck hold the answers to your past and future. If you ask them you will know." She released me then and the warm sensation left with her. "I have given you more than I should, listen well Lily, your answers are here." She pointed at me then everything disappeared.

I could feel the damp forest floor seep into my clothes as I opened my eyes. I was sprawled on the ground. My head lay in Rain's lap as she stared worriedly down at me. "What happened?" Rain rubbed her face with her hands and gave me an anxious smile. "Well we were just walking and then you just fell. You were breathing but it looked as though you was dead." I stood up and brushed the dirt and leaves from my jeans. "I think I went into a vision or something." Rain's eyes widened at me "really what did you see?" She stood up, her knees were wet from where she had been knelt. "I didn't really understand it." Rain nodded and took my arm to link through hers, afraid I might fall again. "Are you alright now?" I felt fine. Drained from staying out all night, but fine despite everything. "Yes thank you, let's get to Amelia's."

We were only few steps from Amelia's door when Rain suddenly stopped. She looked scared and nervous. "What if she doesn't like me, or doesn't want to know me?" For some reason I felt compelled to hug her, and I did. She returned my hug immediately. "She will love you Rain, nobody cannot love you." She sniffed before letting go. I held my hand to her and she took it with a grateful smile. I stepped up to Amelia's door and knocked on it three times. I took hold of Rain's hand again and she squeezed it tightly. I heard Amelia's small footsteps as she progressed to the door. The door opened and Amelia looked at us. She smiled at me and ushered us in to the kitchen where we sat around her little table. Amelia took a seat by Rain and smiled at me "nice to see you Lily who's your friend?" I smiled slightly about to answer when Rain spoke first.

"My name is Rain...my mother was Alice." Amelia looked at Rain and stared hard at her in the eye. She stayed like that for a while, then, a small single tear formed in her eye and fell silently down her cheek. She reached for Rain and folded her into a gentle hug. "How is this possible?" Rain who had been squeezing tightly back and trying to hold in her tears spoke. "She met my dad years ago and had me, but I never got to meet her, she disappeared the day after I was born." Amelia pulled pack and stroked away the stray tears that fell on Rain's face. "She was always good at disappearing, but now I have a part of her back, because she's in you." And we stayed like that for a while. Amelia told us stories of when Alice was younger, and how prone she was to attract trouble. Rain soaked it all in as she had been deprived so long of her mother's memory and presence. Finally after a good few hours I spoke "Cole said that the king thought you might be able to find Alice using your gift through Rain." Amelia smiled gently at me as she held onto Rain's hand. "It's nice of your father to still believe in me but I am not strong enough anymore to use such power. But you Lily, you can." I stood up to place my mug into the sink, my tea had gone cold as I was too preoccupied to drink it when I was laughing at the tales she spoke of. "How can I do it?" Amelia took hold of my hand too.

"I will teach you." She looked at the clock and saw that time hadn't stopped but moved quite fast, night had already come. "You too should get home before it gets too dark. Lily you also need to go home, I know you don't want to but its time." She stood and hugged Rain then hugged me too. We promised to come back soon then we left.

Rain refused to let me walk her home so I was forced to leave her at the entrance to the wood and walk home. I had mixed feelings about going home, such as not being able to figure out what the hell was going on. However I missed home, I missed the sound of Leah's breathing dulling me to sleep. Or the sound of Leo and dads laugh when they were watching something funny on the telly. I even missed the smell of burnt food emanating from the kitchen. Before I knew it, I stood in front of my house. It still looked the same which was comforting. I opened the door and felt the warmth of the fire and the smell of fresh febreeze. The TV hummed in the background.

Dad stepped out of the living room, his hand gripped the frame to support his weight. He looked at me. Stood straight, let go of the wall and opened his arms to me. I went to him and hugged him like I had always hugged him. He had given up his support to give it to me, he had always been strong, and this time he held me up when I was ready to fall down.

Cole

I remember my mother once telling me that we have two reflections, one you see in the mirror and one you see in yourself. Right now I looked at my reflection in the mirror that hangs by my bedroom door. I see a tall skinny pale boy whose eyes I didn't even recognise anymore. Becoming a protector had changed me. Only a few months ago I looked in the mirror and saw a boy, now I saw someone who wasn't quite a man but was closer to that than a boy. When had I aged? That was the person I saw in the mirror. The person I saw inside of me was different. He was stronger, better than the weak pale figure in the glass. He was the me I wanted to be, and that was the difference. I finally understood it now. The person I saw on the outside doesn't have to be me, and the person on the inside is the true reflection of me.

Rain came through the door distracting me from my thoughts. She looked lighter as she came and sat down on my bed. Her eyes no longer held a sombre glint but a shine I hadn't seen before. She smiled at me, but I couldn't managed one back. "Heard anything of Sophie?" My mother had been missing for a whole twenty four hours that's one thousand four hundred and forty minutes, and still nothing. "Nothing, how was Amelia's?" Rain beamed at me, and began telling me about how wonderful she was, about the stories she told. I let her speak because for once she was happy, and despite everything that was going on it made me happy that she had found some light to cling to.

Lily

That night my parents sat me down and explained about my past. Explained how they didn't know where I had come from, didn't know who I was. It was then I realised I had been too harsh on them. None of this was their fault. I hugged them both tight before retreating back to my room. The letter mum had given me before I had left that night felt heavy in my back pocket. Carmen said if I wasn't ready to open it then there was always tomorrow, but tomorrow never truly comes. Leo was with Maria and Leah was at ballet which meant I had the privacy and space to open the letter alone.

Nervously I began to peel open the aged crinkled paper. Before I could reach inside I remembered what Lucas had said only open it when I was ready. Was I ready? The answer was yes. As the days passed and I discovered more of my past I came to realise that I have accepted this along the way, and if I wanted the whole truth then I need not be afraid, but be brave and listen. Inside the envelope lay another letter.

To my dearest child,

Firstly I wish to apologise for the absence I will have in your life. You see it was only a few days before I was due to give birth to you did I realise I was gravely ill. It was an illness that swept through me like a storm. It was then that I knew I would not be strong enough to survive it. It is why I leave you this letter, words cannot describe the love I feel for you and will carry on feeling for you even in death. I know you will be strong and brave just like your father, and hopefully as kind and caring as my own father. I know you will be beautiful and become a great and noble ruler, who is fair and just to your people. I also know you to be special, to be gifted with the gift of dreams and visions, and in this gift I know you will find your true love, who will protect and love you for

eternity. But I also know you to be in danger, your father I am sure will have come up with a plan to keep you safe. I hope that you are like him, for he is the best person I had ever met. I also leave you one last thing, a secret. On the back of this letter is a map. If you are ever lost or in trouble and have no one you can trust then follow this map. It will lead you to my homeland, where my family waits for you, to help and guide you. I hope one day we get to meet but I wish that day be when you have lived a happy and extensive life. Please forgive me for leaving you like this, if there had been another way I would have certainly taken it, to at least know you and hold you at least once, I am sorry.
With all the love I possess,
Your mother, Alana.
P.S if you ever need a quick getaway use the pendent, hold it and picture the place you wished to go.

I felt the tears as they trailed down my cheeks, the pendent hung heavy around my neck. A reminder that it's still there. I then whispered out loud "I forgive you." Then I felt my heart break just a little bit.

Cole

I lay in bed that night, staring at my white ceiling. Listening to Skyla cry quietly in her room. Listening to Rain comfort her when I couldn't, felt Lily's sadness as though it was my own. I felt so hopeless. I had no idea where my mother was. The only clue she had left me was a vague dream about me and Lily being the only ones who could find her, but how? I also felt hopeless because Lily was at home and upset and I didn't know how to comfort her. How can you be there for someone when you need someone to be there for you? There was a knock on my door, looking up I saw Carmen and Jett enter my room and close the door behind them. Both wore matching sympathetic expressions. "How are you Cole?" It was Carmen's gentle voice and soothing vibes that consumed the silent room. I heard Jett punch her in the arm slightly before whispering "what a stupid question Carmen!" I sat up so I could look at them both properly. Carmen hadn't changed since the last time I saw her, she still remained trapped in her pre-teen body and childlike expression. Whereas Jett seemed to change every time I saw him, he had grown taller, his hair darker. His face started to thin out losing its childlike chubbiness. "It isn't a stupid question, I don't know how I am, I feel so hopeless here." Carmen came and sat by me. Placing her comforting hand upon mine filling me with her soothing power. "It's why I and Jett came, we already spoke to Rain to see if it was okay with her to stay with Skyla while we leave." I frowned at them both, so Jett filled in the information I was lacking. "We three are going to do our own search, the others are in Ever and the wood, so I thought we would look in town, somewhere not supernatural." I liked their thinking, if my mother had been kidnapped then her attacker would have taken her somewhere that was inconspicuous. Evergreen was definitely that. "Okay let's go."

I made sure Rain had my mobile number before I left just in case of an emergency. If we were to look in town it meant we wouldn't be able to shift into our wolf forms, but that was okay. I was a protector now and my senses were always on overdrive.

We searched all over Evergreen and still we came up with nothing. It was late when we went our separate ways. Instead of going home I went to Amelia's house. I don't know why, but I felt compelled to go there for some reason. The sky turned thunderous and the heavens opened up releasing a waterfall of rain that soaked me in seconds. I jogged the rest of the way to Amelia's. When I arrived I was about to knock when I heard voices from inside. Slipping away from the door I made my way over to the kitchen window. Inside I saw Amelia standing by the doorway staring down a man whose back was to me. The way he stood was familiar, as was his dark hair and pale skin. I heard his voice vibrate through the glass to my hearing, and I was suddenly filled with dread. "I told you what would happen if you didn't comply!" My father's voice seemed not to effect Amelia in the same way it affected me. Amelia stared hard at him in the eye, something I had never been able to do. "I will not help you with this, now get out of my house. We both know someone will be here to check on things and you wouldn't want to be caught again would you James!" Again? When had my father been here before? I could tell from the way he shifted his feet that he was smiling at her. In his cold and uneasy way. "I will leave this for now Amelia, but I am not a patient person. You will follow my orders next time or else she gets it!" Quickly moving to hide behind the large hedge type bushes that stood by the door I held my breath so he wouldn't hear me breathing as he came out the door. He stepped out and the rain began hitting him too. I hoped the smell of the rain would mask my scent from him, he sniffed the air. My heart bagged heavily in my chest. I begged it to stop so he wouldn't hear it. Frowning slightly he turned on his heel and fleeted the way I had come. I waited a few minutes before stepping out from my hiding place. I checked the coast was clear before letting myself into Amelia's.

I was barely through the door when I felt something hard hit me in the back Amelia's voice screamed at me "come back to taunt me, you've only just left!" Swinging quickly around to avoid another blow I held my hands up in surrender "shhh Amelia it's me." Amelia's wild gaze softened and the frying pan in her hand was lowered. She patted me softly on the shoulder "sorry Cole I thought you was..."
"My father." I finished for her. She nodded slightly at me and led me into the living room. She directed me to a seat and left the room for a minute. I looked around at the room, it was quite modern in light beige. She re-entered with an ice pack in her hand. She took a seat next to me and placed the pack on the side of my neck where she had wacked me with her kitchen utensil. "You heard us then, and sorry for hitting you it's just that...your father drives me up the wall!" I smiled ruefully, I knew the feeling. "Amelia what was my father doing here, what did he mean when he said you better do it this time or she gets hurt?" Amelia sighed next to me. She looked at me deflated, as though she had been putting up a fight and now had finally been defeated. "First of all there's something you need to understand. Your father has always had two vendettas in life. One was to find his mate which he did in your mother Sophie, and two was to find power." I shifted in my seat so I could look her in the eye, it would make it easier to see if she was lying. "Power?" She removed the ice pack from the back of my neck, it was numb now. "Your father has always been power hungry. We initially thought that if he became pack leader that would suffice, but we were wrong."
"Who's the we?" There was silence for a moment then she spoke very carefully "me and the king". When had she spoken to the king? "I don't understand." She stood up from her seat and went to stand by the back door. She looked out the window searching for anyone who could have ears on the walls. "It was back when you were first born, your father began to change his priorities for the welfare of humans, and he no longer

cared about using the pack for good. He was planning to overthrow the king."

"What!" I too stood, sitting down was not helping my sudden unease. She turned and looked at me. I didn't like the sympathy in her eyes, it meant she knew something. Something I didn't want her to know about me. "But I managed to convince him, change him for a while, but only if I found something for him. I promised to look and for a few years my promise worked...until six years ago when he became impatient with me and changed once again." More unease crept through my veins. It seemed everything came back to that day, that year. When my dreams stopped, when I met Lily, when I realised for the first time my father was a monster, when I left. "So that's why he came here to ask you to look again" she nodded at me slightly. "But who was he threatening?" Her gaze returned back through the window her mind far away. "The same person he threatened me with all those years ago" I looked at her hard "Lily." My heart stopped.

Lily

I was in Amelia's house. It looked the same but didn't feel the same letting me know I was in a dream not reality. She stood by her small oak table a photo frame in her hand. The frame held a picture of a little brown haired girl being chased by a handsome man, their smiles were captured perfectly in the shot. "I miss you both you know." She spoke quietly to herself. There was a small knock on the door drawing both of our attentions away from the photo. Amelia made her way out of the kitchen into her hallway that led to the front door. Pulling open the door I saw someone I hadn't anticipated to turn up here. It was James, Cole's father. He looked younger than he did now, more approachable. In his arms was a small dark pale baby boy, who I could only guess to be Cole. "James come in." She smiled carefully and allowed him to step through the door. James let her take Cole out of his arms so she could cradle him. She smiled brightly down at his little face, his bright blue irises shined back at her. "You know why I'm here Amelia." Amelia looked over at James who stood by the door, his eyes were darker than before she let him in. "I can't help you James." He glared at her.

"You promised me you could find her!" His shout vibrated through the house causing Cole to cry, she comforted him while keeping an eye on James. "All I can promise is that I will try, I am not as powerful as I once was." Quick as lightening James was in front of Amelia staring intimidatingly down at her, he took Cole from her arms. "You will more than try or that little princess you've grown fond of will get it!" She stood up and challenged him with her own stare.

"You wouldn't dare touch Lily, because of the prophecy, where your son's life is intertwined with hers!" She pointed at Cole who stared back at her with an innocent face.

"If it comes down to it, I will!" And before I knew it he was out of the door, Cole with him.

I woke with a start, sweat dripped down my spine. The clock read seven thirty. I had fallen asleep after reading the letter but that was an hour ago. The dream clung to me, strangling me. What prophecy? Why is my life connected to Cole's? Who was James searching so hard for?

I got back out of bed and began pacing out my unease, releasing some of my anxiety into the carpet. I pulled out my phone. It rang for a moment before he answered. "Lily what's wrong?" Cole's voice was comforting but this was no time to be comforted. "I had a dream. Your father was threatening Amelia and she mentioned something else." He was deadly silent for a moment then his voice came through the speaker. "What did she mention?"

"That there's a prophecy and it's about you and me."

Cole

I had been leaving Amelia's when Lily had called, which meant I only had to detour my path to get to her house. After talking to Amelia I had fallen asleep on her sofa, when I woke in the morning I found a blanket carefully swung over me and Amelia in her own bed. I left quietly so I wouldn't wake her.

I had barely knocked on the door when it swung open and she hurriedly pulled me inside. Then still holding my arm she dragged me upstairs and into her bedroom. She leant on the door looking slightly distressed. "Lily are you okay?" She looked at me. Her normally bright blue eyes were dark and sleep deprived. Her light blonde hair was displaced around her face from where she had fallen asleep. She shook her head, and I folded her into my arms. Her voice was muffled in my shirt. "Have you heard anything from your mum?" I kept her in my arms, finding comfort in her embrace. "No but I had a dream." She pulled back so she could look at me.

"What did you see?" I sat down on the bed closest to me, and she followed suit.

"I dreamt of her. She was chained in a dark room, she was smiling at me. She asked me to find her, I asked how and she said I needed you, that it had always been me and you...then she disappeared and the dream ended." Lily listened quietly and furrowed her eyebrow at the end, indicating she was thinking. "Maybe she was speaking about the prophecy. Amelia said mine and your life was intertwined somehow, maybe that's what your mum meant." Then a sudden thought occurred to me. I was confused at why it hadn't occurred to me before. "Lily I have to go somewhere, I think I know where I can gets some answers, but I need to go alone." Her blue gaze looked scared and worried. "Where are you going Cole?" I took her hand, it was warm against my skin.

"I need to go and see the king, I know you're not ready to see him yet which is why I must go alone." She nodded at me agreeing.

"Okay but be careful, and call me as soon as your back!" I quickly kissed her forehead, which made her smile. "I promise."

Reaching the wood I shifted quickly. Ever Green faded swiftly into Ever, which swiftly faded to the castle doors. I shifted enough to knock on the door, and like before it was Gwen who answered. She smiled peacefully down at me and allowed me passage through the doors. "Ahh Cole, long time no see, here let me grab you a cloak." She disappeared for a few moments and returned with a billowing ruby velvet cloak, she wrapped it around me so I could shift. "Thank you Gwen." I smiled once I had lost my muzzle. "You're welcome, come I have informed the king of your arrival." We walked the all too familiar corridors until I reached the throne room, where Gwen abandoned me. Inside the stormy grey walls the king awaited me with a kind smile. "Cole nice to see you again, you have come to tell me something I expect." Stepping forward I spoke.

"Yes your majesty, I come to tell you that me and Lily know that there is a prophecy about us." The king stopped smiling.

Lily

It wasn't long after Cole had left that Leah entered the room. At first she didn't seem to notice me sitting on my bed, but then she turned and looked at me as though she didn't recognise me. "Lily is that you?" I came and stood in front of her. My little sister. Whose expression I didn't recognise, she was wary of me. I knelt down on my knees to make myself smaller. "It's me Leah, I haven't been gone that long, surely you haven't forgotten me already." She didn't smile, instead she backed cautiously away from me. "Why are you here?" Confused I tried to take her hand but she flinched when I went near her. "Because this is my home." She shook her head furiously at me.

"No home is where family is, and you're not...family." A tear began to roll down her cheek. Sadness began to choke me. "Leah I am your family, I'm your sister." More tears rolled down her cheeks, but she wouldn't let me comfort her. "No you're not, I heard you, arguing with mum and dad, your adopted and then you left." I went to grab her again but she screamed at me. "No don't touch me, I don't know who you are!" I too began to cry.

Mum burst into the room. She assessed the scene with her doctor gaze before going to Leah and taking her in her arms. Her choice pricked my heart. "What's going on in here, why are you both crying?" Leah buried her face into mum's shirt not answering her. I wiped the tears from my cheeks and stared blankly at mum. "Leah thinks because I'm adopted I'm not family. I tried to hug her and she screamed, she says she doesn't know me anymore." Mum looked deeply at me, waiting for me to show some emotion. Except she couldn't find it, I had locked it away. She turned to Leah and kissed her red hair. "Leah, Lily's your sister you know that." Leah shook her head against mum's chest. "No she's not." I took a breath and stood up and made my way to the door, mums voice halted me. "Where are you going?" I turned and looked at her, saw the way she held Leah, the way she had comforted her. She had automatically assumed that the situation was my fault, that it was I that hurt Leah instead of the other way around. "Out I can see where I'm not wanted." I didn't wait for her response. Amelia was wrong, coming home was a massive mistake.

I had almost made it to the front door, almost. "So you're leaving again, and it never occurred to you that I might want to see you." I turned to see Leo descending the stairs. He still looked the same but his face held a fatigue that wasn't there before. "Thought you might react the same way as Leah." He stepped off the bottom step so he was directly in front of me.

"Lily it doesn't matter to me if you're not biologically my sister, what matters is that you're hurting and there's nothing I can do about it. I can't understand what you're going through, all I know is that I want to be there for you, like I've always been there for you. I want to be your big brother." Tears began to slip from my eyes, dam it my emotions are betraying me. The first tear hadn't yet had chance to fall from my cheek before he had me in a hug. "Lil I'm sorry about Leah, and I'm sorry that you're hurting. She doesn't understand, not really." I sniffed and pulled back.

"It's not just that Leo its mum, she came in and went to comfort Leah first, before asking what was going on. And even when she found out, she made no move to comfort me." Leo looked sadly at me. His sympathy wasn't comforting. I backed away from him so my hand had hold of the door handle. He frowned at me looking hurt. "You're not actually leaving again are you, you've only just come back. We can talk about this, we can explain to Leah." I shook my head. I knew I wasn't ready to come home. "No Leo I can't stay somewhere I don't belong." Knowing he would surely stop me, I pushed quickly down on the door handle and threw myself out the door, leaving it hanging open. He watched as I ran away.

Cole

The king was utterly expressionless and speechless. For once I had caught him off guard. He blinked and suddenly he was back in the present. "I'm sorry but did I just hear you correct, you and my daughter know of the prophecy?" I nodded my head at him and he sunk into his throne. "We don't know what it's about, we just know there is one." The king narrowed his eyes at me for a moment, then smiled carefully. "So that is why you are here, to ask me about it?" I nodded. The king then stood from his throne and walked to the oversized window that framed the perfect roaring ocean. "I cannot tell you, only those who have the ability to see and understand prophecies can tell you." I frowned at his back, and from the way he moved his shoulders I could tell he could feel my confusion burn into him, like an accusation. "And where do I find them?" He turned back round so he was looking at me. "I thought as a protector you would have known, but it is obvious you don't otherwise you would not have asked." He paused to make sure I was listening. Which I was, even when I think I'm not listening, I'm listening. "You and Lily must go together as the prophecy is about you both. You must go to the land of the faeries or as it is known the land of Keva. There you will find your answer to your question." Something screamed inside of me, that whatever the prophecy was it wasn't good, otherwise the king would be smiling right now, instead of looking shocked. "May I ask you one more question your majesty?" The king nodded cautiously. "Christmas day you and my father were discussing something at the table. He asked you to tell me something." The kings pale eyebrows rose, as I waited for him to answer I began to see resemblances in his appearance and expression, that I often saw in Lily. The blonde hair, the blue eyes, the way his eyebrow furrows when he's thinking, the way his smile comes so easy to his face, is so like her. "You wish me to tell you what he wanted me to tell you?" I nodded.

"He asked me to tell you because he said it would be unlikely that you would believe him, that you would be wary of trusting him. Before I answer your question I would like to ask one of my own. How come you are wary of your father?" This was not how I imagined this conversation going. I gulped. "Let's just say we have a strained relationship." He sat back in his throne, looking intrigued and concerned. "And why is that?" If he hadn't been the king I would have said, you only asked for one question. But because he was I bit my tongue. "We disagree on things, or I have done things in the past that have angered him." The king leant forward. His piercing blue eyes searing through me, making me as transparent as a glass jar, except he didn't realise how close to the shelf edge I was. His last question knocked my glass jar from the shelf, shattering my strong glassy shield and exposing my darkest secret. "And did he ever lay a hand on you Cole, I mean did he ever intentionally harm you?" The years of pain and hate and anguish bubbled to the surface, letting one single tear flow from my eye. "Yes." Is all I could manage.

Then the king surprised me even further, by abandoning his throne and pulling me into a hug. His hug worked like magic, I felt control of my emotions again. He pulled back from me but kept his hands on my arms, he looked me directly in the eye. "There is no better man than the man that can stand in front of a near enough stranger, and reveal his heart, and there is no lower of a man who can stand back and watch his own child hurt by their own hand!" His voice held a fierce affliction, and I was suddenly more grateful for being here for this moment that the truth he had revealed to me earlier. "James wanted me to tell you something I cannot tell you, he didn't understand that there are some things that can only be revealed when the time is right. But I can tell you this that six years ago the day you saw my daughter, the day that you left, a connection was made between you both that connects you both together forever. As the years have gone on and circumstances have changed, that bond has been hidden beneath you both, and has now finally started to awaken, I know deep down you know what you feel, there's no denying it. Which means if you thought hard enough you already know your answer." He let go of me, and instead of feeling cold when his warmth left me, I felt as though I was on fire. All the times I had questioned why me and Lily hadn't bonded, at first I thought it was because of Reeve, but I was wrong. All those years ago, the tug that brought me to her, the tingle I felt in my veins, wasn't the anticipation of being seen by a human. No. it was the promise of finding something you don't find every day. It was our bond. We had bonded there on the side of the road. Her soul attached itself to mine, and we didn't even know it.

Lily

I was just wandering the streets when I heard hurried footsteps coming behind me. I swung round to face them, but was instead swung around in the air, by a pair of pale but strong arms, his tattoo glimmering under the night sky,' we keep the stars' in whatever language it was. I laughed and he finally put me down. I looked at him and his pale face was practically glowing. "I guess you found some answers." He nodded, but instead of telling me he stepped closer, he framed my face with his hands and pulled me into a kiss. This kiss was different than before it was full of love and hope, it vanquished all thoughts of home from my mind, leaving me in this moment. When he pulled away he smiled brightly down at me. "I have two things to tell you, the first thing is that, the king told me we both have to go to Keva, which is the land of the faeries to hear the prophecy, because it's about us both." I carried on looking at his face, so happy that something had put a smile on his face, and elevated his spirit a bit. "So what's the second thing?" He bent down and kissed my forehead before stepping back to give me room to breathe. "Six years ago when we first saw each other, what did you feel when you saw me?" I thought back to that day and remember my scorching headache. I remembered his eyes meeting mine and feeling a spark then I felt drained. "I felt like you were taking something from me." His light blue eyes glimmered beneath the stars. He was still smiling. "That's because I did, I took part of your soul and you took apart of mine. We bonded Lily and we didn't even know it." I gasped. It all made sense now. Why I couldn't get his image out of my head, why that despite trying to love Reeve I was always drawn to something more. Because deep down I knew, I had just forgotten. I smiled back at him, and laughed as he spun me around once more. "Your mine Lil and I yours!" I giggled and kissed his lips.
"Forever."

We walked hand in hand on our way in to the woods. We decided that we better go visit the faeries now instead of tomorrow, what was the point if neither of us was going to sleep. I called Amelia. After finding out that after all this time me and Cole had bonded, there was a question burning inside of me. "Do you remember telling me that you knew me and Cole would bond one day, but that we hadn't already?"
"Yes dear." Her voice was a lot softer and fragile over the phone.

"Well me and Cole already have bonded" before I could continue she butted in.

"Yes I know, you bonded six years ago. I only told you that so you could have hope, and also to keep you safe. There are some people you don't want to know that you've bonded."

"Why?" She sighed into the speaker making it vibrate against my ear, I hate when she does that.

"Because there are some people who want to kill you Lily and the easiest way to do that is to kill Cole. If your bond is that strong by killing Cole you will die to."

"Oh." Another sigh.

"Exactly, now if that's all I would like to go to bed. Rain is coming over tomorrow which means you need to be there too, if we have any hope of finding Alice. Be here at ten o clock and bring something sweet, it's been two days since the nurse left something which means if you don't I'll be cranky and you know what I'm like when I'm cranky." Yes I do Amelia yes I do.

"Okay night."

"Goodnight my dear" then the line went dead.

By now we were deep into the forest, I no longer knew where I was. "In about thirty seconds you will pass through the shield and see Ever for the first time." Heart pounding I gripped Coles hand more tightly. I prepared myself to feel something as I passed through the shield, but I felt nothing. The only difference was the sudden change in scenery. We were no longer in the quiet lush wood, but a bustling quaint village, where the scent of sea salt tickled my nose. I looked around completely at awe of the place. It was beautiful, stuck in a time where electricity and modern technology didn't exist. It was refreshing. "Come on Lil we don't want anyone to see you just yet." He began to pull me eastwards, towards the greener parts of Ever.

"Would people really recognise me?" Cole was scanning the paths that led in different directions. He was reading the signs that were in a different language. "Yes, you look so much like them it would be obvious." I knew who he obviously meant by them, my true birth parents, who I had seen in my dreams. He tugged my hand and pulled me down the path that was left.

The quaint see side town faded into the distance, as we sank into a growing countryside. We followed a golden brown path that was narrowed between two green meadows that bedded blush and blue roses. They seemed strange as they sparkled under the moonlight. We had been walking for a while before Cole abruptly stopped as though he had hit a brick wall. He rubbed his head. "Crap I forgot about the shields!" I reached out into the space and felt nothing.

"What shield?" Cole carried on rubbing his head, there was a red patch where he must have hit the imaginary wall. "Each part of Ever has a shield protecting it, it offers protection for the creatures who live inside. Because I'm a wolf I cannot enter without permission." He dropped his hand from his head and flicked his gaze to me "but you can, you're a shadow which means you can enter any of them." I pointed at the vacant space that lay ahead of us, and focused him with a bewildered expression. "You want me to go in there on my own!" He nodded at me.

"Yes so you can find someone to let me in." I gulped suddenly more nervous than before. I smiled weakly at him, before stepping forward, before I could take another step he stopped me. "But whatever you do, be polite, faeries are easily offended." I nodded at him. Breathing in, I stepped through the shield.

Cole and the meadows faded out behind me and I was left in a dark glowing wood. The trees that surrounded me glowed with a fluorescence I had never seen before. Their barks were embedded with glowing gems that twinkled under the cloudless sky. Golden gems glowed as I stepped further into the wood, illuminating my path. The smell of flowers and autumn was trapped here, clouding around me. The sound of laughter and birds echoed between the sparkling branches. "Hello is anyone here?" I called out, hoping I no longer had to be alone. The laughter and the birds stopped, leaving me in silence. Then a voice appeared from behind me. "Welcome Princess we are happy for your visit." I turned around to see a tall woman in front of me. She was deathly pale but had an otherworldly glow surrounding her, her glowing gold eyes twinkled at me. I smiled politely. "And I thank you for allowing me passage, may I ask you to invite my friend in?" The woman smiled and nodded her head. She closed her eyes, then Cole appeared through the shield. He looked at the woman and smiled gratefully at her. "Thank you for allowing me through." She nodded at him. Then held her hand to me and him. As she did I noticed the same black italic tattoo Cole had on his fore arm except the words were different. 'Mundus facit pulchellus'. Immediately I wanted to know what it meant, but her outstretched hand seemed more important. We knew we had to take her hand, not wanting to offend her. Her hand felt like nothing. It felt as though I had grasped air out of the atmosphere. "Please the Queen is waiting for you. My name is Ember I am the Queens only daughter, and you are the lost Princess and you her wolf mate." She addressed us as though she knew us, but it wouldn't surprise me everyone knows more about me than me. "I thought the Queen had many children?" Ember lifted the side of her mouth a little, indicating she was amused. "She has many sons, like I said I am her only daughter." Cole didn't ask anymore instead we were led hand in hand with Ember further into the wood. My intrigue in her tattoo soon enough became too much for me "if you don't mind me asking Ember, but what does your tattoo mean?" Her golden eyes flickered in my direction for a moment before they resumed their gaze on the path ahead. "Like your mates mark, it is a symbol for what we are. My mark identifies me as a faerie, but the words mean 'the world makes us pretty, for we live amongst nature which helps enhance our very beings." So, all the supernatural beings have their own mark like Cole and even Lexi as I remembered her mark. "That makes sense actually, because faeries absorb the nature around them for energy to keep you alive right?" Ember seemed impressed that Cole knew that faeries did that, and maybe a little disappointed that I didn't. Her faith in her princess seemed to be lacking. "Yes Cole you are correct that is what we do."

Soon we reached a clearing, where a throne sat with matching gems from the trees and the same fluorescence as their leaves. Sat there was the woman I had been dreaming about for the past six months. The glowing lady with a willowy figure, her dress, her face and her eyes were the same as seen in my dream. She stood when we neared. She regarded me with her clear eyes, before smiling. Ember let go of our hands. "I'm glad you have finally found me Lily, we have much to discuss."

Cole

I stared at the Queen who directly addressed Lily. How did the faerie Queen know Lily, and why did she want her to find her. I glanced at Lily who smiled numbly back, the Queen flicked her transparent gaze to me. "Ah I see you also brought your mate, you must be Cole Star. To answer your question everyone of Ever knows of Lily, but I personally know her because I frequently came to her in her dreams." She could hear inside my head? She laughed out loud, the sound made me feel weird inside, because it wasn't quite natural. "Yes Cole I can hear your thoughts." Great. Lily flinched suddenly, her phone had begun to ring in her back pocket. How did we even get signal out here? The Queen smiled at her "answer it Lily I do not mind." Lily looked unsure as she pulled the phone out and pressed the answer button. She moved back out of the clearing for privacy.

The Queen's gaze found me once again. Her eyes were making me feel uncomfortable. "You came here to seek the prophecy about you both, and I shall give it to you, but for a price. Lily has already promised me something now it is your turn. You must have figured that nothing is free in this world, or any world for that matter." I shifted my feet.
"What can I offer you, your majesty?" The Queen then opened her hands and against her pale glowing skin was a ring. It was a dull silver band with a glowing emerald sat within it. She offered it to me, and I took it. "I want you to wear this ring, never take it off. That is your promise to me." I slid the ring onto my finger, it was cold and heavy. "May I ask why?" The Queen shook her head at me. "No because it is not my secret to tell, one day you will find out, and one day you may even thank me for it." Before she could say anymore Lily had returned to my side. She looked at me as though she wanted to ask what was going on but knew it probably wouldn't make any sense. "Now that you're both here might as well get on with why you are here. Please Lily Cole stand in the centre of the clearing and hold hands." She waved us into the middle. Lily took hold of my hand, just as more faeries started to appear.

Lily

More glowing faeries appeared at the clearing. They began circling us, holding hands with their neighbours. The floor began glowing gold. Wait I've seen this before. My dream, I had dreamt standing hand in hand with Cole in a golden circle. People chanting. "Cole I've dreamt this before". He squeezed my hand. "It's okay Lil, their channelling each other's power to recall the prophecy." The Queen then stepped into the circle, her dress dazzling me. "Are you ready to remember Lily?" I looked at her "remember what your majesty?" The Queen smiled, her smile made her face glow even more, I had to squint to see her. "Everything. You see Lily, the prophecy was made by you, it was your dream, now it is time for you to remember." She fell silent just as pain seared into my mind.

Flash, a pretty woman with stormy grey eyes looked at me, her smile was breath taking. I could feel her love for me as though she was feeding it into me. Flash, a fair man with sad eyes kissed my soft golden curls, tears stained his cheeks "I will find you again my little Lily, and we will be together again, I love you." The man passed the baby on to a woman with greying hair and blue eyes. Flash, the older lady looked into the baby's eyes, "show me Lily." I then fell further into the darkness, and the pain began to clog in my throat.

She who is born of earth and sky will reconnect the world, and balance out the evil. But she will not go it alone, she must have her own balance, the one who keeps her on the path towards the light, her soul mate. Both who grow stronger together. But evil lies close to both of them, hidden beneath the surface.
Flash, "So it is you."
I couldn't breathe.

I gasped as I was yanked back into reality. I dropped Coles hand so I could squeeze my head, I wanted the radiating pain to stop. I could hear voices around me. "Can someone help her?" Cole was worried, I wanted to tell him I would be okay. Another voice entered the painful space inside my mind. "The past hurts Lily. But to heal it you first need to forgive it." "Why do I need to forgive my past?" Her hand reached out and cooled my pain away with his touch. "Because there's someone in your past you haven't yet forgiven, and whether you know it or not, it's causing you pain." The Queen's voice disappeared along with the pain, and I found myself back in the clearing. Cole looked as though he was about to have a fit. "I'm fine." He nodded slightly at me before turning to the Queen.

"When Lily was just a year old, she saw that both her and your life would be intertwined. Because one day you two will be our saviours."
"And what are we supposed to be saving you from?" The Queen sat down in her throne, and Ember took hold of our hands again, it was time to leave. "You will find out soon, and all I can say is that I'm sorry for when you do." We both left confused. Why would she be sorry? The Queen from what I heard of from the stories Amelia used to tell us when we were little was an emotionless ruler. Strict on her people and regarded her children as mere nuisances. Constant reminders of the many consorts she had taken over the years. Yet, she had regarded us both with some emotion, which meant that whatever was coming, it was bad.

Ember lead us out of the fluorescent forest back to the edge of the shield. She bowed her head to both me and Cole. "It was nice to finally meet you, your highness and you Cole." We smiled at her and told her it was nice to meet her too. Then we stepped out, and once again was surrounded by fields and roses.

Cole

When we made it back into the forest of Ever Green Lily turned to me. "It was Sky on the phone earlier. She wants me to stay at her house tonight, because she says she found something."
"What has she found?" She shrugged her shoulders.
"Have no idea, but I better go especially if I have to see Amelia tomorrow." I nodded.
"I'll bring Rain to Sky's before school, if we're both out of school it looks more suspicious, anyway I need to talk to Jett. He's been avoiding me." She quickly hugged me and ran the rest of the way through the wood. She seemed a bit off since coming back from seeing the fairies. I hoped nothing about the prophecy was bothering her, it was enough to say we were bonded, but soul mates? Pretty sure I wouldn't blame her if she had started freaking out a little bit. I walked slowly home, unravelling the tension in my muscles. I needed to shift more, my wolf was more restless than it was before I received my protector's mark.

When I reached home, I sensed that everyone was asleep, except Dad who had spent the past two nights out looking for my mother. For once in the past six months my bed actually looked inviting. I went to it, and fell soundly asleep.

Lily

I loved Cole, I knew that. There had always been a part of me that knew that. Now with the official stamp of the wolf bond between us, I felt different. My feelings hadn't faltered but a part of me that thought maybe one day I would grow up leave Ever Green behind and marry someone who had never lived here was gone. Instead forever had been laced into my heart the moment I caught sight of his piercing blue eyes. Reality of my situation slapped me in the face as though it was mocking me. But did I really mind? Did I really want to spend my whole life looking for a love that wasn't real, a love that would get me hurt in the end? My answer was no. I wanted a love where I had someone special, someone who stood by my side always. Someone who believed in me when I was ready to crash to the floor, and I guess you could say I found it. Cole was everything I had been looking for and I had left him behind with a brief hug and cold shoulder, because I hadn't been ready to let the thought of our forever sinking in. That thought nearly had me turning back to go to him, then I remembered Sky's urgent voice on the phone. I hurried my pace.

Sky was already waiting at the front door when I made my way up her neat stoned driveway, vacant of the expensive looking vehicles. I had barely reached her when she tugged me briskly through the door by the arm, slamming the door behind her. She looked worried. Her dark hair had been pulled up in a careless pony tail indicating to me that it was that way because she had been worrying and her hair had been getting in her way. She wore her baggy grey trousers and a baggy top, this was what was known as Sky's anxious outfit. When she was seriously worried about something she found herself in a baggy top and soft cottons she was wearing now. "Sky what's wrong?" She looked at me, her eyes startled as though she was a deer caught in the headlights. "Lexi was here." The name of our ex best friend slithered down my back as though it was a poisonous snake, waiting for the attack. I hugged her to me, letting her silently cry on my shoulder. "She came to give me something, that's why I asked you here." She let go of me and removed her bloodshot eyes from my face to the kitchen table where a large old fashioned, leather bound book lay against the marble top. "She gave you a book?" Sky rubbed her eyes as we moved towards the table and took a seat, both of us cringing as the steel chairs squeaked against the marble flooring. "Yeah my mum had picked me up from dance and dropped me off before going back to work, I came in and there she was stood in the foyer looking as though I was the one who had just broken in." She smiled but not in a happy way, more of an ironic slightly annoyed way. "Anyway she didn't look me in the eye when she gave me the book, all she said was that it was the only answer she could give me, then she disappeared in front of my eyes." She tightened the bobble that held her hair in place before pushing the book closer to me. "So before I called you I decided to read it, most of it I don't understand it's in another language, but the parts I did are both interesting and slightly startling." I frowned at the book as I began to turn pages. The pages were old, the colour of toffee, they felt crisp under my fingertips. "What do you mean interesting and startling?" She smiled uneasily at me as I looked at her. "See for yourself." She pointed her finger at the page I had flipped to, and I suddenly knew what she meant.

On the page a woman stared back at me. Her face pale framed by long blonde curls. Her dark blue eyes stared back at me through the paper, her smile familiar. I looked at Sky who had been watching my reaction like a hawk. "Sky this drawing it…" she took my hand in hers and squeezed gently. "She looks like you, I know." My heart began to bang dangerously in my chest, as though the picture had made it go on overdrive, I felt like I was going to pass out. I breathed deeply before reading.

Thousands of years ago, on a day where the veil between Heaven and Earth is open to all those who are living and dead, stepped out the king of heaven. He came to Earth in search of a weapon that would help defeat his brother who had begun a rebellion against his rule. Instead found a woman, whose eyes and heritage intrigued him more than the weapon he had been seeking. The two in time had a child, he was as strong as the mountains he had been born to, and as handsome as the angel who conceived him. On his coming of age birthday he had to make a choice, become mortal, or leave to heaven where he would rule by his father's side. Instead he refused to give his power to the earth or sky and made his own purpose. He created a breed of humans who would protect him from the choice he had once escaped to make. These humans were known as Veil's, those who hold Heaven and Earth in their eyes. Those who had the speed and strength of the supernatural. Their only soul purpose was to protect the family the boy had decided to make for himself. But in such a spell he had to make a loop hole, a way that would make him one day make a decision, the day where he must choose to follow in his mothers or fathers footsteps. His loop hole was a girl. A daughter of his own line, a daughter born of Earth and sky, a daughter who dreamt of the supernatural world of both Heaven and Earth. A daughter who was strong, who was brave. A daughter who would one day accept her place too, and whatever she chose, he would choose too.

I blinked and suddenly I was back in the room, no longer swimming in the text I had been reading. The extract was about Silas, Serena and their son Storm. Sky looked at me with her big blue and brown eyes. *Those with heaven and earth in their eyes.* "Sky are you one of these beings that he created?" She closed her eyes to me, shutting out the reality of my words. I remember once hoping that I could keep Sky out of all this, now I realise I needed her here, and despite my attempts she would still be here because like me, like Cole, like Lexi she was linked to all of this, and there was no out running destiny. "I think I am, it makes sense why sometimes I feel so protective over you." She kept her eyes closed.
"Besides Dad never knew his true family, he was adopted when he was eight, so I maybe that's where I get it from." Sky's Dad like her had the same blue and brown eyes, and guarded smile.
"But wouldn't that make me linked to this bloodline if you're a Veil your purpose is to protect those of Storms bloodline." She smiled before opening her eyes again. She took the book from my hands and flipped to

the very last page. The page had been inked by italic writing, names were imprinted upon the brown paper. "You are linked Lily, look here's your mother's name" she pointed to a name near the bottom, *Alana Lily Greys*, the writing was smudged at the end as though someone had spilled water on it. I got a weird feeling in my chest as I read her name out loud, I felt as though a part of my heart reconnected. Then there underneath it was a name I might not have recognised a few months ago, but now it was clear to me who it was. *Lily Alana Amelia Ever.* Sky rubbed the name with her thumb. "I didn't know you had one middle name, let alone two." I shook my head, neither did I? I had always been just Lily Found.

My name stared back at me, a promise of the life that was waiting for me, a life I had been avoiding since I found out who I really was.

Looking at my name made me decide in that moment. No more running, no more avoiding. It was time I became the person I was born to be. In the morning me and Rain would go to Amelia's to find Alice. Then I would go to Cole and apologise for my blunt behaviour, then I would tell him to take me to my father. I knew I was ready now.

Cole

"Look at me Cole!" Amelia's voice was oddly quiet despite her shouting at me. She looked at me fiercely as though I was a danger to her. "I am listening." She huffed and placed her wrinkled hands on her hips. "I didn't say listen I said look!" But I was looking, then I figured it out. I was so good at looking as though I was paying attention, when really I was just spacing out. I focused, the picture changed. She no longer looked healthy and angry, but sad and empty. Her eyes no longer held the same spark as before. I reached for her "Amelia I don't understand." My hand touched her arm and she was freezing, my wolf recoiling at the scent of death. "The future isn't supposed to be understood Cole, merely observed and accepted. Life and death are the same, you are born into a life, you die and join another" she closed her eyes. "I had to accept that long ago, now

you do too." Then like death she disappeared into the abyss that was the unknown.

I jolted myself suddenly out of my dream, I had moved so quick that I didn't react quickly enough to catch myself before falling. The cold hard floor smashed into my head with a bang, an ache spread through my skull. The door opened and someone's hurried steps came to help me up. "Cole are you okay?" Her touch filled me with her sudden calm and I no longer felt angry at the floor for its brutal attack on my cranium. "Carmen what are you doing here?" I kept my voice quite. She came and sat by me as we both rested against the side of my bed. She sighed. "I needed to talk to you." I flicked my gaze to the clock that hung on my wall. 3:30 Am. Then I flicked my gaze to her. Her face was sullen and tired, she no longer held the tan of summer, her hair had darkened, no longer the golden highlights of before. She wore faded light blue jeans and an oversized jumper that I recognised as one of Reeve's. "What did you want to talk about?" She stood up from where she was sat, and wrapped her arms around her waist. She closed her eyes and I watched a tear fall from her closed eye. "Why is everything falling apart Cole, we were happy once weren't we?" There was a time when we had been all happy. Back when we were younger and our grandparents were alive. "We were happy once." She opened her eyes, then shook her head at me. "No we weren't, we were pretending like we are now!" She moved towards me and took my face in her hands, she looked me straight in the eye, her wolf challenging my own. I thought the move was quite bold for her. "Listen to me Cole, you can stop now. Stop pretending that the fact that Reeve leaving hasn't had an effect on you at all, that there isn't a part of you that wishes that it was you who had left. Don't pretend that the fact that Lily has accepted who she is as a princess and that you're afraid that in the end you will lose her. And definitely don't pretend that you aren't suspicious of your father's intentions since he decided he wanted to be a part of your life again. People don't change Cole!" I looked at her and wondered how she knew after all this time what was really going on. "How did you know about my...Dad?" She let go of my face and sat back, head bowed as though she was ashamed of herself. She shouldn't be she had only stated the truth of things. "The day you came back you were shot by someone." Flashes of the pain and the shooter fleeted into my mind. The shooters face had been hidden beneath the darkness that had surrounded us, I always thought it was a mere hunter, shooting down an animal he thought would fit on the vacant space by his stag head. "I was out walking that night just thinking when I saw him, saw you running." Another image came to me, a brown wolf came to my aid, her colouring a light brown with gold flecks. "It was you wasn't it, you came to help me." She nodded at me, glad I had made the link myself. "Yes I helped you, I managed to pull you home hoping you would be safe, but then I saw the man enter the house and place the gun on the kitchen table I couldn't believe what I saw. Cole the hunter was you're...Dad!" He had tried to be my father again, but that was a lie. The man had inflicted abuse on me for the past six years of my life. Then tried to kill me. The hope that maybe he had been telling the truth hurt more than anything, because I had let myself believe that the impossible was possible. That my father would give up being a power hungry monster who didn't care who he hurt, to be a man of honour and love like his father had been. I wanted to cry, but I wouldn't. I wouldn't let myself cry over a man who had destroyed my life, and was now trying in some way to destroy others. I would stop him. "He saw me bring you back, so he got his own back. I was coming back from patrol, Jett had just left for home when he had entered the clearing. He pulled out a gun and shot me in the leg, just like he had done with you." By now she was crying tears that poured down her cheeks like an endless water fall. "He then pointed the gun at my head...and...he said if I told anyone what he had done to you then...this bullet would go in my head." I pulled her too me and let her cry. She sobbed inconsolably on my shoulder. How long had she kept quite? How long had she had to suffer? "Cole we need to find your mother, I have a very bad feeling her disappearance has something to do with him."

Lily

Sky glumly got ready for school the next morning. It seemed odd for her to do something so mundane despite the fact that we were in the craziest situation ever. I never knew why I hadn't noticed it before. Granted I didn't know the legends about Storms protectors but their personality was evident in Sky. For one the fact that she was going to school despite everything showed that her loyalty wasn't just to me, but to our other friends too, who were unbelievably still unaware of the weirdness that was surrounding them. She went to school not because she thought she might learn something, or afraid she might miss out on the hot new gossip. She went because there was danger lurking behind every corner, our enemies strived in our weaknesses and at school where our closest friends are, our enemies can expose those weaknesses. So she goes.

"Are you sure you're going to be alright at school, I mean Lexi could just pop up there?" Sky looked at me and smiled with a glint in her eye that I hadn't seen before. "I'll be fine, besides if I am what that book says I am then I'll be fine." I rolled my eyes and hugged her tight. As Sky left for school I walked to the opening of the forest where Rain stood waiting for me. Alone. "Where's Cole?" We began walking in the direction of Amelia's house. Rain smiled guiltily at me. "Well last night Carmen came by and they talked, I don't really know what they said but this morning he wasn't in his bed and either was she, their gone, but there was a note for you." She hurriedly pulled out a piece of scrap paper and handed it to me.

Lily don't worry about me, me and Carmen are fine we just think we have a lead on my mum. So were going to find her and bring her home. Find Alice because without her we won't have the full story. It's important. I know if anyone can find her it's you. I love you. Cole.

"Rain what's going on?" She looked at me uneasily.
"You really don't want to know."

Cole

She ran. I ran. Together. Her light brown coat flecked with gold, mine a stormy grey. Our wolves were one, joined by pack. I the protector, her the omega. Her heart yearned for the one who would complete her where my yearned for the girl who already had. We both wanted to keep her safe. We ran together. Our sole purpose the same.

Lily

Cole and Carmen had me worried. Going after Sophie predicated unknown dangers. Cole was a protector but Carmen wasn't. It didn't matter anyway, Cole was reckless when it came to helping those close to him. Me and Rain reached Amelia's five minutes after reading the note. For now I would have to focus on my gift and on Alice, otherwise there was no point.

I sat down in the middle of the living room, the cream carpets softening the cold floor. Spread around me was the dream stone, the heart of fire and a picture of Alice. It was an old picture, she must have been around ten in the image as she giggled and ran from the dark haired man that playfully chased her, that must have been Jack. Rain sat to my left, Amelia to my right. Both of them anxious to get started. "So what am I supposed to do?" Amelia took my hand in hers, I noticed that it was colder than usual. "First you must open your mind, and use the dream stone to search for her like you would when picking a dream." But how was I supposed to find Alice she wasn't a dream? Amelia seemed to know what I was thinking because she added "another part of your gift is that you can enter other people's dreams or dreams they've had before. Many dreams contain fragments of memories from their life, therefore using the stone to channel you, find one of Alice's dreams that could hint to her whereabouts." She spoke as though it was so easy. I had only just started getting to know my power, I didn't yet know how far it stretched or even how powerful I was. I nodded unsure of myself. Rain patted me on the shoulder and placed an encouraging smile on her lips. "Out of anyone I know you can do this Lily, you'll find a way." That's what Cole had said. I breathed deeply before picking up the azure stone and placing it in my palm. But before closing my eyes I looked back at Amelia who smiled at me contently. "Can I ask you a question?" She nodded her greying head at me.
"Did you ever really lose your memories?" She smiled and took hold of my hand once again.
"We all lose a part of ourselves as we take our journey through life, some parts we choose to lose others we don't. I saw that in forgetting for a

while it would keep you safer, but now that you are ready I am letting parts of myself that I had hidden beneath out again in hope it will help." All of these years of us thinking that she was slowly going she was right there looking at us, with both eyes open. Closing my eyes I opened my mind just as the stone began to hum against my palm.

Like before when I had entered Amelia's dreams images crashed past me. I couldn't let myself be distracted by the images, but I found that the pictures were now mismatched events of Amelia's life and my own. A scene from when my first tooth fell out flashed before my eyes, along with an image of Amelia in a white dress. Focus Lily. *Find Alice Cloud.* I decided to use her full name hoping that would lower the chances of me finding someone else. I hoped there's not many people out there with the name Cloud. The images that had cloaked me at the beginning vanished leaving me in a dark room.

The room was so dark that I thought that if I reached out I could actually touch the darkness. Before a panic attack could even come about I was suddenly blinded by a white light. Peeling my eyes open to glimpse at what was going on I found that the scene had changed around me. I no longer stood in darkness but a village surrounded by lush green meadows. The village was small and slightly dilapidated. The houses were crumbling but the roofs stayed sturdy. I could hear in the distance the sound of children's laughter, and birdsong from a Robin that perched on a branch near my head. Stepping forward I found that I was no longer alone. Stepping out of the wood was a girl. She looked no older than fourteen. Her clothes were ripped and muddy, and there was huge red scratches across her arms and face. Her long brown hair was ratty and full of leaves. Despite her dishevelled appearance she had a strong fierceness in her brown and blue eyes.

I followed her as she slowly made her way towards the village. She stopped for a moment, a hiss of pain slipping from her lips and she pulled her top up to expose her left rib cage. A long deep gash ran down her side, exposing blood as it seeped into her shirt. Pulling the top down she breathed deeply and carried on walking. As I got closer to the village I noticed that there was only about eight houses, each of them separate with their own patch of green, where plants bloomed and pumpkins grew. The girl abruptly stopped before she could enter the town, she rubbed her forehead and glowered at the scene in front of her "dam shields! Help! Anyone please I need your help!" Her voice was brittle from lack of water. A boy answered her call. He was slightly older, tall with jet black hair. He frowned at her from the other side of the invisible wall. "Who are you, why did you come here?" Her eyes pleading she pulled her top back again to show her injuries. She placed her tanned hand on the shield that separated them, her innocent pain filled eyes pleading with him. "Please I need your help." The boy looked at her hand for a moment as though he was memorising the lines that were etched into it. He then looked at her face and he faltered. The wall vanished allowing her passage. She quickly passed through losing her footing in the process. Before she hit the ground the boy caught her. "What's your name?" She asked as she stared up at him, his arms still locked around her. He returned her gaze something floating in his dark gaze. "Max, what's your name?" She smiled. "Alice."

Cole

Mum was human which meant the boundary lines between lands didn't count for her. If she was hidden anyway where it would be a place me and the pack couldn't find her. I could count the fairies out, they hated my father for killing one of their own, so I knew they would not help him. My father was also clever which meant he wouldn't dare hide her In Ever where the king's guards were on constant patrol. That left three lands, two of them would allow easy passage, the other would be signing my own death certificate, yet somehow I felt like all this time it did have something to do with the vampires. The fact that the shield around Seth's land had been tampered with and Levi's increasing obsession with me, was starting to make sense now. Who better to be allies with than your natural enemy? From what I heard Seth and my father had a lot in common. Both. Wanted power more than anything. Both. Would also do anything to obtain it. However, this partnership was like having three knives divided by two men, two had already been stabbed in the back of each other, and the third was for the fatal blow, that came when it was time to win.

Our feet had only stepped into Ever for the majority of two seconds before the king's guards had surrounded us. One of them stepped forward, "Cole Star your presence has been demanded by the king in great urgency, please follow me." Carmen looked at me questioningly, her eyes even more earnest in her wolf form. I nodded at her, and because of my rank she followed without hesitation, maybe ties to the pack were harder to break than I thought.

Lily

"What is this place?" Alice asked as she lay on a wooden bed with worn grey sheets. The boy, Max was busy preparing a bowl of hot soapy water. "It doesn't have a name, it's just one of the many small villages that boarder the outskirts of Ever. The king offered us protection but not much else." Alice frowned, her face held so much of Amelia it made me smile. Max drew a chair up so he could sit beside her. "Your cut needs cleaning, then we will be able to see how deep it is." She closed her eyes and only flinched a few times as he delicately cleaned her wound. "Why did you come here of all places?" Her eyes flickered beneath her closed eyelids as she replied, her voice weaker than before. "I ran away and didn't want to be found, so when I saw this place I thought that it would be perfect." Max frowned but kept his attention on her cut. There was a careful way he assessed the wound, it was as though it was the most important job in the world. "You won't need stitches I'll just put a plaster on to keep it clean

until it starts to scab over." She opened her eyes and watched him retreat. "You're different." When Max returned with the plaster he gave her a dubious looked. "How am I different?" She didn't smile, instead she looked at him properly for the first time, searching for something in his expression that would tell her if she could trust him. "You never asked why I was running."

Cole

It seemed that I was forever standing in the king's throne room, with the same cloak wrapped around me to hide my nakedness, and the king standing in front of me knowing everything I wanted to know, but never telling me. "You asked to see me your majesty." The king took a seat on his throne, looking more anxious than before. "Something bothering you your majesty?" Carmen asked politely, she boldly stepped towards him, and placed her hand on top of his, his whole body visibly relaxed. All he could do was stare at her. Carmen feeling like she had offended him stepped back quickly "sorry your majesty I just wanted to help." Her words seemed to knock him back out of his daze. He shook himself then smiled gratefully at her. "I have never felt an Omega's power before that was why I was so stunned. And there is no need to apologise I feel better than I have for days." She blushed not normally thanked for her gift. It occurred to me that she was underappreciated by the pack, her gift was amazing, and we should be more thankful for it. The king then looked back at me "I asked the guards to collect you because my scouts have heard that maybe your mother's disappearance has something to do with James. That means if we are to find her it must be a secret, because if James hears wind of this it puts you both in danger."

"Did you know it had something to do with him?" The king stood and came to place his hand on my shoulder. "Yes, it was Dean Skies who came to me to report your mothers disappearance, I thought it odd then that as your fathers mate that he would be here pleading at my feet to do everything in my power to find her, yet he was nowhere in sight." All this time he hadn't really been looking for her. "Do you have any idea where she could be?" He let go of me, and then to my utter shock he pulled out a long golden sword from where it lay asleep on his belt. He pointed it forward testing its balance. The blade was gold with silver writing engraved into it. The handle was silver with the twisting crest of the shadows embossed onto it. *Evelyn scriptor tactus hanc igni.* "What does the blade say?" The king looked at Carmen who asked the question and lowered the sword so she could look at it she spoke "Evelyn's touch made this fire. What does that mean?" He placed the sword back onto its belt and straightened his cloak. "It's about the legend of Ever, this was the very first royal sword made, it can on be wielded by a Shadow. But back to your previous question Cole. I think I have an idea where she could be, but you're going to need me to get there."

Lily

Time had moved on now. Alice was no longer a small teenager, but an adult. She had grown taller, her skin had the summer glow that days spent outdoors offered. Her eyes held the brightness of happiness that wasn't there before, her hair was shorter now and her face had aged but not her spirit. She sat outside the shield, letting the long grass and wild yellow flowers of the meadows tickle her arms as they fluttered in the wind. "I thought I might have found you here." She didn't look at Max as he took a seat next to her, instead her gaze lay on the sunset that was slowly descending beneath the greenery. Like she, Max had grown older his dark hair was longer now, his body held muscle that hadn't yet developed before, and the way he watched her told me time had brought them closer. He placed his arm around her shoulder but she didn't fold into him like he expected, he let his arm drop. "What's wrong?" His voice was quiet and caring. She stood abruptly and he followed suit. She faced him, small tears brimmed in her tear ducts. "I'm...pregnant." For a moment he stood there stunned, then the next moment he had grabbed her into his arms and swung her around, laughing happily. He kept her suspended in the air, so he could look up and she looked down at his face. "I didn't think you would react this way." She smiled as she let the joyful tears trail down her cheeks. He kissed them away before they could fall, then looked back at her. "I'm going to be a dad?" She laughed and kissed his lips.

Fire began to burn through my body like it had when I had that dangerous fever. I was dragged back into reality screaming from the pain that scorched my brain. Opening my eyes I found myself back in Amelia's living room.

The room was trashed, the sofa had been ripped to pieces and dirty footprints scarred the pristine carpet. Rain lay next to me unconscious, but still breathing. I was about to get up when Amelia came barrelling towards me from where she stood stunned in the room, her gaze frantic and frightened. When she saw me she ran to me and pulled me up by the arms, then crushed me to her in a fierce hug that told me she was saying goodbye. "Listen to me Lily, no matter what happens always believe in yourself, believe in your gift, and believe in your bond. You are a princess in their world but you are also Lily in both. Always remember that, no matter what be true to yourself and you will always know the way!" She let go, my heart beat erratically in my chest. "Amelia?" She then pushed me behind her as someone entered the room...

Three people entered the room, all of them with the same transparent skin and matching black eyes. Lexi and Levi smirked at me from where I was standing, shielded by Amelia. The other man I didn't know. He was tall, with long black hair that was tied back with a leather bow. His features seemed to have been carved out of rock, his eyes older than Levi's. "Amelia it has been a while." His voice was like a razor blade poking at my skin, urging for me to bleed. "Not long enough Seth." The man, Seth smiled bitterly at her. He moved with easy grace about the living room, sliding his porcelain hand over the mantel piece, he came to a stop when his hand hit the golden photo frame that held a picture of Jack and Amelia on their wedding day. He picked it up. "It's such a shame I couldn't make it to your wedding, but I did ensure his funeral." All three of them laughed. I could feel Amelia burning with rage in front of me, I held her wrist. "Oh what happened to this one, Lexi dear take her to him I think she is wanted." Seth asked as he nudged Rain's unconscious body with his shiny black shoes. Lexi moved briskly and picked up Rain as though she weighed nothing. "No stop!" I shouted as I came out from behind Amelia. Seth looked at me intrigued, Lexi didn't move. "My, my, my. When you said she looked like Alana I thought you was joking but she really does doesn't she Levi?" Levi bore me with a hatred filled look and nodded at his father. "Where are you taking Rain?" Seth nodded at Lexi who dispersed into the air along with Rain.

Seth then walked closer to me and began circling me, like a lion with his prey. I could feel his intense gaze as though he was touching me. "You will find out soon enough dear princess." He was just about to reach out to touch my forehead when Amelia pushed me out of the way, glowering at Seth. "You will have to step over my dead body before you will touch her!" Seth simply looked at her. If he had shouted or looked shocked I think I would have been relieved. Instead she received an emotionless stare which made me regret ever leaving her side.

Then. The corner of his mouth curled up into a half smile. "If that is what you wish." Then, everything happened so quickly. Levi grabbed hold of me from behind, one arm around my waist to hold me to his body the other under my chin, forcing me to watch the scene that played out in front of me. Seth had grabbed hold of Amelia, his iron grip around her neck. Choking her. "This would all have been easier if you had just loved me instead, I offered you more than that mutt and yet you still chose him. Well now you can rot in death with him." Quick as a viper he sunk his long fangs into her neck exposing a vein, and allowing blood to stream furiously from the wound. He let her go, and her frail body hit the floor with an ugly thump. "Amelia?" My voice broke as tears streamed down my face and my heart ached to be near her. "Levi let her go, it is not time yet." Levi let go of my chin, then whispered in my ear before releasing me fully "until the next time princess." Then like Lexi they vanished into thin air.

I quickly ran over to Amelia and turned her body over. She was breathing but barely. I quickly placed my hands around her wound in an attempt to stem the flow of blood. I took her hand and her eyes peeled open to look at me. "Hold on Amelia, you'll be fine." The tears were endless now. She smiled sadly at me. Her hand was cold, her lips purple. "It's time to let go

now Lily, you'll see me again someday." I choked on my tears.
"No hold on you're not leaving me, not like this! I need you please stay." I could feel her pulse slowing in my hand her eyes closing. "I love you Lily." I crawled down next to her and held her close to me. "I love you too Amelia." Then her heart stopped beating against me ear, and I knew I had lost her.

Loving someone means that despite where they are you love them forever. A part of them becomes a part of you, so when you lose them, you feel like you've lost a part of yourself, a gaping hole in your soul. They say time heals you of this wound, but that's just a lie. Time only reminds you of how long you have until you see them again. Time just reminds you of what you've lost. Amelia had told me this long ago. I hadn't believed her then, but now with her cold body propped motionless against me as I screamed for her to open her eyes again. To breathe, to tell me everything was going to be alright. I couldn't help but believe that she was right.

An ambulance came fifteen minutes later after a neighbour had reported a scream. When they reached us they realised that it had been my scream who had alerted the neighbours. I cried and cried. Screamed until I had nothing left inside of me. She still didn't wake up, she was gone and a part of me was as well.

My mother and my terminally ill father arrived to the scene, looking as shattered as I felt. They took one look at me, broken and heartbroken covered in Amelia's blood and folded me into a hug, something I had taken for granted. Then they took me home, and allowed me to cry, not once did they ask what happened, not once did they ask why I was there or where I had been. They just let me cry.

Cole

I could feel Lily's heart shatter into a million pieces, feel the burn of anger course through her veins. But I was here, and she was there. I couldn't get to her, which made it even more soul shattering. The king had been speaking to one of his guards, his face full of sorrow and remorse. We were a few miles from Ever, making our way towards the outskirt towns. The king thought my mother could be there, it was isolated, shielded and dangerous to those who are used to being kept inside shields. The king returned to us, his face grave. "There was an incident at Amelia's house." Carmen looked anxiously towards me.

"What kind of incident?" The king breathed in, before speaking.

"Seth took Rain and killed Amelia." Carmen gasped, tears springing to her eyes even though she didn't know Amelia she would cry for her anyway. My dream, Amelia had been trying to warn me about death, she knew it was going to happen. "What about Lily?" Carmen was asking all the questions I should have been asking, but I was too startled by the realisation. Why hadn't I been listening? "She's upset but not hurt, her adoptive parents collected her and took her home." The two kept talking, when something hit me. My mother had said we needed both me and Lily to find her, that together we were stronger. I felt a bit insensitive, but I knew she would understand. Hopefully.

The phone rang only once when she answered. "Cole?" The king's attention zeroing on me, as he heard his daughters voice for the first time in fifteen years. Her voice was flat and broken from crying, I wanted to hug her. "Are you okay, I'm sorry I'm not there?" She sniffed.

"You need to find your mum, besides I'm being coddled enough by mum and dad I think they're afraid I'm going to lash out or something." I understood.   "Anyway that's not why you called, I know you need something I can feel it." She laughed slightly. Probably shocked that she was so in tune with me now. "I need your gift, I can't find my mum without you, apparently were stronger together, but will it even work over the phone, but I don't want to push you I mean you've been through a lot today?" There was a pause before she answered. "Cole its fine at least something good might come out of this day, anyway I want to help it might keep me from thinking about it. Yeah it will work but you need to open your mind to me, I'll use the dream stone to find you." The phone went dead then, and I realised she meant now. I closed my *eyes* and let down all my defences and let her walk in.

Lily

Due to the bond Coles mind was easier to find compare to Alice's. He stood in the dark room waiting patiently for me. He opened his arms to me but I shook my head "no we don't have time for that, here give me your hands." He didn't argue. With his hands laced with mine and our eyes closed I could feel our power charged between us. An image began to focus into my mind.

Long overgrown meadows, dilapidated houses. Vacant of life. A fire had been through here recently, the ash still sprinkled across the ground. One house still remained. Untouched by the flames. Blink. A dark mouldy cellar held prisoners a woman and man. Both chained and battered.

The image disappeared and I was back in the dark room. Coles grasp more urgent now. "I know where they are, there in one of the abandoned villages, a fire recently passed, in a basement she isn't alone." Cole nodded and let go, but before I cut the connection I kissed him. He kissed me back but it didn't last long. Pulling back I looked him directly in the eye. "Be careful, come back to me." He kissed my forehead and smiled sweetly at me "always." Then the connection broke and he was gone.

Cole

When my eyes re-opened I couldn't decide whether I felt better about seeing Lily, or worse because I was leaving her again. The king waited patiently for me, he looked different in his fighting gear compared to his normal entire. "Do you have more of an idea now?" He asked. Carmen was looking at me as though she was going to have a heart attack, I had forgotten she didn't know about my gift, it had been Reeve that knew. "Yes, she's in one of the buildings in an abandoned village, a fire had been through there recently." The king looked thoughtful for a moment, then he started walking. "I know where she is, follow me."

Lily

After waking up again from seeing Cole I lay feeling empty on my bed. Mum checked every hour if I was okay, Leo walked past my room every ten minutes trying to sum up the courage to come in and comfort me. Leah didn't come in, in fact when I got home she planted herself in the living room with some dolls, ignoring my presence in the house. But I was gone past caring now. When the door knocked I expected it to be mum, so I turned my back tired of giving her the same two words over and over again "I'm fine." The door closed behind them as they came and sat down on the end of my bed, maybe not mum she was too scared to cross over into the room, instead hung by the door. Rolling over I found my dad looking sadly down at me. He looked worse than he did before, and I felt suddenly bad for causing him any stress. I had been selfish this past week. He didn't ask if I was okay, he didn't ask what happened. Instead he took hold of my hand and pulled me to him so he could hug me. Wrapped in my dad's arms I began to cry again overwhelmed by more emotion. He stroked my back comforting me. "It's okay to cry and not be okay. Nobody would blame you, it's been a hard week for us all, but it's been worse on you. I won't ask what happened today, only that you bring me into the loop about everything else."

I pulled away from him. He asked me to explain who I was, but where would I even start, how would I even get him to understand. But the way he looked at me told me no matter what I said he would believe me, and he would be there for me. Because despite who I was I would always be his little girl, and he would always be my father. "Okay but keep an open mind." He nodded, then the past six months of my life came tumbling out of my mouth, and with each word I began to feel lighter again.

The police arrived a while later. Two of them, one female with a friendly face sat in front of me. The other a stern looking man sat next to her. My mother and father flanked me, both of them knew the truth now, both of them knew what really happened. Both of them had taken everything in their stride. My mother took hold of my hand from under the table. "Please could you tell us your account of what happened four hours ago?" Amelia had been dead four hours. Dead. Gone. I shook myself. "I went to go and visit her an hour before, we were just talking when someone entered the house. Amelia tried to protect me, then she died." The woman wrote everything I said down onto a note pad, the scratch of pen on paper created an annoying sound that made me want to reach out and stab her with the pen. Totally irrational I know. "Why were you not at school?" The male police officer interjected. It was my mother who answered him, her voice stern and uncompromising. "We let her have a day of since the night before she found out she was adopted, we thought she needed a little time to accept it." Her hand squeezed mine tighter. The woman officer looked at me with more sympathy than before. I liked her, but I wanted to punch her. What was wrong with me? "Is that what you went to Mrs Clouds for, to speak to her about this?" She smiled. How could she smile when she was talking about someone that was now dead? I nodded at her. "Did she offer any enlightenment on the subject?" I sighed and nodded. "She said that it didn't matter who I was to others it was who I was to myself that mattered." The woman smiled slightly and wrote once again on her pad. "Can you identify your attacker?" The male officer asked, strictly business with him, he hadn't let his guard down once, not even unfolded his arms. Yes I could there was three of them all evil malicious vampires, one loved Amelia, another was an ex best friend and the last one just had a serious life threatening vendetta against me. "No I didn't see a face, but I think they were male." The woman placed her note pad back into her pocket then stood from the table. The man followed suit. "Thank you for your time Miss Found, if we need to contact you again then we will, we suggest that maybe you see a therapist, losing someone is hard enough without actually witnessing their death." Bit blunt, but no chance. I nodded and my father led them out of the door, saying goodbye politely, but by the look on his face the officers had rubbed him the wrong way as well. Before they were out the door the male officer turned giving me a stern look with a raised eyebrow, "why do you think a man entered Mrs Cloud's house and slit her throat in mid-daylight?" I looked levelly back at me and raised my eyebrow in response "isn't that your job officer?" And with that they were gone.

"Lily I think you need to go and get some sleep, it's been a long day." My mother finally let go of my hand and stood. She looked down at me her hazel eyes sad. They both had reacted well to what I had told them, apart from the part where I was a princess which out of it all seemed the only plausible part. I think it's because they knew one day I would have to leave, and become a part of this world. They weren't ready for that yet. I stood and hugged both of them tight, then ascended the stairs.

Before I could reach my room Leo stopped me. His eyes were red from crying and his face strained with the promise of what he wanted to say, but couldn't say. Instead he hugged me tight, tighter than he had ever hugged me before, then he let go and retreated back into his room. Leo had never had trouble in the past to tell me how he felt, but now everything had changed, and so had he. Back into my room I clambered into bed with the dream stone firm in my hand. I never got to the end of Alice's dreams, now that Amelia was dead and Rain was still missing we needed her more than ever. It just made me sad that she never got to say goodbye.

"I have to go, I won't be gone long." Alice smiled sadly up at Max's face who did not look happy at her suggestion. "I don't care I don't want you to leave at all!" She carefully took a hold of his face and kissed him carefully on the lips. His hands automatically reached out to stroke her swollen belly. Time had moved on once again. She pulled back and smiled at him. "I have to go, I never really got to say goodbye, this might be my only chance." He sighed but he was clearly defeated. "You know time has moved on for them all, you're supposed to look older than you actually are." Her eyes filled with a mischievous glint. "So are you, besides this is why I can go back. All this time they would be looking for someone who's aged twenty years. They won't recognise me!" He didn't look convinced. She kissed him quickly then she let him go. "I'll be back in a few days." He looked pained as he watched her walk away, as she disappeared he pulled out a glorious ruby from his pocket. He smoothed the glassy surface with a careful hand. "I think she forgets we don't live forever." He spoke out loud into the silence.

I didn't recognise the house Alice now stood in but the little boy she sat talking to I would remember anywhere. Cole. He was no older than three. His jet black hair was more curly than it is now and his eyes larger against his pale skin. "Can I tell you a secret?" Little Cole nodded his head with enthusiasm, she smiled amused by him. "Will you keep it though?" He laughed then held out his tiny pale pinkie finger at her "you can't break a pinkie promise." Her eyes shined as she took hold of his little finger with her own. Then she pulled out a stone that was identical to the one Max had, she let him hold it. Against his white palms the stone looked redder than it had before. "This stone is special. It comes from a bigger stone that was made to protect the daughters of Storm." Cole's big eyes turned to her intrigued. "What does it do?" His voice soft nearly a whisper. She smiled back at his curious face. "It gives me power, it allows me to be faster and stronger than normal people, allows me to escape danger if I have to. But if you sleep with it under your pillow it stops time for a while, but eventually it will catch up to us again." He frowned and looked back at the stone. "What do you mean?" She carefully took the stone back and placed it into her pocket again. "I mean I won't grow old for a while, but eventually all the years I have stalled will catch up with me." She stopped then took his small hands into hers.

"Promise me that you won't tell anyone about this, in time you will forget, because in time everything that matters is eventually forgotten, but don't tell for now. I just wanted for someone other than someone like me to know. To see what it feels like to let go of a secret that had been hidden beneath."

I quickly awoke again the heart of flames that hug around my neck scorched my skin reminding me of its presence, perhaps if it hadn't been on the floor at Amelia's I would have been able to fight Levi. The stones were replicas of the stone I held around my neck, which meant that the story of Storm is true, that my mum was one of these daughters too, and so was I. The memory also answered an unanswered question from before, how did Alice still look so young? It was the stone it kept her that way, but not forever. That's what Max had meant. Cole knew her secret but had never said anything. Maybe she had been right that with time he would forget the conversation. Then again he had only been about three. I needed Sky. No I needed to find Rain. No I needed to go find Cole and help him find his mum. There was so many things that needed to be done, yet I couldn't even think about doing them. Amelia was gone. Stop Lily she would have wanted me to do something. I quickly stood up and left my room, after putting them through hell I thought I would be best if for once I actually told them what I was doing. I found them in the kitchen, both looked as though they needed to catch up on a weeks' worth of sleep. They looked up when they heard me enter. "I need to go find Sky so we can go find Rain." It still felt strange to say everything out loud. The only part that they didn't know was that Cole was a wolf, it was against the law for humans to know so I couldn't tell them. Anyway I thought maybe that extra bit of information might just tip them over the edge. Mum looked as though she would rather say no to this little expedition but knew I'd probably leave with or without her permission. Dad spoke up "do you want one of us to go with you?" I thought he was brave to ask, but I would never ask him to do this. I knew trying to save Rain would be dangerous seen as her kidnappers were a bunch of blood thirsty immortals, and I was human, well almost. I shook my head "no me and Sky can handle it but if I..." then suddenly I choked. I was about to say if I don't come back then I'm sorry for what I put you through and that I loved them but the words never came. My parents came to my rescue and enfolded me into a warm comforting hug. They knew what I was going to say. Then they let me go. I kissed them both on the cheek before stepping out of the front door.

I needed to be brave. Strong. Amelia had been both till the very end. I wanted to be like her. I breathed in. Today had been one of the worst days of my life and I was desperate to find some hope somewhere. But first we had to find Rain.

End of part three.

Holding onto anger is like drinking poison and expecting the other person to die.

Buddha.

Cole

The outskirt villages weren't as impressive and complete as the rest of Ever. Instead they were small collections of houses and fields each surrounded by an invisible shield. We stood in front of one of these villages now. The shield separating us from the community that had recently been engulfed in flames. The grey ash scattered in the wind. It was silent. It was a ghost-town. The king stepped forward and placed his hand on the invisible wall. The air shifted where his hand fell against the transparency. Then, the shields outline blazed a shimmering gold before crumbling to the ground where we stood. We stepped forward.

The atmosphere was sharp against me. Screaming something bad had happened here recently, something we couldn't see. Carmen shivered next to me, her wolf picking up the same vibes as me. Her normally composed face was anxious, she stayed close to me. The guards fanned out ahead of us, swords drawn in defence as they checked for impending danger. The king also guided his own sword from his belt. I felt useless in my human skin and borrowed clothes. We followed the king as he progressed towards the only house that still stood, his face cautious.

The guards returned from their search to stand by their king's side as we entered the house. The door was unlocked and creaked as it opened.

Inside the house held one room. It was bare of anything that suggested someone had once lived here. The wooden floor however told a different story. Etched onto the wood were scuffed foot prints both human and...wolf. Betrayal and anger made a sudden appearance catching me of guard. I thought I had my emotions under control. Mixed in amongst the prints was traces of blood. The blood had turned brown which suggest it had been there a while. "There's nothing here." Spoke the king, his voice quiet. He turned to leave when Carmen spoke "wait look!" She moved to the other side of the room quickly where a rug lay tattered in the corner. She tugged the rug back to expose a hidden door that lay in the floor boards. The king frowned "how did you know that was there?" Carmen looked up at him and smiled. "Clearly you haven't watched enough movies." The king's only response was for him to raise one of his pale eyebrows. Turning back to the door she tugged it open, the latch creaked. Then before anyone could stop her she jumped through it, disappearing into the unknown.

Lily

It was late...really late. I worried that Sky was in bed. However when I reached her lavish house the kitchen light illuminated the drive, and Sky's small silhouette sat at their pristine marble table. I went up to the window and knocked carefully. The sudden sound made her jump but when she saw my face she smiled and quickly came to the door. When the door opened her face immediately crumpled into one of sympathy. I held my hand up to her before she could speak. "I can't talk about it now, but I'm okay but I need your help." Her face changed instantly. She pulled me inside. Her eyes held a glimmer I hadn't seen yet, was It excitement? "What can I do?" I looked at her, and she looked back at me. We were equals. "I'm really hoping you're as badass as that book says you are." Her eyes glittered again and a smile spread across her lips, I guess I had my answer.

Cole

All of us stared shocked at the now open trapped door that Carmen had just disappeared through. The king then stepped forward his guards shadowing his movements. He glanced at me "I will go in first then you follow." His pale gaze flicked to his guards "stay here just in case someone comes, you will know if we need you down there." The guards didn't argue. Instead took defensive positions around the room. The king then crouched down and slid through the door. I followed.

My feet made a loud thud when they hit the concrete floor. The room wasn't dark, a small trail of light beamed through the room from the only window that hadn't been blacked out by age. The room like upstairs was vacant and unlived in. However the erratic heart beats of someone behind the door on the far side of the room suggested different. The king stood by Carmen who had safely got here before either of us. She stared at the door. The king raised his sword again as we progressed towards it. My heart began to beat faster, I was nervous for some reason. It seemed like my body was only just catching up with everything that was going on. The door squeaked open as the king pushed it with his hand. Inside the room was littered with candles, all of them burning. The floor was dirty and blood stained most of it. Then. There in the far corner chained to the wall by ancient looking shackles was my mother and a man I didn't recognise. Both of them unconscious. Both looked tattered and bloody. My heart leapt at the sight of her, but my mind curled in anger. Who would do this to her?

I quickly found myself next to her. Reaching out I gently shook her body awake, afraid I might break her in her fragile state. Her eyes slowly peeled open. Her normally shiny green eyes had darkened and were blood shot.

She stared at me, her mouth opening and closing as though she couldn't quite get what she wanted to say out. "Cole." Her cracked voice finally managed. I took her hand in mine, it was cold. "Yeah mum it's me, we're here to get you out." She suddenly looked alarmed and quick as a flash she shot up. She was standing but couldn't move properly because of the chains, her ankle seemed to be broken too. "No you have to go before he comes!" The king stepped towards her and left Carmen to bring the unknown man around, he was still unconscious. "Sophie we are here to help you, but I would like to know who you are so afraid of." His voice was soft as she spoke, but she flinched at every word. Her face changed then, she looked deadly. I almost didn't recognise her. "All these years have been a lie. He loved me once you know, but then losing her was the worst thing to ever happen to him. It drove him crazy! He became obsessed with power, he wanted her back but she was gone. He's evil and I hate him!" Her voice had grown stronger as she shouted on, tears still slipped from her eyes. She looked brave and strong but at the same time looked as though she could crumble under any more pressure. She was mountain that had been weathered by the wind for many years, and now the rocks she was made from had begun to fall. "Who are you talking about mum?" She looked at me and her face changed again, she became softer but the rage was boiling to the surface. "You of all people should know. How long did you have to put up with him hurting you, how long has he tried to make you weak? You know who I mean Cole! The sick man that claims the title of your father." I don't know why her words surprised me. We had guessed a while ago this whole thing had something to do with my father. But hearing her say it made it so much worse. She was his mate. How could he ever hurt her like this? Then again I was his son how could he hurt me? "Sophie you mentioned that he lost someone and it was in losing her that he became like he is now. Who were you talking about?" My mum didn't look at the king, instead the tears became too much for her and she crumpled to the floor. Her sobs tearing at my heart. She shook her head defiantly. "He doesn't know." She whispered finally. The king bent down to be at her level. His pale eyes calm and caring. "Who doesn't know?" She curled her knees up into her chest and made herself smaller. "Cole. He doesn't know about her." I to then bent down to see her better. I took her hand once more. She didn't look at me. "Who don't I know mum?" She sniffed and her shoulder began to shake as my sobs racked her body. "About your sister" her eyes then did look at me and they held so much sadness in them that I thought I could cry her tears for her. One last tear dropped from her eye and she squeezed my hand tight. "Cole you had a twin sister."

Lily

Before we could go anywhere I had decided to fill Sky in on everything I found out in Alice's dreams. She listened intently and never once broached the subject of Amelia. "So everything leads back to the guardians. You, your mother and now Alice?" She was right everything did lead back to them. "But what I've been wondering is what was she running from and why did she disappear?" Both of these questions had flittered through my mind over the past few months. Yet like most of the questions we had we were no nearer to finding the answers. Right now my priority was finding Rain, but where would we even start looking? "So if Lexi took her that means she would have to take her to a place that a vampire could get to." I recalled Cole telling me that the shields between lands prevented different creatures from entering. That meant that Lexi, Levi and Seth would need to go to a place they could enter. "So where does that leave?" I really should have paid more attention to Cole when he spoke about the lay of the land, but he had mostly talked about this when I hadn't been ready to accept it yet. "I think it leaves the woods, the land the vampires live in or…Ever Green." Sky let out an exasperated sigh and pulled her hair up into a tight pony tail. She looked at me and answered sarcastically. "So not many places then."

The three of them were smart which meant they probably wouldn't hide her in a place that could be easily gotten to, or a place that had witnesses. It occurred to me then though it was pretty obvious. The shield around their land kept creatures out which meant the wolves couldn't enter. Which makes it perfect. "I think I know where to find her, but I can tell you now it's going to be dangerous." Sky suddenly looked nervous then. Despite what that book said about her she still looked like my small fragile friend. Yet at the same time she didn't, she looked strong and brave. And I really needed to stop underestimating her. "But how would we get in, I'm pretty sure they won't just let us walk through?" I had already thought of that, she was right they wouldn't just let us through and stand by as we took back Rain, who they had purposely stole in the first place. No I was counting on something, I was counting on who I was. Cole had told me once that only Shadows could pass through each of the shields without permission which meant that hopefully my heritage might just come in handy.

Cole

Twin sister. Twin sister. I had a twin sister. I thought maybe if I let it swirl round in my head for a while it would finally sink in. Twin, I had been a twin. I could feel both my mother's and the king's gazes on me. Waiting for my reaction. That made three of us. I blinked. "I...was a twin?" I managed the words but they didn't feel right in my mouth. My mother closed her eyes, and when she did I could see her taking in all of her emotions and locking them away. When she re-opened them, they were dead. Empty. However she re-claimed my hand and managed to keep her voice strong. "Yes you were. You were both born beautiful and healthy. We named her Nova Grace, after your grandmother. You both looked exactly alike it was strange." She took a breath. The king had moved to leave us to our private conversation to help Rain, the man was still unconscious. "You were both taken for a test, they said that something with your lungs wasn't right. They lied to us Cole. An hour later they brought you back but Nova was gone, the doctor said she had died, we never saw her again." I let my hand slip from hers as I stood up, soaking up the story. Nova Grace, it had a weird irony as our last name was star.

"When you said they lied, what did you mean?" She too stood up, but the shackles kept her chained to the wall. "She didn't die someone took her, it's why he got so worked up. He wanted her back so did I. But I thought his determination was because of his fatherly love for his child but I was wrong. Your sister was special Cole, she could see things in her dreams." If that was the case then why hadn't I been taken too? My sister had been kidnapped as a new born because of the gift she had that I also shared, there must have been another reason. "How did you know she had been kidnapped?" She sniffed her eyes blazing for a second. "That women Amelia, she had the same gift. She dreamt about it and told him. She's the reason he turned bad!" The accusation in her voice ripped into me as though she was cutting me with a knife. Angry I turned to her, my own accusation in my voice. "Yeah well she's dead." I could see the words sink in but they had no effect on her what so ever. Wounds cut too deep to heal now.

"Cole, I know you're probably angry that we didn't tell you, but there was never the right time. James asked the king to explain it to you at Christmas but in the end he couldn't. It had to come from one of us." I looked to the king who was immersed in trying to revive the man. So that was what he had originally wanted to tell me. Finally some questions being answered. "Why does he want her back then, if it's not for the obvious family reasons?" Her mouth didn't move, but I got an answer. I remembered only months ago when we had come back here that, that voice would send shivers down my spine and unease to cling to my stomach. Instead the voice only filled me with anger. "I wanted her power, dreams hold many possibilities, possibilities that I need to get what I want." I turned around to face my father. He wore a black shirt and black jeans that matched his jet black hair. His blue eyes so like mine stared at me. His stance was defensive, and coiled like a snake ready to strike. Looking closer I noticed his shirt wasn't actually black, but stained with dark blood. The guards. I didn't know this man, but that was a lie it was the man I had known for the past six years of my life. I hated him. "Where's Rain?" My father walked forward confidently, he pushed past me and reached for the chains that were clasped around my mother's wrist. He tugged them and the chains fell from the wall, another tug and she was forced to move towards him. With each step she cringed away from him. He smiled as though nothing was wrong. "I will take you to her, Skyla and the pack are waiting there too." He then flicked his icy gaze to the king. He cocked his head to one side then smiled, his smile made me feel sick. "Ahh your majesty, you may take that young man back to the palace, I left you one guard who will help carry him. This is a family matter. Carmen you will also follow." Carmen compelled by his Alpha tone stood and came to stand reluctantly next to him. The king looked at me, I nodded. He didn't need to get himself killed over this, Ever needed him more than I did. Looking as though he would rather take his sword and stab my father through the heart, he picked up the man into his arms and went back through the way we had come. When he was gone my father turned to us all. "Now come I have some people I want you to meet."

Lily

Sky had never been to Ever let alone go through the whole of the woods. Without Cole to guide me I had to let my natural instinct take over and help guide me through the dark trees. It was strange that my feet knew exactly which way to go without my brain even processing it. Today had been a long day, the sky still dark promising an eternal night, refusing to let go of this day like a stubborn child. In many ways I wished this day would just end, so that tomorrow could come and everything would be different. Yet, in another way I didn't want it to end, I wanted the day to end in a good way, so that could counteract all the bad. But really all of this was just a distraction from Amelia's death.

Sky stood clutching my hand as we neared the entrance of Ever. Stood in front of me like an impossible phantom was the shield that protected Ever. I could feel its radiating power sink into me as I reached out. I was about to enter this world without Cole at my side, but it didn't matter because Sky was there. My best friend, my protector. I could hear her gasp as we stepped forward, the sudden change in scenery took me by surprise too, the first time. "It's beautiful." I nodded at her. It was, beautiful and quaint. "Look there's the castle Lily, that's where your dad is!" She pointed in the direction of the towering grey palace. A weird feeling spread through me as I gazed at it, the strong walls and sapphire flags were all most familiar. She took my hand and tugged me towards it, her face eager and excited. "Come on Lil, go see him!" I planted my feet firmly on the ground and managed to tug my hand free. Panic began to rise. She stopped. "No we need to find Rain, I'm not ready for that yet." Sky came and stood in front of me, her blue and brown eyes glistening with understanding, she then folded me into a delicate hug. Her voice whispered in my ear. "Okay but when you are promise me that I can be there with you." I let her go and she stood back I smiled at her "I promise now let's go, Rain needs our help."

We managed to get to the cross roads between the different lands. I had been here before when Cole took me to see the fairies. He had managed to navigate the signs better than I had. We were stuck. Which name had the vampire land been? Sky began progressing down the left path not even looking at the signs. "Where are you going?" I asked as I tried to keep up with her. She looked over her shoulder at me and smiled, it was almost smug. "Vamps live in Kolga so that's the way we're going." Frowning I followed, my instincts telling me to trust her judgement. Weird.

The path was long and was starting to get more treacherous with every step. The path was no longer a nice even dirt road, but a winding stone slip where my feet slid along the granite rock. Sky however didn't even falter. Her steps so sure and precise. She didn't even sway. "So...have you just morphed into a ninja or something overnight?" I could hear her faint laughter despite her being quite a few steps in front of me. "I think it was a gradual transformation. But now that I know the truth I've being paying attention to it more so I think I'm improving. Why do you ask?" Her theory made sense because it applied to me too. Mine had also been gradual but the more I paid attention and learned the stronger that I became. "Because you managed to read the signs fine, and I feel as though I'm going to break my neck on these rocks and you haven't even lost your balance yet!" The same light laughter floated to my ears just like before. She was obviously enjoying being the stronger one in the situation for once. Sky then stopped a few steps in front of me, looking up. There she stood by a sign post that pointed back the way we come, or up. The towering foreboding mountain looked sternly down upon us, as though we were truly unworthy of its presence here. Sky spoke out loud "et lapis iste, quem scalis nunc in sanguine currit in eam."

"What does that mean?" Sky looked back at me, then looked back at the sign where the writing was engraved. "Men have scaled this stone, now there blood runs within it." I wanted to ask how she understood the language, but I didn't. "Well that sounds promising." She grimaced at me silently agreeing with me. Then she started forward placing her hand on the rock and began to climb. "Sky what are you doing!" She didn't looked back when she answered instead carried on climbing. "This is the only way, you want to save Rain or not?" She was right, I guess. Following her lead I placed my hands up on to the rock and began to pull myself up. The rock was hard against my palm. I forced myself not to look down. My fear of heights was certainly being put to the test right now. I felt free as I climbed. No longer bound to the earth like mortals, free to climb into the heavens and seek out forever. Yet, another freeing feeling was that my life hanged in the balance between my own hands and the rock that I now clung too. Danger had a strange sense of freedom, it was thrilling.

Sky had scaled the rock a lot quicker than I had and patiently waited at the top, her eyes excited. She took my hand as I neared her and pulled me up into the mouth of the mountain. The cave was dark and menacing. Waiting to swallow us whole. "Follow me." I didn't even hesitate as she led me into the darkness. That was my first mistake.

Cole

One of the worst feelings in the world is being forced to follow someone you know that will hurt you in an instant, but an even worse feeling is letting others follow them too. I held my mothers and Carmen's hands in my own. Both trembled with fear. My father strode gracefully like he always did ahead of us. His hands holding the chains that bound my mothers. The climb up the mountain that led into Kolga had drained my mother. She was a ghost, trailing behind a monster. I had never been inside the vampire world until now. The shields that protected it made that so. But my father passed through the shield as though he was a welcome visitor. As though he was a long lost friend that they were eager to see.

Kolga was mostly made of stone and dirt. It was a harsh scene that easily compared to its occupants. It was devoid of life. The sun didn't hit the landscape well here either, it was almost like the rock intentionally refracted the light away from it and let it bounce somewhere else. He led us towards the stone mansion that stood boldly against the sky. The stone it was made of was darker than the stone of the mountain, its presence here put my wolf on edge.

When we reached the door my father rapped loudly upon it, the sound echoed through me making me shiver. The door opened and there stood in the door way was Lexi. Her skin was even more porcelain than before, her eyes dark and cold. She smiled at my father with familiarity. "James everyone is waiting on you." He pulled the chains that bound my mother which forced her to stand by him. He smoothly placed his arm around her shoulder and returned Lexi's smile. "Good."

Lily

The darkness didn't last long, the tunnel eventually opened out into the light and we were able to see land again. Well, I wouldn't exactly call it land. The landscape was a harsher stone than the mountainside, lifeless and empty. Sky stepped forward to leave the tunnel but was suddenly stopped in her place. "I think we've found the shield." Stepping closer I felt the power of the barrier. Following my instincts I lifted my hands and placed my palms onto the invisible wall. The shield shuddered under my presence, then, it began to glow a bright shiny gold. The shield then began to crack and tear, pieces of the gold fell around my feet, the presence of the barrier disappeared and I knew we then could pass through.

This high up the altitude began to make my head buzz, oxygen levels lower than normal. The large expanse of land was vacant of life, or anyone. It was excessively quite. "So where do we go?" Sky pointed into the distance where a dark growing mansion stood. "I think there would be a good start."

Cole

The mansion was as dark as it was on the outside. The theme was seriously outdated. There was a lot of rich greens and reds as I walked along the stretching corridor. The smell of death and blood was potent in my senses. Carmen flinched at every sniff. Her heart was erratic in her chest. I squeezed her hand. Her dark brown eyes found mine and for once in her life she didn't seem calm. I managed a small smile which she reluctantly returned without much enthusiasm. My father led the three of us into a room. Room isn't quite the right word for it, it was more of a dining hall except without any furniture. Instead in the middle of the room lay a dark penetrating podium in which two, charcoal thrones stood gracefully. The floor around the podium was scarred with scratches and blood. There, sat in the burnt thrones was Levi, his usual cocky smirk printed onto his face. Then next to him was an older man. His hair was longer than Levi's, held back by a leather bow. His eyes eons older than the man next to him. This must be Seth.

Seth rose when we entered. His stony features moulded into a smile. "Ah James so good to see you again." My father abandoned the rest of us and made his way to Seth to shake his outstretched hand. "Likewise Seth." My father didn't even twitch from the presence of him let alone his touch. It amazed me how he managed to keep control, whereas my wolf scrapped at my insides begging to get out. Seth's eyes then flicked to us, his smile faltered for a second but was quick to rearrange his features. "These must be your wife and son, and also young Carmen am I right?" My father nodding in agreement with him. Seth slowly approached us, my father on his tail. He stretched his ivory hand out to me, waiting for me to shake it like my father had. My hand didn't move. After a moment Seth dropped his hand and annoyance spread across his face. "I understand why you wouldn't want to shake my hand boy, but it is only polite to shake the hand of the one who invited you into their home." I managed to stare blankly back at him. Then suddenly an image of Amelia popped into my head, she was smiling telling me everything would be okay. This man had killed her. He didn't deserve my politeness. "Kidnapping isn't the same thing as an invite." Levi hissed, then he was beside his father in a second. My mother jumped at his sudden nearness. "Father you let him speak to you in this way?" Seth held a hand up to his son to quieten him. His eyes never left mine. "Come let us reunite you with your pack." And for the first time since coming here my father's smile slipped from his face.

Lily

As we approached the mansion the more alarm bells started going off in my head. Warning me that as soon as I stepped inside these walls I was unprotected. But Rain needed me. The door was unlocked enabling us to step inside easily without alerting anyone else. Inside the smell of blood which had a metallic rusty smell wafted in to my nose. It made me feel sick. Sky pulled on my hand. "This way." She led me down a long corridor coloured in dark greens and reds. Black curtains dressed the faded walls. I watched the way Sky scanned around her, the way she relied on her senses to guide her. Yet it seemed she wasn't relying on the right sense. "Well look who we have here." Dam Sky you forgot hearing. We turned cautiously to find Lexi waiting behind us. She looked different. Despite her being eternal and damned never to grow old again she looked older. Her skin was paler, eyes darker and her smile more malicious than before. I could no longer picture the happy go lucky girl she once was. "It seems that you both have a death wish otherwise you wouldn't be here, then again you might have come to try and save your mate from his impending death." My heart jolted. Cole was here? Sky took hold of my wrist, keeping me in control. "Take us to them." Sky spoke. Her tone took Lexi of guard, but she composed herself as she turned. "Very well, follow me."

"Do you ever get the feeling that something bad is about to happen and you can do nothing about it?" Sky whispered to me as we followed Lexi willingly into our impending doom. I laughed in a humourless way. "All the time Sky. My life is just one big bad thing that I can't do anything about." Lexi also let out a slightly sadistic chuckle, which made my skin crawl. "Ah Lily we are the pioneers of our own life, you are the ones that choose the path that will take you through it. So really if your life is just one huge problem then maybe you need to do something about it." I hoped she could feel the red hot glare that I was giving the back of her head. From the way she rolled her shoulders and twitched a little bit, she could. That made me smile just a little bit. "So what's it like being a vampire Lex, I mean what does it feel like to be dead?" Sky spoke out loud, her words becoming bolder as she went on. Her confidence seemed to have grown a lot since the last time she spoke to her. Even though I couldn't see Lexi's face I could picture it contorted in annoyance, she never did like people asking questions about her. "Oh you know it has its perks, the speed, strength, eternal youth you know." Sky rolled her eyes at me.
"Well I don't actually know seen as I'm not like you. But if there are perks there must be some downfalls too, what are they?" I didn't understand what Sky was doing, was she intentionally trying to get us killed quicker? Lexi spun to face us, her face eerily still, frozen. "I guess you could say the downfall is that eventually one day I will have to watch everyone I love die, while I stay here." Sky's fierce expression faltered, that was her first mistake. Lexi's eyes changed then, it seemed impossible but they became darker. "Wait did I say that was a downfall, I mean that is the absolute perk of this whole thing." She then opened the door she stood in front of and pushed us briskly inside, her hands freezing on my skin. She didn't stay instead pushed us through and shut the door behind her, the lock clinking into place.

Cole

I looked up as the door opened and two familiar figures were pushed inside. My heart plummeted when I saw the recognisable halo of blonde hair. Lily and Sky turned to face us, shock carved their features. Hector, Dean, and Jett all stood at once and bowed at Lily. They each muttered "your highness" before re-seating themselves. Lily blushed slightly then looked to me. I reached for her and she folded herself comfortably into my arms. I felt more complete now with her here, despite her being in more danger for being so. "What are you doing here?" I whispered into her ear, taking in the scent of her fruity shampoo. She returned my question in my own ear, her breath tickled my neck. "We came to get Rain." We pulled back, feeling the force of the packs gazes on us. Lily blushed again then moved to Carmen who was waiting to hug her too. Sky stayed near the door suddenly unsure of her presence here. I beckoned her closer and hugged her too not wanting her to feel left out. She sighed against me, and muttered something in my ear that she knew I would be able to hear. "She hasn't spoken about her, but that doesn't mean she doesn't want to." Right Amelia. She pulled back and went to sit by Carmen who eagerly stretched her hand to her. Carmen had been starved of friends so I couldn't really blame her. Lily moved to my mother whose chained hands reached for her. My mother's eyes watered as she hugged her. Lily hugged her back tight, then let her go to frown at the chains. "Who...what...why are you here?" She managed to stutter out.

My mother took her hand and squeezed it. "I think you better sit down, it's a long story and a lot to take in." Lily looked to me and I nodded at her. Then she folded her legs in on herself and sat. She waited for my mother to speak. But she didn't. Instead she looked at me. I nodded, took a deep breath then I began to speak. The secrets and lies of my life spilled out of me, and I watched the faces of my pack, of my mate change.

Lily

His voice was tortured as he spoke. His years of abuse and lies scattered across the burgundy floor. His face stayed vacant of emotion. I watched the packs expressions as well as his. All of them hurt and angry that this had been going on for so long, but the worse thing was...that they didn't even know. Sophie looked as though she was being strangled as he spoke, the hurt and hate of a man she thought loved her instead turning out to be the man she never wanted, a man nobody would ever want. It was when he started talking about his twin sister and the fact it was James who shot him and Carmen that Dean lost it. He stood quickly, his fist bunched together, ready to punch whoever was necessary. It was then I noticed that Dean and Hectors wives weren't here, which made me wonder if he had left them out of this, or had them somewhere else. Maybe with Rain. "How could he do this? How could he do that to his mate, his child, his pack?" Carmen came to stand by her father and placed a calming hand on his shoulder. His body visibly relaxed under her touch. "Your anger is useless here, save it for when you need it." Hector then too stood, he raised his shoulders and also placed a hand on Dean. They both looked deadly and angry. "She is right Dean, and believe me you will need that anger if we're ever going to get out of here."

I ignored them and went straight to Cole. I took his hands and looked up into his beautiful pale blue eyes. "Cole, I'm so sorry for what you've been through." He smiled slightly. And reached up to brush my cheek softly. He then bent down to kiss me sweetly on the lips. He pulled back but his face was still close to mine. "You don't need to be sorry, do you want to know why?" I nodded and he smiled the sweet smile I loved so much, the one where his dimple appeared on his cheek. "Because I found you, everything in my past is forgotten when I'm here in the present with you." I smiled and kissed him back, hoping my love for him could be felt through the kiss. Someone coughed and we were forced apart. Our spectators still looked angry but they were amused by us. "Cole." Dean called to Cole as we broke apart. Cole nodded at him as he took my hand. I felt better now that I was close to him. "We follow you now Cole." Then in a sequence, Dean, Hector, Jett and Carmen all bent down on one knee and bowed to him. His mother smiled slightly but it was terribly forced. "Your Alpha now Cole." I could feel Cole's heartbeat beat against my wrist as it picked up the pace.

"Well isn't this a wonderful turn of events." With all the commotion none of us even registered the door opening. James stood tall and brooding in the doorway. His icy gaze on Cole. As Cole looked up to look his father in the eye a flash sparked between the two. James stumbled back, blinking hard, whereas Cole stood tall, even stronger than before. When James readjusted himself he glared at Cole. "You an Alpha, your barely a protector!" His voice was almost a snarl, his face twisting into a vicious smile. A low rumbling growl emanated from inside Coles throat. The pack came to stand around him, the same sounds coming from them too. Sophie me and Sky were pushed behind them, safe behind the barrier of bodies.

James began to laugh, it was almost as scary as his snarl. "Your naïve Cole, challenge me when you're ready." Cole stared at him his glare deadly. Then there was a pop behind us, someone grabbed me from behind, they were strong and very very Cold "I told you when I killed that girl in the street, that this is only the beginning." I recognised Levis voice. He only had hold of me for a moment before the heart of flames began to blaze on my chest. He let go quickly scorch marks burning into his transparent arms. His deadly eyes landed on me. Screams sounded around me as Levi launched forwards too quick for me to react and with the strength of a bull he pushed me through the large bay window behind me, allowing me to fall. Glass splintered around me scratching and tearing at my skin, and I felt myself plummeting to the ground, my life literally flashing before my eyes. Just as my face was about to hit the floor someone caught me. Whoever it was they were warm and strong. I saw a familiar pair of eyes before my vision disappeared and I blacked out.

Cole

It was too late. My reactions reacted too slow to stop Levi as I watched the glass shatter around Lily as she fell. "No!" I shouted as I raced towards the window, but Seth and Lexi were suddenly in the way. Seth shook his head at me. "You should have shook my hand in the beginning." Without even thinking I punched him square in the face sending him flying into the wall. Lexi hissed at me. The pack surrounded me, Sky and mum staying by the corner. Protecting one another. My father walked up to Seth and helped him up. Seth glared at me his face darkening. At the same time his and Lexi's fangs slipped from their gums and dad phased into his black wolf. His teeth snapping.

I glanced at Dean who nodded at me, then I looked to Sky. She read the message in my eyes. "Get out!" She nodded too. I let out a growl which was nearer to animal then human, then we all phased. Dean and Hector flanking me, Carmen and Jett behind. Seth hissed then launched himself forward. With a growl we all followed suit.

Lily

"Lily wake up. Come on Lil I need your help. Lily!" The voice became more urgent the longer my eyes stayed shut. The warm hands gently shook me awake. Peeling back my eyelids I looked up to a face I hadn't seen a while, but I had surely missed. "Reeve, is that you?" He smiled and nodded as he pulled me up into a hug. He had saved me. I would be dead without him. "Yeah it's me Lil, look we can't stay here the others need our help." He pulled me up to my feet. I looked down at my body that was bruised and tattered with scratches from the glass shards. "We need to find Rain." He nodded then took my hand and pulled me towards a back door that was covered in weeds. "Where have you been, have you been okay, does anyone know you're here?" Reeve placed a finger on my lips and smiled. "I'll answer your questions when we're out of here okay." I nodded, get a grip Lily!

Reeve examined the door for about two seconds before kicking it down with one swift movement. I looked at him in disbelief. He shrugged. "I saw someone do it in a movie once, I've always wanted to try it." I laughed at him as we went through the entry way. It was cold. The walls and floor were the same aged stubborn stone as the mansion. Metal bars shielded off areas with their rusty stance. "We're in a dungeon aren't we?" I whispered to Reeve who was scanning the place with his chocolate gaze. He nodded slightly at me.

The dungeon was a maze of discoloured rock. I relied on Reeve to get me out of here. Cole and the rest were still here somewhere above me, I could feel Coles anger as though it was my own. I knew that they all will presume I was dead, nobody could survive that fall. "Can I ask you just one question?" Reeve chuckled besides me. He looked different. His hair was shorter than before, his eyes more serious. He looked like he had aged in his plain black jeans and long sleeved top. "I forgot how impatient you are, yes ask your question then." I smiled ruefully.

"Where did you go, when you left?"

"At first I didn't go far. For the first two days I went into the town hoping some inspiration would hit and I would know where it was I wanted to go. But I didn't so I decided to follow my feet. They took me everywhere, other villages just like Ever Green. It was amazing." And I could see just how amazing it was from the happiness that radiated of him as he spoke. "So why did you come back?" He frowned for a moment lost in a memory. "I guess you could say I was always on my way back, but yesterday I got a horrible feeling in my stomach, like something bad was going to happen. So I ran back here and found that everyone was gone." So how did he find us? I didn't have to wait long he seemed to know what I was thinking. "I found mum and Aunt Lila first, they were with the king. It was them who told me that James had turned up and taken Cole and Carmen, and that James had kidnapped Jett and the others earlier so I had to hazard a guess. My instincts told me that he would be here so I followed them, I went through the tunnel and suddenly remembered that there was shield, but that didn't matter because it was gone." I laughed uneasily and he looked at me. "Yeah that was my fault, I kind of brought it down when me and Sky got through." He looked at me slightly impressed. "Anyway I was just walking when I heard you scream and watched Levi push you, do you know what I didn't even know I could move that fast!" He was making a joke but his humour was misplaced. If he hadn't been quick enough I really would be dead, and that was no laughing matter. "Well thank you for saving me." He smiled crookedly at me. "Like I said before I don't mind saving a damsel." I blushed as I remembered what else he had said the last time he had said that to me, which was when I went nearly flat on my face again running around the school track. That seemed years ago. He was just about to add something when a heart wrenching scream pierced the silence. Reeve became more alert, his eyes dilating and muscles began to contract, he shook himself and his body stopped changing. He looked at me, but his eyes held more wolf than before, maybe he wasn't in full control. "I think we've found Rain." We turned a corner and I saw what he meant.

Cole

As soon as we attacked more vampires filled the room, appearing out of nowhere. I could feel my pack fighting around me, Dean and Hector staying close to Carmen and Jett who weren't protectors yet, who haven't even been in a scrap yet. But my attention was on my father and Seth. Lexi was busy fighting Dean. Her fangs nipping at his fur but not close enough to get to the skin, her arms were covered in his scratch marks. "Do you want him or do you want me to take care of him?" My father looked at him alarmed, Seth smiled slyly down at him.
"Don't tell me your feeling sentimental, he is just a boy nothing else. If he doesn't die then you can't control the pack. You must challenge him!" My father growled at him. My hackles began to rise. Whatever my father's choice I was fighting one of them. But Seth didn't give him a choice, nor did he give me enough time to react before his stone hard body smashed against mine.

I scrambled away from him, getting my body back of the ground. I growled and snapped my teeth at him. But he wasn't far behind me. His hands pulled at my fur as my claws sank into his pristine skin. I noticed that everyone around us has stopped fighting, instead they all watched Seth try to sink his teeth into my skin. I rolled which made Seth's grip on me collapse, feeing me. My pack quickly moved to flank me once again. The remaining vampires that Hector and Dean hadn't got to surrounded Seth and Lexi, my father flanked him too. I quickly examined my pack, we were all bleeding in some way, but we were fine. "Join us Cole and you can have everything you want, power, and friendship family. You don't need a mate, all she would have done is hold you back." I growled loudly hoping he could sense my anger. My mate was dead because of him now he will die too. I ignored my heart shattering as I thought about Lily, as I hunched down ready to pounce.

Lily

There. Laid upon the cold stone was Rain. Her body was sprawled across it in distress, her face stained with tears. But she was silent. I started towards her but Reeve stopped me with his hand on my arm. "No something's wrong look at all the blood." I looked back at her again and saw what he saw. Blood splattered the stone around her and flecked her skin. I tugged my arm from his grip and went to her. Her skin was ashen and freezing as I bent down to touch her, but my touch didn't even make her twitch. I examined her body to see countless bruises and bite marks on her ankles and wrist, her breathing was shallow. "Reeve look bite marks do you think they...?" I let my question hang there in the quiet hoping he would get what I was meaning. He shook his head at me and also bent down to examine her. I didn't know how well Reeve knew Rain but I was suddenly protective of her. "Lily these aren't Lamia bites there...wolf." The word startled me despite me hearing it nowadays on a regular basis. "Why would a wolf bite her?" Reeve carried on examining Rain as he answered. "I don't know, we were always told you could only become a wolf if you were born this way, not bitten." I frowned at him so he clarified. "But that wouldn't stop someone trying." I smoothed away one of Rains soft brown curls that had become clustered with dirt and blood. "So do you think James did this?" Reeve nodded. He then slipped his arms underneath her frail motionless body and picked her up into his arms. Her limp head fell against his shoulder. "Cole told me that she was dying and James thought he could save her by biting her, but neither of us actually thought he might do it."

We started back the way we came, the maze seeming longer than it had before. "We have to go back and get the rest of them." Reeve carried on in his long stride, forcing me to jog to catch up. He shook his head defiantly. "No I'll go back and you can get Rain to safety." He wasn't the only one who could be stubborn. "No how about I go back and you get Rain to safety." He huffed and stopped so he could turn and glare at me, I mirrored him the best as I could. "You're not a wolf Lily, the only way were getting out of here is a fight. You have no battle strategy."

"And you do!" He sighed expatriated. My stubbornness wasn't making him laugh anymore now. "So if we both go what about Rain, who will take her?" Good question, but before I could answer someone else did. "We will." Both of us turned around quickly Reeve pushing me behind him automatically. But we needn't have been worried, it was Sophie and Sky. "Lily your alive!" Sky squealed as she ran to hug me, I could feel her tears as she buried her face in my neck. "Yes I'm fine Sky. Reeve saved me." She pulled back and awarded Reeve with the best smile she could summon at this present time. Reeve quickly returned it before turning to Sophie. "How did you two escape, what about everyone else?" Sophie hadn't taken her eyes of me since she arrived, but as Reeve spoke she directed her emerald sight onto him. "It was Cole he's Alpha now, as everyone attacked he pushed us out of the room. The rest are still in the room as before they were fighting. But Lily I think Cole needs to see you, as his mate I can't imagine the pain he will be in thinking you're dead it might make him reckless." I nodded at her, I knew the pain he was in, I could feel it piercing my heart every second. Reeve frowned slightly. "You bonded?" Reeve handed Rain over to Sky who opened up her arms to accept her. Before they left Sophie turned to me, her eyes holding the protective glint of a mother who wanted to protect her child. "Be careful, both of you. Seth is dangerous and cruel and he has already tried to kill you once, he won't hesitate to do it again. Bring them all home safe Lily including yourself!" With that they both turned left through the back door in hope of not being recaptured, and getting Rain to safety. That left me with Reeve and his unanswered question. Maybe I should have taken Rain after all. "Reeve...we...we were always bonded, from the moment we saw one another on the side of the road all those years ago." His frown deepened and his voice became more strained.

"How was that even possible, you would have known?" I had vowed to myself that when the day came when I would see Reeve again I wouldn't hurt him anymore. Now here I am breaking my promise. "Reeve we didn't know, honestly." He didn't answer instead sharply turned his body back around and strode off. His only words were. "Well we better hurry, we wouldn't want your mate to do something stupid."

Cole

I could feel my muscles bunching up, coiled. Ready to attack. The presence of my pack following my lead was exhilarating. The vamps lips curled into a snarl their ivory teeth snapping. But before I could even leap forward, or before they could jump, there was a blast of white light. I flinched away from it. It was out of this light that two figures emerged. One a brown wolf with brown eyes. Reeve. The other a beautiful angelic girl I never thought I'd see again. Lily. Reeve came to stand by his father and Carmen and Lily took her place in front of us all. Her shoulders back, eyes bearing into each of our enemies. Her voice rumbled through us, her intent only for them who caused us harm. "My name is Lily Alana Amelia Ever princess of Ever" her eyes glowed slightly her power from her acceptance of herself and the power that had stayed hidden beneath so long radiated out of her. "You will bow!" I watched in shock as one by one the vampires began to bow to her, she kept her gaze on Seth and my father, who under her intense gaze also followed her order. Reluctantly.

"Good now that I have your attention. You will let us leave without any further harm. You will also leave this place too and find refuge in a place where I will never have to see or hear from you ever again. Well everyone except you!" She pointed at Seth, who glared at her with hunger in his eyes. If she hadn't been a Shadow, then she would have been dead. "You can stay and rot in here for all I care, count it as punishment for killing Amelia. You will not leave!" Her power ripped through him and he fell further onto his knees. He picked his head up so his glare could reach her. "You will pay for this young princess, you have more enemies out there than us. Just because you order us away doesn't make us disappear." Lily then to my utter dismay and surprise. Moved towards him. She bent down so she could be at level with him. She smiled a complete sarcastic smile. She then pulled the heart of fire from around her neck and placed the ruby coloured gem against his chest. The stone blazed a white hot flame. Seth began to writhe in pain but Lily kept her hold on him tight. The others were forced to watch due to Lily's order. She then let him go. "I wanted you to feel the pain I felt when you made me watch you kill my great grandmother. I wanted it to burn into your heart too, but seen as you haven't got one, the stone burned through the ice of your evil." She stood and came back to stand in front of them. "You will not move until we are off the mountain side!"

She then turned on her heel and walked back the way she had come. The pack following her lead. Before I reached the door I looked back at them. Frozen in a bow. My father's icy gaze found mine, the ice had now melted into the fire of fury. But I couldn't feel anything for him. He was no longer my father. He was no longer anything. Just a man who risked everything for power, only to lose more than what he had gained.

By the time I caught up with the rest of them we were already at the tunnel. Lily stopped at the entrance and lifted her hands back to the air. A golden shimmer began to build around her hands, slowly spreading further, upwards and across. "You will not allow Seth passage through." The shield sparked and then disappeared into nothingness. The rest had started to make their way back down the mountain, but I waited for her. My mate. She was alive, she was amazing, she was beautiful. There was so many emotions flitting through my head as I looked at her. She bent down and kissed the fur on my head. "Let's go home."

Reeve

It had been two days since everyone found out the truth, since Lily forced Seth to stay trapped in Kolga while the others we allowed to be free. Two days since she had told me her plan, it had seemed crazy at the tIme. Now, looking back it didn't seem so insane. We had been nearly at the room when she had stopped me, her blue eyes excited despite knowing she might not come out of this thing alive. "Battle strategy?"
"What?" She laughed slightly then glanced around her to make sure no one was there to hear her. "Yeah I didn't think so, so here's the plan." And that's when she explained it. How she was relying on her Shadow instincts and her own power to get us out of here. She would use the bright light that the dream stone created when she wanted to delete a dream to

distract them while we entered. How she was relying on the fact that her mother was a Guardian, who could control every supernatural creature. How she would make Seth pay for Amelia's death by forcing him into isolation. It had seemed reckless and crazy at the time. Now it was utterly brilliant.

Sky had waited for us at the crossroads splitting main town Ever into the different lands. She explained that Sophie had taken Rain to the king to be healed. And that was when we spit ways again. Lily not ready for that part of her life yet decided to return to Ever Green with Sky to help her parents plan Amelia's funeral. Cole knew he needed to be with his pack, but had left for at least an hour for the past two days to check on her. Each time jealousy tugged at my heart strings, but I ignored it. She would never be mine and I needed to accept that. But how?

Cole

I looked at her and she stared back. Blue battling maroon. Challenging me. Unlike my mother and the others Rain and I hadn't yet left the castle. We were both being held captive here, Rain more than me. I was free to come and go as long as I did come back to fill the king on what was going on. Rain however had to remain chained to the wall. Her body unpredictable and changing. You see my sadistic father had gone along with his plan after all. He had bitten Rain, and now she was changing. Or, dying more rapidly than before. We didn't know this was the first time anything had happened like this. We were born this way not bitten. It was impossible and yet as I watched her convulse and shake I thought that maybe it was possible. If this had happened to a normal Mortalis, a normal human then the venom that was hidden in our canines would just pass through your system, affecting nothing in its wake. But Rain wasn't normal, not only was her natural biological defences down due to her dying already she was an ancestor of a strong werewolf line which meant her body would react differently to the bite. She had known when she had come to live with us that it would happen eventually, we all did, and yet I hadn't actually believed it would.

Rain stood panting, bound to the castle walls in the lower dungeons. Her forehead was beaded with sweat, clothes shredded from near changes, mouth curved in pain but she was tiring now. As the new appointed Alpha it was my job to make sure she made it through. I tried to recall the first time that I had changed. I was ten, it was painless. It was almost like breathing. I inhaled and the heat of the change ran through my body, I exhaled and I was a wolf. As easy as that. It was similar from what I heard from Reeve, Jett and Carmen, quick and swift. Not this an agonised change, slow and steady. She suddenly let out a pain filled scream, tears were now pricking at her eyes as her pine arched into more of a curve, I could hear the bones splintering as they rearranged themselves. Her nails had begun to darken and extend into claws.

She had been in this state of pain and change from the moment she reawakened two days ago. She had healed miraculously from the injuries she had sustained. When she had opened her eyes I had been too immersed in my relief that I didn't detect the shift in mood with her until it was almost two late. Her eyes had dilated and she had sprung quickly at unexpecting nurse who had been helping her. I had caught her just before she had got enough momentum to lunge. Hence why she was now chained. Sometimes the wolf's instincts were too much to take at first, you learnt how to control it though. She screamed again but this time I heard words within the noise. "What's happening to me?" She knew really what was happening to her, her brain was just hoping that it wasn't true. "My father bit you, we think that you're becoming one of us." Her teeth gritted so tight that I could hear them scrape against one another. She managed to talk between gritting her teeth and crying. "Ha he did it then, actually thought he was joking." There was no humour in her statement. She didn't want this, the monster had decided it for her. I moved forward so I was in front of her. Come on Cole you're the Alpha, she needs your help! I took her shaking sweaty face in my hands and forced her to look directly into my eyes, she gasped as she began to feel the Alpha power sear into her, she managed a grimace at me. "You're going to be okay Rain, you've been through so much so this cannot be the end. You're the bravest strongest person I know. You've looked death in the eye many times and all you did was laugh and shake him of, this is nothing compared to that" she began to smile for real this time. Her heart rate began to slow to normal again. It was working. "I know you didn't want this, but things happen at least now you won't doubt how strong you are, now you won't have to worry about dying, we're with you Rain, always." I released her then feeling the spike of the change heighten. I stepped back and watched her skin ripple away being replaced with fur, watched her face elongate into a muzzle. The chain that held her to the wall suddenly broke as her back cracked forcing her down, but four furry legs were there to catch her. She didn't move, instead she kept her eyes still on me. I looked back at her and saw the shining dark hazelnut brown wolf that stood in her place.

Rain

I do not fear the world, but I do fear my reflection, for I am scared that it will one day show me somebody I do not recognise, and I fear that person will be me.

Pain was a mere understatement for the way I had been feeling for the past two days. Agony wasn't even a strong enough word to justify the immense ache and snap of my bones as they began to reshape. I knew what I was becoming long before I had asked Cole to clarify. A wolf. A werewolf. Was that now my destiny? Did I even believe in destiny? I knew now that the dark ominous loom of my death had now been postponed, but I wasn't comforted. I wanted to live don't get me wrong, but I didn't want this.

I knew it was nearly over when my spine finally caved in too tired to withhold the change any longer. It forced me onto all fours where my arms and legs lengthened and bulged changing to front legs and hind legs. I felt the cold stone floor beneath my padded paws. When it was over I kept my eyes on Cole. Too scared to even glance at the mirror they had left abandoned by the door, waiting for this moment. Cole stayed where he was, drifting in the door way. His smile however brightened the room and lightened my heart a little bit more since the change. "You don't need to be afraid of your reflection Rain, your wolf is a part of you, but it's not all of you." Knowing he would probably just use his Alpha power on me I used my own free will to look at myself in the mirror. There in the shiny glass was a plain hazelnut wolf. She was strangely beautiful. Not at all what I thought I would look like. "I'm going to shift too, then we are going home where the pack will accept you, before you freak out that just means they will scent you so that they will be able to recognise you." Before I could even bob my heavy new skull he had disappeared through the doorway, a minute later returning in his stormy grey fur. It felt so long ago since I met him in the clearing. We were both new people now. Like he did in the clearing he waited for me, and like before I followed.

Cole

I wasn't prepared for the emotions that bombarded me as we arrived home. I hadn't been back here since the day we went looking for my mum. This is the place where everything had started. I hated it and loved it at the same time. I wanted to leave but then stay it was confusing. Yes this place reminded me of the monster but it was home. That was that. Mum and Skyla were the first to meet us. Skyla had been safely looked after by Delia and Lila while everything had gone on. It seemed Dean had an idea something like this would happen, so he left Delia a note explaining for them to go into the town and disappear until someone called. They had been safe, but all I kept thinking about was, what if no one had called? What would they have done? Both of them placed a kiss onto our foreheads, Skyla giggled as the spiky tufts of fur on my head tickled her. She beamed at Rain "you're so pretty." My mum nodded at her with a smile before tugging Skyla by the hand out of the way. Lila and Delia then came out and echoed mum and Skyla's actions, both of them mumbling compliments on Rains new appearance. They two moved to where the other two stood, Delia took hold of Skyla's hand and Lila took hold of Delia's. They would never be wolves, well we didn't know about Skyla yet but the three women never would be. But they were pack, they were here to accept her too.

I moved and planted myself in front of Rain, my back to the others. Rain fidgeted uncomfortably under everyone's gaze. Then one by one the others began to join us, slowly creating a circle around Rain, leaving her in the middle. There was Dean and Reeve who were almost identical in their wolf forms as they were in real life. Both a light brown with darker patches here and there, Dean however had small hints of grey now in his fur. Then there was Hector the stark snowy white wolf patched with grey. Lastly Jett and Carmen emerged taking their places in the circle. Jett a nimble sandy brown that matched his natural hair and Carmen the same brown as her father and brother except highlighted with streaks of gold. Following my lead each of us stepped forward to take a sniff of Rain, she was still, frozen in a storm of fear and anxiousness. It surprised me when her scent filled my nostrils that she still smelled of cinnamon, her natural scent. Her eyes then began to grow wider as one by one we began to bow, belly's to the ground, eyes and nose down. Accepted. We all then looked up to the once dark sky. The sun had begun to peak above the trees. Sunrise.

The women moved quickly placing towels around each of us as we began to shift back with the sun. Rain remained stuck both in her wolf form and from shock. Carmen who was now wrapped carefully in a towel stepped towards her. Her brown hair flowing in the breeze as she did. Then she placed her palm against Rains head. Rain shivered and as quickly as the rest of us she shifted back. Carmen helped her to her feet. She smile brightly at her "welcome to the pack Rain."

Rain

I stood in the centre of my room hoping that the painted flowers I had created on my walls would calm me like they had done before. I could feel the early morning light creep up my spine as it trailed through my window. I wrapped my arms around myself. My body felt different. Stronger, fuller. I was no longer weak and fragile but strong and maybe even slightly a bit more invincible. I heard my bedroom door open and close as someone entered. The scent of the wood filled the space around me. Cole. It was strange how I knew it was him before he had even had chance to speak, how I recognised him from the way he smelled. "How do you feel?" I glanced over my shoulder and found Cole as he moved to sit on my pristine bed. I wanted to hit him for ruffling my perfect cushions. I restrained myself and answered his question instead. "Better I guess, you?" He looked away which gave me a moment to look at him. He had changed too. I hadn't noticed it before, too in pain and my normal human eyes wouldn't have picked up the subtle difference. However they did now. His expression was harder, almost older. As though his eyes had aged and his body had not. His muscles were more defined than before, and even though we were in one of the most mundane of settings I could detect the slight ripple of the Alpha power on him. Different. "I don't know how to feel just yet." I guess we had that in common.

"How's Lily?" He had let his eyes drop now to his forearm where his protector mark was, forever inking his skin with his purpose and destiny. "She seems okay. She's helping her family organise Amelia's funeral, I think she's just trying to distract herself though." From what? From what I had been told it was Lily who had saved us all with her totally hidden badass skills. I guess like me and Cole she didn't know how to feel about that yet. "Can I ask you a question?" I sat down on the wooden floor. The cool ground soothed the fever that was brewing inside of me. Was I still ill? I nodded at him. "You never told me about your life, where did you live? How did you meet my father?" I laughed at him slightly.
"I'm pretty sure that was more than one question, but I get the idea." He sat up so he was looking at me intently. Waiting for me to start. "I lived in a small village on the outskirts of Ever. It was a small community only three other families lived there along with us. It was just me and dad and the other families, we were all close, but not close enough for the adults to answer my questions about my mum. I guess they knew it hurt my dad too much when he heard about her, so I long ago accepted I wouldn't learn anything about her there. I was about ten when they first realised I was ill, I would come home from playing out with the other kids and have huge headaches, it didn't matter how much water or sleep I got the pain was still there. One day I was just playing when my head scorched and I passed out. Dad said that they couldn't wake me up so he had to take me

to a human hospital. They scanned me and found that I had a tumour on my brain, and the headaches were caused by added pressure from the tumour, my dad knew about my heritage and couldn't risk the human doctors detecting anything about me that could get us into trouble, so that's when he went looking for help somewhere else. I guess that's where he met your dad. I remember him coming home one evening and told me he had a cure, but told me I had to go away and that I would be different. I hadn't really known what he meant until I saw you in the clearing. I haven't been back and I haven't seen him since."

I had barely finished before Cole was in front of me pulling me up from the floor. Then he pulled me into a hug. "You can see him again if you want to. When we found my mum there was another man there, the king took him back to help him, his name is Max he told the king he was your father but I wasn't sure." I pulled away from him and looked at his face, pale and earnest. He wasn't lying. "Is he okay?" I asked and let worry dip into my tone. Cole nodded reassuringly. I moved to the door then and looked back at him, me waiting this time. And like I he didn't even hesitate as he followed me.

Lily

Amelia's funeral had been my only thought for the past two days. I didn't want to think about the likelihood that Rain might die changing into a wolf, didn't want to remember how much Cole had lost, I didn't want to think about how somehow I knew what I was going to do, how I had let my power control me. How I saved everyone. Remarkably. Sky had been stuck to my side like a limpet on the sea shore ever since we had got back, only leaving to change and shower. Currently we were immersed in the flower arrangements. We had come to some sort of unspoken agreement. Neither of us would talk about what happened. I stared at the red and pink roses mum had picked for the arrangement, they didn't look like something Amelia would have chosen. Sky was looking at me. I could see on her face that she had been looking for a way to broach the subject cleverly, she was about to break the unspoken promise. "Why did you only keep Seth there, why not the others?" I knew this particular question had been coming, so for a while I had been coming up with some scenarios to the answer. "Seth killed Amelia and I knew deep down that he would kill again so I couldn't risk it, the other vampires I don't know so I cannot judge reasonably what they would do, I guess I wanted to give them the chance to prove that they aren't like him, that vampires don't have to be like they are in the stories." As I spoke I made sure my eyes remained on the flowers. I see from the corner of my eye Sky shift in her seat, becoming more intent than before. "But what about Levi he nearly killed you, and James and Lexi? I'm pretty sure they've all proven to you what's in their hearts Lil." I pushed the magazine of petals away from me. Then I sucked up the courage and looked at her. "I guess there's a part of me that thought, or hoped that they might change. That James would realise his mistakes and be a proper father, or Lexi realise that she doesn't have to be so cold and evil. That she could still be our friend despite everything. And Levi, well I don't really know why I didn't lock him up to, I guess I pitied him in some way."

I watched as my words sank in, she didn't smile but her eyes had lightened a fraction more than before. "Do you know why you're going to be great Lil?" I shook my head at her so she took my hand. "Because you have hope."

Rain

The king met us outside his throne room. He was dressed in his normal formal attire, minus the billowing cloak. He seemed smaller, younger without the velvet blanket. He regarded Cole as though he was an equal, along the way they had formed a bond that had become unbreakable. I was suddenly jealous. I envied the way that Cole easily got people to like him, how easily he gained peoples trust. The king then moved his pale eyes to me and regarded me differently too. He took my hand in his, mine looking bronzed and glowing against his ghostly pale one. He shook the hand carefully. "I'm glad that you made it Rain, I can sense you will be a great wolf." I managed a smile at him. My nerves nibbling in on my insides. Where was my dad? The king released my hand and pushed the great double oak doors open that led into the throne room.

There, stood in amongst the cool stone walls was my father. The past six months had aged him considerably. My father didn't age, or he hadn't for a long time. But now I saw flickers of grey in his dark hair, slight wrinkles starting to crease his eyes. His tanned face was taut and cut but when he caught a glimpse of me he managed to glow and smile. "Rain!" He cried. I left the king and Cole behind and ran to my father's open arms. As soon as I reached him his strong arms enveloped me into a desperate hug. The smell of cinnamon filled my senses, erupting images of my old life into my mind. He smelt like home. "Rain I've missed you very much!" His slight common Ever accent flickered into his voice. I pulled back and saw tears leaking from my father's eyes, I brushed them away and smiled up at him. "I've missed you too dad." He smiled brightly back and took my hands in his. He cocked his head to the side watching me, his eyebrow raised. "You seem different, are you…?" He didn't finish. But then again he didn't need to, I knew what he meant. I nodded my head at him, not able to speak. His smile then began to sparkle. "So you're okay now?" This time I didn't have to answer even though I wanted to. "Yes she's okay now and fully accepted into my pack." Cole and the king had finally stepped into the room after giving us space to reunite. My father then watched Cole, observing him too. Then he released one of my hands to stretch it out to Cole. "My name is Max, your Cole right?" Cole had taken my father's hand and shook it carefully, he nodded at my father as he said his name. "I guess I have a lot to thank you for, not only have you saved my daughter's life, but you saved mine. It was you, and you your majesty who saved me from that man." Cole flushed slightly under my father's thanks, the king merely smiled and nodded at him.

"I guess you have a choice now Rain, you can live with us, or you can live with your dad." Cole let his voice hang in the air. "But what about the pack?" Cole smiled his charming smile, it was a smile I recognised he pulled when someone said something he liked to hear, or if someone had said something to make him laugh. "No matter where you live Rain, you will always be pack."

Lily

I do not fear death, merely the unknown life I will live once I have left this world. Death is the goodbye, moving on is forgetting the soul that was once mine.

Time moved like it had always moved. Slow, then swift the next. Days had passed since saving everyone on the mountain. Days had passed since Rain had become a wolf and had been reunited with her father. Which meant days had passed since Amelia had died. Today was a day I had been dreading ever since she had died, because now I really had to let go and say goodbye. But I didn't know if I was ready to do that yet. Today was her funeral.

I stood alone in the bathroom staring at my reflection. My long blonde hair had been tied back in a long droopy ponytail. I left my face bare because makeup wouldn't hide the shadows beneath my eyes, my eyes were already red. I hadn't cried. My body was just preparing me to. I looked pale under the dim light, the deep black dress I was wearing didn't help, I pulled at it. There was a knock on the door. They didn't let me answer when they entered. It was Sky. She too had her masses of hair held in a ponytail and wore a simple black dress. She didn't hug me, she didn't ask if I was okay, because she understood that it would have been a stupid question. Instead she took my hand in hers and led me out of the bathroom and down the stairs to where my family was waiting.

Cole and Rain were meeting us at the churchyard, so Sky had agreed to come with me. My mother held her Grandmother's hand. Both had similar bloodshot eyes. They both looked at me as I descended. My grandmother hadn't known what to say to me when she found out I had been there when Amelia had died. I felt that the information had created a distance between us. We hadn't been all that close to start with, but now. The distance seemed gaping. My granddad stayed close to the door, his comfort was in Leah's hand as he held onto it tightly. Amelia wasn't his mother but when his own mother had died when he was twenty, Amelia had taken him under her wing and cared for him too. Leo came to stand by me and like Sky he took my hand. With their hands in mine I felt like I had the strength to continue. I took a breath then took a step out the door.

Cole

I remembered the first time I ever met Amelia. She had known what I was and wasn't exactly warm about it, but as time went on I began to understand the hurt she had endured. Her husband like me was a wolf, and like me and Lily were bonded for life. She had been protecting us both. It felt too late now to appreciate what she had done. She was gone, destined to become a memory just like Jack had become.

Rain waited in the living room for me. She had been up bright an early slowly getting ready. She had only known Amelia a while but she was family, apart from her dad she was the only family she had left, as we still didn't know where Alice was. She let her brown curls free and wore a black dress she had borrowed from my mum. Her eyes were red. I stepped through the door and she turned towards me. The change into a wolf had changed her, she was stronger more grown up than before. But today with her bloodshot eyes she still reminded me of that girl I found not so many months ago. A girl who needed me and my family to look after her. "Are you ready?" Nobody could really be ready for this. She nodded and followed me outside where Carmen, Reeve, Jett and my mother waited. I quirked my eyebrow at them. Carmen stepped forward. "We're coming for support, we don't abandon pack when they need us." Carmen's words brought Rains eyes closer to tears than they already were. She managed a watery smile towards them. My mother stepped forward to take Rains hand. "I may not be your biological mother but when Cole brought you home that day you became my daughter, so I'll be with you through this holding your hand Rain." I smiled at my mother. Rain started to cry but pulled my mother to her and hugged her tightly.

My mother automatically wrapped her arms around her, comforting. I could hear Rain whisper. "Thank you."

Reeve came and stood by me. He like me wore simple black trousers and shirt with a darker black tie. "When you came back I bet you didn't expect all this to happen." He was right. When I had come home I had expected what had been happening for the past six years of my life. Nothing. Occasional abuse and then moving on to a new place. Never had I expected to be going to school, to meet Lily, for Reeve to leave for a while, for Lily to be who she is, for her to be my mate. For my father to be an ally to Seth, for people dying. For everything that had happened in the past few months. "Don't you feel like this is just the beginning that something bigger is starting?" Reeve looked warily at me, but I knew he knew what I meant. He agreed with me whether he could admit it out loud or not. This was not the end, it was just the beginning. Levi hadn't been lying that day when he killed that Mortalis girl on the street. "Reeve Cole are you ready?" Mum called to us as we began to leave for the church.

Lily

The church was airy and quiet. I sat on the front bench with my family, Rain and the others sat behind me. I thought Rain should have been next to me but my Grandmother had just wanted us. She didn't want to believe that Alice might be alive let alone her having a daughter. Deep down she must still be hurting from Alice's disappearance. Amelia had written in her will that she had wanted her friends to speak at her funeral. I didn't know anyone who spoke but it was nice. They shared stories of her from her younger years which made us laugh and cry. It became clear that all through her life she remained loyal and protective over the people she loved. It made my memories of her stronger which I appreciated. I didn't want to forget her.

She had also asked if I would speak at her funeral too. I was the only family member she had asked. I felt honoured, but scared. I've never spoke in front of an audience before. Then a memory flashed into my mind. Me standing in front of a group of supernatural beings and taking control. I could do this. I stood up slowly and made my way to the pedestal where the others had spoken from. I took a breath and cleared my throat, which had become blocked with emotion. I unfolded my piece of paper. And began to speak.

"Hi, for those of you who don't know me I'm Lily. Amelia was my great grandmother." I paused and watched everyone's eyes bear into me. Breathe Lily. "Amelia was a very special person, not only to me but to everyone in this room. Her friendship and love touched us all in different ways and I know I'm not the only person who is thankful for that. She has taught me a lot of things in the years I had grown up knowing her. One was to never swear in front of a police officer." People began laughing all remembering that particular incident where she had cussed out a police officer, she would have been arrested but the officer seemed to be well humoured, everyone in Ever Green knew of her swearing habits anyways. "Another is to never put a cake in the microwave." Again laughter. "but most importantly she taught me that no matter what happens in life, we all have to be true to ourselves, because if we aren't living for ourselves then what are we really living for? And its only now do I realises she has always wanted me to answer that question, so my answer is we live for those we love, for without love there is nothing. And we love you Amelia, and in that love your memory will live on forever in our hearts and memories." The last word came out more of a splutter as emotion had overwhelmed me and the tears were endless. I wasn't alone, I saw that nearly everyone was crying.

My grandmother stood when I came down from the stand she took me in her arms and hugged me. She spoke through her tears. "Thank you Lil, she would have really liked that." I let her go and sat back down.

When the service was over we all followed the coffin out into the churchyard to watch her be lowered into the ground. Cole had finally found me and was stood at my side as we watched. His hand was in mine comforting me even though he wasn't really doing anything. He

whispered quietly "et reversus est in anima ad corpus rediit ad Silam et Serenae." I frowned as I looked up at him. "What does that mean?" He stepped forward hand still in mine, to place a rose onto the lid of the coffin, he stepped back and spoke. "It's an old prayer we say when someone dies, it means let the soul return to Silas and body return to Serena." Recognition dawned on me. They were the names from the story. "You mean Serena and Silas from the story?" He nodded as we began to move away from the coffin so others could place flowers. "Yes Serena is the queen of the earth, and in our legends all bodies come from the earth and are created by her, the soul is a heavenly thing so it comes from Silas and is created by him." I pulled him to stop, I glanced around at everyone who was watching the coffin descend into the ground. "So god is them they are our creators?" Cole shrugged at me.
"It's what we believe in, every religion is different I guess you could say this is ours." So what god did that make Storm? I knew he could control the supernatural and created the Guardians, but what else was he?

Rain

I knew it would be difficult to say goodbye, but I didn't think it would be this difficult. I hadn't known her long, but hearing stories about her from over the years I felt angry that I never got the chance to fully get to know that person, before she was viciously taken from me. I didn't have much family as it is and now it seemed suddenly a lot smaller. My mother had been a vacant seat in my life, my father had been caring and everything I would want in a father except for the fact that we weren't allowed to talk about my mother. Then there was the Stars and the pack, even though James had threatened to tear them apart they came back stronger, held together by family. I wanted that. Others I could fall back on when I made mistakes or I was scared. I thought that Amelia would be that person, then she died. Leaving me drowning in a world full of wanting. Then I became a wolf and I got my father back, I got a family. Yet, it didn't feel like enough. There was still apart that was missing, and I didn't know what would fill it. My mother, someone else? I didn't know.

Sophie had stayed with me the entire time, holding my hand. Somewhere along the way I had gained a mother, like she had said earlier I had become her daughter the moment I came to them, I guess she became my mother in that way too. I watched Amelia's coffin being lowered into the ground before I let Sophie steer me away. Lily's words kept replaying in my head. "We live for those we love, without love there is nothing." It was scary how right she actually was. Nobody wanted to live in a world where they had no one to love or to love them. I guess now I understood why my dad didn't want to talk about my mum, apart from me she was the only thing he had to love in this world. He had no family as he was orphaned at the age of three, abandoned in a small village full of people who didn't have family either. He grew up learning how to fend for himself, and when he was old enough, he learned how to leave that place and find somewhere new. I admired him for that, to be able to do what he did takes a lot of strength, but even he has his limits, I just guess she was one of them.

Carmen and the others had left after the service which left Cole and Lily waiting for us by the gate. Carmen had organised a 'girly' night for me, Lily and Sky. I didn't really know what that entitled but I couldn't wait anyway, I needed something to keep my mind of everything for a while and I think Lily would agree. Sophie smiled at them both and spoke to Lily. "Sky said she will bring your stuff over when she comes, Carmen told me to tell you that you will have fun." Lily managed to smile slightly. She knew what Carmen could be like. Lily had changed a lot from the past few days, she wasn't so light anymore. It was as though her sorrow was sucking the life out of her leaving behind a cracking shell. But there was a glimmer of her still in her eyes. I think like I, we needed time to adjust to the things we have lost and gained. "Excuse me miss, but are you Rain Cloud?" I turned around to face the voice who had spoken, which had been strangely formal. Then again it was a funeral.

There stood a woman. She had short brown hair, tanned skin. One sparkling blue eye and another a glowing brown. Her smile was familiar like I had worn it myself. I managed to nod at her and her smile brightened. Her heavy accent that I didn't recognise but knew it wasn't local shrouded around me like a shield. "My name is Alice Cloud, I am your mother."

Lily

I stared at Alice Cloud hoping to find something in her expression that I could forgive for putting me through so much trouble trying to find her, only for her to turn up out of the blue anyway. I didn't. Instead I found unmistakable characteristics of both Rain and Amelia. It made my eyes sting with more tears. Rain hadn't said a word since Alice had revealed herself. She simply stared at her in total shock. I couldn't really blame her, it was a rational response. Alice smiled again not ever indicating she was uncomfortable with this surprise reunion. "I can't believe how grown up you are, you were just a baby when I…" she didn't finish, but it seemed to snap Rain out of her daze. She glared up at Alice. "What when you abandoned us!" Alice flinched at the anger in her daughters tone, but she couldn't have not thought that this might have been a problem. "I can explain that if you will let me." Rain didn't say anything. Instead Sophie pulled Rain back so she was behind her. Then she switched on full mother bear mode. She stared down Alice. "What are you doing here Alice?" Alice frowned at my mother, sensing the undercurrent of a woman who would definitely take her down if she threatened any of her children, including Rain. "I came to say goodbye to my mother and too see my daughter." Sophie narrowed her eyes at her, not for one second blinking. "You've had plenty of time to see her and Rain, why now?" Alice suddenly began to look ashamed and sad. A single tear slid down her cheek and I saw Sophie falter a moment, just a moment. "I couldn't. I wasn't even supposed to be here today but I had to come…to say goodbye. I never wanted this." She wiped the single tear off her cheek quickly as though she was ashamed it was even there, that she even had enough sentiment to cry. "What about Rain then?" It was me who spoke up this time. Alice looked at me for the first time and I knew from her expression she saw the uncanny resemblance to me and my mother. She smiled.

"Well little princess if we find somewhere private I will explain everything, for what I have to say links to you, to your mate and to my daughter, and because of this I have come back when I should not."

Cole

My mother didn't let Alice anywhere near Rain as we made our way out of the churchyard. I didn't know if it was because she didn't trust Alice or the fact that she just didn't like Alice. Either way her mothering instincts were on over drive. We decided to go back to our house to talk. I texted Reeve to tell Carmen the girls would be a bit late coming over. I knew he knew something was going on but he didn't ask, he knew I would tell him eventually.

When we got home I asked Lily to take Rain and Alice into the living room so I could talk to my mother alone in the kitchen. She made herself busy making hot drinks for everyone even though she hadn't offered them anything yet. "Mum what are you doing?" She carried on messing around with the over used kettle. I moved the kettle away from her and she frowned at me. "I was making coffee but the kettle doesn't want to work." I arched my eyebrow at her and she quickly moved over to the fridge to collect the milk. "We both know that's not what I meant, but if you need me to clarify here it is. What are you doing Alice needs to speak to Rain you cannot stop that." I said it softly but she reacted as though I had shouted. She dropped the milk carton that was in her hand and shouted back at me. "Yes I can Cole! Do you want to know why? Because I've been more of a mother to that girl than that woman in there has, she will not just show up here and take her!"

Before I could say anything Alice appeared in the door way. My mother glared at her. "That is not why I am here, and even if it was she would be given the choice and I'm pretty sure she would choose you guys over me." My mum didn't answer her instead she picked up the carton of milk and made her way back to the kettle. "Why don't you go and get Skyla from Deans she won't like if you're away for too long, while we will talk." I thought she might argue, but she didn't. Instead she left softly through the deck doors. Alice raised her eyebrow at me, a slight smile tugging at her lips. "It seems your Alpha power works on humans too." Weird I hadn't been using it had I?

We moved back into the living room. The three of us sat on our small sofa while Alice remained standing in front of us. She began fiddling with the button on her jacket. She was nervous. When she looked up her expression seemed to have tired and aged since five minutes ago. She looked sad. "First things first I need to apologise to all of you, especially you Rain. I've been absent in your life for so long and I'm sure you've needed me at some point and I wasn't there, but I'm trying now." Rain didn't speak but she nodded her head. Alice then flicked her gaze between me and Lily. "And I apologise to you two for spending so much time trying to find me, I see you saw some of my memories in your dreams Lily, but the spell I have on me would have prevented your gift from ever showing you where my whereabouts was." I saw Lily frown, out of the both of us, her gift was definitely stronger. "So are you going to start explaining, we know you're sorry but apologies aren't what we need now?" I knew I sounded harsh but we needed some answers. She closed her eyes and sighed. Then nodded her head. "Firstly you must be wondering why I haven't aged, I should be in my late fifties but I look around twenty well it's because of this." She pulled a glowing red ball out of her pocket. The way orange flames flickered around the surface seemed familiar. At the corner of my eye I saw Lily pull out her pendent, the stone was identical to the ball. Familiar. Alice smiled. "This is just a small part of the heart of flames, my leader cut them from the pendent and made them for a selected few. It keeps us strong and stops us aging for a while, but they don't work forever, eventually I will start to grow old like you three do." Lily smoothed her fingers over the glowing surface. "So does this stone affect me too?" Alice replaced the ball back inside her pocket and nodded at Lily. "The heart of fire was made for the daughters of the Guardians, it helps them be strong and enhances their powers, and it doesn't stop aging unless you want it to."

"Want it to, what does that mean?" Alice shifted her eyes back to me again. Unlike Sky her eyes made me feel uncomfortable when they settled onto me. "The heart of fire can be commanded, you can ask it to make you stronger, to enhance your powers, to live forever and it will give you that. But only the daughters can do that, the stone doesn't work for everyone in the same way it does for the daughters." It made sense, it burned the supernatural, and only had limited power for people like Alice. Lily spoke again. "Max had one didn't he, Rains dad I saw it in one of your memories?" Alice looked pained at the mention of Max. But she nodded at Lily. "You told Cole once what it does, but you also said he would forget, why did you tell him?" Alice had told me about the stone, when?

Alice nodded at her again. "Because I knew one day you would see the memory and understand what these stones do, that one day I will grow old again, so if you ever did find me you would understand I would either be young or old." Rain stood up and for the first time since the church she spoke. "But dad has aged, not a lot but he has." Alice's eyes suddenly lightened a shade. "He's alive, he's okay?" Rain nodded at her, and Alice visibly relaxed, she had thought he was dead. "It's probably because he didn't want to be a part of it anymore, he must have guessed that the Guardians had taken me away and didn't want a part of it. But most importantly he would have wanted to be there for you, to not risk leaving like it did."

"So your like Sky, you're a protector of the Guardians, that's why you have a blue and brown eye, you're a Veil?" Lily's voice had grown stronger with each time she had spoken. "Yes like your friend I have Heaven and Earth in my eyes, she is another reason why I am here, she is old enough now to come and train. I was around her age when I went to the Guardians, by then I had found Max and we went together. We learnt the rules and how to be a Guardian, and when it was time we were given our stones." I got up from the sofa and went around the other side so I could stand behind Lily. "Why did you run in the first place?" Alice folded up her legs and sat on the floor. She suddenly looked a lot younger there on the carpet. "I was running away from Seth, he knew who I would grow up to be and wanted to use me to get to Storm, so I ran. Even though I didn't really know who I was at that point I knew it was important for me not to let him get to me." I couldn't imagine what had been going through her head, fourteen years old and forced to leave everything she knew behind to save someone she didn't even know yet. Admirable really.

"So how does this all link to me, Lily and Cole?" Alice looked surprised that we even had to ask, like the answer was so obvious. "Well firstly you're my daughter which means you have Guardian blood too, so when you're old enough you might become one too. You wouldn't be a Veil but you would still have the power of the Guardians within you. I haven't be allowed to come back because I've been on a mission, but I came back because you needed warning. When you hit the age of sixteen and

suddenly you get this impulse to go somewhere and fight now you will know what it is. And Lily well her mother was a daughter. Her father Warren was Storms only son and Alana was the only child, which means that Lily is the only direct Guardian apart from Storm. And where Lily's involved so is Cole because she is his mate and because of the prophecy." Rain frowned at me and Lily. "What prophecy?" Lily reached up and took my hand, needing my comfort. I cleared my throat. "Lily and I apparently will help rid the world of evil, together." Surprise seemed to smack Rain across the face, she looked sceptical. Alice rose from the floor her eyes were on my hand that held Lily's. "When did you get that ring?" I looked at my hand and noticed the dull silver ring with a green stone planted on wrapped around my finger. "The fairy Queen gave it to me why?" I had forgotten I even had it, it was so light that I didn't even feel the pressure of it on my finger. Alice looked intrigued, probably thinking why we would go to the fairies in the first place. "Because it's a very rare ring, it's a life ring. It allows you to restore a life if someone has died, but only one life. What did you give to get it?" So I had the power to restore someone's life if they had died, I thought of Amelia, what would it be like to have her back again. "I didn't give anything she gave it to me, it was my promise to her, and I'm supposed to never take it off." Alice shrugged.
"Strange I don't know why she would ask you to do that."
"So what now?" Rain asked. Everyone looked at her. What did happen now? Alice sighed and smiled at her. "You and Lily have a sleepover and I need to go, he will want me to report back." Rain looked suddenly alarmed. "But...you will come back right?" Her voice was unsure and wavering. Alice took the few steps that there was separating them and took her in her arms. They both held each other tightly. Both had tears streaming down their faces. "I will come back, it was easier when I didn't know you but now, I don't think I can stay away. Do you want me to come back?" Rain pulled back to look at her mother. Their faces and colouring were so familiar. Rain smiled up at her. "Yes I want you to come back." They hugged again before Alice let go of her. She then looked at me. "I know what you're thinking Cole, about bringing my mother back but it won't work. They have to want to come back." If I hadn't known Amelia I wouldn't have understood what she had meant, but because I did, I knew. Amelia would be at peace with her husband now, she would be finally complete and happy. I nodded at her. "I will come back tomorrow, tonight

go and have fun that's what she would have wanted. Then tomorrow we can deal with everything we have to deal with." We all nodded, she squeezed Rains hand before letting go and leaving.

Rain sighed deeply before turning to Lily and smiling. "So a sleepover, what's that entail?" We both laughed at her.

Lily

I decided to put everything that has been going on behind me, just for tonight. We were all staying at Carmen's house, and the boys were all staying at Cole's. It had been obviously Carmen's idea and none of us had the heart to say no. However I'm thankful we didn't, we all needed the distraction. With our PJ's on and hot chocolate handed out I finally felt at ease and normal. It had been so long since I had felt that way. "Right everyone has to tell who they have a crush on, apart from Lily because she's boring and has a mate already." We all laughed at Carmen so as it was her idea we made her start. She blushed and ducked her head slightly. "It was this boy I met in Ever when we were there for Christmas, I met him in the village." Sky nudged her in the elbow her eyebrow raised and amusement glowing on her face. "Oooh what's his name, what's he like? Wait most importantly what kind of supernatural being is he?" We all laughed and Carmen's blush deepened. "His name is Ronan and he's a...witch." Rain and Sky laughed. She finally looked up at everyone, her smile was radiant. "Well he just said he had magic but didn't mind if I called him a witch, anyways Sky it's your turn." Sky didn't even indicate she was uncomfortable when she answered. "Sean unfortunately." I began to laugh at her and she followed me. The other two were slightly blank. Sky filled them in. "He's a boy from our group of friends at school, by the way everyone thinks you've been off for so long because Amelia was ill and then she died." I stopped laughing. Way to put a downer on things. Rain chimed in. "What about Cole then?" Sky scrunched up her face which meant she was thinking. Her face cleared and she spoke. "I think his and Reeves lack of attendance was down to a close family member dying who didn't live close by." Everyone nodded.

"Okay enough with the heavy stuff, who wants to watch a film, and something that's funny. We definitely haven't laughed enough tonight." Everyone gladly agreed. But the topic of school stuck in my head. I had agreed with my parents that after today I would return to school. It was after all my last year. After that I could decide whatever I wanted, whether that was staying on to the schools sixths form, college or nothing. But none of that seemed important now.

The next morning came too quickly. Rain would go back to Cole's house where she would wait for Alice to come back. Carmen would stay here and do whatever she does when everyone else is out. And me and Sky, well we found ourselves back in our ugly old fashioned uniform, dreading the fact that we had double maths first thing. Outside, Reeve, Jett and Cole waited for us. All five of us slowly made our way out of the lightening forest into the late January air. The warm breeze promised spring and change. Cole took my hand as we reached school. Although school felt completely pointless and stupid I was happy to be here, to have something normal in my life for once. And with Cole's hand in mine and my friends around me, I knew even If I didn't want this, I could do it anyway.

Cole

We had barely made our way into the hallways when we were ambushed by Sean, Luke and Ella. "Where have you all been, are the rumours true?" Sean for once in his life looked angry, which was strange to his normal laid back demeanour. I raised my eyebrow and accepted the man hug he gave me. "What rumours?" Sean looked back at Luke and Ella who had quietly made their rounds, hugging us all. Luke finally spoke his voice cool. "That your all in some kind of trouble, nobody buys the dead relative thing apart from Amelia, so what is really going on?" Lily glanced up at me, her blue eyes worried and sad. "Listen me and Reeve had to go for a while a family friend did die and our families needed us, and obviously Amelia died so." Sean took my shoulder and smiled slightly. I had forgotten how comforting his presence was. He had been my first real friend, a friend that I hadn't already known. "It's okay Cole, we knew that what Sky told us was true, anyways we're glad your back." The bell rang shrilly bursting the bubble around us. Ella laughed and smiled at us all, she then grabbed hold of Lily and Sky's hands and pulled them down the corridor. "You don't know how relieved I am to have you back, Maths has been even more dreadful without you two." I could hear the rumble of laughter as students entered the hall to go to their classes. Reeve and Jett made themselves scarce desperate to find their own group of friends. Sean carefully grabbed me and Luke by the shoulders and pushed us towards the math department. "We have a lot to tell you bro, school started to get interesting in your absence." "How so?" Luke smiled his face lighting up in amusement, while Sean visibly cringed awaiting for the story Luke was so desperate to tell. "Eight words my friend: Jasmine, public breakup, dinner hall, Sean sporting stew!" As I laughed Sean good heartily wacked Luke around the back of the head for good measure. I looked at him "you've got problems man". Sean smiled and winked. Grabbing me and Luke by the shoulders as we headed down the dreaded maths corridor. We entered the classroom I had walked in for my first class here a few months ago. Sean looked over at the girls sitting laughing in the corner, clearly ignoring the equations on the board. He looked over at me, quickly glancing away from the daggers Jasmine was sending his way, "Girls, who needs them?"

Rain

I didn't know why I was nervous. I had already met my mum, seen what she was like, saw what she looked like. So why did today feel different? I guess it was because yesterday I hadn't anticipated seeing my mum, yesterday I had planned to cry a years' worth of tears as I forced myself to say goodbye to Amelia. Then, Alice showed up and disrupted everything I was feeling. Today, however I knew she was coming. So why couldn't I control what I was feeling?

I stood in front of the bathroom vanity. My room didn't yet have a mirror. I didn't want to add more furniture as my home was now uncertain. Would I live here with the Star's like I had for the past five months, or did I return to the outskirt town where I had once grown up and left? Today was full of questions, skirting along the uncertain side of the spectrum. There was a knock on the bathroom door. I turned and opened it to find little Skyla smiling up at me. She had been my bundle of sunshine in the growing grey storm that was my life. Although I had been ill and weak, she made me feel as though I had all the energy in the world. She was, my favourite kind of person. Someone who just by being themselves could make you feel better about yourself without changing you, or themselves. She was a lot like Cole in that way. Even though Cole had been through a lot in his life, and now the struggles and demands of the pack fell onto him, he still managed to put everyone else's feelings before his and make things better.

"Will you plait my hair?" Her voice was soft and small like a child's voice should be. Bringing me out of my train of thought I nodded and watched her clamber onto the closed toilet seat. She smiled which scrunched her eyes slightly. Her eye was still slightly bruised from when she had been attacked, a pink scar tattooed the side of her face, a constant reminder of what happened. She spoke as I began to run my brush through her ebony hair. "Are you going to live with your daddy now?" Her voice was sad, and it took me a while to realise she was crying. I stopped brushing her hair and came to kneel in front of her. Her bottom lip trembling as she fought to keep her tears in check, as though it was a skill she had been taught a long time ago. "Do you want me to live with my dad?" She shook her little head with exaggeration. Then leant forward so she could hug me. Her little arms not reaching the whole way around me. "No I want you to live here, so you can be my sister." I squeezed her to me in response. I had always wanted a sister, and she filled the space perfectly. The Star's had offered me a family and I couldn't just ignore that, but I couldn't abandon my father either. I let her go and took her hand instead. "I have an Idea, come on."

Cole

Life began to balance itself out again after Amelia's funeral. We all began attending school again every day, and every night I found myself with my pack running perimeter lines, teaching Rain the ropes. Lily and Sky studied the book Lexi had given them to learn more about the Guardians and what it all meant to them, and quizzing Alice on the subject whenever she was around, because true to her word, Alice came back. As the weeks went on Rain and Alice formed a relationship that had been vacant to them for fourteen years. Rain couldn't choose between wanting to live with us or her father, so she settled with both. The last abandoned house in the clearing we lived in was small and more dilapidated than ours had been, but with a few nights and weekends we got the place looking pristine, perfect for the two of them. So it was there where the last werewolf families stayed, the Stars, the Skies, the Moons and the Clouds.

Weeks had passed since the day on the mountain. Nobody dared mention my father's name. To the pack he was no longer a member. In fact he was now the enemy. To my mother he was no longer her mate, she refused to say or hear his name, and wished to cut his memory out of her life. And to me and Skyla, he was just a man who had helped bring us into this world, but he was no father. Then there was my other sister, my twin. Whether she was alive or not, he wanted her. I hadn't known her, but I owed her the chance to never know who our father was. Which meant if she was alive, I would find her before he did, and I would bring her home again.

To do this however would require leaving. I didn't trust that he wouldn't come back. I didn't trust that he wouldn't come back to finish was he had started. I knew I had been right, everything was starting. There was no way this was all over. If I knew anything about my father it was this. He wouldn't give up until he got what he wanted. Lily had postponed time, not stopped it. Yes Seth was trapped in the vampire land, but how long for, how long would it be before someone figured out a way to get him out. And even if he didn't get out his son was still out there, Lexi and the other vamps were still out there. And there's nothing scarier than a group of revengeful vampires.

I decided to make three promises, all three of them I would keep. Number one, stop my father and his army of vampires in whatever they are after, whether that's power or my twin sister. Number two, be a proper Alpha, let me not be the second Star to let them down. And number three, to always love and protect Lily, no matter what happens. Never did I want what happened to my parents happen to me and Lily.

I thought in my next decision I was keeping all three of my promises. Well that's what I told myself as I wrote the note. I knew they wouldn't see it that way, especially Lily.

This all started with me, me and my twin sister. Therefore it's my duty to at least find out what he wants, so we can find a way to stop him. We need that advantage, because without it we are blind. Dean you will look after the pack while I'm gone, and Reeve you will teach Rain, you were always a good teacher and she needs you. I don't want to leave, but I have too. And I have to go alone, because alone none of you can get hurt. Tell Lily I love her and that I'll be back soon. Don't be angry, its better this way, I'll be back soon.

Cole.

I left the note on the kitchen side knowing one of them would find it when they came in. Probably my mum, I could picture her crushed face now, and it killed me, but I carried on walking. Looking up at the sky I saw the night sky cascading over us like a huge shadow following its body that was morning. Breathing in a quickly shifted. Ignoring the spike of guilt that shot through me I pushed my body on, feeling the forest disappear underneath my paws, and the promise of night disappearing on the horizon. I ran faster.

Lily

Cole's note was clear. He blamed himself for what happened and now he thought that by going out on his own he could sort everything out again. But he was wrong. We were stronger together, not alone. Just as everything was starting to go back to normal, he decides to leave. It had been days, and with each passing day the ache of missing him grew and grew, when it got to the point where it was nearly unbearable. I had avoided going to his house as it reminded me so much of him, but today I felt like I needed to be close to him.

The once naked forest had begun to dress itself again. Replacing its stark nakedness with a covering of green. Daffodils had begun to bloom in their yellow beauty. Spring was in full swing. Birds twittered to one another as I walked, clouds ran across the sky exposing hues of blue that I hadn't seen in months. When I reached the houses I found that everyone was out on the front decks. The smell of a bonfire reached my nostrils before my eyes caught sight of it. In the middle of the floor was a small fire burning away, laid amongst it were clothes and other belongings that looked familiar. Carmen was the first to spot me. "Lily!" She shouted as she ran off the deck to hug me. Nearly spilling her glass of lemonade on my shirt. When she let go I waved at everyone who smiled happily back. "What are you all doing?" Sophie came off the deck to hug me and pass me a dark blue shirt with the name James printed on the back. I frowned. "We are all saying the stuff James has done to hurt us, then throwing his crap into the fire. It's a way of releasing our hate without releasing it on each other." I looked around and saw that everyone each held a belonging of his. Did he hurt everyone here? "Carmen why don't you go first?" Carmen nodded at Sophie and her once calm happy face crumpled into one of hurt and anger. She threw a photo frame into the flames and it hissed. "For shooting me in the leg." Her voice was empty. So that was him. I looked towards her but she shook her head. Sophie went next, throwing her wedding album into the flames. Her voice was hard and devoid of emotion as she watched the memories become charred in the fire. "For everything." I watched everyone as each person took their turn. The kids looked away, and the adults took a swig out of the beer bottle they were holding. His effect was still with them despite this, and despite the fact that he was gone.

It was then my turn to throw something into the fire. Personally he had only made me uncomfortable and plotted my demise, but he hadn't actually done anything. Before I could say anything, someone joined me. It was Reeve. He smiled sadly down at me, then he took the hand that was holding the shirt and made me drop it into the flames, then he spoke. "For Cole."

Reeve

I watched his belongings burn in the fire along with everyone else's. He had managed to hurt us all in some way, but the one he hurt the most wasn't even there, and that hurt even more. I knew Cole had left to find answers that might help us in the long run, but really he had left because of his guilt. There will always be a part of him that blames himself for the change in James, even though it couldn't possibly be his fault.

The problem with Cole was, he wanted to save the world and everyone that lived in it. It didn't matter to him whether they were good or bad. It didn't matter to him if they had hurt him or not. All that matter to him was whether he thought they could be saved or not. Whether they were worthy of redemption. And one day that will be his down fall, because one day he will believe in someone who can't be saved. Then there will be no one to save him.

In life you love and lose, that's what he had once taught me. Right now Cole will feel like he's losing, but what he doesn't realise is, without James in his life, he's actually winning.

Rain

I stood in the door way to the living room in my new house and watched my father fret in front of the mirror. Smoothing down his already smooth hair, brushing off none existent dust on his shirt. "Are you okay?" He looked up at me. I didn't really look like my dad, but I was a lot like him. The way he surveyed things, the way he handled a situation. And the way he fidgeted when he was nervous. He sighed heavily. "It's just...I look different since she...left." I moved towards him and hugged him. "You look fine dad, and I'm sure aging a few years won't change anything, in fact she might find you more attractive now." I could feel the rumble of laughter in his chest. I let him go and smiled. Before he could say anything the doorbell went. I winked at him quickly before skipping to get it.

Swinging the door open I found my mother waiting for me. It was still strange to see her even after her frequent visits over the past few weeks. She too was fidgeting. I took her arm and pulled her in. Then I pushed her quickly into the living room. Both of my parents stared at one another, as though they couldn't quite believe what they were seeing. My father blinked first. "You haven't changed." He smiled carefully. Mum then blinked, the side of her mouth curled up into a sly smile, which only made my father's smile wider. "But you have." They slowly took steps towards each other, keeping their eyes on each other's. "I stopped using the stone." Their smiles got brighter the closer they got, and when they were directly in front of one another, I thought their smiles were going to blind me. Just kiss already! "I think a few years suit you." My father leaned in and so did my mother. He smiled the smile he used to use on me whenever I did something funny. "You're a bad liar." And then they kissed. I sighed in relief, and when they broke apart I came to them so I could join in the group hug. I finally had them both again. I couldn't remember a time I had been happier than in that moment.

Carmen

Now that everyone knew the real reason how I had been shot that day, the hate for James seemed to have spiked up a level. Especially with my dad who had been James best friend since they were at school. In the weeks that Cole had been gone, dad had took it upon himself to be the best step in Alpha he could be. Somewhere deep down I think like Cole he blamed himself. Out of us all, he was the one who knew him the best, even if he hadn't known him the longest. So why didn't he notice? I could never blame anyone for James, apart from James. And if anyone was to blame it definitely wasn't Cole or my dad, how could they know that he would turn in to this person?

With Cole's absence, things seemed to seep into the sullen uncertain atmosphere of before, the time when he had been gone for six years and we didn't know if he was coming back. Somehow this felt the same as before, except this time, he had chosen to go.

Lily

When Amelia died, she told me to be true to myself, no matter what. At her funeral I promised to do just that, and I promised I would meet my real father, for how can I be true if I don't even know the other side of me yet?

I stood in the middle of my living room. My mother and father sat together on the sofa holding hands, and Leo was sat next to them with Leah on her knee. Since Amelia's death, Leah had come around and apologised for the things she had said, and I had forgiven her. Though it had hurt at the time, there was no point still crying over it. Them sat like this, all together reminded me of a dream I had once had. A dream when in this life I didn't exist. I looked at my father first, a skinny sallow man, who was once bright and healthy before his cancer took his glow away from him. I looked to my mother next, small next to my father, bright ginger curls and pale complexion. Leah next, I didn't really need to memorise her, for she was mums exact copy. Then there was Leo, tall, brown hair and bright eyes, dads copy. This isn't a forever goodbye I kept telling myself over and over again. I will see them again. Leo spoke first. "You have to go now don't you?" I nodded, I could feel the tears battling against my eyes. They all stood up and came to hug me together. One massive group hug.

"We will miss you." My mother whispered into my ear. I noticed I wasn't the only one crying now. "I will miss you guys too." They squeezed harder, then they let go. All of them had tear stained faces, even Leo and dad who didn't cry at anything. It only made me leaving worse. I looked over to dad, my heart squeezed a little bit. "Will you be okay?" He sniffed before bobbing his head up and down. "Yes Lil as long as you are." Mum handed me a photo frame with a picture from a few years ago. We had gone to the beach, and a passer-by took a photo of us all on my father's demand.

We all looked so happy. "So you won't forget us." The tears began falling faster and I pulled them quickly into another hug. Squeezing my eyes shut, I breathed. "I could never forget you." Then I had to let them go. It broke my heart to leave. To wave goodbye not knowing when I would see them again, not knowing what things would be like when I did see them again.

Smiling and waving goodbye for the last time I turned my back on them, and forced my feet through the front door. All the while convincing myself that this is what I had to do, even though it hurt so much to do so.

Ever was a truly beautiful place. The spring air brought the smell of salt and flowers from the meadow to my right. The sun danced off the quaint buildings and shimmered off the flapping sapphire flags of the castle. It was time. For so long I had been finding excuses, diversions from this very moment. To meet my real father. Without Cole here, I was going it alone, but it felt right that I come on my own terms, without anyone else. Because it would be my decision, nobody else's.

I walked slowly, allowing the scenery to consume my thoughts, calming my nerves. Before I knew it I had made it to the large stretching wooden bridge that lead to the wide double doors that was the entry to the castle. There intertwined with the velvety green vines were pale ivory lilies. The petals soft and stark against the weathered wood. My eyes pricked with sudden tears. I moved forward.

I hesitated at the door. Did I knock? Did I just enter and announce myself? Thankfully someone else decided for me as they pulled open the doors. For the barest of moments there was silence, then there was a shrill squeal before strong arms had hold of me and enveloped me into a hug. "The last time I saw you, you were a baby. My how beautiful you have grown!" The lady finally let go of me, and allowed me to catch my breath as she stole it from me in her bear hug, it also gave me time to look at her. She was an older woman with a pristine white uniform and a tight slick bun. Her eyes seemed strangely familiar, as though she had looked me in the eye a fare few times. Her eyes glistened with tears and excitement. "My name is Gwen, you wouldn't remember me, but come in come in, we've all been waiting for you!" We? She gently took my hand and led me down a stretching corridor that was lined in red carpet. "Come come, your father cannot wait to meet you."

We walked for a while, I thought the corridor would never end, but eventually it did. She stopped outside another set of double doors that I guessed led to the throne room that I had seen in my dreams. I turned around and noticed the paintings which hung proudly on the stone walls. Generations of kings stared back at me, sharing the same light hair and gaze as my own. Family. Then on the painting nearest to me was a picture of my mother. Her smile radiated warmth to me, making me feel as though she was here with me. "I wish you had got to meet her, she was truly wonderful, and I see that you are very much alike." I moved my gaze back to where Gwen was. I didn't speak, knowing the tears I was holding back would fall furiously. I had cried enough today.

Without another word she pushed against the wooded door allowing me passage. I looked around the room. It was the same as it had been in my dreams. The same stormy grey stone, stark red throne, the golden emblem of the Shadows engraved on the walls. I could even hear the sound of the ocean crash against the shore from the window at the back of the room. Then, there in the middle of the room was my father. His back was to me but I knew it was him. From the deep burgundy cloak that hung on his shoulders, his fine halo of pale hair, and the way he cocked his head which suggested he had heard me enter. The doors closed behind me.

He turned around. His face so like mine held so much happiness, but tears stained his cheeks. His smile faltered as emotion consumed him. Fighting everything I was feeling I slowly moved towards him. His light gaze followed my progress, the set of shock apparent on his face. I finally stopped in front of him. I looked up at him, took a breath then I spoke. "Hello... father." He smiled his first bright smile and took me into his arms. He smelled of the spring air and the salt of the sea. He smelled like home. "Hello my little Lily..."

Epilogue

A storm was coming. But that's not what she smelled. It was adventure on the wind, and it shivered down my spine.

Atticus

Lily

Our moment was quick and fleeting as the doors to the throne room were
pushed forcibly open by an elderly woman, who had a fierceness in the
way she moved. Her fierceness was directed at my father. "I hope you are
not keeping my only grandchild from me Pace!" My father's laugh
rumbled from behind me, he carefully pushed me forward his voice in my
ear. "That is my mother Primrose, she missed you nearly as much as I
did." I managed a small smile, but my nerves were getting the better of
me.

Primrose stared at me as I slowly approached her. Her light eyes only
getting brighter with each of my steps. I was now close enough to smell
the potent scent of flowers that seemed to spiral around her. She was
practically bubbling, waiting for me to make the next move.
"Ermm...hello..." she didn't let me finish before she had grabbed me to
hug me to her. She was warm. "Call me grandmother, or if you're not
ready just Primrose." I hadn't thought of that, not being ready to call my
relatives by what they actually were. When I said hello to my father I had
called him father, because it felt right to do so. Besides if I have to accept
who I am then I might as well accept who they are. I squeezed her back "I
think grandmother will be fine." I could feel her beaming smile even
though I couldn't see her face. Eventually she released me and took my
hand instead. "Your aunt and uncle are waiting in the garden if you're up
to meeting them." I looked at my father who had by now come to stand
next to me. He regarded me with a concerned look, as though I might
explode from all the attention. "Only if you want to right mother?"
Primrose nodded but did a bad job at hiding her disappointed look. I

shook myself mentally and smiled at her "I would love to meet them, well properly this time." And with that she pulled me back through the corridors, my father laughing as he tried to keep up with us.

The garden as Primrose had referred to it wasn't actually a garden at all. In fact it was a large expanse of sand that stretched to the sea. The tranquil waters lapped at the sand, as it moved with the tide. Large trees bordered the edge of the sand. Bright purple flowers hung from the leaves enveloping me in their sweet scent, which did a good job at blocking out the salt of the sea. Then there stood at the water's edge was my aunt and uncle, both of their gazes were captured by the horizon, where heaven met the sea.

My father approached them first. "Dia, Brother Lily is here to meet you." My aunt Dia was the first one to approach me. She looked the same as she did in the forest. The same pale sallow skin, dark hair, green cloak and a friendly familiar smile. "It's nice to finally meet you properly this time dear one, I am your aunt Dia." Unlike the others she held her hand to me, I took it and felt the same thing I did when she touched me in the wood, a strange warmth. Her eyes twinkled. Stepping back she allowed her husband to approach me. Like his wife Lucas hadn't change from the last time I had seen him in the Skies living room, the day he had given me the heart of flames. "Nice to see you again Lily, it makes me happy that you chose to come home." I nodded at him, afraid to use my voice. Even though he was family, the way he spoke made my skin crawl. Maybe it was just nerves.

Primrose, Dia and Lucas left the beach after we exchanged a few words, wanting to give my father time alone with me. Together we stood at the edge of the surf, not stepping in but not stepping away either. We looked out at the expanse of moving turquoise water, letting the sound of the waves fill the silence. "I wanted you to know that even though you are here, that doesn't have to change the way you live your life. I want you to carry on with school and see your friends and have your freedom. I don't want you to lose that just because you chose to be here." I turned to look at him, but he carried on looking out at the ocean. I liked that he didn't want me to feel caged here. "But what about protection, Cole seemed to think I was safe when I wasn't here, but now I am and you want me to carry on being normal isn't that dangerous not only for me but for you too?" He finally turned to face me so I could see the conflicting emotions pass across his face. "I want you to be happy, and if the cost of your happiness is me being in danger then so be it. This seems like the only way I can think of to try and make up for the past fifteen years of your life that I have missed." Instead of answering him I hugged him. I took in the smell of his clothes and the way his heart beat felt against my ear, and the way despite everything he was willing to put me first. Because even though he hadn't been a part of my life he was still my father, and in this moment he was closer to becoming my dad.

We stayed like that until the sun began to dip in to the ocean. A daughter holding onto her father trying hard to fill in the gaps in her heart. And a father holding onto his daughter, who was the anchor to the sea of doubt and fear he was now floating in. In the past few months the world and my life have become a scary unknown place, but finally it feels real, all the secrets that had been hidden beneath had now been exposed. Revealing holes and scars, which needed help to heal. Everything had changed; which forced me to accept a one crucial point. This was merely the beginning...

28065618R00190

Printed in Poland
by Amazon Fulfillment
Poland Sp. z o.o., Wrocław